Collected Works of
the First Korean Female Writer
Kim Myeong-sun

Collected Works of the First Korean Female Writer
Kim Myeong-sun

발행일 2022년 4월 5일

지은이 김명순   **번역** 현채운   **표지 디자인** Amelia Tan
펴낸이 손형국
펴낸곳 (주)북랩
편집인 선일영   **편집** 정두철, 배진용, 김현아, 박준, 장하영
디자인 이현수, 김민하, 허지혜, 안유경, 한수희   **제작** 박기성, 황동현, 구성우, 권태련
마케팅 김회란, 박진관
출판등록 2004. 12. 1(제2012-000051호)
주소 서울특별시 금천구 가산디지털 1로 168, 우림라이온스밸리 B동 B113~114호, C동 B101호
홈페이지 www.book.co.kr
전화번호 (02)2026-5777   **팩스** (02)2026-5747

ISBN 979-11-6836-249-9 03810 (종이책)   979-11-6836-250-5 05810 (전자책)

Collected Works of
the First Korean Female Writer
Kim Myeong-sun

한국 최초 여성 **작가 김명순 작품집**

—

Translated and edited by **Hyeon Chaewun**
현채운 번역 & 편역

북랩

**Author:
Kim
Myeong-sun**

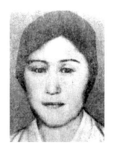

Kim Myeong-sun was born in Pyeongyang on the 20th of January in 1896. Her father was the county administrator of Pyeongannam-do Province and her mother whose penname was San-wol was a concubine of a gisaeng background. Kim Myeong-sun was a pioneering Korean female writer and one of the first to publish her books called *Fruits of Life* and *Gift of a Lover*, a collection of her short stories and poems. Further, she worked as a literary critic, playwright, journalist, actress, and was a translator that was proficient in five languages. She was the first to translate English writer, Edgar Allan Poe's *The Assignation*, French writer, Charles Baudelaire's *The Flowers of Evil*, and German writer, Gerhart Hauptmann's *Lonely Lives*. Also, she graduated summa cum laude from Jinmyeong Girls' School. Afterward, she went abroad to Japan and attended school in Shibuya, but after being socially disgraced by becoming a rape victim of Lee Eung Jun, even as she finished her last semester, her name got removed from the list of graduates. As she had profuse talent in writing early on, at the age of 21, she made her debut as a writer with *Mysterious Girl*, which was awarded second prize. Later on, as she went on to create stories that reflected on the plights of women of low-class, she published 170 literary pieces, such as *Looking Back*, *Tan-sil and Ju-yeong*, and *In the Dead of Night*, leaving important traces in the history of Korean literature.

**지은이:
김명순**

김명순은 1896년 1월 20일 평양에서 태어났다. 김명순의 아버지는 평양 남도의 고을 군수인 김희경이며 어머니는 산월이라는 필명으로 기생 출신의 첩이었다. 김명순은 첫 한국 여성 소설가이자 『생명의 과실』과 『애인의 선물』이란 단편소설과 시집을 묶은 출판집을 낸 몇 안 되는 작가다. 그 밖에도 평론가, 극작가, 기자, 배우로 활동을 하며 5개 국어를 능통한 번역가였다. 영국 작가 애드거 앨런 포의 『상봉』, 샤를 보들레르의 『악의 꽃』과 게르하르트 하웁트만의 『외로운 사람들』을 최초로 번역했다. 또한 1912년 진명여학교 보통과를 우수한 성적으로 졸업했다. 이후 일본으로 유학을 가서 시부야의 국정여학교를 다녔지만 1915년 이응준으로부터 강간을 당한 사회적 오명으로 인해 졸업생 명부에서 삭제되었다. 이후 귀국해서 숙명여자보통고등학교와 이화여자고등보통학교를 다니게 되었다. 일찍부터 글쓰기에 재능이 많았던 김명순이 1917년 21세에 쓴 「의심의 소녀」란 단편소설은 2등으로 문단에 등단하게 되었다. 그 후 「돌아다볼 때」, 「탄실이와 주영이」와 「심야에」 등 낮은 사회적 신분이었던 많은 여성의 시련을 비추는 글을 창작하여 170개의 작품을 펴내어 한국 문학의 역사에 중요한 발자취를 남겼다.

Hyeon Chaewun is a student at Ewha Womans University, majoring in International Studies. Her debut work is *Selected Works of Na Hye-seok, the Korean Pioneer of Women's Liberation*. It has garnered attention for being the first book in Korea that translated Na Hye-seok's works into English. Chaewun was first immersed in Na Hye-seok, a New Woman in the early 20th century, 100 years ahead of her time. Subsequently, as she discovered other New Women of the same time period who actively challenged themselves to rise above the social barrier, she started exploring Kim Myeong-sun, the first Korean female writer. Coincidentally, the fact that Kim Myeong-sun was born in the same year, 1896 as Na Hye-seok and faced different but similarly fierce battles in their lives sparked her interest. As a young reader of the 21st century, she became deeply inspired by Kim Myeong-sun, who also had passion for creative writing and fought her way through thick and thin to unleash her talent in a male-dominant literary society. Chaewun ventured into the English translation and Korean edits of the works so that Kim Myeong-sun's literary pieces would be resurrected especially at a time now when the world needs to learn more about such a female literary prodigy.

현채운은 국제학을 전공하는 이화여자대학교 학생이다. 그녀의 데뷔 작품은 『Selected Works of Na Hye-seok, the Korean Pioneer of Women's Liberation』이다. 이는 국내에서 나혜석 최초 영문 작품집으로 주의를 끌었다. 채운은 20세기 초에 100년을 앞서간 신여성인 나혜석 선생님에 푹 빠져들게 되고 이어 사회의 장벽을 뚫기 위해 도전한 동시대의 다른 신여성이자 최초의 한국 여성 작가인 김명순을 흠모하게 되었다. 김명순은 나혜석과 같은 해 1896년에 태어나 닮은 듯 다른 치열한 삶이었던 점이 더욱 그녀의 관심을 끌었다. 그리고 21세기의 젊은 독자로서 현채운은 창작에 대한 열정과 남성 중심적인 문학사에서 자신의 재능을 펼치려고 고군분투한 김명순 작가에 깊은 감명을 받았다

이러한 천재적인 여성 문학가를 더욱 찾아내고 배워야 하는 오늘날, 채운은 김명순의 작품이 다시 부활될 수 있도록 영문 번역과 편역을 도전하게 되었다.

Designer:
Amelia Tan
(Jin Hye-rin)

Amelia is a professional and multitalented visual designer and illustrator, with extensive experience in multimedia and print design. She has completed her associate degree course in Advertising Graphic Design in The One Academy of Communication Design, Malaysia and involved herself in numerous projects from brand and corporate identity (BI CI), publication, packaging design, advertising campaign and not forgetting, book cover illustrations. Besides that, she also possesses a Bachelor's Degree in Film Digital Media in Dongguk University, Seoul, South Korea. Her designs and illustrations come with a specific objective in mind and she has an excellent eye for detail. Her positive attitude and effective use of communication drives her passion to create and design, which has been the engine that drives her entire life of creativity. One of her recent cover artworks was featured in *Selected Works of Na Hye-seok, the Korean Pioneer of Women's Liberation*.

디자이너:
아멜리아 탄
(진혜린)

1994년 출생. Amelia (진혜린)는 전문적인 시각디자이너이자 일러스트레이터로서 멀티미디어 콘텐츠 및 인쇄 디자인 분야에서 다양한 활동을 하고 있다. 말레이시아에 있는 예술 대학 The One Academy of Communication Design에서 광고 및 그래픽 디자인 전공으로 이수했으며 브랜드와 기업 아이덴티티(BI CI), 출판물, 패키지 디자인, 광고 캠페인, 책 표지 일러스트레이션까지 포함한 수많은 프로젝트에 참여했다. 그 외에도, 영상에 남다른 관심이 생겨 동국대학교 영화영상학과에 진학했고, 학사과정을 수료했다. 그녀는 창의적인 사고를 갖추고 자신의 디자인에 대한 열정으로 멋진 작품들을 만들어 내며, 그 작품은 긍정적인 마인드와 에너지를 느끼게 한다. 최근 표지 작품 중 하나는 나혜석 선집 한국 최초 영문판 『Selected Works of Na Hye-seok, the Korean Pioneer of Women's Liberation』에 실렸다.

Translator's Introduction in English

When I first read Kim Myeong-sun's short stories, I delved into it with a feeling of anticipation and curiosity, for they were penned by the first Korean female writer. During the early 20th century, when Korean literature was dominated by male writers, *Mysterious Girl*, published in 1917 was a rare gem, born out of the mind of a young woman, 21 years of age. Kim Myeong-sun's *Mysterious Girl* was published one year earlier than the 1918 debut work, *Kyeonghee* by Na Hye-seok, another prominent female writer. It was an extraordinary feat for Kim Myeong-sun at the time to have clinched second prize with *Mysterious Girl*, a debut novel while competing against a sea of young literary aficionados in Joseon. Thereby, the story of a young girl, Beom-nae, whose past had been shrouded in mystery, hence the title, *Mysterious Girl* came out into the world.

Other than the fact that she is a pioneering female author and one of the earliest modern novelists, it is Kim Myeong-sun's works themselves that make her all the more deserving to be recorded in the history of Korean literature. It's because of her beautiful prose filled with elaborate metaphors and similes on nature that bring to light the sophistications of people and the society that engirdled them. It's the fact that she uniquely conveyed the reality of Joseon's class hierarchy and gender discrimination to a society that turned a deaf ear to the voices of minority. Further, it is that upon reading her work, regardless of time and space, the readers could be teleported to the historical upheaval surrounding the nation and its people as Korea fell victim to Japanese colonization from 1910 to 1940s. And it is that her work serves as a telescope that let readers look into the life of the writer, who aspired to break the social stigma that she suffered as the daughter of a concubine, a gisaeng. In fact, it would be everything above that would make Kim Myeong-sun's works resonate with the readers.

What started with a curiosity as to what I would find from her stories evolved into my deep connection with the struggles of each individual female protagonist, Beom-nae, Seonrae, Soryeon, and Tan-sil that represented Kim Myeong-sun herself. Each protagonist carried a piece of Kim Myeong-sun that when the shards coalesced together to form a mirror, it reflected her background as a giseang, concubine's daughter and the turbulent Korean society, swayed by colonial and patriarchal oppressors.

What is interesting about the dawn of the 20th century is that as the modern ideology of feminism from the West seeped in, globalization conjoined with localization, giving birth to the glocalization of Korea. Thereby, 20th century Korean women, New Women began sublimating it in the form of art, that is literature. Here, New Women, inspired by modern ideals, came to long for free love against arranged marriage customs and liberation from a patriarchal class system that discriminated against concubines and gisaeng. The New Women that set off the first waves of Korean feminism are representatively Kim Myeong-sun, Na Hye-seok, Ho Jong-suk, and Kim Iryeop. Among these 4 women, I was first inspired by the bold stroke of Na Hye-seok's pen that astutely criticized the double standards and gender norms that trapped Joseon women in their lives. What started with a mere inspiration that had me diving into Na Hye-seok's works blossomed into passion to translate stories by other Korean women writers in history as well. Initially, when I translated Na Hye-seok's works and published *Selected Works of Na Hye-seok, the Korean Pioneer of Women's Liberation*, I wasn't aware at that time of other classic female writers in Korea that contributed to women's movement and to kindling profound waves in modern literature. In fact, while there were people who knew Na Hye-seok, they were mostly unfamiliar with other woman writer of the same time period, Kim Myeong-sun. I wondered why that was the case, asking myself, why only a select few were remembered, while other writers just as deserving and admirable fell into oblivion. Perhaps, that was none other than the fact that the close-minded society that persists to this day has not taken kindly to writers who shed light on different viewpoints, that is, the perspective of the 'Other,' which diverges from the conventional themes of the mainstream literary community. Perhaps, it was because Kim Myeong-sun was born in an inferior social status as the daughter of a concubine, a gisaeng and was later defamed in society, being the victim of sexual assault. Or, perhaps, it was because there was no loved one, a supporter, a friend or a family member to pass on her stories by the time she, in her destitute state, was at her deathbed. All of the reasons I mentioned above could serve as an explanation as to why classics written by women like Kim Myeong-sun did not come to be as widely read in Korea. Also, such reasons speak to the harsh conditions the writer was in as she had to brave through slanders by the mainstream male literary society to chase for her freedom and make her voice heard. For instance, after Kim Myeong-sun suffered sexual assault in her school days, a number of male writers concertedly spread scandalous rumors about her that denounced the victim rather than the rapist. In fact, one of Korea's widely known authors of the time, Kim Dong-in created a literary piece, modelled on Kim Myeong-sun, which grossly violated her character. Here, the incident of Kim Myeong-sun being a rape victim was wholly distorted in Kim Doing-in's novel, where her character was written off as a woman who indulged in debauchery. In response, Kim Myeong-sun sought ways to defend herself, her honor in a world that gravely misunderstood her based on her history of being a child of a gisaeng scarred by sexual abuse. It was through literature that she spoke her truth. Thenceforth, *Tansil and Ju-yeong* was born. It was her response and resistance as well to the groundless social blame that left the mark of a scarlet letter on her.

Further, Kim Myeong-sun sought freedom through her constant pursuit of education in a world where girls were expected to hunker down in their homes to take up sewing and household chores for filial piety. Her love of learning, especially in both Korean and foreign literature made her find the courage to not limit herself to the education in Korea and study abroad in Japan. Thus, she became well-versed in 5 languages, mainly English, German, and French. What is admirable about her is that with her mastery of languages, as she engaged in translation of Edgar Allen Poe's English work, *The Assignation*, Charles Baudelaire's French poetry, *The Flowers of Evil*, and Gerhart Hauptmann's German play, *Lonely Lives*, she went on to expand her horizon of the world. Inspired by such works, her literary venture actively took off, where she began to let out her voice as a leading modern Korean writer with 170 of her own literary creations. What's more, during a period when a vast majority of short stories were released in newspapers or magazines, she was the first woman to have published her book called *Fruits of Life*, a collection of her short stories and poems.

To delve into the author's autobiographical novel, *Tan-sil and Ju-yeong*, the impression that one could get from the main protagonist, Tan-sil (penname of Kim Myeong-sun) is that of a female Hong Gildong. Although Tan-sil is in no way a will-o'-the-wisp who fights the tyranny of the authorities like Hong Gildong, she is similarly an illegitimate child who tries to overcome the stigma attached to her social status. Here, Hong Gildong and Tan-sil both struggle to break out of the fetters of social class as an illegitimate child. However, an important distinction has to be made between the two. Hong Gildong is an idealistic fantasy about the son of a minister and a concubine with a clear happy ending. This is because despite the lowborn status as an illegitimate son, he defeats the tyrannical forces and ascends to a position as a king. On the other hand, *Tan-sil and Ju-yeong* is much more of a realistic tale that portrays the internal struggle of Tan-sil that does not end even in the last page. It could be likened to a perpetual journey for Tan-sil. While mistreated for being the daughter of a concubine, her ironclad resolve to conquer her background through education faces perpetual collision against a corrupt society that hinders her capabilities. It is a journey that goes on and on and on without a definite resolution. The texts from *Tan-sil and Ju-yeong* manifest Tan-sil's resolve to prove her worth, regardless of class, gender, or nationality;

Yet, when even the students who did not have better grades than her set off for Japan, China, or America to study, Tan-sil was not at ease. Not only that but ever since she was a child, she brimmed with the hope to fulfill all her aspirations that were felt to the very marrow of her bones. She always thought,

'I was terribly looked down on for being the daughter of a gisaeng or the daughter of a concubine in an inferior circumstance. The country that I'm growing up in is weak and ignorant, the times that it historically outcompeted others were scant, and it was always looked down on by strong countries. But I need to get out of this circumstance. I need to get out. During the time that a maiden from another country is playing after learning

five letters, I cannot but think of learning twelve letters without frolicking around. When others are finding honor on the surface, I cannot but foster my inner skills. In order for the one line of insult and the one inch of hatred to turn to glory in the future, by learning and thinking with all my energy, I have to become a woman of virtue who above all wouldn't hear the despicable name, 'concubine.' To do so, I cannot but excel in my studies alone and hide my flaws instead, as I'm not the daughter of a virtuous woman, unlike maidens from other households.' (Kim, 1924, p. 213-p. 214)

Despite the similarity of being an illegitimate child, there is another point of distinction between Hong Gildong and Tan-sil. It would be that Joseon's strict social hierarchy (Yangban/ Upper-class-Commoner-Cheonmin/low-class including gisaeng, concubine, and the children of concubine) is the only hurdle for Gildong, but Tan-sil faces the triple burdens of being a woman, the daughter of a concubine, and the colonized.

As for, *When Looking Back*, what is noteworthy is Kim Myeong-sun's critical view of how the freedom of an individual, for instance, free love was oppressed by the Joseon social structure. Due to the Joseon social custom that ironically permitted the widespread practice of men to have concubines, but plastered a scarlet letter over women who committed adultery, Soryeon, the main female protagonist eventually chooses not to cross the line. Yet, even as Kim Myeong-sun did not paint a revolutionary female character from *When Looking Back*, she showcased Soryeon's raw, heartfelt emotions of sorrow and anger at the injustice, and the hidden desire for freedom that many other women of the time would have felt. The texts from *When Looking Back* exuded the anguish of a young woman, Soryeon and the individual's longing for free love beyond the customs entrenched in family lineage and matrimony;

> *Yet, starting from when they met, they could not be closer than as people who had merely known each other and as it was not right to stir up love or romance again in the midst of it, their destiny fixed the seal on conditions that neglected freedom under the social system.*
>
> *Yet, as Soryeon had such a pleasant meeting with him, wouldn't she have wanted to meet in a quiet place just for the two of them and laughed in joint bliss and felt joint sorrow? While from having been wrapped up in the skirt trails of old morality, it may have been Soryeon's rationale that she could not get out of the rigid custom, how on earth could she block out the natural demands of nature? Yet, in their case, they hid such emotions and Hyo-sun felt displeased, as if the blending of ice and boiling water were sprinkled over him. This was because as his wife found her way to this place to be educated under the tutelage of Madam Ryu Educk and with Soryeon as the assistant teacher, the thoughts he had of Soryeon in the previous days seemed like*

an attempt to grasp the forbidden fruit (Kim, 1923, p. 75).

Seonrae, another short story by Kim Myeong-sun is filled to the brim with such beautiful literary prose that depicts nature, especially the hill, currents, and breeze through the personification of human nature. Here, the writing technique that Kim Myeong-sun uses are metaphors and simile, which create a rhythm that flows smoothly with the sequences of the story. It is interesting to take note of the way music and art are described in the story, which symbolize the ever-changing, advancing currents of life that flow. For instance, in *Seonrae*, the main character, teacher Kim talks about the shifting trends of art from 'impressionism,' 'post-impressionism,' 'futurism,' to 'expressionism,' and the chaos that occurs from the changes. By presenting the transition in artistic style and people's difficulties in embracing the novelty of expressionism, it serves as a metaphor for the world's resistance to change. Thus, in the short story, Kim Myeong-sun shows her critical view of people's lack of openness to new things. This could be clearly seen from the main character, teacher Kim longing solely for a woman named Seonrae, who unlike the inflexibility of the world, is free and unstilted with her own perspective like a flowing tune. It is this experience of change from meeting the woman, Seonrae that eventually induces him to reflect on his own flaws as an artist and for the first time discover who he is as he takes the first steps like a "not fully grown blood-stained child." As such, through *Seonrae*, Kim Myeong-sun conveys the importance of embracing change, where deep self-reflection and discovery of one's identity follows. That is in order for one to grow from the change and become the true artist that could create and weave a flowing tune.

Other than short stories, it was through the language of poetry that Kim Myeong-sun communicated her loneliness and lament, struck by the loss of her mother and the bygone times that would never return, an aching nostalgia in her aged days. Throughout Kim Myeong-sun's childhood, her relationship with her mother was strained from external forces, namely Joseon's patriarchal class system that looked down on her mother for being a gisaeng and concubine. For being in the lowest rung of the Joseon class system and its occupation of entertaining men, a discriminatory social perception as lowly and dissipated stuck to gisaeng. Concubines also received an inferior social treatment as seen from how even when they had a child of their own, they were not accepted as a part of the family. As such, Kim Myeong-sun was catcalled and harassed for being the child of a mother who was a gisaeng and concubine and failed to get a sense of belonging to the head family (paternal family). It was her mother's social status that stood in the way of Kim Myeong-sun being accepted in society, which was what had made the mother-daughter relationship rocky in her youth. Later, as Kim Myeong-sun grew past her childhood, as it shows in her poems, it must have eventually dawned on her that it wasn't her mother's fault, that her mother was not to be blamed for who she was. One could feel from her poems the realization that hit her in later years. That it was the fault of the corrupt society overrun by many destitute families selling their daughters (her mother) into gisaeng house. That it was the fault of the patriarchal society that encouraged men to engage in concubinage, but ironically pointed fingers at women who were concubines and gisaeng. Representatively, *In the Dead of Night*, a poem written in her 40s makes clear how much she misses and grieves for her mother. In a world where she was marginalized and isolated, it shows how her mother was the sole person to comfort her, love her, and accept her for who she was. The huge indispensable presence of her mother in her life even in her mother's absence is strikingly manifested in the lines of the poem, *In the Dead of Night*;

> *In the beautiful flowerbed, in the merry banks of a stream*
> *the time I cried out, brother, sister, friend*
> *is all a past, but at least,*
> *my mother who's gone now*
> *she who shares my blood and flesh*
> *seems to know my life and my love*
> *At the sorrow coming from passing through the shadowy kingdom of the dead*
> *every night every moment*
> *I shed tears*

During the process of translating Kim Myeong-sun's short stories and poems, what I found most challenging was finding the right balance between literal translation and liberal translation. It was because the author had her own unique way of expressing, which I believed should remain as it was, undiluted. But simultaneously, in order for the meaning of certain Korean phrases to be understood clearly in English, there were times when I had to carry out my own interpretation and struggle to pass on the spirit of the author in another language. Yet, despite gasping at the long winding sentences from Kim Myeong-sun's works that seemed to stretch on forever, what made me push through was also ironically the long, winding sentences. The sentences brought out such a beautiful, literary writing style of Kim Myeong-sun that subtly captured the restrained emotions in a scenery, without resorting to 'telling,' but rather using the 'showing' technique that got me immersed. Above all, I have come to admire the words that she left for future generations, on the revictimization of the sexually abused and discriminatory treatment regarding blood lineage that has passed on to the present days. Whether it came in the form of Beom-nae with a mysterious past, Tan-sil bogged down by society's prejudices against a rape victim, and Soryeon, grieving from the social oppression of women of inferior lineage, Kim Myeong-sun brought every part of herself in her characters. May the fruits of life Kim Myeong-sun sowed through her creation bloom again in the 21st century···.

Translator's Introduction in Korean

'김명순, 한국 최초의 여성 작가'라는 기대감과 깊은 존경심으로 김명순 선생님의 작품을 처음 맞이하게 되었다. 남성 작가들이 주류였던 20세기 초, 1917년 출판된 『의심의 소녀』는 21살의 젊은 여성에 의해 탄생된 진귀한 보석이다. 심지어 김명순의 『의심의 소녀』는 또 다른 훌륭한 여성 작가, 나혜석의 1918년 데뷔 작품 『경희』보다 1년 더 일찍 세상에 나왔다. 그 당시 수많은 조선 문학 청년들과의 경쟁에서 『의심의 소녀』, 김명순의 첫 작품이 2등으로 당선된 것은 눈부신 업적이다. 과거의 미스터리에 휩싸인 어린 소녀, 범네의 이야기로 소설 『의심의 소녀』는 세상에 나오게 되었다.

그만큼 한국 여성 작가의 선구자이며 첫 근대 소설가인 김명순은 한국 문학에 이름이 새겨질 만한 가치가 있다. 왜냐하면 사람들과 그들을 둘러싼 사회의 복잡함을 나타낸 자연의 은유와 의인화를 통한 정교한 문장 구조의 아름다운 산문이었기 때문이다. 그리고 조선의 신분 계급과 성차별의 현실을 소수의 목소리에 귀 기울이지 않는 사회에 특별함으로 전해졌고, 더욱이 김명순의 작품은 시공간의 제약과 상관없이 1910년부터 40년대 일본의 식민화 속의 역사적 혼란의 시대로 순간 이동이라도 되는 듯 빠져들게 하기 때문이다. 또한 김명순의 작품은 첩, 기생의 딸이라는 오명을 깨는 것을 갈망한 작가의 삶을 통해 현재까지 이어지는 여러 여성을 향한 사회적 편견을 더욱 직시하는 망원경이 되기 때문이다. 위에서 언급한 모든 것은 김명순의 창작물을 통해 앞으로도 수많은 독자들에게 울림을 줄 것이다.

그녀의 이야기에서 어떠한 모습을 찾게 될지에 대한 번역자, 독자의 호기심으로 시작하여 김명순 자신을 대표하는 각 여성 주인공, 범네, 선례, 소련과 탄실의 시련에 깊은 공감으로 진화했다. 각 주인공은 작가의 일부분을 담아서 조각조각이 함께 만나 거울이 되며 김명순이 기생, 첩의 딸이었던 배경과 식민, 가부장적 억업자들에 의해 휘둘렸던 그 당시 한국 식민지 사회가 그대로 비추어진다.

20세기의 동이 텄을 무렵이 흥미로운 점은 서양에서의 모던 페미니즘의 사상이 넘어와 세계화globalization, 지역화localization가 맞물리면서 한국에서 글로컬화glocalization로 재탄생되었다는 것이다. 그것은 바로 20세기 한국 신여성들의 의식의 확장이 문학이란 자신의 예술로 승화되어짐을 말한다. 여기, 신여성들은 모던 사상에 감화되어 첩, 기생을 차별한 가부장적 신분제도로부터의 해방과 중매 결혼 관습에 반발한 자유 연애론을 열망하게 되었다. 이러한 한국에서의 첫 페미니즘의 돌풍을 불러일으킨 신여성들은 대표적으로 김명순, 나혜석, 허정숙과 김일엽이다. 필자는 이분들 중에 조선 여성들의 삶을 억누른 이중 잣대와 젠더 규범을 날카로운 통찰력으로 비판한 나혜석의 필력에 처음 감명을 받았다. 이후 그 감명은 역사 속의 한국 여성 작가들의 이야기를 번역하고자 하는 열정으로 이어졌다. 처음, 나혜석의 작품을 번역해서 『Selected Works of Na Hye-seok, the Korean Pioneer of Women's Liberation』을 첫 출판했을 때만 해도 여성의 움직임과 한국 문학에 커다란 발자취를 남긴 다른 고전 한국 여성 작가들에 친숙하지 않았다. 사실, 대부분 나혜석은 알지만 다른 여성 작가, 김명순은 잘 모른다. 이후 이에 대한 이유가 궁금하게 되었고 왜 극소수의 작가들만 사람들의 기억 속에 남으며 충분한 자격이 되고 존경스러운 다른 분들은 왜 잊혀 왔는지 의문이 들었다. 아마도 다른 견해, 소위, '타자'의 관점을 보여 준 작가를 받아 주고 싶지 않은 획일화된 사회가 지금까지 이어져 왔기 때문일 것이다. 또한 김명순은 첩, 기생의 딸로서의 불우한 신분으로 태어나고 이후 강간 피해자로 사회에서 꼬리표를 달게 되면서일 수도 있다. 아니면, 사랑하는 사람, 후원자, 친구, 또는 가족이 곁에 없는 채로 극히 빈곤한 상태에서 돌아가셨기에 그녀의 이야기를 쉽게 전할 방도가 없었을 것이다. 방금 위에 언급한 모든 원인들이 왜 김명순과 같은 여성이 쓴 고전이 한국에서 널리 읽히지 않았는지 설명해 줄 수 있다. 또한, 그러한 원인들은 자유를 쫓고 목소리를 내기 위해서 주류 남성 문학 사회의 멸시에 맞서야 했던 여성 작가의 혹독한 상황을 비춘다. 예를 들어, 학창 시절 김명순이 강간을 당한 후 여러 남성 작가들은 한목소리로 가해자보다는 피해자를 헐뜯는 악성 루머를 퍼트렸었다. 사실, 그 당시 한국에서 잘 알려진 김동인 작가는 김명순을 모델로 한 문학 작품, 『김연실전』으로 김명순의 인격을 극도로 모독하였다. 그녀가 성추행을 당한 사건을 완전히 왜곡시켜 김명순의 캐릭터를 방탕한 여자로 그렸다. 기생의 아이에다가 성적 학대를 받은 사연을 바탕으로 그녀를 대단히 오해하고 있는 세상에서 김명순은 자기 자신, 자기의 명예를 지키기 위해 나섰다. 바로 문학을 통해 그녀는 자신의 진실을 보여 주고자 하였다. 이에 『탄실이와 주영이』가 탄생하였다. 주홍 글씨를 새긴 사회의 근거 없는 비난을 향한 답변이자 저항이었다.

또한, 효녀로서 바느질과 집안일을 하도록 집에 박혀 있는 것을 원하던 세상에서 김명순은 끊임없는 공부와 탐색을 통해 자유를 추구했다. 한국과 외국 문학에 대한 그녀의 열정은 한국에서의 교육에 한정하지 않고 일본으로 유학 가서 공부하는 용기를 찾게 해 주었다. 이에 그녀는 5개 국어, 한국어, 일본어는 물론 영어, 프랑스어, 독일어에도 능통하게 되었다. 그리고 더욱 의미 있는 점은 이런 언어의 능숙함으로 에드거 앨런 포의 영문 단편소설, 『상봉』, 샤를 보들레르의 프랑스어 시집, 『악의 꽃』과 게르하르트 하웁트만의 독일어 희곡 『외로운 사람들』 등 여러 작품의 번역 활동으로 시야를 넓혀 갔다는 점이다. 이어 170편의 소설과 시를 창작하며 최초 근대 작가들 중 손꼽히는 일인으로서 자신의 목소리를 세상에 내놓았다. 심지어, 대부분 신문이나 잡지에서만 작품이 공개되던 당시 김명순은 소설과 시로 구성된 『생명의 과실』이란 자신의 책을 출판한 첫 여성이다.

작가의 자전적 소설, 『탄실이와 주영이』에 들어가자면 주인공, 탄실이(김명순의 필명)로부터 받을 수 있는 인상은 '여자 홍길동'이다. 비록 홍길동처럼 권력자들의 횡포를 맞서 싸우는 신출귀몰한 인물은 아니지만 탄실도 자신의 열등한 사회 신분에 따른 오명을 극복하려 하며 비슷하게 아버지는 높은 신분인 군수이고 어머니는 첩이다. 홍길동과 탄실이는 사생아로서 신분의 쇠사슬에서부터 벗어나기 위한 끊임없는 투쟁을 한다. 하지만 둘 간을 구분해야 할 중요한 차이점이 있다. 『홍길동』은 대관과 첩의 아들을 그린 이상적인 판타지이며 길동은 낮은 신분에도 불구하고 포학한 세력을 물리쳐 왕이 되는 분명한 행복한 결말이다. 하지만 『탄실이와 주영이』는 훨씬 더 현실적인 이야기로서 마지막 페이지까지 끝나지 않는 탄실이의 내적 갈등을 비춘다. 이는 탄실이의 계속되는 험난한 여정이라고 할 수 있다. 첩, 기생의 딸로서 학대를 당하지만 탄실이는 공부를 통해 자신의 혈연의 불리함을 극복하려고 하는 강철 같은 의지가 부패한 사회와의 지속적인 충돌로 이어져 가기 때문이다. 『탄실이와 주영이』에서 나오는 다음과 같은 구절은 신분, 젠더, 국적과 상관없이 그녀의 가치를 증명하기 위한 의지를 보여 준다;

"자기보다 성적 좋지 못한 학생들도 일본이나 청국이나 또는 미국으로 공부하러 출발할 때는, 심지가 편안하지 못했다. 그뿐 아니라 어릴 때부터 골수에 사무친 모든 결심을 달할 가망이 아득하였다. 그는 늘 마음속으로

'나는 남만 못한 처지에서 나서 기생의 딸이니 첩년의 딸이니 하고 많은 업심을 받았다. 그리고 내가 생장하는 나라는 약하고 무식하므로 역사적으로 남에게 이겨 본 때가 별로 없었고, 늘 강한 나라

의 업심을 받았다. 그러나 나는 이 경우에서 벗어나야 하겠다, 벗어나야 하겠다. 남의 나라 처녀가 다섯 자를 배우고 노는 동안에 나는 놀지 않고 열두 자를 배우고 생각하지 않으면 안 된다. 남이 겉으로 명예를 찾을 때 나는 속으로 실력을 기르지 않으면 안 되겠다. 지금의 한마디 욕, 한 치의 미움이 장차 내 영광이 되도록 나는 내 모든 정력으로 배우고 생각해서 무엇보다도 듣기 싫은 '첩'이란 이름을 듣지 않을, 정숙한 여자가 되어야 하겠다. 그러려면 나는 다른 집 처녀가 가지고 있는 정숙한 부인의 딸이란 팔자가 아니니 그 대신 공부를 잘해서 그 결점을 감추지 않으면 안 되겠다.' (김명순, 1924, p. 292-p. 293)

이렇게 사생아란 공통점이 있는 반면 홍길동과 탄실 간의 또 다른 차이점이 있다. 길동에게는 조선 사회의 엄격한 신분 제도만이 장애물이지만 탄실은 여성, 첩의 딸, 그리고 그 당시 식민지화되었다는 삼중 억압을 받는 다는 점이다.

김명순의 『돌아다볼 때』에서 주목할 점은 개인의 자유, 예를 들어, 조선 사회의 구관습에 의한 자유 연애의 탄압을 비판적으로 본 시각이다. 남성들은 여러 첩을 둘 수 있는 행위를 허용하면서 모순적으로 간통을 행한 여성은 주홍 글씨를 새긴 조선의 사회적 관습 때문에 소련, 여주인공은 결국 선을 넘지 않게 된다. 『돌아다볼 때』에서 김명순은 개혁적인 여성 캐릭터를 그리지 않았지만 불의로 인한 소련의 진심 어린, 정제되지 않는 비애와 울분의 감정과 그 당시 많은 여성들이 느꼈을 법한 자유를 위한 숨겨진 열망을 보여 준다. 『돌아다볼 때』에서 다음과 같은 구절은 소련이라는 여성의 고통과 혈연, 결혼주의에 얽매인 관습에서 벗어난 자유연애의 갈망을 표출한다;

"하나, 그들은 만나는 처음부터 두 사람은 다만 아는 사람으로 밖에 더 친할 수도 없고, 다시 그 가운데 사랑이라거나 연애라거나 한 것을 일으켜서는 옳지 않은 것으로 그들의 운명인 사회 제도의 자유를 무시한 조건에 인을 쳤었다.

하나 소련은 그들의 그렇도록 반가운 만남을 만났으니 조용한 곳에 단둘이 만나서 한 기꺼움을 웃고 한 설움을 느껴 보고 싶지 않았을까? 아무리 구도덕의 치맛자락에 싸여 자라서 굳은 형식을 못 벗어나야만 한다는 소련의 이성異性일지라도 이 당연한 자연의 요구를 어찌 막을 수 있었겠느냐. 그러나 그들의 경우는 그들의 그러한 감정을 감추고 효순은 그 부인을 류애덕 여사의 보호 아래 수양시키려고 찾아오고 소련은 그 조수가 될 신세이니 전일의 생각이 확실히 금단의 과실을 집으려던 듯해서 그 등 뒤에서 얼음물과 끓는 물을 뒤섞어 끼얹는 듯이 불쾌했다." *(김명순, 1923, p.112-p.113)*

김명순의 또 다른 작품, 『선례』는 특히 언덕, 물결과 산들바람 등 자연을 그리는 아름다운 산문을 통해 인간의 단면을 비추는 의인화를 했다. 여기에서 김명순이 사용하는 글쓰기 기법은 은유와 직유이고 이는 이야기의 전개가 부드럽게 흐르는 리듬을 만들어 주었다. 이 이야기에서 삶의 변화하고 계속 나아가는 흐르는 물결을 상징하는 음악과 미술의 묘사가 아주 흥미롭다. 예를 들어, 『선례』의 주인공 김선생은 '인상파,' '후기 인상파', '미래파'에서 '표현파'로 바뀌어 가는 미술의 트렌드와 변화에 따른 혼돈을 이야기한다. 예술적인 기법의 바뀜과 표현주의의 새로움을 받아들이기까지의 많은 사람들의 시련은 변화에 반감 있는 세상을 묘사하는 은유로 볼 수 있다. 따라서, 김명순은 이 단편소설을 통해 새로운 것에 열린 자세를 가지고 있지 않은 사람들에 대한 비판적인 시각을 보여 준다. 이는 주인공 김 선생이 세상의 경직됨과 달리 흐르는 곡조와 같이 자유롭고도 자신의 주관이 있는 선례를 유일하게 동경하는 것을 통해 볼 수 있다. 선례와 같은 여인을 만난 변화의 경험을 토대로 김 선생은 비로소 화가로서의 자기 허점을 성찰하고 "다 자라지 못한 피투성이의 아이"처럼 첫 발걸음을 하면서 자신을 처음으로 발견하게 된다. 이에 『선례』를 통해 김명순은 깊은 자기성찰과 정체성을 찾아가는 과정이 따르는 변화를 맞이하는 중요성을 토로한다. 바로 변화로 인해 성장해서 흐르는 곡조를 창조하고 빚어내는 진정한 예술가가 되기 위해.

김명순은 단편소설 외에도 시라는 언어로 자신이 나이 먹은 날 절대로 돌아오지 않을 지나간 시간들, 가슴 아픈 향수와 사랑하는 어머니를 잃은 고독과 비애를 토로했다. 기생, 첩이라는 이유로 어머니를 업신여겼던 조선의 가부장적 신분 사회로 인해 어렸을 적 김명순은 어머니와의 관계에서 여러 시련을 겪었다. 그 당시 기생은 가장 낮은 신분으로 미천하고 방탕하다는 사회의 차별적 시선을 받았기 때문이다. 게다가 첩은 자신의 아이가 있음에도 가족의 일부분으로 인정받지 못했고 열등한 존재로 취급당했다. 이에 김명순은 기생에다 첩이었던 어머니의 자식으로서 조롱과 학대를 받았고 큰집(아버지 쪽 가족)에 소속감을 느껴 보지도 못했다. 어머니의 신분은 김명순이 사회에서 인정받는 데 있어 걸림돌이 되었고 이는 어렸을 때 모녀간의 충돌을 일으켰다. 어린 시절을 지나온 후 결코 어머니의 잘못이 아니었고 탓할 것이 아니라고 깨닫게 되는 김명순의 모습을 그녀가 쓴 시에서 느낄 수 있다. 결국 기생집에 딸(자신의 어머니)을 팔았던 수많은 빈곤한 가족들이 득실거렸던 부패한 사회의 잘못이라는 것이라는 깨달음과 함께. 남성들이 첩을 두는 관습이 장려되었지만 모순적으로 기생, 첩이었던 여성들에게 손가락질하는 가부장적 사회에 책임이 있다는 것을 느꼈던 것이다. 김명순이 40대에 쓴 『심야에』라는 시에서 얼마나 잃어버린 어머니를 그리워하고 슬퍼하는지를 볼 수 있다. 또한 소외되고 고립되어 왔던 세상에서 어머니가 유일하게 다독여 주고 자신의 모습 그대로 사랑하고 받아 주셨던 모습을 표현한다. 어머니의 부재 속에서도 자신의 인생에서 없어서는 안 될 어머니의 커다란 존재가 『심야에』의 구절에서 절절히 나타난다.

> 아름다운 꽃밭에 즐거운 시냇가에
> 오빠야 누나야 동무야 부르짖던 일
> 다 옛날이었고 그나마
> 지금은 안 계신 내 어머니
> 나와 피와 살을 나누신 그이가
> 내 생활과 내 사랑을 아시는 듯
> 유명계幽明界를 통하여 오는 설움에
> 밤마다 때마다
> 눈물을 짓는다

김명순의 단편소설과 시를 번역하는 과정에서 가장 힘들었던 점은 직역과 의역의 밸런스를 찾는 것이었다. 작가 자신만이 표현하는 고유함이 있기에 그대로 살려 내서 희석되지 않도록 해야 한다고 생각했다. 하지만 동시에 어떤 한국말 구절은 영어로 분명히 이해되기 위해서는 나의 해석을 실행해야 하면서 작가의 혼을 다른 언어로 옮겨질 수 있도록 노력하는 힘든 과정이었다. 비록 김명순의 작품에서의 길고 굴곡진, 영원히 이어져 나갈 것 같은 문장에 숨이 막힐 것 같은 순간이 있었지만 그것을 뚫고 갈 수 있었던 것은 모순적으로 그 길고 굴곡진 문장이었다. 그 문장은 말하기보다는 보여주기의 기술로 장면에서의 절제된 감정을 미묘하게 잡아내서 빨려 들게 하는 아름다운, 문학적인 문체를 발현하였다. 무엇보다도 현대 사회에 존속하는 성적 학대에서의 2차 피해와 혈연을 둘러싼 차별적 대우에 관해 미래 세대를 위해 남긴 김명순의 글이 큰 울림이 되었다. 미스터리한 과거를 가진 범녜, 강간 피해자를 향한 편견으로 억눌린 탄실이나 열등한 혈연의 여성으로서 차별을 겪는 소련을 통해 김명순은 자기 자신의 모든 일부분을 끌어 내었다. 창작으로 심은 김명순의 생명의 과실이 21세기에 또다시 꽃피워지길….

편역을 하며

　이번 김명순 작품집 영문번역은 한국 여성 고전이 계속해서 세계에 널리 알려지기를 바라는 마음으로 이어진 두번째 도전인 만큼 또 다른 특별함으로 느껴졌다.

　우선 김명순 선생님의 1925년 발표된 『생명의 과실』은 한국 여성 최초의 문학 작품집이라는 점에서 의의가 깊다.

　더욱이 김명순 소설은 그때 당대의 주류 남성 작가들과 견주어도 뛰어난 작품성이 인정된다. 그리고 무엇보다 소설로서의 흥미로운 소재와 주옥같은 언어의 유희로 표현된 탄탄한 구성은 현대 소설과 비교해도 대단한 작품성이 느껴진다는 점이 더욱 놀라움이다. 더불어 본인은 독자로서 작품 속 그 시절 주인공인 여성들의 험난한 삶 속에서 특히 그들이 직면해야 했던 사회 장벽과 억제된 남녀 간 사랑이 그대로 녹아든 애달픈 이야기에 깊이 빠져들게 되었다. 이는 선생님 원본 작품을 많은 독자들과 공유하고 싶은 열정으로 이어졌고 편역 작업 또한 도전하게 되었다.

　편역을 하며 어려운 고어이기에 해독이 쉽지 않은 어휘는 괄호 안에 주석을 달고, 또한 원본의 의미가 훼손되지 않는 범주 안에서 현대어로 바꾸어 독자들이 좀 더 쉽게 이해하도록 했다.

　많은 사람들이 영문번역본과 더불어 김명순 선생님 원본 작품집을 만나는 감동을 기대하며….

CONTENTS

1. Fiction

2. Poetry

1. FICTION

Mysterious Girl

1

When entering as far as 2 ri (0.8 km) into the east bank of Tae-dong river in Pyeongyang, a neighborhood called New Village stands. The neighborhood is not that small. The appearance of the village or the houses is not the least bit abject and farming takes up most of the occupation. In this village, there is an eight to nine-year old girl named 'Beom-nae' who is so beautiful that she was suspected of being a flower and was utterly meek, a complete opposite to her name 'Beom.' As it was two years ago that the girl came to this village, she abruptly moved from somewhere with an old man aged sixty with white hair, Hwang Jinsa and has come to reside here. A few months later, a woman around thirty years of age came to Beom-nae's house, but she was an outlander as well. Even in the absence of work, it appears that the livelihood of Beom-nae's household is content without a single guest visiting them even once a year and without bonding with the village people. All the while, within this village, the incident in Beom-nae's house became a subject of mystery that in the monsoon season of summer and in the long night of winter, it has turned into a topic of discussion between smokers of tobacco pipes.

The beautiful girl named Beom-nae seems to desperately hope to be friends with the neighboring girls. Should Beom-nae seize the opportunity and stand there looking at the neighboring girls gathering wild herbs, the girls would be so enraptured by the beautiful features of Beom-nae that they would end up staring vacantly at each other. At this time, the old man with white hair always definitely calls out,

"Hey — Beom-nae — Hey — Beom-nae." Beom-nae looks behind with a pitiful look and returns home. Also, another thing that arouses mystery is that the three people respectively use the language of an outlander. The old man has the pure Pyeongyang dialect, Beom-nae uses the standard language without a dialect, and the woman's diction is from Yeongnam. And Beom-nae calls the old man, 'Grandpa,' and refers to the woman as 'Eo-meom' (Slang for mother or housemaid depending on the context). The country boys who did not understand the ways of the world wondered if the woman was the mother of Beom-nae. Other than this, the village people purposefully did not bother to know the details of Beom-nae's household.

2

It was the summer season, two years since they moved to the village.

On a market day, the old man opportunely went out at around 2 in the afternoon and did not return home until it was a rather dark evening. As Beom-nae could not fight off boredom, she opened the door ajar and stood, looking ahead. At that time, as she saw the daughter of the village foreman, Teuksil wandering about in search for her mother, she cautiously presented just her white face outside of the door, grinned at Teuksil who was staring at her, and said furtively,

"Are you Teuksil?"

Teuksil said cheerfully in her village dialect,

"Yes, where did your grandfather go?"

Putting a smile on her comely face, Beom-nae said,

"He already headed to the city······."

Before finishing her words, her eyelids, which were like the gingko peels flushed. The two girls momentarily went silent.

Teuksil asked, "Don't you have a father?"

"My father lives in Seoul with his concubine and his elder sister······."

Once again, her eyelids flushed.

"As for those who are now with you, how are you related to them?"

"One is my grandfather and one is my housemaid who cooks rice······."

As the conversation between the two girls gradually became amicable, from afar, the refined and harmonious features of the old man were seen. Beom-nae warmheartedly said to Teuksil,

"Come over here to play again tomorrow" and quickened her pace, holding onto the clothes sleeves of the old man, immensely pleased with his return home. The old man pulled Beom-nae's wrist and while entering a blush clover gate, he said,

"Were you bored?"

While they lived in the same village as next-door neighbors for two years, it was the first time that Beom-nae conversed with Teuksil like this.

3

While it used to be a stifling midsummer, as the awaited autumn season arrived without notice, the leaves of the paulownia tree feebly dropped from the clear, cool wind and even this year, the Chuseok holiday that did not cease to return yearly came back. Whether it was the city or the countryside, regardless of age or sex, those paying their respects at their family grave prepared alcohol and food and headed in the direction to the northern village from early morning to pray for the repose of the deceased spirit of each ancestor, parent, husband, wife, and child. Beom-nae and the old man from the neighborhood's New Village were also amongst them as they must've been heading to someone's grave. In no time, the sun slanted to the westside of Moranbong and at the side of Rungnado (Island in Taedong river of Pyeongyang), the weak flow of the small waves was girdled by the color of gold.

As the grave visitors who had been bustling in the early morning and daytime have now come to a pause, already, below Cheonglyubyeog (Cultural heritage in Moranbong of Pyeongyang), on the new highway, mildly drunk people who mumbled alone and were on their way back were beginning to be sighted at intervals.

One could see the shadows of the two people, the young and the old who crossed the Taedong river, heading to the neighborhood's New Village, and with a rustle, made the sand reverberate. Here was the old man and Beom-nae, returning home, extremely fatigued. The black hair that fell hanging down to the tip of Beom-nae's toes was glossy and slick. The two white cheeks were carved as if out of a marble and a couple of strands of frontal hair were hanging down, blown by the cool breeze that came from time to time, adding to her beauty. She was clad in fresh, light navy-blue skirt made out of summer silk, a straw-colored lined jeogori (upper garment of Korean traditional clothes), and pink shoes. In truth, she stood out in the midst of the ordinary girls of the New Village. The old man was silent and the girl was silent as well. The sorrow that a young child is not bound to have, along with a wearied complexion was shown on the comely face of the girl. At the riverbank, there were country people preparing dinner. While this was not the first time they saw her, on this day, curiosity being aroused even more, they held her in the limelight. Among them, one kid said, "I wonder where the child came from. How pretty she is." Also, one child said,

"Despite seeing her every day, she always looks pretty. I'd like to once get a long look at her as much as I can." Another child asked while laughing,

"Beom-nae, where have you been?"

Beom-nae merely smiled with her eyes at the country people and followed the old man with her mouth shut. At this time, there was a gentleman who could not be easily discerned as to whether he was a foreigner or a Korean, looking at this side with his eyes pressed against the binocular outside the Taedong river, at the second floor of the Western-style house of a thick towering wall. The gentleman urgently called the servant boy. Upon receiving the master's order, in front of the door, the servant boy hung the paper lantern at the green little boat, swiftly rowed toward the riverbank and by the time the boat reached it, the old man and Beom-nae had already entered the New Village.

The gentleman left the direction to the New Village and headed for a path to a different village. When the gentleman returned to the riverbank with a disheartened look, as it was a time when the round moon did a million people in dark places a favor by extending its clear rays in Dongcheon, outside of the Taedong gate in Pyeongyang, the light was dazzling. It was a place where night was like day. As it was said to be a good day today, on the river, a skiff that was boating lit up the ruby-like lamp and the Pyeongyang folk song (Mournful tune of a folksong of the northwestern province) was sung from the coalesced sounds of men and women, which rose and fell. The gentleman stood by the riverbank, looking ahead, as if dispirited. After a long-while, he feebly went on the boat, rowed back, got off at the other side, and stepped into the villa of director Cho. The gentleman seems to be a resident of the villa.

4

At the riverbank, among the country people who saw the countenance of the gentleman, there was a person called the 'mother of a lass' who often went about poking her nose in other's business. So that she could also see Beom-nae whom she missed, she came over to Beom-nae's house and informed them of the incident with the gentleman. The old man was not that surprised and guilelessly thanked the mother of a lass. After the mother of a lass left, with the elapse of around two hours, the old man and Beom-nae visited the house of the village foreman to bid farewell to the village neighbors all of a sudden. This was the only time that the old man visited the village foreman's house ever since he had moved to this place.

The village farmhands carried the seven to eight crates and the rest of the furniture to the riverbank and from behind the old man and Beom-nae, the woman from Beom-nae's house and the compassionate neighbors came following out to bid farewell, although they had not reached the extent of a deep bonding. At the riverbank, at last, there was a boat that went downstream.

The serene waves reflected the convivial color of the moonlit night.

As the boatman informed that all was set, the old man gradually took his leave of the neighbors who came out to bid farewell. The village people chimed in to celebrate the departure of the outlanders. Even the sound of the mountains and streams merged together. Beom-nae's white face received the moonlight and looked desolate. The countenance of her shivering with a snowy quilt wrapped around her seemed to be as if she had caught a cold. Beom-nae concluded her farewell in her quivering voice and holding the hand of the old man, walked briskly in quick steps, and while getting on the prow of the boat, she turned her head and with her luster-filled round eyes, she looked at the village people one more time······.

As the night wore on and it was silent everywhere, the Taedong river that held the million-year secret since the old days made the sound of the waves as if to speak of the past and the present. The sound of the paddle rowing the boat excruciatingly, adamantly broke the silence of the dead of night. As the boat went as far as about 30 meters downstream, when Teuksil said, "Beom-nae, goodbye —" from the other side as well, Beom-nae said, "Teuksil, goodbye —" The sound was heard tremulously like the sound of a zither. There, the country people held such diverse discussions until the boat afar was dimly seen and the rowing sound ceased to be heard that they were not even aware of the tide coming in and dousing their feet. The village foreman heard the evening incident from the mother of a lass, pondered on it with his head tilting, and after a long-while, he asked her,

"Okay, where was the gentleman coming from?" As the mother of a lass was quite farsighted, she said,

"He pressed his eyes against the pitch-black thing at the second floor of the towering house, looking……."

The foreman tilted his head once again. After a long time, as if he had at last resolved the mystery of many years, he said,

"I get it. Beom-nae is baby Gahee, the birth-child of director Cho's wife who committed suicide in spring."

As if everyone heard something terrifying, their eyes widened. Letting out a deep sigh, the village foreman cried out, "Pitiful child!"

5

As the only child, Gahee was a spitting image of the strikingly beautiful director Cho's wife who committed suicide due to the family's turmoil several years ago, out of concerns that Gahee would also take after her mother's wretched destiny, her maternal grandfather renamed her, calling her Beom-nae, a crude name.

As the mother of Gahee was a renowned beauty at the time in Pyeongyang castle, she was lured by the earnest desire of director Cho who was on a summer vacation there and became his wife. The wife was an only child of a man of wealth, official Hwang, which was why at the age of fourteen, even as her mother passed away, her father, official Hwang did not even get remarried and raised her like she was the apple of his eye. Who would have intended for things to happen as they did? How could the splendid palanquin become entangled in thorns? Director Cho was a good-for-nothing yangban (upper-class). He was fond of seeing flowers in full beautiful bloom, deft in making objects, and adept at archery and gunnery. He switched wives three times and even replaced dozens of concubines. He sought entertainment in the red-light district, even harassed girls of the countryfolk, and frolicked all around day and night in his villa. She got married to him and gave birth to her daughter, Gahee. However, as it was difficult for her physical beauty not to fade away, the debauchery of the husband grew alongside with the wife's misfortune. The concubine that newly came in snatched away her husband's love for her. The husband also cut off all his relations with his relative. The daughter of his ex-wife seized the opportunity at all times to slander the wife. Even as the wife wanted love, she could not get it, even as she wanted freedom, she could not get it, and even as she asked for separation, he turned a deaf ear and from being suspected, abused, trapped, and disheartened, she ended up having an ailing body, from which she committed suicide at the villa of Pyeong-yang. The young 24-year-old woman, who was like a flower of the human world, took her own life with a knife one day in April when even a tiny unnamed grass, trampled on the ground by the feet of people and the hooves of horses, blossoms. As the grievous death of the pitiful wife spread far and near at that time, everyone felt it. As the ancient proverb said, 'It is subsequent to an absence of a person that one is missed even more,' afterward, director Cho came to his senses to some degree and grieved to a certain extent. Yet, it was too late. Afterward, director Cho loved Gahee even more than he did when his wife was living. Yet, as her maternal grandfather, officer Hwang feared director Cho's concubine's devious scheme get all the love from director Cho for only herself, her grandfather and Gahee took the path of a pitiable vagabond. When would the balmy day of springtime come back for pitiful Gahee, a vagabond — After the passing of three seasons, summer, fall, and winter, spring was bound to come again — A pitiful child of a pitiful mother······.

(November, 1917)

의심의 소녀

1

평양 대동강 동쪽 해안을 이 리쯤 들어가면 새마을이라는 동리가 있다. 그 동리는 그리 작지는 않다. 그리고 동리의 인물이든지 가옥이 결코 비루하지도 않으며 업은 대개 농사다. 이 동리에는 '범네'라 하는 꽃인가 의심할 만하게 몹시 어여쁘고 범이라는 그 이름과는 정반대로 지극히 온순한 8, 9세의 소녀가 있다. 그 소녀가 이 동리로 온 것은 두어 해 전이니 황진사라는 육십여 세 되는 젊지 않은 백발옹과 어디로선지 표연히 이사하여 거한다. 그 후 몇 달이 지나서 범네의 집에는 삼십 세 가량 된 여인이 왔으나 역시 타향인이었다. 하는 일은 없으나 생활은 흡족한 듯이 보이며 내객이라 고는 일 년에 한 번도 없고 동리 사람들과 사귀지도 않는다. 그런 고로 이 동리에는 이 범네의 집안 일이 한 의심거리가 되어 하절 장마 때와 동절기인 밤에 담뱃떼들 사이의 이야기 거리가 되었다.

범네라는 미소녀는 그 이웃 소녀들과 사귀기를 간절히 바라는 것 같다. 혹 때를 타서 나물 캐는 소녀들을 바라보고 섰으면 그 이웃 소녀들은 범네의 어여쁜 용자容姿(용모와 자태)에 눈이 황홀하여져 서로 물끄러미 바라보고 있을 때에 백발옹은 반드시 언제든지

"야 — 범네야 — 야 — 범네야" 하고 부른다. 범네는 가엾은 모양으로 뒤를 돌아보며 도로 들어간다. 또한 의심을 일으키게 하는 것은 삼인이 각각 타향 언어를 쓰는 것이라. 옹翁은 순연한 평양 사투리요 범네는 사투

리 없는 경언京言(경성 말)이며 여인은 영남 말씨라. 또 범네는 옹더러는 '할아버지', 여인더러는 '어멈'이라고 칭호한다. 물정 모르는 촌 소년들은 그 여인이 범네의 모친인가 하였다. 촌사람들도 이렇게 외에는 범네의 집 내용을 구태여 알려고도 아니하였다.

2

그들이 이사하여 온 지 만 이 년이나 지난 하절이라.

어떤 장날 마침 옹은 오후 이 시경에 외출하여 어슬어슬한 저녁때까지 귀가치 않았더라. 범네는 심심함을 못 이김이던지 싸리 문 안에서 문을 방긋이 열고 내다보고 섰다. 그 때 동리 이장의 딸 특실이가 그 어머니를 찾아 방황하는 모양을 보고 살며시 문 밖으로 흰 얼굴만 나타내어 자기를 쳐다보는 특실이를 향하여 미소하여 은근하게

"네가 특실이냐?"

특실이는 반가웁게 그 지방말로

"응 너희 할아버지 오데 가셨니?"

범네는 어여쁜 얼굴에 웃음을 띠며

"벌써부터 성내에 가셨는데……."

말 마치기 전에 은행 껍질 같은 눈꺼풀이 발그레하다. 두 소녀는 잠깐 잠잠하다.

"너는 아버지는 안 계시니?"

"아버지는 서모하고 큰 언니하고 서울 계시구……."

또다시 눈꺼풀이 붉어진다.

"지금 같이 있는 이는 너의 누군가?"

"외할아버지 하고 밥 짓는 어멈이다……."

두 소녀의 담화가 점점 정다워갈 시에 멀리서 옹의 점잖고 화평한 모양이 보였다. 범네는 특실이를 향하여 온정하게 "내일 또 놀러오너라" 하고 걸음을 빨리 하여 옹의 옷소매를 붙들며 옹의 귀가를 무한히 기뻐한다. 옹은 범네의 손목을 끌어 싸리문으로 들어가며

"심심하든?" 한다.

범네가 이같이 특실이와 이야기 한 것도 이 년이나 한 동리 앞 뒤 집에 살았지만 처음이더라.

3

혹독한 서중暑中(더운 여름 동안)에 기다리던 추절이 기별 없이 와서 맑고 시원한 바람에 오동잎이 힘없이 떨어지매 년년이 변치 않고 돌아오는 추석 명절이 금년에도 돌아왔다. 도都(도읍)에나 비鄙(마을)에나 성묘 가는 사람이 조조(새벽)부터 끊일 새 없이 각기 조선祖先(조상), 부모, 부처(夫妻), 자녀의 고혼故魂을 위로키 위하여 술이며 음식을 준비하여 남녀노소를 물론하고 북촌 길로 향한다. 새마을 동리의 범네와 옹도 누구의 묘에 가는지 기중에 끼었더라. 어느덧 해는 모란봉 서편에 기울어지고 능라도 변에 연연涓涓한(잔잔한) 세파細波는 금색을 대帶하였다(금색의 띠를 이루었다). 이슬아침과 주간에 그리 분요紛擾하던(북적대던) 성묘인들도 지금은 끊어져 벌써 청류벽 아래 신작로에는 얼근히 취하여 혼자 중얼거리며 돌아오는 사람이 사이사이 보이기 시작하였다.

대동강 건너 새마을 동리를 향하고 바삭바삭 모래를 울리는 노유老幼(노인과 어린이) 두 사람의 그림자가 보인다. 심히 피로하여 귀촌하는 옹과 범네라. 범네의 발 뒤꿈치에 내려드리운 검은 머리가 제 윤에 번지르하다. 대리석으로 조각한 듯이 흰 양협(두 뺨)에 앞이마 털이 한두 올 늘어져 시시

로 불어오는 청풍에 빛날리어 그의 아름다움을 더하였다. 풋남순(연한 남색)인 치마에 담황색 겹저고리 입고 분홍신을 신었다. 실로 새마을 동리 소녀들과는 '군계중에학'이라. 옹도 무언, 소녀도 무언. 소녀의 어여쁜 얼굴에는 어린 아해(아이)에게는 없을 비애에 지친 빛이 보인다. 강안에는 석향(저녁)을 준비하는 촌부들이 있다. 처음 보는 바가 아니로대 이날은 더욱이 호기심을 일으켜가며 주목한다. 기중 한 아이

"어드메 살던 아해인지 곱기도 하다." 또 한 아이

"늘 보아도 늘 곱다. 한 번 실컷 보았으면 좋겠다." 또 하나는 하하 웃으며

"범네야 어디 갔다 오니?" 하고 묻는다. 범네는 촌부들을 향하여 눈만 웃으며 입 다물은 채 옹의 뒤를 따른다. 이때에 대동강 외 우뚝 솟은 난벽卵壁의 이층 양옥에서도 이편을 향하여 망원경을 눈에 대이고 바라보는 외국인인지 조선인인지 분별키 어려운 신사가 있다. 신사는 급히 상노를 부른다. 상노는 주인의 명을 받아 문전(문 앞) 녹색 소주小舟(작은 배)에 제등을 달고 속히 저어 강안을 향하여 배 대었을 때는 이미 옹과 범네가 새마을에 들어갔을 때이라.

신사는 새마을 가는 길을 두고 다른 동리의 길로 향한다. 그 신사가 낙심한 안색으로 강안에 돌아왔을 때에는 동천에 둥근 달이 맑은 광선을 늘이어 암흑한 곳 몇 만민에게 은혜 베푼 때이니 평양 대동문 외에는 전등빛이 반짝반짝 불야성이오 강 위에는 오늘이 좋은 날이라고 선유하는 소선小船이 루비 홍옥 같은 등불을 밝히고 남녀 성을 합하여 수심가를 부르며 오르락내리락한다. 신사는 실심한 듯이 강가에서 바라보고 섰다. 한참 만에 힘없이 배에 올라 도로 저어 저편에서 내리어 조국장의 별장으로 들어갔다. 신사는 그 별장에 사는 사람인 듯싶다.

4

강안에서 신사의 모양을 본 촌부인 중에 '언년어멈'이라는 남의 일 참견 잘하는 사람이 있다. 보고 싶은 범네도 볼 겸 범네의 집을 찾아가 신사의 일을 고하였더라. 옹은 별로 놀라지도 않으며 천연스럽게 언년 모에게 감사하였다. 언년 모가 돌아간 후 두 시 가량이나 지나 옹과 범네는 갑작 동리 이웃에게 고별하려고 이장의 집을 심방하였다. 옹이 이장의 집을 심방함도 이사 왔을 시와 이번뿐이라.

동리 머슴들이 행담行擔 칠팔 개와 기타 기구를 강안으로 나르고 옹과 범네의 뒤에는 그 집 여인과 인심 후한 이웃 사람들이 별로 깊이 사귀었던 정도 아니건만 전별차餞別次(작별 인사차) 따라 나온다. 강가에는 마침 물아래로 가는 배가 있다.

잔잔한 파도는 명랑한 월야의 색채를 비치었다.

선인船人이 준비 다 됨을 고한대 옹은 서서히 전별 나온 이웃 사람들에게 고별하였다. 동리 사람들은 소리를 합하여 여중旅中의 안녕을 축하였다. 그 소리에 산천까지 소리를 합하였다. 범네의 흰 얼굴은 월광을 받아 처참히 보인다. 백설 같은 담요를 두르고 오슬오슬 떠는 모양이 감기에 걸린 것 같다. 범네는 떠는 목소리로 인사를 마치고 옹의 손을 잡고 차박차박 걸어 뱃머리에 오르다가 고개를 돌리며 둥글고 광채 있는 눈으로 동리 사람들을 한 번 더 본다……

밤은 깊어 사방이 적막한데 옛적부터 기 억만 년의 비밀을 담은 대동강 물이 고금을 말하려는 듯이 가는 물결 소리를 낸다. 배 젓는 노 소리는 지긋지긋 철썩철썩 심야의 적막을 파한다. 배가 물아래를 향하여 삼단(약 30미터)쯤이나 갔을 때에 특실이가 "범네야 잘 가거라 ―" 하매 저편에서도 범네가 "특실아 잘 있거라 ―" 한다. 그 소리가 양금 소리같이 떨리어 들린다. 촌인들은 배가 멀리서 희미하게 보이고 노 소리가 안 들릴 때까지 그

곳에서 의논이 분분하여 물이 밀어 그들의 발을 적시는 것도 몰랐더라.

이장은 저녁 때 일을 언년 모에게 듣고 머리를 기울여가며 생각하더니 한참 만에 언년어멈을 향하여

"그래 그 신사는 어디서 옵디까?" 물었다. 언년어멈은 원시遠視(먼 시야)를 잘 보는 양이라

"저기 보이는 우뚝 솟은 이층집에서 시커먼 것을 눈에 대고 보더니……."

이장은 또 한 번 머리를 기울였다. …… 한참 만에 이제야 비로소 수년간의 의심을 푼 듯이

"알았소. 범네는 그렇게 봄에 자살한 조국장 부인이 낳은 가회라는 아기구려."

일동은 무슨 무서운 말을 들은 듯이 눈이 휘둥그레진다. 이장은 한숨을 지으며

"불쌍한 아해!" 하고 부르짖는 듯이 말하였다.

5

이는 연전年前(몇 년 전) 가정의 파란으로 인하여 자살해버린 과히 아름다운 조국장 부인을 꼭 닮은 일녀 가회니 그 어미의 비참한 운명까지 닮을까 염려한 그 외조부가 개명하여 투박한 이름, 범네라 하였다.

가회의 모친은 평양성 내에 그 당시 유명한 미인이기 때문에 피서차로 왔던 조국장의 간절한 소망에 이끌리어 그 부인이 되었었다. 부인은 재산가 황진사의 무남독녀이니 십사 세에 그 모친이 별세하매 그 부친 황진사가 재취도 아니하고 금지옥엽 같이 기른 바이라. 누가 뜻하였으리오. 그 옥여玉輿가 형극으로 얽히게 될 것일 줄이야. 조국장은 세세로(보잘것없는) 양반이라. 농화弄花에 교巧하고 사적射的에 묘妙하다. 그는 세 번 처를 바꾸

고 첩을 갈기도 십여인이라. 화류에 놀고 촌백성의 계집까지 희롱하였고 그의 별업別業에서는 주야를 전도하고 놀았다. 부인이 그에게 가嫁하여 그 딸 가희를 낳았다. 그러나 육肉의 미美는 싫어지지 않기가 어려운 것이매 남편의 난행은 부인의 불행과 같이 자랐다. 새로 들어온 첩은 남편의 사랑을 앗았다. 남편은 친척 간에도 끊었다. 전처의 딸은 매사에 틈을 타서 부인을 무함誣陷한다. 사랑을 원하여도 얻지 못하고 자유를 원하여도 얻지 못하고 이별을 청하여도 안 들어 의심받고 학대받고 갇혀 비관하던 나머지에 병든 몸을 일으켜 평양의 별장에서 자살하였다. 길바닥에 인마(사람과 말)의 발에 밟힌 이름 없는 작은 풀까지 꽃피는 사월 모일에 인세人世(인간 세상)의 꽃일 이십사 세의 젊은 부인은 단도로써 자처自處하였다. 가련한 부인의 서러운 죽음이 기시에는 원근에 전파되어 모든 사람이 느끼었더라. 고어에 '사람은 없어진 후 더 그립다'는 것 같이 그후 조국장은 얼만큼 정신을 차려 얼마큼 서러워도 하였다. 그러나 늦었더라. 그후 조국장은 부인 생시때보다도 가희를 사랑하였다. 그러나 그 외조부 황진사는 조국장의 첩이 그 총애를 일신에 감으려고 하는 간책이 두려워 가희와 함께 가엾은 표랑의 객이 되었다. 하시에나(언제나) 표랑객인 가련한 가희에게는 춘양려일春陽麗日이 돌아올는지 ― 절기는 하추동夏秋冬 삼계三季가 지나면 다시 양춘陽春이 오건만 ― 불쌍한 어머니의 불쌍한 아해……

(1917. 11)

When Looking Back

1

It was summer night. As the ray of the moon that was becoming round on the 12th day was misted up like a silver thread in the dewy atmosphere, it languished in plenty of sorrow that meandered around the pond.

In the meadow which held the dew, as the fireflies came in and out, it glimmered, as if it was from a pearl in the air mingled with the dewdrops that received the moonlight or from the spark of the meadow.

Soryeon halted her footsteps and sat by the pond as if to doze off. The wind blew downward from the hill and the lotus leaves swayed limply as if to kowtow obsequiously in the direction toward Soryeon. The sorrow that seemingly made an unheard-of-southern singer of chang (Korean traditional narrative song) pause was faint before one's sight.

It was as if her musing kept her from discerning whether the unnamable incidents before her eyes were from the past or the future.

While the children stared at the sky, outside of the westward fence of Choi Byeong-seo's gloomy, silent house, they called out to each other with sounds of flattery.

"One star, one for me, Two stars, two for me, three stars, three for me, hundred stars, hundred for me, thousand stars, thousand for me."

As these young voices penetrated to the very bottom of her chest, she said in her quivering silvery voice, 'When we've passed through this world under one principle and one belief as one unified life, why on earth would we be separated in the south and the north? And, even as we coincidentally gather again in one space, couldn't it not have been the case that we could neither meet nor weep?'

When agonizing over whether to meet him again or not, while saying, 'Yet, isn't it the case that there is no one who wouldn't let us meet and that is, when we're about to gather in the same meeting hall?' as if to see through the murkiness of this thought, the crickets ceaselessly echoed their chorus.

Now, on this night, it is as if the clearness of the summer night sky crossed the galaxy toward the middle of the sky, and as if Orpheus's geomungo (Korean musical instrument with six strings), thrown into the midst, serenely played out a melancholic tune.

The ancient story made by the people of the past who looked up to the eternal sky piled up above her head once again, arousing sorrow.

Wet with dew, Soryeon went into the three-compartment backroom on this day as well. She was about to lock the door, but having the door of the room open, she stopped stretching her foot and stood absent-mindedly.

Just at the time, there were sounds of people passing the bottom of the hill of Changjeon-ri.

"This is the house, right?"

"Right –"

"Mr. Song, Okay – let's go up the hill and see her just for a moment. You used to have such a good friendship with her, but why would you be punished for a crime that's keeping you from meeting her?"

"What! Even if it's not that, think about it. Would there be a sense of honor in breaking someone's tranquil happiness?"

"If so, why don't you just dispose of even that lingering thought like washing it off······." The footsteps of people talking came close all the way below the brick wall, which Soryeon faced while standing.

"Mr. Lee, this isn't even about a ghost or an animal but a person's gloom. Now – it is futile, so let's go down. What consolation would there be to look around while standing outside of the layered brick wall piled high up?" said he and as one footstep hurriedly came down,

"Mr. Lee, please go right ahead and clearly master the musical accompaniment of Ms. Y a bit more."

With that, the other footsteps behind it also seemed to come down in sync.

Soryeon stood at the spot, as if she once again turned into a pillar of salt. As this moment elapsed, she soon inwardly cried out.

'Oh-it is the voice of Mr. Song. If it's not him, would there be anyone with such a voice? That is right, right.' And while she tried to jump all the way down to the bottom of the brick wall in stocking feet (One's feet with traditional Korean socks on) and open the backdoor, there was no way to open the door that was securely bolted with a lock fastened. She hurriedly went to the front of the pond and standing on her tiptoe on top of the cornerstone of a stone lantern, she looked beyond the brick wall. And yet, the new wide highway merely shone brightly in the moonlit night and as if it was empty, at the end of the road, while the shadow of a person may be faint, its presence was dubious.

As if Soryeon was disheartened, she took off her beoseon (traditional Korean socks) as she came up to the wooden porch and stepped into the room.

As if to replay memories with mere thought, Soryeon securely locked the summer door and sunk into thoughts of the bygone days.

One year prior to that time, in spring, Soryeon who graduated with good grades from S School as an English Literature major, as expected, became an English teacher from S School in Kyeongseong from spring and taught students with such a beautiful pronunciation. She had a rather amicable relationship with the students and while she may have been slightly treated like a child by the teachers, she had nothing to worry. However, from that spring, Soryeon became haggard day by day.

It was said that her becoming haggard could be because she had grown up solely under the supervision of her strict aunt since a child or it was said to have been because she suffered from a lingering regret, though she had turned down offers from an aristocrat, pretending to be smart and saying that she could not wed him due to their different social status.

Yet, the truth about her would overturn such a sickening nonsense and build a story that could not be cast away.

2

The following year that Soryeon became an English teacher from S School, at the end of April, when the whole school went on a field trip, she got to visit the Meteorological Observatory of Incheon, leading the students in their third year of high school and mingling with other Japanese teachers.

At the time, the day Soryeon found her way to the Meteorological Observatory of Incheon was one of the days when as usual, the weather was quite murky, but even so, as the raindrops sprayed from moment to moment, it was as if the spring cold that penetrated all the way to the marrow of her bones was crushing like her shoulders became stripped of the thin padded jeogori (Korean traditional jacket) she was clad in.

As the teachers and students vacillated, they were guided into every machine room and listened to the explanation of a young scientist who possessed a lofty presence, as if he had descended from heaven and with a voice that once heard, could not be forgotten forever.

With the young scientist in front, roughly 40 teachers and students went up and down from one basement to another basement and from stairs to the other stairs.

Most diligently raising such a white cheek with reddish, crimson color, the young scientist explained, "Do you get it, do you get it?" While studiously listening, Soryeon nodded her head as if she occasionally understood.

After showing them around the facilities of all the machine rooms, the young scientist ushered them into the sitting room to treat the S School teachers with a cup of tea. There, they shared each other's business cards and Soryeon, upon finding out that he was a young Korean man, could barely keep the roots of her ears from being flushed. Yet, addressing Soryeon whose cheeks inflamed, Song Hyo-sun brought all of the softness to the surface in Korean words as he whispered below her ear,

"I thought you were a student. It's cause' you look very young."

At this moment, Soryeon for the first time came to know the aroma of the opposite sex. Until now, she had thought the smell of men as unclean, but when this went against her expectation and when she realized something strange, wherein, she anticipated coming closer to his body, he spoke again, "Since when were you at the school? Do you teach only English? Don't you have any hobby in science?"

And blushing to the roots of her ears, she listened to Mr. Song's hushed words.

She was consumed by helplessness and a secretive feeling, where her whole body wished to rely on the strength of a wall and hide inside a serene and tidy room alone.

Even so, she hoped that Song Hyo-sun would not come close to her. At times like this, as if Hyo-sun was also overwhelmed with the same feeling, he went on to speak less to her and next to the other Japanese teachers, he talked to them with a clear voice in Japanese. While sending looks of immense favor in Song Hyo-sun's way, the teachers carefully looked at Soryeon. And as their eyes all held envy of Soryeon, they seemed to look up to the fact that she sat close to the young scientist. When leaving the meteorological observatory, Hyo-sun and Soryeon rather quietly talked,

"In which part of Seoul do you live?"

"I live in Sungui-dong."

"Is it your birthplace?"

"No, it's not."

"Then, is it an inn?"

"No, it's my aunt's house I've grown up in."

"Then, your parents are not present?"

"Yes······."

With that, she was about to turn her heel and after a long while, she said,

"Then, good bye."

At this moment, Hyo-sun stood blankly, as if he was thinking of something and spoke,

"Who is your aunt?"

"Well – She is Ryu Educk of E Hakdang."

"Then, you have a relative who is a brilliant adult. If I make a visit, would you pretend not to know me?" he said.

Like this, Soryeon exchanged words with Hyo-sun, mingled with the students, and came down to the mountain ridge.

After that, she came to have utterly unforgettable sufferings. Even in the street (It was because he said that he would be coming to visit her) and even when she seemed to catch sight of the lively gait of a handsome man with wide chest, she wondered if it was really him. All the while, day by day, she grew haggard and came to realize hardship in everything. Even if it would be just once, she wanted to meet Hyo-sun again. As her admiration for Hyo-sun eventually went all the way from sensibility to spirituality, she came to newly take up a hobby in science and⋯⋯she went so far as to cradle a wish to meet him in an eternal voyage. Day and night, she prayed that she would meet him again. Even if it was for a moment, the emotions indicative of a beautiful purity had taken root in the nest of an unforgettable memory inside of her pure heart. Still, she could not help but be at a loss. No matter how much of a firm resolve she had, she merely wanted to meet him with her own eyes, forgetting the impression she gained from the one-time meeting, where she newly came to explore science.

Eventually, with her praying day and night coming to no fruition, as she was not able to meet him, it was to a point where she fell victim to a lingering illness. To her as a maiden, all the men other than Song Hyo-sun looked as worthless as bits of straw. Yet, disregarding that, there were never few who made the vain efforts to ask Ryu Educk to be wed to Soryeon.

While she did not clearly say that it was due to the exhaustion of decently raising a niece without parents for ten years or due to caring for Soryeon's future, Ryu Educk merely wanted to get Soryeon married as soon as possible. On some occasion, Ryu Educk spoke of how it was a shame that the 30 won Soryeon received as an hourly teacher's salary was meager.

When Soryeon suffered from this, she could not set her mind at ease even more. As she must have realized how life was tougher than expected and lonesome, and because the more she ascertained how much her aunt's lessons for her was Janus-faced, the more she could not find what was clearly wrong about it, the hot, hot tears automatically rolled down the pale cheeks. Even if it wasn't so, it was just that day and night, during the time that she was a maiden, she so awfully got a taste of the worries and loneliness of a desolate circumstance. One day, she forgot to eat and sleep and suffered from pain that could not even be clearly named, as if she was laid up with a fever. She was just like an ailing person and so, she was reluctant to go to S School. Yet, inevitably, if she were not to go there, she could not help her aunt make a living.

While day after day, directing her two burning eyes of her longing for a person to the wide street, she frequented S School, but later on, she lost so much of her physical strength that she dropped her eyes to the ground and did not even look at the people passing by the street. At this time, even though it was easy for a maiden's emotion, which for the first time missed a person, to be hyper, Soryeon effortfully repressed her feelings and inwardly hid the secret that she was longing for something. As such, finally, she came to think about all of the lives and even among the livelihood of women, she pondered on how Joseon women have lived and how they would go on to live. Also, while comparing everyone's livelihood, the heart that yearned to know about science tremored with anticipation like it was when a child who had left one's hometown merely heard the name of one's hometown.

At a certain time, whether it would be physics or astronomy, the name of the academics appeared to be the byword for Song Hyo-sun. Yet, when Soryeon could not find such thoughts in her friends, how much of a disappointment and loneliness she must have felt. While she was a maiden who was already over 20 years old, the worries that for the first time were exceptional prompted her to put on an almost shameful behavior.

At some time, she assiduously asked a teacher of natural sciences in S School and at a certain time, she carefully listened to women's stories of the bygone days and she would come to her senses on how much of an erroneous livelihood they have been having. Still, as day by day, Soryeon's health would only worsen, the brusque Madam Ryu Educk could not help but be surprised. In the meanwhile, as Soryeon was sick at heart, which had nowhere to go to, she could not make an effort at being in the group of women in natural sciences, and she ended up carrying around a type of literary work after teaching English at S School and returning home. It was because there, the entire world did not appear to be troublesome. While the other day, she even studiously reviewed the piano lesson, as it was naturally easy for her heart bearing a deep secret to lose hope, which was like the reddish evening sunlight akin to the evening dusk, she sunk into a gloomy meditation, hesitant to even let out her inner voice. How much of a misery she must have felt as she stood on the slope of the back hill and gazed at the evening sky. If anyone had known what was going on in her mind, despite it not being something of romance, they would have embraced her and taken pity on her, expressing the deepest condolences for the general sufferings of people. Yet, no one's sympathy was directed to her. Carrying around a type of literary work, she came to feel diffident around her aunt (It was because according to Ryu Educk, being educated was about getting a graduate degree to earn a living) and bearing a dark secret at heart, she got suspicious looks from teachers at school and students whispered about her. While opening her pitch-black eyes widely and explaining herself with them, she said, 'No, it's not like that. But rather, a memory unbeknownst to you that my mind was powerfully struck by is troubling me like this.' Yet, this failed to be communicated to anyone and the teachers simply said,

"The suffering of a maiden – she'd be considerably vain."

"Well, it's frustrating. Why did Soryeon miss the opportunity at the time when Ms. Ryu Educk was dead set on it? The aristocrat already went through the wedding ceremony……"

"How pitiful. How could Soryeon have lost out on that spot? Pretending to be too smart is a harm as well."

They muttered amongst themselves and asked,

"Why are you growing thinner like that? Miss Ryu Soryeon. Is there a need for you with a lovely figure to suffer? You could be easily getting whatever happiness……"

"Take good care of your health. Would an incident that has already passed be of use? Look for another opportunity next time."

And they gave absurd sympathy that was directly irrelevant. Each time, Soryeon came to realize shame and insult to no end, felt as if she was a useless person in this world, and even, a superstition arose, where it seemed right to perpetually hide the secret about Song Hyo-sun.

Everything gloomily tried to make her mind plunge only into a dark place.

Yet, as expected, she missed Song Hyo-sun. She could not forget him. So, whenever there was talk of marriage, she turned it down. While Madam Ryu Educk asked her why, it was not because of her dissatisfaction that the other side was uneducated, not because of her being modest about her low social status, and not because she was in an unbearable circumstance from not having wealth.

But rather, she missed Song Hyo-sun from the Incheon Meteorological Observatory who was possessed of trustworthiness, modesty, and vigor, who with a lofty voice, concealed all audacity and said,

"If I make a visit, would you pretend not to know me?"

If not for the shame that came from her patience and genuine longing, she might have gone to the Incheon Meteorological Observatory, but as if to wait for the tactful tip of the fingers, the white keys of the piano, whose lid was closed, could not make any sound and was merely silent.

3

Ryu Educk was a sister of Soryeon's father, five years older than him and her hometown was in Bakcheon district in the northside of the peninsula. The father of Ryu Educk was a strict elder who earned the name, Ryu Jinsa as Seonbi (classical scholar) of a certain period in Korea. Yet, because of a son that he unfortunately saw in his late years, he terribly fretted himself and even before his son turned 20, he passed away. Even before this, as Ryu Educk turned 15, while she got married to Official Lee, not only was the wrangling between Seonbi (Ryu Educk's father who had a higher status) and Official (Ryu Educk's husband who had a lower status) vicious, but as Ryu Educk's husband was a scumbag into debauchery, he went about doing all sorts of bad deeds and then, ended up abandoning the house and his wife, leaving them altogether. As such, Ryu Educk who became a grass widow at a still young age lived with her family, but as she was on bad terms with the legal wife of Soryeon's father, she spent the days, crying and sighing during what was commonly the fairest point in time for women. As she was the earliest to receive the civilization's light of dawn that for the first time shed on Joseon, she started to attend chapels to wish for the afterlife and within a lonely life, where her heart had nowhere to head to, it found joy in learning as she studied and amplified her knowledge day by day. Yet, as it was with a majority of women in the district's peninsula, she was someone that failed to get the ray of hope other than superstitious beliefs. However, in an environment where she eternally lost her love for men, she did not intend to get married again and instead, she set her goals on education. Perhaps, owing to her destiny, she stepped on a relatively gentle route in reaching up here. After becoming a widow, under the protection of her mother, she received school fees, studied, and did not have much temptation coming from outside and so, she was not a sturdily unmoving rock that taunted the currents of the seaside. So, she tended to be biased and could not let go of pretending to be the only one innocent. Yet, her strict and simple mannerism in church earned the respect of all the churchgoers and young students. So, as she was able to study there and not lose her job, she came to live a life in the most secure position. Afterward, her parents who always inflicted worries on her passed away at the end of the month.

Ryu Kyeong-hwan, Soryeon's father deserted his legal wife and found substitutes for women once a few months. Then, he got obsessed with Soryeon's mother and there, while he came to find joy in seeing his adorable daughter, perhaps from being under some kind of curse, for her entire life, Soryeon's mother let out deep sighs, rarely smiled, and she was apt to wash her tears that came out on end with the hem of her skirt. Even then, as it must have been that Soryeon's mother could not bear it any longer from the deep sorrow amassed together, in the year Soryeon turned 11, she passed away. Up to this point in time, Ryu Kyeong-hwan, who squandered almost all of the family fortune, left Soryeon under the care of his sister and went back to his past wife. But during fall, no less than one year from then, he passed away from indigestion.

From that time onward, under the care of her aunt, day by day, Soryeon grew physically and mentally just as her small bones thickened, but the opportunity to melt the layer of ice embedded in the very bottom of her heart did not arrive again easily. There was a flaw in Ryu Educk raising Soryeon, which was that she left a lonely shadow on Soryeon's face. While she may not have been miserly about clothes and school fees, when Soryeon got sick, though it was not the case of being late in finding a medicine, Ryu Educk was somewhat careless and forlorn. The carelessness and forlornness seemed to wane a bit after Soryeon completed her studies, but at the end of her anger-laden speech or her talk about marriage, Ryu Educk said unfailingly,

"It's because you resemble your mother, and that is why there's such a thing as bloodline," and Soryeon heard the unpleasant words.

Even as she heard such words, she merely believed it to be an irony of her aunt and while she did not ponder on her bloodline, Soryeon who did not receive compassion eventually did not get to be an exuberant person and along with such personality, as the dark shades became amply embedded, even the needless tears were frequent.

When Soryeon who was in such a state met Song Hyo-sun from Incheon, she came to know warmth, where somehow, her whole body felt as if it would melt. Yet, as if she had the same dream again, it was like an apparition which someday, she could not help but try not to forget with all her strength.

One night, when Soryeon had been thinking a lot about Song Hyo-sun, she had a strange dream.

It was a place like the Shimogamo Jinja of Kyoto rarely seen in Joseon. Surrounding the shrine yard, set in a wide forest with trees, the creek with rapid currents flowed and next to the bridge that stretched out of the shrine, a gigantic zelkova tree stood, and on top of the highest branch that could be remotely seen, the indigo flower with six leaves, edged with gold was floating in the air like the moon. At the bottom, the creek just as ever made the gushing sound while rapidly flowing down. Upon looking at it closely, in the creek, the raft that was not seen until now was being carried away and on top of it, a young woman, lying sideways, was being swept away as she gazed only at the south. As her whole body was chilled, while she tried to come to her senses, something shrieked into her ears, saying, the thing being washed away is You! You! and it let out an ear-splitting sound until her entire body went numb.

Soryeon tried to shake her body and make a sound, telling herself, I woke up, I woke up, in order to open her eyes, but even then, they would not open, and the scary raft flowing in sync with the rapid currents was vivid before her eyes.

In the meanwhile, as she had awoken, she laid her hand on her chest and soothed her body, which had been in slumber with clothes on.

As she awakened, while she had thought that she dreamed of her one-time trip to Kyoto, every time she mused over Hyo-sun, for some reason, she came to think of the dream as something of an ominous sign.

4

Yet, as there was a saying, 'When the time comes, the hardened rocks also open their chest and spout the spring water that soars up from underneath its depths, out on the ground,' Soryeon, who in the daytime, prayed that she would meet him and who due to her failure to meet him, suffered from sleep paralysis at night, finally met Hyo-sun.

It was the summer, just two years ago. One day, Madam Educk was concerned for Soryeon's health and as such, it was a time when she had been advising Soryeon to retire from teaching at S School. Madam Educk, who wrote down the light labor and study hours and had been deeply chiding at her to care for her health, threw a piece of paper at Soyreon as if something she forgot abruptly came to mind and asked her to buy peach for making ice cream, saying that a guest would be coming.

Every time a guest was coming, Soryeon waited around, mulling over whether Mr. Hyo-sun would not be coming, but as day after day, he did not turn up, she stood up dejectedly, wondering what guest would be arriving again today, and walked all the way out to the front of Changgyeongwon and got on the tram. In the blistering afternoon of the summer days, Soryeon could not disobey as it was ordered by her aunt and went all the way to Jin Gogae and bought the aromatic soft peach. At the time, Madam Educk said,

"As Song Dal-seong who's helped a lot with the Young Women's Association is coming, go dress up in new clothes and nimbly entertain him."

When she heard these words, Soryeon was taken by surprise that it was a person named Song, but as the name was different and because she knew who he was, she was reassured to a certain extent.

That day, in the evening, a gentleman over 40 and a young gentleman aged 25 to 26 walked the sand-covered ground near the Technical Junior College in merry steps that were neither lazy nor hurried, heading to Sungui-dong.

The sky spread out the heart of a maiden and as if to wrap up the white ball of cotton in the silk wrapping cloth, it once again thinly unfurled the light pink that had a purplish light spinning, appearing to have engulfed the summer clouds, and at one end of the pearly horizon, the women came and went to gather water from the well. It was as if in an attempt to forget the exhaustion of the day when the sky and the ground were hot, the evening wind cooled and drowsy tunes were exchanged.

As Soryeon had seen from a certain scenario book that she was starting to read these days, she adorned the dining table with blue grape vines, went to the kitchen, and said to her aunt, "Madam, please look at how I set the dining table."

As Madam Educk, whose expression of joys and sorrows was usually not evident, beamed upon seeing Soryeon's wits, she said,

"That kind of trick is your forte."

As Soryeon was well aware of her aunt's habit, she was by all means struck by a celebratory occasion that she spoke to her aunt in succession.

"What kind of guest would be receiving such a good treatment of ours?" and

"Why of all times did you invite the guest in the evening?"

"Would only one person be coming?"

In one of rare moments, when Soryeon's aunt was setting up ice cream while joyfully talking, the unfamiliar sound of footsteps was heard from the yard and called out,

"Come here."

Upon hearing this sound, as Soryeon's aunt halted her conversation, a woman named Yeongbok who was wiping the dishes by their side immediately rose to her feet and said,

"Ah, guests have already arrived." Then, she went down to the front of the yard. Madam Educk also hurriedly washed her hands and after rising up, she was about to step into the room but instead, she went out to the yard facing the guests. She completed her greeting with a voice ripe with friendliness and it also seemed like she was greeting another person whom she saw for the first time.

At this moment, as Soryeon felt her heart beating for some reason, she could not bear it any longer without standing up and looking out. Raising her body that was trembling like the poplar trees, she looked out of the kitchen door – At that very moment, what would Soryeon have seen? As if her whole body turned rigid, she could not move around freely and so, she was going to turn her head, but could not even do so, and stood blankly, looking out.

Yet, a little while later, upon seeing Soryeon sitting nonchalantly and setting up the ice-cream, Ryu Educk, who made her guests be seated and returned to the kitchen, said,

"We have three guests."

After being speechless for a long time, Soryeon asked in a trembling voice,

"Who are these people?"

Madam Educk who hastily put food on the plate momentarily halted the movement of her fingers and said indifferently,

"Right, I did not tell you. Well – from now on, a student is coming to our house. It's a 25-year-old woman named Yoon En-sun.

Her husband, Mr. Song Hyo-sun, the nephew of Mr. Song Dal-seong returned after completing his studies in university from Tokyo and is living in Incheon."

Soryeon unwittingly cried out,

"Then, it's Mr. Song Hyo-sun from Incheon Meteorological Observatory."

At this moment, as if a bit astonished, her aunt asked,

"How did you know that he was in Incheon Meteorological Observatory? I was greeting him just now."

At this point, while Soryeon thought for an instant that she had made a mistake, she spoke without constraint,

"Uh, it was from being on a trip to Incheon Meteorological Observatory."

And in an attempt to hide her complexion, she turned around to the other side and opened the lid of the tea kettle, which was lifting a sweet fragrance as it boiled.

When the food was all prepared like this and the dining table was set, Soryeon and Hyo-sun were not able to exchange a lot of words, because they met as if they were trying to cross a log bridge face-to-face, in front of surveillants, their respective uncle and aunt, who were like the cliff. But under the 12-point luminous intensity of the lightbulb's red light, their flushed faces, overjoyed at seeing each other to the point of radiating a deep bluish hue, drew the surrounding attention.

Yet, starting from when they met, they could not be closer than as people who had merely known each other and as it was not right to stir up love or romance again in the midst of it, their destiny fixed the seal on conditions that neglected freedom under the social system.

Yet, as Soryeon had such a pleasant meeting with him, wouldn't she have wanted to meet in a quiet place just for the two of them and laughed in joint bliss and felt joint sorrow? While from having been wrapped up in the skirt trails of old morality, it may have been Soryeon's rationale that she could not get out of the rigid custom, how on earth could she block out the natural demands of nature? Yet, in their case, they hid such emotions and Hyo-sun felt displeased, as if the blending of ice and boiling water were sprinkled over him. This was because as his wife found her way to this place to be educated under the tutelage of Madam Ryu Educk and with Soryeon as the assistant teacher, the thoughts he had of Soryeon in the previous days seemed like an attempt to grasp the forbidden fruit.

5

Starting from the following day, Song Hyo-sun's wife, Yoon En-sun came to stay in Ryu Educk's house.

As originally a woman of the past who had grown up in a family entrenched in the old custom, she was Song Hyo-sun's wife, who undid the hair that she had braided behind her ears when she was a child, as a so-called traditional ritual of getting married. Yet, as they each had grown up in a separate course of life, revering something different, there was no knowledge they shared in any way and no assimilation of unified thoughts and emotions. As such, they could not be friends who could move forward in unity, stepping on the same path eternally and aiding each other. Yet, as the structure of society was still bound to knock over a person who demanded freedom, his footsteps could not head straight up towards the path of freedom, which was the ideal goal. And, half of his heart was a great deal higher up than the ground and as for the other half of his heart, it was merely by way of sympathizing with a pitiful woman, En-sun that he sent her to the School for Wives managed by the Young Women's Association, as if to suppress his burning emotions for ideal.

As Song Hyo-sun sent En-sun to school, praying that the seed planted late would grow more quickly than the tree planted earlier on a rich soil and even anxious that she would review what she would learn, (Without being able to by himself tell this apart from his unconscious wish to meet Soryeon), Hyo-sun came to knock on the door of Madam Ryu Educk.

Yet, Soryeon did not have the strength to teach Yoon En-sun who knew nothing but the Korean alphabet and it somehow got to a point where things like En-sun reviewing her studies were negligently considered and there were a lot of times that En-sun consulted solely in food, clothing, and shelter (bare necessities of life).

In the meantime, Hyo-sun came over once a month and once

on two holidays and left after praising Madam Educk. Each time, while Hyo-sun and Soryeon became further apart, Hyo-sun and Madam Educk got along and En-sun and Soryeon got closer.

Eventually, as Soryeon and Hyo-sun whose closeness derived from knowing each other disappeared, if they happened to meet in a deserted place, they faltered and seemed to pretend not to know each other to the point that they could not greet one another. As it has turned out like this, during the time that En-sun and Soryeon studied and did housework under one inspection, on the cool autumn days, in the golden-like forest of gingko tress, the leaves fell and with the long winter coming, when tangerine peels piled up from people peeling them off in the room, snow barely managed to melt like an elder loaded with a heavy baggage crossing the long hill.

In the meanwhile, En-sun and Soryeon exchanged a lot of past stories they kept in their heart. People instantly praised them for having a sibling-like relationship upon seeing their closeness. Yet, in the complexion of Soryeon who treated En-sun like a sibling, it could not conceal the troubled look that seemed to be enduring something.

As Soryeon herself was often frail, she could not assist in the efforts of her aunt and talked about leaving her aunt's home in the future permanently. And En-sun shared the enviable story that her cousin was now living a life, joyfully collecting money as her cousin studied even when harassed, without heeding the objections of parents and uncle, while growing up in the same house with her. Yet, their closeness did not last long and as the days became warm, a crack started to form.

In the spring days, as it became mottled with heat haze in the far and near part of the flat plain, above the horizon where not even a bud sprouted, just in time, Soryeon got engaged.

How cornered must Soryeon have felt while undergoing this moment. Although in her heart, still, the impression of Song Hyosun only deepened and did not in the slightest wane, it was a circumstance where she did not have any choice but to marry someone else! Who should she confess this to? She lapsed into a severe depression.

Once again, even when she pleaded that she would lead an independent life by getting a job and not cause harm to her aunt, even the first time around, her aunt, having gotten knowledge somewhere, said,

"You can't because of your bloodline."

And the second time around, she intimidated her,

"It doesn't all turn out the way everyone wants it to."

Soryeon's body once again withered. As the cold spell of tedious winter went away, people's desire to play surged rapidly in their chest, but in Soryeon's heart, the cold spell accumulated day by day and so, a sheet of ice got embedded in her chest.

As there was nowhere to relieve such lonely emotions, she furrowed her eyebrows and although she grudgingly prepared clothes for the future (marriage), she shed boundless tears from the sorrow whose cause could not be exactly explained, while holding a book (Traditional old book) and reciting the following words.

Isn't someone calling me

In the middle of the night In the middle of the night

The small boat that could not hang the lamplight

would not lose its paddle and yet,

not having the will to row ahead

Isn't someone calling me

Isn't someone calling me.

Beneath the ice Beneath the ice

Life that fails to receive the light

would not lose the ability to flow and yet,

it could not get the degree of heat to melt

Isn't someone calling me

Isn't someone calling me.

Oh Oh Oh Oh

Light, the degree of heat and light

Hoping for it to come out in one place and yet,

not seizing the opportune time

Isn't someone calling me

Isn't someone calling me.

If

If spring melts me

In the rock crevice, the plantain fruit would blossom, blossom

If, If.

If I seize the opportune time,

I would open the rock and pour, pour my heart.

If, If.

6

That year, as the spring was somewhat ripe, Soryeon's pallid body that had shocked people who saw her bloomed like a flower.

Song Hyo-sun came over to Ms. Ryu Educk's house frequently, in search of his wife. And hearing Ryu Educk say that she was going to get Soryeon married to Choi Byeong-seo from Pyeongyang, as if to oppose this, he said,

"If a person like her is already put into the family system, who would be carrying out social activism? If Joseon's family system is fairly good, it won't be the case that she couldn't work after getting married, but······perhaps, she would fall into the well without being able to pump out the well water and without being able to build the dike again. Please bring her further out into society," and closed his mouth. Upon hearing these words, Soryeon was truly grateful. So, she thought to herself, 'Then, Mr. Hyo-sun hopes that I live on in this society meaningfully.' Also, as if her heart could not let go of such a meaning, it cried out, 'Let's get out of the tethers of the family system.'

Afterward, a few days later, saying that he was going to Japan to write a doctorate thesis, as Song Hyo-sun stopped over at Ms. Ryu Educk's house, he got the opportunity to talk to Soryeon.

In the holiday morning, Madam Ryu Eduk and Hyo-sun went out early, but Hyo-sun returned first and greeted Soryeon who was reading a book at the edge of the wooden floor. He said,

"Spring has so clearly arrived. What is the book you're reading?"

Feeling ashamed of Hyo-sun's cold shoulders that had vacillated between pretending to know her or not know her until this moment, she thought, 'Why did you stop bestowing kindness, which seemed like it would persist as you followed me? If you were a bit kinder to me, my heart would've softened.' Yet, because on this day of all days, as Hyo-sun became urgently kind to her, with the helplessness once struck by this, while she felt happy, she thought, 'What happens if the door locked in my heart opens? It would be at the very moment that I would commit a horrifying sin' and said equivocally,

"Yes. It really has become spring"

and called over En-sun who had been cleaning her room, unaware of her husband's arrival and with her face quickly flushing even more, she promptly said to Hyo-sun,

"It's Hauptmann's *Lonely Lives.*"

and could not finish her words. Seeing En-sun come out to the wooden porch, as if Soryeon had been saved, she said,

"Ms. En-sun, he's come already."

En-sun looked back and forth between Soryeon's face and Hyo-sun's face and at the question from her husband, "What were you doing?"

she said, "I've been cleaning the room" and pursed her lips.

At this opportunity, immediately rising to her feet, Soryeon went to the cupboard placed in the corner of the wooden porch at the other side and pulled out a tea set.

Hyo-sun abashedly eyed Soryeon's equivocal attitude that looked as if she was shot to pieces and said,

"Teacher Educk hasn't come back yet?" and smiled. Soryeon held the tea set she pulled out and said,

"Yes, she hasn't returned yet. She went out with you."

Then, she headed to the kitchen and seemed to try to safeguard her duty as the host of the house.

After a long while, Soryeon came out, carrying and getting tea from a person who cooked rice named Yeongbok.

In the meanwhile, Hyo-sun was studiously eyeing the book that Soryeon put down after reading. And then, as Soyreon put the tea in front of him, he said,

"Up to which part of the book did you read? Is it the first time you're reading it? I also quite enjoyed reading this book."

As she also offered tea to En-sun who was sitting in front of Hyo-sun face-to-face, as if Soryeon was merely surprised, she could only say,

"Yes, yes."

Hyo-sun took a close look at Soryeon's attitude, but as if it wasn't that unfamiliar, he said,

"In Hauptmann's *Lonely Lives*, there are people like us. While you still may not have read until the very end, it is rare for a famous foreign piece like this to wring the heart of a Joseon youth," and blankly opened his luster-filled eyes.

Soryeon sat nearby En-sun's side and once again simply replied,

"I just managed to read all of it now."

Lowering his eyes that had been staring at the sky, Hyo-sun gazed at Soryeon for a long time and in his soft voice, he said,

"I don't know if you've thought about it yet, but in the book, there is a man like me who has a mother, a wife, and a child but is the loneliest in the world. When I was studying abroad, I did not read it with that much feeling, but after coming back to this land, I think that there is nothing like it that could beautifully soothe our heart that much."

Finally, at this moment, carried away by her instinctive impulse that was fond of stories, Soryeon said frantically,

"Then, you think that Johannes and Mahr truly loved each other······Right······?"

and opened her radiantly colored eyes like a bell. At this moment, grinning slightly, Hyo-sun said,

"Miss Soryeon, it isn't that they came to love each other. Through the past and the future, we set up one ideal and there, we come to love something reasonable and have been doing so.

Yet, such an ideal love is not only rare for people but also if there is a resonance in ideology and psychological comfort and if fortunate, an approval for not splitting up would arise. While the exchange of approval in the script is a lot more extravagant than it is in Joseon, the circumstance of Johannes kneeling down under the domination of old morality is common in Joseon. Speaking of which, we are buds just starting to sprout while they are trees growing."

For a long while, Soryeon lowered her head and after ruminating, she said,

"Then, couldn't it not be said that people try hard to seek love or lose it? Also, even if we wait to grow until the moment we blossom, eventually, doesn't the sorrow like the relationship between Johannes and Mahr not cease? At that moment, a new tragedy would arise again."

"Yes, Miss Soryeon. It is a lie that a person seeks love or loses it. A person has love in oneself and it is nothing but a case of being awakened from something and eventually having a clear awareness in life. The tragedy like the one you mentioned in *Lonely Lives* of course could not be evaded until wherever it is, a person first makes one's destiny and goes on to dominate the world and until the life of colluding with everyone in the world is abolished."

"So, that Johannes –"

and Soryeon dithered over something and then, said,

"Does Johannes also get destroyed eventually from falling into the trap of old morality? As I don't know philosophy, I don't have a clear idea on Darwin or the theory of Hegel that he knows, but the female student called Mahr comes to know everything about his theory and about him, which absolutely resonates with her. It turns into a relationship where it's difficult for them to split up."

"Yes –"

and Hyo-sun turned his head as if he found it a bit strange and replied.

"That······Johannes met an ideal friend. Yet, he certainly could not live with her let alone console the friend for one or two more days. So, the friend does not even indicate where she's heading and goes away, but leaves one strange statement. That is, even though the two people are split up, it's to live under one principle and one goal. As they believe in the same theory, it's to live carrying out a lot of the same actions by behaving in accordance with the theory. However, Johannes dies, drowning in the lake, without thinking of translating his acute bodily emotions into a long-time faith in the future. He is quite a lonely man."

And Hyo-sun stared at the sky once again. En-sun followed suit, staring at it.

Yet, after looking down at her hand on her knees, Soryeon, inserting strength into the end of her words, said,

"Of course,"

and she uttered,

"That······Johannes is a person who couldn't have faith?"

"No"

and Hyo-sun threw another powerful glance at Soryeon and

said,

"While it may not be like that, he was a lot more cornered than Mahr. Whoever it is, even if one may not be Johann Wolfgang von Goethe, one could not believe in a vague theory and would instead, demand a vigorous life."

At this moment, as if to bring life into a marble statue, Soryeon unwittingly said,

"Then, say Johannes solved the difficult problem by taking his own life. What about Mahr?"

As if to respond to these words with the utmost interest, Hyo-sun said,

"Oh-"

and was opening his mouth when from the sound of En-sun's words,

"The tea is getting cold"

he at last came to his senses after having quite forgotten the presence of his wife and cursorily looking at her, he said,

"Right!"

and moistened his throat that was dry from talking.

"That is because Mahr was afflicted with a helpless life circumstance"

and rummaging through the bookshelf, he found one spot and continued his words.

"Isn't that so? She said that she would study and study until she would indeed not even turn a side-glance. That is, while we certainly don't know the true intention of the author, as to whether she took off to finally seek the theory or whether she was hiding her face with the book in order to forget her misery, she eventually hit the road."

At this time, as if Soryeon was perplexed, she said,

"Then, don't you think that they are different from each other? Wasn't Johannes far ahead of her? Also, isn't it that Mahr could never trust Johannes? If not, would Mahr have more potential for future growth than Johannes?"

and questioned like a young student asking a teacher.

"No, their environment was different. While the two may have hoped to live together like anyone, Mahr believed that Johannes would be returning to the old life even if it was missing her, not only because Mahr completely believed in the spiritual world, but also because contrastingly, Johannes had an object of old morality. Yet, as long as he got to know the warmth of his hometown, what kind of person would be continuing a tasteless, lonely life again? While the author wrote up till' there and sealed the case······."

He finished his words and grabbed the cookies that were laid in front of him. And then, he said,

"Miss Soryeon, a person could never say that one could live only when one physically merges with the other person, whoever it is. While that'd be fine for people who didn't get to circulate affection without knowing how to improve from resisting this world, don't we delicately see everything in our surrounding from knowledge about a single object? It is merely fortunate that the awareness in life we get from the object is clear. However, I think that the case of women is actually closer to the case of Johannes. It is the case of Joseon women above all, but I don't think that is morally right."

And he stared at Soryeon who was in deep thoughts.

7

Soryeon's face turned pale. Her lips even turned a deep blue.

En-sun had been sitting still, but then, pouring tea, she went to the front of the table. After looking in the mirror hanging in front, without noticing that her own eyes held spite, En-sun shot her gaze at Hyo-sun staring down at the front of the yard like everything was agonizing after ending the conversation with Soryeon, which was performed as if in a harmonization of breaths.

At this time, as the two people realized the gaze from behind that shone as it got reflected, they turned around simultaneously. It was right at this moment. The two faces with the beauty of intellect and the speculative face that merely suspected something gathered in the mirror, like sharply forming into a triangle.

At once, Soryeon who became a tad pale, as if the two eyes reflected a black jewel, turned and said,

"Ms. Ensun. As there are sweet potatoes I boiled in the cupboard, please take them out. While it may not be tasty because I carelessly made them with my hands······."

At these words, En-sun wordlessly brought the tea kettle out, placing it in between Soryeon and Hyo-sun, went into her room, and came out, holding a bag of candy drop and chocolate, put them on the woodblock, and as if she was reluctant, she faltered before pulling out the sweet boiled potatoes from the cupboard.

Instantly, the smell of burnt eggs, butter, and milk made up the sweet aroma and radiated above the serene porch that was shone by the spring sunlight. With the seeming dexterity that was about to put back the delicious-looking thing, En-sun asked with a lump in her throat,

"Are you going to eat this?"

Wearing a weak smile, Hyo-sun wordlessly looked at En-sun, then at Soryeon, and turning his head, fixed his eyes on the sky. Soryeon looked sorrily at En-sun's displeased complexion and with her unsteady breathing, she ended up saying,

"Put that worthless thing back."

In accordance with what Soryeon said, En-sun put back what she had taken out and returned to her seat.

The sky manifested a clear smile and as if it cared for what people thought, it cleared up rather low. In the yard, above the ground where steam rose up densely, the cripple flower and dandelion had bloomed. In the flower bed, the peony that grew by a handspan and the plantain, which grew by a couple of squares were fluttering in the serene spring wind amidst the unnamed flower foliage.

The tea was lifting the thin steam as the sunlight glared down the southward porch in the broad daylight of a spring day and along with the cookies, appeared to have departed from the memory of the people of this world.

However, after a long while, En-sun broke such serenity and in a choked sound, she offered, "Please have some tea."

In their faces, not even the tiniest disagreeableness was mixed in their affectionate faces, which seemed to be off into space, thinking the same thought as the two (Hyo-sun and Soryeon) stared at the sky and then, looked down at the ground.

It was at this moment. For some reason, since then, it was thought that Hyo-sun and Soryeon got closer while En-sun and Soryeon grew distant······Until now, in this world we have seen all the things that used to be attached become detached and all the things that used to be detached become attached. It is also the case when we're choosing between the ddeok (rice-cake), kimchi, fruits, and meat we eat······! There is no time that we don't see such a thing day after day. Yet, there, we try to build a country that has no such thing as splitting from one another and try to build a country that would not be broken up. Yet, day after day, we split up and during the time that we meet, we witness change day after day. At last, people who possessed both physicality and spirituality were finally not able to overcome their weakness and came to break up the country from revealing the cracks to destiny and lose the opportunity, which is why we start to cry and laugh in the east and west and stray in the north and south.

Here, Soryeon's destiny was certainly set on where she would go. Over several days that Hyo-sun was staying, En-sun spent the day with speculation and suspicion, Madam Educk was not idle in her rigorous surveillance, and all the while, the legal wife of Soryeon's father came up to Seoul under the pretext of sightseeing and following along with many people's suspicions, she told tales about Soryeon.

"Who knows how she'd behave when she takes after her mother?"

As if he was abashed, Hyo-sun would only direct a look filled with sympathy to Soryeon and kept silent. Even prior to this, Soryeon and Hyo-sun reflected all their action back to each other, questioned each other on every suspicion, answered everything commandingly, and were subservient to each other in all deeds. Over these past couple days, En-sun could not stop shedding tears and whispered something frequently to Madam Educk.

At this, Madam Educk took on a tactful attitude to Hyo-sun and was busy trying to finalize Soryeon's marriage. During this brief period, Hyo-sun once again acted like he pretended not to know Soryeon. And then, he quickly prepared to set off for Tokyo. In the meanwhile, once again, his father, Song Do-seong came up to Seoul from the province and took Hyo-sun away to an inn. Soryeon had happily spent the few days with the man she longed for like a dream. However, everything passed by like a dream.

From the threats of her aunt and the legal wife of her father, she hastily accepted getting wed to Choi Byeong-seo.

Madam Educk went back to showing a cordial attitude to Hyo-sun. Day by day, Soryeon grew haggard again. En-sun's complexion relaxed. Yet, at the same time that the complexion of Hyo-sun's face teemed with unpleasantness, ridicule, and sharpness, it seemed to obediently take in the mildest behavior. Madam Educk effortfully ushered Choi Byeong-seo into the house. Byeong-seo courted the good graces of aged women with his money that was commonplace. Every time Byeong-seo turned up in the doorstep, even the woman called Yeongbok received him with open arms.

Byeong-seo tried to pleasantly get along with Hyo-sun and bantered,

"You have a bachelor's degree! A Bachelor of science!"

Mr. Choi plastered cream over his dark face and removed the grease from his coarse hair in imitation of Hyo-sun's looks. While this showed the incongruous features of Hyo-sun's pale, lofty face and Byeong-seo's copper-colored cantankerous face, Hyo-sun who was mild and moreover, did not wish to be under any restraint did not want to be perturbed in any way and tried hard to compromise.

While doing so, he seemed to really hold Byeong-seo who was a law graduate from Meiji University of Tokyo in high esteem. And he did not fix his habit of looking up at the sky.

Yet, he occasionally said, "It is said that a person who doesn't break harmony in the surrounding would be the only happiest one and someone who goes way beyond and breaks up everything but still is able to skillfully regroup is the only great being. Also, while targeting something that is incongruous with a person is like a thief, as much as a person does not know the origin of one's own life, one would not have started such a life by oneself and so, could not take responsibility for everything, which is why mere efforts are needed."

Byeong-seo scoffed at Hyo-sun's words, saying that they did not seem like words from a bachelor of science. Still, Hyo-sun ended up wordlessly staring at the sky.

Instead, Soryeon wanted to cut down on these distressful days and quickly head to Byeong-seo's house. Yet, as it did not turn out according to such an intention, she toiled under anyone's gaze.

Subsequently, even as Hyo-sun was leaving for Japan, he dragged the disappointed but speechless Soryeon to the backyard and left words like such.

"Ms. Soryeon, I am just happy that one time, we got to live on Earth and bond with each other like this. As we got to know each other now, the only thing that's needed is to live a life where we are conscious of one another and make the efforts to meet at the same point of unity. Later, Ms. Soryeon would be having a harmonious family with Mr. Choi Byeong-seo. Also, you wouldn't forget me, your like-minded unforgettable friend, which happened to be an uncoincidental opportunity. I would go on to endure adversity and work hard like you. Okay-isn't it refreshing? We don't have destruction that sweeps over Johannes and Mahr. Okay-how welcoming it is if we think that the Mars that we're studying would be like our Earth. Also, how surprising it would be if we think that we could make a passage there. Yet, we don't cut back on the right of time to solve things by itself. It is merely that in the meanwhile, a person is allowed to do only what one works hard on."

At this moment, Soryeon could not suppress her closeness to him that overflowed from her chest and stood close to him, crying out,

"O-Oraboni (Meaning older brother but not denoting a sibling relation here; rather, a Korean term of endearment referring to a male who's older than her)."

With his head turned, Hyo-sun spoke,

"Nu-i (Meaning younger sister but not denoting a sibling relation here; rather, a Korean term of endearment referring to a female who's younger than him)"

and wheeled around first, going to the front yard.

At this time, opportunely, it was the evening of spring day. Above the sky, a lark cried out from a remote place, just as it was possessed of sorrow, heightening its emotion.

Later on, as if everything had been there from the very beginning and as if everything had not been there, Soryeon came to live in Mr. Choi's house. However, as Byeong-seo who did not have faith in her said that while he could respect Soryeon, he could not love her, he meddled with other women whenever he wanted to and deserted the house. Even so, he was not shameful in abusing Soryeon who worked hard on her household chores, as if she was a person filled with flaws. All the while, Byeong-seo's mother occasionally came over and harassed Soryeon, as if her son's affection had been taken away by Soryeon. Yet, Soryeon endured through it, worked, studied, loved everything, and lived on, softening people.

Afterward, even if Soryeon would go to Seoul, she who had been coincidentally suspected by En-sun and Madam Educk could not meet Hyo-sun.

Afterward, Hyo-sun earned a doctoral degree. Also, he hid at Incheon Meteorological Observatory and piled up his research. Yet, it was heard that because he was in a feud with his wife, he was living a single life and avoiding women.

Hearing this, all the more, Soryeon was not idle in her labor, learning, and love. While she had been like such, on this night, seized by her musing, outside the brick wall, she plaintively listened to the voice of Hyo-sun who came to lecture again. As the summer night dragged on, her whole body trembled.

Yet, the tedious thought at the back of her mind made her fall asleep and hours later, she brought her respiration during sleep to a brief halt and opened her eyes in a flash. It appeared that Byeong-seo still had not come back yet. At this moment, all the things that did not seem to be present were there. In the wide three-compartment room, how much she had hoped for freedom despite how fettered her body was?!

Whatever it is, isn't Soryeon's desperate hope for freedom in the photograph of Rodin's *Danaid* hanging on the wall by the ondol floor, in Longfellow's *The Arrow and the Song*, an English poem embroidered on a jade-green scroll made out of white silk at the bedside, and in the painting of an unnamed waterfowl struggling to get out of the distant family sphere, an act of freedom as it clung to a club and was bound by it? How could Soryeon who looked back on all these things hope for there to be no merging of two flows that encircled Rungnado of Taedong River? The flows would break down the dike!

Yet, after such a moment, they would say, it was inherited by bloodline, that it was adultery.

What would the refreshing courage of a person who earned freedom at this moment be called?

Wouldn't it be said, 'What things did you name? Which name are you averse to and despise? Amongst them, don't you insult beautiful things?' Who would guarantee things? Who is as pure to the point of being able to block the outcry? What kind of adult pronounced judgment on it?

While nodding her head, Soryeon gave her approval in front of a deity that could not be seen. The sky that had been dark began to grow light above the Taedong river.

It is natural that on the day the night broke out into dawn, Soryeon went all the way to the meeting hall, listened to Hyo-sun's lecture, and was moved by it. Also, regardless of whether that is the case or not, like the spring water flowing in harmony with eternal life, it is guaranteed that she would live life refreshingly.

Even as dawn arrives on this day, she would assess every living being and take it out of Choi Byeong-seo's house that is actually hers. Who wouldn't know the true master of the house?

The master of the house would be sound, gentle, and respected.

With that, it was the instinct of a person who lives on to effortfully wait for the 'moment.'

It was natural that their world would be devoid of En-sun, Byeong-seo, and even Madam Educk.

[November 29th, 1924]

돌아다볼 때

1

여름밤이다. 둥글어가는 열이틀의 달빛이 이슬 내리는 대기 속에서 은실같이 서려서 연못가를 거니는 설움 많은 가슴속에 허덕여든다.

이슬을 머금은 풀밭에서 반딧불이 드나들어 달빛을 받은 이슬방울과 어우러진 공중의 진주인지 풀밭의 불꽃인지 반짝반짝한다.

소련은 거닐던 발걸음을 멈추고 연못가에 조는 듯이 앉았다. 바람이 언덕으로부터 불어 내려서 연잎들이 소련을 향하여 굽실굽실 절을 하듯이 흐느적거렸다. 무엇인지 듣지도 못하던 남방南邦의 창자를 끊는 듯한 설움이 눈앞에 아련아련한다.

마치 그의 생각이 눈앞에 이름 지을 수 없는 일들을 과거인지 미래인지 분간치 못하게 함과 같다.

음침히 조용한 최병서 집 서편 울타리 밖에서는 아이들이 하늘을 쳐다보면서

"별 하나 나 하나, 별 둘 나 둘, 별 셋 나 셋, 별 백 나 백, 별 천 나 천"

하고 노란 소리들을 서로 불러 받고 주었다. 이 어린 소리들이 그의 가슴속 맨 밑까지 들어서 '왜, 결합된 한 생명같이 한 법칙 아래 한 믿음으로 이 세상을 지나면서 하필 남북에 헤어져 있다가, 우연히 또 한 성에 모이게 되어서도 만나지도 못하고 울지 않으면 안 되었느냐' 하고 애달픈 은방울을 흔들었다.

'그러나 아무도 우리를 못 만나게 할 사람은 없는 것이 아니냐, 같은 회당에 모일 몸이' 하고 또다시 만날까 말까 오뇌할 때, 이 생각의 아득함을 꿰뚫는 듯이 귀뚜라미들이 그들의 코러스를 간단이 없게 울렸다.

여름 밤하늘의 맑음이 하늘 가운데로 은하를 건너고 그 가운데 던져버렸다는 오르페우스의 슬픈 거문고를 지금 이 밤에 그윽이 들려주는 듯하다.

구원久遠한 하늘을 우러러 옛사람들이 지은 옛이야기가 또다시 그 머리 위에 포개져서 설움을 북돋운다.

소련은 이슬에 젖어서 역시 이날도 뒷방 세칸 속으로 들어갔다. 그는 문을 잠그려다가 방문을 열어놓은 채 발을 늘이다 말고 우두커니 섰다.

이때 마침 창전리 언덕길 아래로 지나는 사람들의 음성이

"이 집이지?"

"송 군, 자- 언덕 위로라도 올라가서 잠깐이라도 보게그려. 그렇게 맑은 교제 사이였는데 못 만날 벌을 받을 죄가 왜 있단 말인가."

"원! 그렇지 않더라도 생각해보게. 남의 잠잠한 행복을 깨뜨릴 의리가 어디 있겠나."

"그럴 것이면 그 연연한 생각조차 씻은 듯이 없이 하든지……" 하면서 이야기하는 발소리를 들은 소련이가 향해 선 벽돌담 밑까지 가까이 오면서

"이 군, 이것이 유령幽靈도 아니고 동물도 아닌 사람의 우수憂愁일 것일세. 자- 부질없으니 내려가세. 겹겹이 벽돌로 쌓아높인 담 밖에 와 서서 본다기에, 무슨 위로가 있겠나"

하고 한 발소리가 급급히 내려가면서

"이 군, 어서 가서 Y양의 반주伴奏할 것을 좀더 분명히 익혀주게"

하매 그 뒤로 다른 발소리들도 따라 내려가는 듯하다.

소련은 또다시 소금 기둥이 된 듯이 그 자리에 섰다. 이 순간이 지나자 그의 마음속은 급히 부르짖는다.

'오- 송 씨의 음성이다. 그이가 아니면 어디서 그런 음성을 가진 사람이

있으랴, 그렇다 그렇다' 하고 그는 버선발로 벽돌담 밑까지 뛰어 내려가서 뒷문을 열려고 하나, 빗장을 튼튼히 찌르고 자물쇠를 건 문이 열쇠 없이는 열려질 리가 없었다. 그는 허둥지둥 연못 앞으로 가서 석등용 주춧돌 위에 발돋움을 하고 서서 담 밖을 내어다보나 달밤에 넓은 신작로가 빈 듯이 환히 보일 뿐 저 편 길 끝에 사람의 그림자 같은 것이 가물가물할지라도 긴가민가하다.

소련은 실심한 듯이 방 마루로 올라오면서 버선을 벗고 방으로 들어갔다.

소련은 생각만이라도 되돌려보겠다는 듯이, 여름 문을 꼭꼭 잠그고 지나온 생각에 잠겼다.

그때의 1년 전 봄에, S 학교 영문과를 좋은 성적으로 졸업한 소련은 그 봄부터 역시 경성에 S 학교 영어 교원이 되어서 그 아름다운 발음으로 생도들을 가르쳤다. 그와 생도들 사이도 지극히 원만하였고 또 선생들 틈에서는 좀 어린이 취급을 받았을지라도 근심거리가 없었다. 하나 소련은 그 봄부터 나날이 수척해갔다.

혹여 그의 수척해감을, 그가 어릴 때부터 엄한 그 고모의 감독아래서만 자라나서 그렇다 하기도 하고, 어떤 귀족과 혼설婚說이 있던 것을 영리한 체하고 신분이 다르니까 할 수가 없습니다, 하고 거절은 하였지만 미련이 남아서 번민한다고 하기도 하였다.

그러나 그의 사실은 이런 구역이 날 헛소리들을 뒤집어엎고 버리지 못할 이야기를 짓는다.

2

소련은 S 학교 영어 교사가 된 그 이듬해 4월 하순에 학교전체로 수학여행을 하게 되었을 때, 고등과 3년생들을 이끌고 다른 일본 선생들 틈에 섞여서 인천측후소仁川測候所로 가게 되었다.

그때 일기는 매일같이 구물구물하고 그러면서도 빗방울을 잠깐잠깐 뿌려보기도 해서 웅숭그리게 뼛속까지 사무치는 봄 추위가 얇은 솜저고리 입은 어깨를 벗은 듯이 으스러뜨렸었는데 소련이가 인천측후소를 찾은 것도 이러한 날들의 하루였다.

선생들과 생도들은 얼버무려서 모든 기계실에 인도되어 자못 천국에서 내려온 듯이 고상한 풍채를 가지고 또 그 음성이란 한번 들으면 영원히 잊히지 않을 젊은 이학자의 설명을 들었다.

젊은 이학자를 앞에 두고 40여 명의 선생과 생도는 지하실에서 지하실로 층층대에서 층층대로 올라갔다 내려갔다 하였다.

젊은 이학자는 가장 열심으로 그 희던 뺨에 불그레한 핏빛을 올리면서……

"아시겠습니까, 아시겠습니까?"

하고 설명했다. 소련도 열심으로 들으면서 가끔 알아듣는 듯이 고개를 끄덕여 보였다.

모든 기계실의 설비를 구경시키고 나서 젊은 이학자는 S 학교 선생들에게 차를 대접하려고 응접실로 인도하였다. 거기서 그들은 서로 명함을 바꾸었는데 소련은 그가 조선 청년인 것을 알고 귀밑이 달아오르는 것을 간신히 참고 있었다. 그러나 송효순은 뺨이 발개진 소련에게 조선말로 그 부드러움을 전부 표면에 나타내서

"나는 당신이 생도인 줄 알았어요. 아주 어려 보이니까요"

하고 그의 귀밑에 속삭였다. 이때에 소련은 처음으로 이성異性에 대해서 그 향기로움을 알았다. 지금까지 사내 냄새는 그리 정하지 않았던 것으로만 알았던 것이- 그 예상을 흐리고 이상한, 그 몸 가까이만 기다려지는 무엇을 깨닫게 되었을 때, 또다시

"언제부터 그 학교에 계셨습니까? 영어만 가르치세요, 과학에 대해서는

아무 취미도 안 가지셨어요?"

하고 그 달아오르는 귀밑에 송 씨의 조용한 말을 들었다.

그는 온몸이 무슨 벽의 튼튼함을 의지하고 싶기도 하고 자기 홀로인 고요하고 정결한 방 속에 숨고 싶기도 한 힘없음과 비밀스러운 기분에 취했었다.

그는 그러면서 송효순이 그의 몸 가까이 오지 않기를 바랐다. 그럴 때 효순도 같은 기분에 눌리는 듯이 점점 말을 없이 하고 그 옆에서 다른 일본 선생들과 어음(語音)불분명한 동경 말로 이야기를 했다. 선생들은 송효순에게 대단한 호의를 보이는 듯한 시선을 보내면서 소련을 유심히 바라보았다. 그리고 그 눈들이 모두 소련을 부러워해서 그 이학자의 몸 가까이 앉은 것을 우러러보는 듯하였다. 측후소를 떠나올 때 효순과 소련은 특별히 조용하게

"서울 어디 계세요?"

"저 숭이동…이에요."

"거기가 본택이십니까?"

"아니 그렇지 않아요."

"그럼, 여관입니까?"

"아니요, 제가 자라난 고모의 집이에요."

"그럼, 양친이 안 계십니까?"

"네……"

하고 그는 발뒤꿈치를 돌리려다가 또 한참 만에

"그럼 안녕히 계십쇼"

했다. 이때 효순은 무엇을 생각하는지 멍히 섰다가

"고모 되시는 어른은 누구세요?"

"저- E 학당의 류애덕이에요"

"그러면 훌륭하신 어른을 친척으로 모시는구먼. 혹시 찾아가보면 모르

는 체나 안 하시겠습니까?"

하고 이야기를 했었다.

소련은 이처럼 효순과 이야기를 바꾸고 생도들 틈에 섞여서 산등성이를 내려왔었다.

그 후로 그는, 도저히 잊지 못할 번민을 가지게 되었다. 그는 길거리에서라도 (그이가 자기를 찾아와 본다고 하였으므로) 혹여 넓은 가슴을 가진 준수한 남자의 쾌활한 걸음걸이를 볼 것 같으면 그이나 아닌가 하게 되었다. 그럴 동안에 그는 점점 수척해가고 모든 일에 고달픔을 깨닫게 되었다. 그는 단 한 번이라도, 다시 효순을 만나고 싶었다. 그의 그리워하는 효순에 대한 동경은 드디어 감성으로부터 영성에까지 미치게 되어 그는 새로이 과학에 대해서도 취미를 가지게 되었고……영원한 길나들이에서라도 만나지라는 소원까지 품게 되었다. 그는 밤과 낮으로 그이를 다시 만나지라고 기도했다. 잠깐 동안이었을지라도 그 아름다운 순결을 표시한 듯한 감성이 정결한 마음속에 잊지 못할 추억의 보금자리를 치게 하였던 것이다. 하나 그의 마음은 망설이지 않을 수 없었다. 아무리 굳센 의지가 있다 할지라도 단 한 번의 만남으로 얻은 감명이 걸핏하면 새로이 연구하려던 과학 같은 것도 잊어버리고는 다만 자기의 눈으로 만나고만 싶었다.

그는 드디어 밤과 낮으로 기도하던 보람도 없어 만나지지 못하므로, 시름시름 병을 이루게까지 되었다. 그 처녀의 마음에서는 송효순 이외의 모든 남자들은 초개같이 보였다. 그러나 그러함은 돌아보지 않고 류애덕을 향해서 소련에게 청혼을 하는 사람들은 결코 헤일 만치 드물지 않았다.

류애덕은 부모 없는 조카를 남부럽지 않게 10여 년 기른 피로로 인함인지, 또는 그의 장래를 위함인지 분명히 말을 하지 않으나 다만 하루바삐 그를 결혼시키고 싶어 했다. 어떤 때는 소련의 30원 받는 시간 교사의 월급이 너무 적어서 수치라고도 했다.

소련은 이때를 당해서 그 마음을 더욱 안정할 수가 없었다. 그는 얼마나 삶에 대해서 맹랑하고 쓸쓸한 일인 것을 깨달았었는지 또 그 고모의 교훈이 얼마나 표리가 있었던지 헤아려보면 헤아려볼수록 분명한 그릇됨을 찾아낼 수도 없건마는, 뜨거운 뜨거운 눈물이 저절로 그 해쓱한 뺨을 굴렀다. 다만 그는 밤과 낮으로 그렇지 않아도 처녀 때에 더더군다나 외로운 처지의 근심스러움과 쓸쓸함을 너무도 지독하게 맛보았다. 그는 어느 날은 침식을 잊고 이 분명히 이름도 지을 수 없는 아픔을 열병 앓듯 앓았다. 그는 흡사히 병인같이 되어서 S 학교에 가기를 꺼렸다. 하나 그는 하는 수 없이 거기 가지 않으면 고모의 생계를 도울 수 없었다.

그는 매일같이 사람 그리운 불타는 듯한 두 눈을 너른 길거리에 살펴 보이면서 S 학교에를 왕래하였으나 나중에는 아주 근력을 잃어서 눈을 땅 위에 떨어뜨리고 길 지나는 사람들을 쳐다보지도 않았다. 이런 때 처녀의 처음으로 사람 그리는 마음이 그대로 들떠지기도 쉬웠지마는 소련은 힘써 자기의 마음을 누르고 무엇을 그리는 그 비밀을 속으로 속으로 감추어서 드디어 모든 삶에 대해서 생각하게 되고 또 여자의 살림살이들 중에도 조선 여자의 살아온 일과 살아갈 일에 대해서 생각하게 되었다. 또 모든 사람의 살림살이들을 비교도 해보면서 과학에 대하여 알고 싶어지는 마음은 마치 고향을 떠난 어린이의 그것과 같이 이름만 들을지라도 가슴이 두근거려졌다.

어떤 때는 물리학이라든지 또는 천문학이라든지 하는 학문의 이름이 송효순의 대명사나 되는 듯했다. 하지만 소련이 스스로 그 동무들 간에는 그런 마음을 찾아볼 수 없는 것을 볼 때 얼마나 섭섭함과 외로움을 알았으랴. 그는 벌써 20이 넘은 처녀인데 이 처음으로 남 유달리 하는 근심은 그에게 부끄러운 듯한 행동거지를 하도록 시켰다.

그는 어떤 때는 S 학교 이과 선생에게 열심히 물어도 보고, 어떤 때는 여인들의 지나온 이야기에도 귀를 기울여보고, 그들이 얼마나 그릇된 살림살이를 하여왔는지도 정신 차리게 되었다. 하나, 소련의 건강은 나날이 글러갈 뿐이어서 그 쌀쌀스러운 류애덕 여사도 놀라지 않을 수 없게 되었다. 이러할 틈에 소련은 그 향할 곳 없는 마음에 병까지 들게 되었으므로 이학과 여인들의 모둠에도 힘쓰지 못하고, S 학교에서 영어를 가르치고 집으로 돌아오면 문학서 유를 손에 들게 되었다. 거기에는 모든 세상이 힘들지 않게 보이는 탓이었다. 전일에는 피아노도 열심으로 복습했지만 깊은 비밀을 가진 마음은 자연히 어스름 저녁때와 같이 불그레한 저녁 날빛 같은 희망조차 잃어버리기 쉬워서 캄캄한 명상에 빠져 마음의 소리를 내기도 꺼려졌다. 그는 얼마나 뒷동산 언덕 위에 서서 저녁 하늘을 바라보고 처창함을 느꼈을까. 만일 누구든지 그이의 마음을 알면, 비록 그 연애란 것이 아닐지라도 사람들이 일반으로 가지는 번민을 그렇게도 깊이도, 삼가롭게 함을 얼싸안고 불쌍히 여겨주었을 것이다. 하나 그에게는 아무의 동정도 향해지지 않았다. 그는 문학서 유를 들고 고모의 눈치를 받게 되고(류애덕의 교육은 생계를 얻기 위하여 학교 졸업을 받는 것이 주장이었으니까) 어두운 마음의 비밀을 품고는 학교에서 같은 선생들의 의심스러운 눈치를 받고, 생도들의 속살거림을 받았다. 그는 그 눈들에 대해서, 은근히 검은 눈을 둥그렇게 뜨면서, '아니요, 그렇진 않아요. 하지만 당신들이 모르는 내 마음에 힘 있게 받은 기억이 나를 이같이 괴롭게 해요' 하고 눈으로 변명했다. 하나 그 마음이 아무에게도 통하지는 못하고, 같은 선생들은 단순히,

"처녀의 번민- 상당히 허영심도 있을 것이지."

"글쎄 답답해, 류애덕 씨가 완고스러운데 그때 왜 소련은 기회를 놓쳤던고. 벌써 그 귀족은 혼인 예식을 지냈다지……"

"불쌍해라, 그런 자리를 놓치다니. 너무 영리한 체하는 것도 손해야"

하고 자기네들끼리 중얼거리기도 하고,

"왜 그렇게 수척해가시오, 류소련 씨. 그런 귀여운 자태를 가지고 번민 같은 것을 가질 필요야 있습니까. 아무런 행복이라도 손쉽게 끌어올 것을……"

"몸조심을 잘하세요. 이왕 지난 일이야 쓸데 있습니까, 또 다음 기회나 보시지요"

하고 직접 아무 관계 없는 기막힌 동정을 해주었다. 소련은 이런 때마다 수치와 모욕을 한없이 깨닫고, 자기가 마치 이 세상에 쓸데없는 사람인 것 같기도 하고 또 송효순에 대한 비밀을 영영히 숨겨버려야만 옳을 듯한 미신이 생기기도 했다.

모든 것이 다 - 어둡게 그의 마음을 어두운 곳에만 떨어뜨리려고 했다.

하나 그는 역시 송효순이 그리웠다. 잊히지 않았다. 그래서 그는 혼인 말이 있을 때마다 거절했다. 그 고모 류애덕 여사는 그 연고를 묻지만, 저편에 학식이 없다는 불만족들보다 자기가 신분이 낮다는 겸손보다 또 재산이 없노라는, 감당 못 할 정경에 있다는것보다,

"찾아가도 모르는 체 안 하시겠습니까?"

하던 믿음성과 겸손과 활발함을 갖추어 보이고, 또 고상한 음성으로 모든 대담스러움을 감추어버리던 그 인천측후소의 송효순이 그리웠다. 그는 그 참을성과 진정한 그리움에서 나온 부끄러움이 아니면 인천측후소를 찾아갔을지도 모르겠지만, 다만 재치있는 손끝을 기다리는 듯한, 덮어놓은 피아노의 하얀 키가 아무 소리도 못 내고 잠잠할 뿐이었다.

3

류애덕은 소련의 아버지보다 다섯 해 위 되는 누이였으며, 그의 고향은 반도 북편에 있는 박천 고을이었다. 류애덕의 부친은 한국 시대의 유자儒者로 류 진사란 이름을 얻은 엄한 노인이었으나 불행히 늦게 본 아들 때문에, 속을 몹시 태우다가, 그 아들이 20도 되기 전에 그만 이 세상을 떠나버렸다. 이보다 전에, 류애덕은 열다섯 살이 되자, 그 이웃 이 주사 집으로

출가를 했으나, 유자와 관리 편 사이에는 일상 설왕설래가 곱지 못했을 뿐 아니라, 류애덕의 남편은 불량성不良性을 가진 병신이었으므로 갖은 못된 행위를 다 하다가 집과 처를 버리고 영- 나가버렸다. 그러므로 아직 어려서 생과부가 된 류애덕은 흔히 친정살이를 했으나, 그도 소련의 적모와 사이가 불합해서 가장 고울 을녀乙女의 때를 눈물과 한숨으로 보내다가, 조선 안을 처음으로 비추는 문명의 새벽빛을 먼저 받게 되어서 후세를 바라려고 교회당에도 다니게 되고, 또 공부까지 하게 되어서 쓸쓸한 삶의 향할 곳 없는 마음을 배움으로 재미 붙여 나날이 그 학식을 늘렸으나 그 역 반도 부인의 태반이 그러하도록, 미신적迷信的 믿음 외에는 달리 광명을 못 받은 이였다. 그러나 그 환경에서 남성에 대한, 사모할 마음을 영구히 잃어버린 그는 다시 출가할 마음을 내지 않고 교육에 뜻을 두게 되었다. 그는 운명이 그러한 탓인지 여기에 이르도록 비교적 순한 경로를 밟아오게 되었다. 과부가 되자 그 모친의 보호 아래 학비 얻어 공부하게 되고 또 밖으로부터 들어오는 유혹은 아주 없었으므로, 그는 해변가의 물결을 희롱하고 든든히 움직이지 않는 바윗돌은 아니었다. 그러므로 그는 편벽했으며 자기만 결백한 체하는 폐단을 버리지 못했다. 그러나 교회 안에서 그 엄하고 단출한 행동은 모든 교인과 젊은 학생 들의 존경을 받게 되었다. 그래서 그는 그 안에서 공부하고 또 직업을 잃지 않게 되어 가장 안전한 지위에서 생활하게 되었다. 그 후에 늘 그에게 근심을 끼치는 그의 양친은 한 달 전후하여 이 세상을 하직하고 소련의 부친 류경환은 본처를 버리고 몇 달에 한 번씩 계집을 갈다가, 소련의 어머니에게 붙들려 거기서 귀여운 딸을 보고 재미를 붙이게 되었으나 어떠한 저주를 받음인지 소련의 모친은 평생 한숨으로 웃음 짓는 일이 드물고, 걸핏하면 치맛자락으로 거푸 나오는 눈물을 씻다가 그도 한이 뭉쳐 더 참을 수가 없던지 소련이가 열한 살 되던 해에 이 세상을 하직해버렸다. 이때에 이르러 거의거의 가산을 탕진한 류경환은 소련을 그 누이에게 맡겨버리고 다시 옛날 부인을 찾아갔으나 거기서 1년이 못 된 가을에 체증으로 세상을 떠났다.

그때부터 소련은 그 고모의 보호 아래, 잔뼈가 굵어진 듯이 몸과 마음이 나날이 자라는 갔으나, 그의 마음속 맨 밑에 빗박힌 얼음장을 녹여버릴 기회는 쉽게 다시 오지 않았다. 류애덕이 소련을 기름에는 소련의 얼굴에 쓸쓸한 그림자를 남기도록 한 흠점이 있었다. 비록 의복과 학비를 군색하게 하지 않을지라도, 병났을때 약을 늦춰 써줌이 아닐지라도 어딘지 모르게 데면데면하고 쓸쓸스러웠다. 그 데면데면하고 쓸쓸스러움은 소련이 공부를 마치게 되었을 때 좀 감해가는 듯했으나, 어떠한 노여운 말끝에든지 혹은 혼인 말끝에든지 반드시

"너의 어머니를 닮아서 그렇지, 그러기에 혈통이 있는 것이야" 하고 불쾌한 말을 들었다.

이러한 말을 듣고도 소련은 그 고모의 역설인 줄만 믿고, 자기의 혈통을 생각지 않았으나 온정을 못 받은 그는 결국 쾌활한 인물이 되지 못하고, 그 성격에 어두운 그늘이 많이 박히게 되어서 공연한 눈물까지 흔하였다.

그러한 소련이 인천서 송효순을 만났을 땐 무엇인지 온몸이 녹을 듯한 따뜻함을 알았다. 하나 그것은 꿈에 다시 꿈을 본 것 같이 언젠가는 힘을 다해서 잊어버리지 않으면 안 될 환영幻影일 것 같았다.

소련은 송효순을 몹시 생각한 어느 날 밤에 이상한 꿈을 보았다.

-조선 안에서는 흔히 보지 못하던 교토 시모가모가와진자下鴨川神社 안 같은 곳이었다. 넓은 나무 숲속을 이룬 신사 뜰을 에둘러 물살 빠른 내가 흐르고 신사 밖으로 나가는 다리 옆에는 큰 느티나무가 서 있어서, 그 까마득히 보이는 제일 높은 가지 위에는 여섯 잎으로 황금 테두리를 한 남빛 꽃이 달처럼 공중에 떠 있었다. 그 아래는 여전히 냇물이 빠르게 좔좔 소리를 내면서 흘러내려갔다. 자세히 본 즉 그 냇물에는 지금까지 보이지 않던 뗏목이 떠내려가는데, 그 위에 젊은 여자가 빗누운 채 흘러 내려가면서 남쪽만 바라본다. 온몸이 으쓱해서 정신을 차리려 하여도 무엇이 귀에

빽빽 소리를 치며 저기 떠내려가는 것이 너이다! 너이다! 하고 그 귀를 가를 듯이 온몸이 저릿저릿하도록 소리를 지른다.

소련이 눈을 뜨려고 몸을 흔들어보고 소리를 내어보려 하여도 내가 깨었거니, 깼거니 하면서도 눈이 떠지지 않고 무서운 뗏목이 빠른 물을 따라 흘러가는 것이 눈에 선했다─

그럴 동안에 그는 잠이 깨어서 가슴 위에 손을 올려놓고 등걸잠을 자던 그 몸을 수습했다.

그는 깨어서 한번 여행 갔던 교토를 꿈꾸었다고 생각했으나, 그 꿈이 무엇인지 효순을 생각할 때마다 무슨 흉한 징조같이 생각되었다.

4

그러나 '때가 이르면 굳은 바위도 가슴을 열어, 깊은 속 밑에서 솟아오르는 샘물을 땅에 뿜는다'는 듯이 낮에는 만나지라고 기도하고 밤에는 못 만나서 가위눌리던 소련은 드디어 효순을 만나게 되었다.

바로 지금부터 2년 전 여름이었다. 하루는 애덕 여사가 소련의 건강을 염려하여 그더러 S 학교는 퇴직하라고 권고할 때 가벼운 노동 시간과 공부 시간을 써놓고 곰곰이 타이르면서 몸조심해야 한다고 하던 애덕 여사는 급히 무엇을 잊었다 생각난 듯이 종잇조각을 소련에게 던져주며 손님이 올 터라고 아이스크림 만들 복숭아를 사 오라고 일렀다.

소련은 매일같이 손님 올 때마다 혹시 효순 씨가 오지 않나 하고 기다렸으나 매일같이 오지 않았으므로, 오늘은 또 어떤 손님이 오시려나 하고 풀기 없이 일어나서 창경원 앞까지 걸어 나와 전차 위에 올랐다. 그 찌는 듯한 여름날 오후에 소련은 고모의 명령이라 어기지도 못하고 진고개까지 가서 향기로운 물복숭아를 사왔었다. 그때도 애덕 여사는 말하기를

"우리 여자 청년회를 많이 도와주시는 송달성 씨가 오실 터인데 새 옷을 가려 입고 민첩히 접대하라"

하고 일렀다. 이 말을 들을 때 소련은 송이라는 데 깜짝 놀랐으나 이름이 다르고 또 그이를 아는 터였으므로 얼마큼 안심하였다.

그날 저녁에 40이 넘은 신사와 25, 6세의 젊은 신사는 게으르지 않고 급하지 않은 흥거운 걸음걸이로 공업전문학교 근처의 사지砂地를 걸어서 숭이동을 향하여 갔다.

하늘은 처녀의 마음을 펼쳐서 비단 보자기에 흰 솜덩이를 싸듯이 포돗빛 도는 연분홍을 다시 엷게 풀어서 여름 구름을 휘몰아싼 듯하고 보안 지평선 한끝에서는 여인들이 우물물을 길어 오고 길어 갔다. 마치 하늘과 땅이 더운 때 하루의 피로를 잊으려고 저녁 바람을 식혀서 졸린 곡조를 주고받는 듯하였다.

소련은 요사이 보기 시작했던 어느 각본 책에서 본 대로 파란 포도 덩굴로 식탁을 장식해놓고 부엌으로 가서 그 고모에게

"아주머니 식탁 차려놓은 것 보세요"

했다.

일상 회로애수喜怒哀愁의 표정이 분명치 않은 애덕 여사도 소련의 재치 있음을 보고 희색이 만면해서

"그런 장난이야 네 장기지"

하였다. 소련은 그 고모의 습관을 잘 알기에 무언가 암만해도 경사나 당한 듯해서 연해 그 고모에게 말을 걸어본다.

"어떤 손님이 이렇게 우리의 공대를 받으십니까"

하기도 하고,

"왜 하필 저녁때 청하셨어요"

하기도 하고,

"꼭 한 분만 오실까요"

하기도 했다.

숙질(류애덕)이 저녁때 드문 버릇으로 재미스럽게 이야기하면서 아이스크림을 두를 때 뜰에서 낯선 발소리가 들리며

"이리 오너라"

하고 불렀다. 이 소리를 듣고 소련의 숙질(류애덕)이 하던 이야기를 그칠 때 그들의 옆에서 그릇을 닦던 영복이란 여인이 냉큼 일어서며

"에이구, 벌써 손님이 오신 게로군"

하고 뜰 앞으로 내려갔다. 애덕 여사도 허둥지둥 손을 씻으며, 일어나서 방 안으로 들어가려다가 뜰로 마주 나가서, 사교에 익은 음성으로 인사를 마치고 또 다른 처음 보는 사람에게 인사를 하는 듯하였다.

이때 소련은 무엇인지 가슴이 두근거려서 일어서서 내다보지 않고는 더 참을 수 없었다. 그는 사시나무같이 떨리는 몸을 일으켜서 부엌문 밖을 내다보았다- 그때야말로 소련의 눈에 무엇이 보였을까? 그는 온몸이 굳어지는 듯이 자유로 움직일 수 없어서 그 머리를 돌리려다가 그러지도 못하고 우두커니 서서 내어다보았다.

그러나 조금 후에 손님을 좌정하고 부엌으로 돌아온 류애덕은 예사롭게 앉아서 아이스크림을 두르는 소련을 보고

"손님이 세 분이다"

하고 일렀다.

소련은 한참 말 없다가 떨리는 음성으로

"그이들이 누구입니까?"

하고 물었다. 총총히 그릇에 음식을 담던 애덕 여사는 그 손끝을 잠깐 멈추고 예사롭게

"참, 그 이야기를 네게는 아니 했었구나. 저- 이제부터, 우리집에 학생이 한 분 온단다. 윤은순이라고 스물댓 살 된 부인인데 그 남편은 송달성 씨의 생질 되는 송효순 씨라고 하고 동경서 대학을 마치고 돌아와서 인천 계

시다고 하시더라"

했다.

소련은 은연중에,

"그럼 인천측후소에 계신 송효순 씨인 게지요"

하고 부르짖었다. 이때 그 고모는 좀 놀라운 듯이

"그이가 인천측후소에 있는 것을 네가 어떻게 알았니? 나는 지금 막 인사를 한 터이다"

하고 물었다. 이때 소련은 잠깐 실수했다고 생각했으나

"저, 인천측후소에 여행 갔을 때요"

하고 스스럽지 않게 말하고 그 낯빛을 감추기 위해서 저편으로 돌아서서 단 향내를 올리며 끓고 있는 차관 뚜껑을 열어보았다.

이같이 되어서 음식 준비가 다 되고 식탁을 차려놓았을 때 소련과 효순은 삼촌과 고모 사이에 또 절벽 같은 감시자 앞에서 외나무다리를 마주 건너려는 듯이 만났으니까 많은 이야기를 서로서로 바꾸지는 못하였으나 12촉 전등 불빛 아래 그들의 붉은 얼굴에 남빛이 돌도록 반가워하는 모양은 그 주위의 시선을 모았었다.

하나, 그들은 만나는 처음부터 두 사람은 다만 아는 사람으로 밖에 더 친할 수도 없고, 다시 그 가운데 사랑이라거나 연애라거나 한 것을 일으켜서는 옳지 않은 것으로 그들의 운명인 사회 제도의 자유를 무시한 조건에 인을 쳤었다.

하나 소련은 그들의 그렇도록 반가운 만남을 하였으니 조용한 곳에 단 둘이 만나서 한 기꺼움을 웃고 한 설움을 느껴보고 싶지 않았을까? 아무리 구도덕의 치맛자락에 싸여 자라서 굳은 형식을 못 벗어나야만 한다는 소련의 이성異性일지라도 이 당연한 자연의 요구를 어찌 막을 수 있었겠느냐. 그러나 그들의 경우는 그들의 그러한 감정을 감추고 효순은 그 부인을 류애덕 여사의 보호 아래 수양시키려고 찾아오고 소련은 그 조수가 될 신세이니 전일의 생각이 확실히 금단의 과실을 집으려던 듯해서 그 등 뒤에서 얼음물과 끓는 물을 뒤섞어 끼얹는 듯이 불쾌했다.

<h1 style="text-align:center">5</h1>

그 이튿날부터 송효순의 아내인 윤은순은 류애덕의 집에 와서 있게 되었다.

그는 본래부터 구가정에서 자라난 구식 여자로, 어렸을 때 그 이른바 귀밑머리를 마주 푼 송효순의 처이다. 하나 지금에 이르러 그들은 각각 딴 경위에서 다른 것을 숭상하며 자랐으니 그들 사이에는 같은 아무런 지식도 없고 똑같을 아무런 생각과 감정의 동화도 없으므로 서로 도와서 영원히 같은 거리를 밟아 똑같이 나아갈 동무는 못 될 것이나, 사회의 조직이 아직도 자유를 요구하는 사람은 넘어뜨려버리게만 되어 있는 고로 그의 발걸음을 이상理想의 목표인 자유의 길 위로만 바로 향하지 못하고 그 마음의 반분은 땅 위에서 위로 훨씬 높이고, 또 반분으로는 다만 한 가련한 여자를 동정하는 셈으로 이상에 불타오르는 감정을 누르는 듯이 은순을 여자 청년회가 경영하는 이문안 부인학교에 넣었다.

송효순은 은순을 학교에 넣고 늦게 뿌린 씨가 먼저 뿌린 건땅 위에 나무보다 속히 자라라는 기도로 복습할 것까지 염려해서(자기도 모르게는 소련을 만나보고 싶은 마음은 스스로 분간치 못하고) 류애덕 여사의 문을 두드리게 되었다.

그러나 언문밖에 모르는 윤은순은 소련이 가르치기에도 너무 힘이 없었으므로 어찌하면 그의 복습 같은 것은 등한等閒히 여겨지게 되고 의식주에만 상담하는 일이 많았다.

그동안에 효순은 한 달에 한 번 두 공일에 한 번 찾아와서 애덕 여사에게 치하를 하고 갔다. 그럴 때마다, 효순과 소련 사이는 점점 더 멀어져가고, 효순과 애덕 여사 사이는 친해지며 은순과 소련 사이는 가까워졌다.

소련과 효순은 마침내 아는 사람으로의 친함조차 없어져서 사람 보이지 않은 곳에서 만나면 머뭇거리다가 인사를 하지 못하도록 서로 몰라보는 듯하였다. 이같이 되어서 은순과 소련 사이가 한 감독 아래 공부하고 살림할 동안에 서늘한 가을날들이 황금 같은 은행나무 숲에 잎 떨어져가고, 긴 겨울이 와서 사람들이 방 안에서 귤 껍질을 벗겨 쌓을 동안에 늙은이가 무거운 짐을 지고 긴 고개를 넘듯이 간신히 눈 녹았다.

그동안에 그들은 많은 마음속 옛이야기를 서로 바꾸었다. 사람들이 얼른 그들의 친함을 보고 형제들 사이 같다고 칭찬했다. 그러나 은순을 친형같이 대접하는 소련의 낯빛에는 무엇을 참는 듯한 고난의 빛을 감출 수 없었다.

소련은 흔히 자기가 몸이 약해서 그 고모의 노력을 돕지 못하고, 또 장차는 영구히 그 고모의 집을 아주 떠나야 할 이야기를 하고, 은순은 자기의 사촌이 자기와 한집에서 자라나면서 그 부모와 삼촌들이 말리는 것도 듣지 않고 학대를 받아가면서 공부를 해서 지금은 재미나게 돈 모으고 산다는 부러운 이야기를 했다. 하나 그들의 친함은 오래지 못하고 날이 따뜻함을 따라 틈이 생기게 되었다.

봄날에 아지랑이가 평평한 들의 먼 곳과 가까운 곳에 싹도 내지 않은 지평선 위에 아롱질 때 마침 소련은 그 남편과 약혼하게 되었다.

이런 때를 당하여 소련은 얼마나 난처하였으랴. 그 마음속에는 아직 송효순의 인상이 나날이 깊어가면 깊어갔지 조금도 덜어지지는 않는데 다른 사람과 결혼하지 않으면 안 될 경우! 그것을 누구에게 호소해야 할지? 그는 심한 우울증에 걸렸다.

그는 다시 그 고모에게 직업을 얻어서 독립생활을 하면서 그 고모에게 폐를 끼치지 않겠노라고까지 애원하여보았으나 그 고모는 어디서 얻은 지

식인지 제1에도

"핏줄이 있어서 안 돼"

하고 제2에도,

"아무나 다 - 마음먹은 대로 되는 것은 아니야"

하고 을렀다.

소련은 또다시 그 몸이 쇠침해져갔다. 지루한 겨울의 추위가 풀려 사람들의 마음속에는 놀고 싶은 마음이 모락모락 자라건만 소련의 마음속에는 나날이 불어가느니 그 가슴속에 빗박힌 얼음장이었다.

그는 이 쓸쓸한 심정 풀이를 향할 곳이 없어서 눈살을 찌푸리고 장래 의복 준비를 마지못해서 해보기는 하나 딱히 원인을 말하지못할 그 설움에 서책을 들고는 한없는 눈물을 지으며 이 아래 같은 문구文句를 읊었다.

　누구 나 부르지 않나

　밤 가운데 밤 가운데
　등불을 못 단 작은 배는
　노를 잃음도 아니련만
　저어 나갈 마음을 못 얻어
　누구 나 부르지 않나
　누구 나 부르지 않나.

　얼음 밑에 얼음 밑에
　빛을 못 받는 목숨에는
　흐를 줄을 잃음도 아니련만
　녹여 내일 열도를 못 얻어
　누구나 부르지 않나

누구 나 부르지 않나.

오오 오오
빛光과 열도熱度더위와 빛
한곳으로 나오련만
옳은 때를 못 얻어
누구 나 부르지 않나
누구 나 부르지 않나.

만일에

만일에 봄이 나를 녹이면
돌 틈에서 파초 여름을 맺지요 맺지요
만일에 만일에.

만일에 좋은 때를 얻으면
바위를 열어 내 마음을 쏟지요 쏟지요
만일에 만일에.

6

그해 봄이 적이 무르녹아서 소련의 파리하던 몸은 보는 사람들의 마음을 놀라게 하리만치 꽃송이처럼 피어올랐다.

송효순은 류애덕 씨 집에 자주 그 아내를 찾으러 오게 되었다. 그리고 저는 소련을 평양 최병서에게로 결혼시켜 보내겠다는, 류애덕 여사의 말

을 듣고는 반대하는 듯이

"그런 인물들을 가정 안에 벌써부터 넣어버리면 이 사회 운동은 누가 해놓을는지요. 조선의 가족 제도가 좀 웬만할 것 같으면 결혼은 하고도 일을 못 할 배 아니지만⋯ 아마 우물에 빠져서는 우물물을 치지도 못하고 제방堤防을 다시 쌓지도 못할걸요. 좀더 사회에 내놓아보시지요"

하고 입을 다물었다 한다. 소련은 이런 말을 듣고 참으로 감사하였다. 그래서 그는 마음속으로 '그러면 효순 씨는 내가 이 사회에서 의의 있게 생활해 나가기를 바라시는구나' 하고 생각해보았다. 또 그 뜻을 저버리지도 못할 듯이 그의 마음이 '가정 밖으로 나가자' 하고 부르짖기도 했다.

그 후에 며칠이 지나서 송효순은 박사 될 논문을 쓰러 일본으로 가겠다고 하면서 류애덕 씨 집에 머무르게 되어서 소련과 말해볼 기회를 얻게 되었다.

어느 공일 날 아침에 류애덕 여사와 효순은 일찍이 외출하였는데, 효순이 먼저 돌아와서

"아주 봄이 완연히 왔습니다. 그 보시는 책이 무엇입니까?"

하고 마루 끝에서, 책을 보던 소련에게 인사했다. 소련은 지금까지 효순의 아는 체 마는 체하는 냉정함에 무색하여 다만 '그 따라다니면서 할 듯하던 친절을 왜 그쳤나. 그이가 내게 좀더 친절이라도 하셨으면 이 마음이 풀리련만' 했었다. 하나 이날따라 효순은 급히 그에게 친절해졌으므로 막상 닥쳐놓으면 그렇지도 못하다는 심리로, 기쁜 듯하기는 하면서도 '이 마음에 잠긴 문이 열리면 어찌하나. 그때야말로 무서운 죄악을 지을 테지' 하고 어름어름

"네 아주 꼭 봄이 되었어요"

하고 자기 방을 치우느라고 그 남편이 온 줄도 모르는 은순이를 부르고 나서 급히 더 한층 그 얼굴을 붉히면서 효순을 향해서 얼른

"하우프트만의 『외로운 사람들』⋯"

하고 말을 마치지 못하고 은순이가 마루로 나오는 것을 보고는 구원을 받은 듯이

"은순 씨, 벌써 오셨는데요"

하고 일렀다. 은순은 소련의 얼굴과 효순의 얼굴을 번갈아 보아가면서 그 남편의

"무얼 했소?"

하는 물음에

"방 치우느라고"

하고 입을 오므렸다.

이 틈에 소련은 얼른 일어서서 저편 마루 구석에 놓인 찬장 앞으로 가면서 다기茶器를 꺼냈다.

효순은 소련의 낭패한 듯이 어름어름하는 태도를 민망히 눈여겨보면서

"애덕 선생님은 아직 안 돌아오셨습니까?"

하고 웃었다. 소련은 다기를 꺼내 들고

"네. 아직 안 오셨어요. 선생님과 같이 나가셨는데"

하고 부엌을 향해 가며, 주인 된 직분을 지키려는 듯했다.

한참 만에 소련은 차를 영복이라는 밥 짓는 이에게 들려 가지고 나왔다.

그동안에 효순은 소련이 보다 놓은 책을 열심으로 보고 있었다. 그러다가, 소련이 그 앞에 차를 놓을 때는

"이 책 어디까지 읽으셨어요, 처음으로 읽으세요? 저도 이 책을 퍽 흥미롭게 읽었지요"

하고 말을 걸었다. 소련은 효순의 앞에 맞앉은 은순에게도 차를 권하면서 다만 놀라운 듯이

"네, 네"

할 뿐이었다. 효순은 소련의 태도를 눈여겨보기는 하나, 그리 생소치는 않은 듯이

"이 하우프트만의 『외로운 사람들』 가운데는 우리 같은 사람이 있지요. 아직 맨 끝까지 안 보셨을지 모르지만 이와 같이 외국의 유명한 작품이 조선 청년의 가슴을 속 쓰라리게 하는 것은 드뭅니다"

하고 말하면서 그 윤택한 눈을 멍히 떴다.

소련은 은순의 편으로 가까이 앉으며 또다시

"지금 겨우 다 보았습니다"

하고 간단히 대답했다. 효순은 하늘을 쳐다보던 눈을 아래로 내려서 소련을 이윽히 바라보며 그 부드러운 음성으로

"아직 생각까지 해보셨는지 모르지만, 책 속에는 저와 같이 부모가 계시고 처자까지 있어도 세상에서 제일 외로운 사람이 있습니다. 저는 외국서 공부할 때는 그렇게까지는 그 책을 느낌 많게 보지 못했지만 이 땅 안에 돌아와서는 그렇게 우리의 흉금을 곱게 쓰다듬어주는 것은 없다고 생각합니다."

소련은 이때 비로소 이야기를 좋아하던 그의 본능의 충동에 이끌려 정신없이

"그럼 그 요하네스와 마알은 서로 참사랑을 합니다그려……네……?"

하고 영채 있는 눈을 방울같이 떴다. 효순은 이때 미미히 웃으며

"소련 씨, 사랑하게 되는 것이 아닙니다. 우리는 과거와 미래를 통해서 한 이상을 세우고 거기 합당한 것을 사랑하는 것이고 그렇게 살아온 것입니다. 그러나 그러한 이상적 사랑은 사람들에게는 흔하지 않을 뿐 아니라, 그렇게 사상의 공명이 있고 정신상 위안이 있으면 용해서는 헤어지지 못할 인정이 생길 것입니다. 그 각본 속의 인정 교환은 조선의 상태에 비하면 훨씬 화려하지만 무엇인지 그 요하네스가 구도덕의 지배 아래 그 몸을 꿇게 되는 사정은 조선에 흔히 있는 사실입니다. 말하자면 우리는 이제 움 돋는 싹이고 그들은 자라나는 나무라고 하겠지요."

소련은 한참 머리를 숙이고 생각하다가,

"그럼 사람은 애써서 사랑을 구하거나 잃어버린다고 말할 수 없지 않습니까? 또 우리가 더 자라나서 꽃필 때까지 기다리더라도 결국 요하네스와 마알의 사이 같은 슬픔도 끊어지진 못합니까. 그때에는 또 새로운 비극이 생길 터인데요."

"네, 소련 씨. 사람이 사랑을 구한다거나 잃는다는 것은 거짓말입니다. 사람은 자기 자신 속에 사랑을 가지고, 어떤 대상으로 하여금 그것을 눈깨우게 되어서 결국 분명한 생활 의식을 가지는데 불과한 일이니까요. 또 말씀하신 『외로운 사람들』 속의 비극같은 것은 물론 어느 곳에든지 사람 자신이 그 운명을 먼저 짓고 이 세상을 지배해 나가게 될 때까지 또, 세상의 모든 사람들과 결탁해서 사는 것을 폐지하기까지는 면치 못할 일입니다."

"그래서 그 요하네스-"

하고 소련은 무엇을 머뭇거리다가

"그 요하네스도 구도덕의 함정에 빠져 멸망합니까? 저는 철학을 모르니까 그가 아는 다윈이라든지 헤겔의 학설을 분명히는 모릅니다마는, 그 마알이라는 여학생은 아주 그의 이론에 그의 모든 것을 다 아는 고로 절대로 공명이 됩니다 그려. 아주 헤어지기는 어려운 사이가 되는 거지요."

"네-"

하고 효순은 좀 이상한 듯이 머리를 돌리다가 대답한다.

"그…… 요하네스는 이상적 동무를 만났습니다. 그러나 반드시 같이 살 수도 없고 그것은 고사하고 그 동무를 하루 이틀 더 위로할 수도 없지요. 그래서 그 동무는 가는 곳도 아니 가리키고 가버리지만 한 가지 이상한 말을 남기고 갑니다. 즉 두 사람이 헤어져 있지만 한 법칙 아래서 한 뜻으로 살아 나가자는 것이지요. 그들은 같은 학설을 믿으니까 그 학리에 적합한 행동을 해서 여러 가지 똑같은 사실을 행해 나가면서 살자는 것이지요. 그렇지만 그 요하네스는 그 극렬한 육신의 감정을 오히려 장래 오랜 믿음으로 이끌겠다는 생각을 저버리고 호수에 빠져 죽지요. 참 외로운 사람입니다"

하고, 효순은 또다시 하늘을 쳐다보았다. 은순도 덩달아 쳐다보았다. 그러나 소련은 무릎 위의 손길을 내려다보다가

"그럼"

하고 럼이란 자에 힘을 넣으며,

"그…… 요하네스는 믿음을 가지지 못할 사람입니까?"

"아니"

하고 효순은 소련을 향하여 다시 힘 있는 시선을 던지며

"그렇지도 않을 테지만 사정이 마알보다, 더 난처하였습니다. 누구든지 괴테가 아니라도, 회색 같은 이론을 믿지는 못하고 생기 있는 생활을 요구하겠지요"

하였다.

이때 소련은 대리석상에 생명을 불어넣는 듯이, 자기도 모르게

"그럼 그 요하네스는 그 목숨으로 어려운 문제를 해결해버렸습니다 그려. 그러나 마알은?"

했다. 효순은 이 말을 가장 흥미 있게 대답하려는 듯이.

"오 -"

하고 입을 열다가

"이 차 다 식습니다"

하는 은순의 말소리에 그 아내의 존재를 아주 잊었다가 비로소 정신 차려서 그를 걸핏 쳐다보고

"참!"

하며 이야기하느라고 말랐던 목을 축였다.

"그 마알은 생활을 어찌 못할 경우를 당해서"

하고 책장을 뒤지다가 한곳을 찾아놓고,

"아닙니까? 공부해서 공부해서 그야말로 옆 눈도 뜨지 않겠다고 했구먼요. 그러니까 종내 학리를 구하러 길 떠나는지 또 괴로움을 잊으려고 책으로 얼굴을 가리려는지 작자의 본뜻은 분명히 모를 일이지만 종내 길 떠나지요"

하고 말끝을 이었다.

이때 소련은 난처한 듯이

"그럼 그이들은 서로 다른 것 같지 않습니까? 요하네스는 더 앞서지 않았습니까? 또 마알은 요하네스를 절대로 믿지 못하는 것 아닙니까? 그렇지 않으면 마알이 더 많이 요하네스보다 발전성發展性을 가졌던지요?"

하고 어린 생도가 선생에게 묻듯이 물었다.

"아니오, 그들의 환경이 달랐습니다. 그 두 사람은 누구나 똑같이 함께 생활해 나가기를 바랄 것이지만 마알은 아마 심령心靈의 세계를 완전히 믿을 뿐 아니라 또 요하네스에게는 구도덕이 지은 대상이 달리 있었으니까 마알은 자기가 아니라도 요하네스는 그 옛날로 돌아가 생활할 줄 믿었겠지요. 그러나 그 고향의 따뜻함을 안 이상에야 어느 목숨이 또다시 무미한 쓸쓸한 생활을 계속하려고 하겠습니까? 작자는 거기까지 쓰고는 막음을 했지만……"

하고 말끝을 그치고 그 앞에 놓인 과자를 집었다. 그러고 나서

"소련 씨 사람은 절대로 누구와든지 꼭 육신으로 결합해야만 살겠다고는 말 못 할 것입니다. 그것은 정을 유통시켜보지 못하고 이 세상에 대항하여 발전이라는 것을 모르는 사람에게는 능할 것이지만 우리는 한 대상을 앎으로 그 주위의 모든 것까지 곱게 보지 않습니까? 단지 그 대상으로 인해 얻은 생활 의식이 분명한것만 다행하지요. 하지만 여자의 경우는, 오히려 요하네스에 가까우리라고 생각해요. 더군다나 조선 여자는 그렇지만 그것이 옳은 것은 못 됩니다"

하고 생각 깊은 듯이 소련을 바라보았다.

7

소련의 그 얼굴은 해쓱하게 변했다. 그는 입술까지 남빛으로 변했다. 은순은 가만히 앉았다가 차를 따라 탁자 앞으로 가서 그 앞에 걸린 거울 속을 들여다보다가 자기 눈에 독기가 띤 것을 못 보고, 효순이 소련과 숨결을 어울리듯이 하던 이야기를 그치고 모든 것이 괴로운 듯이 뜰 앞을 내려다보는 것을 보았다.

이때 두 사람은 뒤에서 반사되어 비치는 시선을 깨달으면서 똑같이 뒤를 돌아다보았다. 이때이다. 두 지식미를 가진 얼굴과 다만 무엇을 의심하고 투기하는 듯한 얼굴이 뾰족하게 삼각을 지을 듯이 거울 속에 모였다.

이 한순간에 두 눈은 검은 보석을 비춘 듯이 해쓱해진 소련이 머리를 돌리며

"형님 그 찬장 안에 고구마 군 것이 있으니 내놓아보세요. 내 손으로 아무렇게 해서 맛이 되잖았지만……"

했다. 은순은 그 말에는 대답 없이 차관을 갖다가 소련과 효순 사이에 놓고 자기 방으로 들어가서 드롭스 봉지와 초콜릿 봉지를 들고 나와서 목판에 담고 또 꺼린 듯이 주춤주춤하다가 찬장에서 고구마 군 것을 꺼내었다.

이 찰나에 계란 탄 냄새와 버터와 젖 냄새가 단 향기를 지어서 봄빛이 쪼인 고요한 마루 위에 진동하였다. 은순은 그 맛있어 보이는 것을 도로 들이밀어버리려는 듯한 솜씨로

"이것 잡수세요?"

하고 목이 메어서 물었다. 효순은 말없이 미미히 웃으며 은순을 바라보고 소련을 바라보고 고개를 돌려 하늘을 쳐다보았다. 소련은 은순의 불쾌한 낯빛을 미안히 바라보고 숨결 고르지 못하게

"그까짓 것 그만 넣어버리세요"

하고 말해버렸다. 은순은 소련의 말대로 내놓던 것을 들이밀어버리고 다

시 앉았던 자리로 와 앉았다.

하늘은 맑은 웃음을 띠고 나지막하게 사람들의 생각을 돌보는듯이 개어 있었다. 뜰에는 모락모락 김이 오르는 땅 위에 앉은뱅이와 민들레가 피어 있었다. 화단에는 한 뼘이나 자란 목단과 또 두어 자나 자란 파초가 무엇인지 채 알지도 못할 꽃 이파리들 가운데서 고요한 봄바람에 한들거리고 있었다.

차와 과자는 봄날 대낮의 남향한 마루로 들이쪼이는 볕에 엷은 김을 올리면서 이 세상 사람의 기억에서 떠나 있는 모양이었다.

그러나 한참 만에 은순은 이 고요함을 깨뜨리고 그 목멘 소리로

"차를 잡수세요"

하고 권했다.

하늘을 쳐다보고 땅을 굽어보던 두 사람은 듣는지 마는지 무슨 똑같은 생각을 같이 하는 듯이 정밀한 그들의 얼굴에는 조그만 잡미雜味도 섞여 보이지 않았다.

이때였다. 무엇인지 효순과 소련 사이가 가까워지고 은순과 소련 사이가 동떨어져 나간 듯이 생각된 지가……우리는 지금까지 이 세상에서 모든 붙었던 것들이 떨어지는 것을 보고 모든 떨어졌던 것들이 붙는 것을 본다. 우리들이 먹는 떡과 김치와, 과실과 고기를 생각할 때에도……또, 그렇다! 우리는 매일같이 그런 것을 안 볼 때가 없다. 그러나 우리는 거기서 서로 헤어짐이 없는 나라를 짓고 나라를 깨뜨리지 않을 경우를 지으려 한다. 하나 우리는 매일같이 헤어지며 만나는 동안에 매일같이 변함을 본다. 필경 육신과 영혼을 양편으로 가진 사람들은 약함을 끝끝내 이기진 못하고 운명에게 틈을 엿보여서 나라를 깨뜨리기도 하고 경우를 잃기도 해서 동서에 울고 웃게 되며 남북에 헤매게 되는 것이다.

여기 이르러 소련의 운명은 그 갈 곳을 확실히 작정했다. 효순이와 있는 며칠 동안을 은순은 투기와 의심으로 날을 보내고 애덕 여사는 혹독한 감

시를 게을리하지 않았으며 그 중에 소련의 적모는 서울 구경을 핑계하고 올라와서 이 여러 사람의 눈치에 덩달아

"제 어멈을 닮아서 행실이 어떠할지 모르리라"

고 말전주(남의 말을 좋지 않게 전하여 이간질하는 것)했다. 효순은 난처한 듯이 동정 깊은 눈치를 소련에게 향할 뿐이요, 침묵을 지키게 되었다. 이보다 전에 소련과 효순은 모든 행동을 서로 비추어 하게 되고, 모든 의심을 서로 물으며, 모든 것에 또 명령적으로 대답하며, 모든 행동에 서로 복종하였다. 이러한 며칠 동안을 은순은 눈물을 말리지 못하고 애덕 여사에게 자주 무엇을 속삭였다.

이에 애덕 여사는 효순에게 정중한 행동을 취하며 속히 소련의 혼인을 작정하려고 급한 행동을 했다. 이 틈에 효순은 소련에게 또다시 안 체 만 체한 행동을 했다. 그리고 속히 동경 갈 준비를 했다. 그런 중에 또, 송도성이란 그의 부친은 시골서 올라와서 효순을 그 여관으로 데려가 버렸다. 소련은 꿈과 같이 그리운 사람과 며칠 동안을 기껍게 생활했다. 하나 모든 것은 꿈같이 지나가 버렸다.

8

소련은 그 고모와 적모의 위협에 급히도 최병서와의 혼례를 허락하였다.

애덕 여사는 다시 효순에게 상냥한 태도를 보였다. 소련은 다시 나날이 수척해졌다. 은순의 낯빛은 편안해졌다. 그러나 효순의 낯빛은 거슬림과 비웃음과 날카로움으로 충만되어 있으면서도 제일 온화한 행동을 낙종諾從 (마음으로 받아들여 진심으로 따라 쫓음) 하는 듯했다. 애덕 여사는 힘써서 최병서를 그 집으로 이끌어들였다. 병서는 흔한 금전으로 나이 먹은 여인들의 환심을 사버렸다. 병서가 문안에 이를 때마다 영복이란 여인까지 그를

대환영하였다.

병서는 효순과 기껍게 사귀려고 하며,

"학사! 이학사!"

하고 빈정거렸다.

최 씨는 그 검은 얼굴에 크림을 칠하고, 그 거센 머리에 기름을 빼게 해서 효순의 모양을 본떴다. 효순의 창백하고 고상한 얼굴과 병서의 구릿빛 같은 심술궂은 얼굴은 서로 맞지 않는 모양을 보였으나, 순하고 게다가 아무런 구속도 받기 싫어하는 효순은 아무 편으로든지 건드려지지 않으려 하고 애써 타협하려 하였다.

그러면서, 동경서 명치대학 법과를 졸업한 병서의 학식을, 더할 나위 없이 높이 알아주는 듯하였다. 그리고 그의 버릇인 하늘을 쳐다보는 표정은 고치지 않았다.

그러나 저는 이따금씩

"사람이 그 주위에서 조화를 깨뜨리지 않는 사람만 가장 행복될 것이고, 또 훨씬 넘어서서 모든 것을 깨뜨리고도 능히 세울 수 있는 사람만 위대하다고 설명했다. 또 사람이 어울리지 않는 대상을 요구하는 것은 도적과 같지만 사람은 사람 자체의 생활의 시초를 모르느니만치 그 생활을 스스로 시작하지 못했을 터이니까 전부 책임질 수가 없어서 노력만이 필요하다"

고 이야기했다.

병서는 효순의 말을 이학자의 말 같지 않다고 비웃었다. 그래도 효순은 아무 말 없이 하늘을 쳐다보고 말았다.

소련은 차라리 이 괴로운 날들을 어서 줄여서 속히 병서의 집으로 가기를 원했다. 그러나 그 역시 그 뜻대로 되지 않아서 그는 아무의 눈에든지 보이도록 번민했다.

그 다음에 효순은 일본으로 떠나면서 섭섭해 하면서도 말을 못하는 소련을 뒤뜰로 끌고 가서 이 같은 말을 남겼다.

"소련 씨, 우리가 한때에 이 지구 위에 살게 된 것과 또 이렇게 사귀게 된 것만 행복됩니다. 이제 우리는 서로 알았으니까 서로 의식하며 힘써서 같은 귀일점에서 만나도록 생활해 나가는 것만 필요합니다. 이후에 소련 씨는 최병서 씨와 단란한 가정을 지으시겠지요. 또, 우연치 않은 기회로 영영 잊히지 못하도록 맘이 맞던 한 동무가 어디서 당신과 똑같이 고생하며 힘쓸 것을 잊지 않으시겠지요. 자 - 유쾌하지 않습니까? 우리에게는 요하네스와 마알에게 오는 파멸은 없습니다. 자 - 우리는 우리가 연구하는 화성이 우리의 지구와 같다고 생각하면 얼마나 반갑습니까? 또 통행이 된다고 생각하면 얼마나 놀랍습니까? 하나 시간이 홀로 해결할 권리를 아끼지 않습니다. 다만 사람은 그동안에 힘쓰는 것만 허락되었습니다"

하였다. 소련은 이때 그 가슴속으로 넘쳐흐르는 친함을 억제하지 못하고 그 앞으로 가까이 서며

"오-오라버니"

하고 부르짖었다. 효순은 얼굴을 돌리고

"누이"

하고 먼저 돌아서서 앞뜰로 왔다.

이때는 마침 봄날 오후이라. 하늘 위에서는, 종다리가 한 있는대로, 감정을 높여 먼 곳으로부터 울어댔다.

그 뒤에 소련은 모든 일이 맨 처음부터 있었던 듯이 또 모든 것이 없었던 듯이 최 씨 댁으로 와서 살게 되었다. 그러나 믿음을 가지지 못한 병서는 소련을 공경은 할 수 있지만 사랑은 할 수 없노라고 하면서 마음 내키는 대로 계집을 상관하고 집을 비웠다. 그러고도 부족한 것이 많은 사람처럼 애써서 가정 일에 힘쓰는 소련을 학대하기도 부끄러워하지 않았다. 그런 중에 또 병서의 모친은 이따금씩 와서 그 아들의 애정을 소련 때문에 앗긴 듯이 소련을 들볶았다. 그러나 소련은 참고 일하고 공부하고 모든 것을 사랑하고, 사람들의 성격을 부드럽게 하며 살아왔다.

그러나 그 후에 은순이와 애덕 여사에게 우연히 의심을 받게 된 소련은 서울 가더라도 효순을 만날 수 없었다.

그 이후 효순은 박사가 되었다. 또 인천측후소 속에 숨어서 연구를 쌓았다. 그러나 들리는 말이 그 부인과 불화해서 독신을 지키며 여자들을 피한다고 했다.

그 소리를 들으면서 소련은 더욱 자기의 노동勞動과 수학修學과 사랑博愛을 게을리 하지 않았다. 그러던 것을 그는 이 밤에 이런 생각에 붙들리고 또 강연하러 온 효순의 음성을 그 담 밖에서 애달프게 듣고있다. 그는 여름밤이 깊어갈수록 온몸을 떨었다.

그러나 지루한 뒷생각이 그를 잠들게 하고 몇 시간이 지난 뒤에 그는 잠자던 숨결을 잠깐 멈추고 눈을 번쩍 떴다. 여전히 병서는 들어오지 않은 모양이었다. 이때에 모든 없는 듯하던 것이 있었다. 넓은 세 칸 방 속에, 그의 취미는 얼마나 부자유한 몸이면서 자유를 바랐던고?!

아랫목 벽에 걸린 로댕의 「다나이드」를 사진 찍은 그림이며, 머리맡에 롱펠로의 「화살과 노래」란 영시英詩를 흰 비단에 옥색으로 수놓은 족자며, 또 이름 모를 물새가 방망이에 붙들어 매여서 그 자유인 오촌五寸가량의 범위를 못 벗어나고 애쓰는 그림이 어느 것이나 자유를 안타깝게 바라는 소련의 취미가 아니랴? 이런 것들을 뒤돌아보는 소련의 마음이 어찌 대동강의 능라도를 에두른 2류二流가 합쳐지지 않기를 바라랴? 흐름은 제방을 깨뜨린다!

그러나 그런 때에 그 뒤로서는 유전遺傳이다 간음姦淫이다 할 것이다.

이때에 자유를 얻은 사람의 쾌활한 용감함이 무엇이라 대답할까?

'너회는 무엇을 이름 짓고, 어느 이름을 꺼리며 싫어하느냐? 그중 아름다운 것을 욕하진 않느냐' 하지는 않을지? 누가 보증하랴? 누가 그 부르짖음을 막을 만치 깨끗하냐? 어떤 성인聖人이 그것을 재판하였더냐?

소련은 머리를 끄덕이며 보이지 않는 신 앞에 허락했다. 컴컴하던 하늘은 대동강 위에 동텄다.

소련이 이 밤을 샌 이날에 그 회당까지 가서 효순의 강연을 들을 것과 감동할 것은 당연한 일이고 또 그렇든지 말든지 영원한 생명에 어울려 샘물이 흐르듯이 신선하게 살아나갈 것은 보증된다.

그는 이날이 새어서도 최병서의 집인 자신 (소련)의 집에서 모든 생명을 견주고 내놓을 것이다. 그 집의 참주인이 누구인지 누가 모르랴?

집주인은 건실하고 온화하고 공경될 것이다.

그리고 힘써서 '때'를 기다리는 것은 생활해 나가는 사람의 본능이라 하겠다.

그들의 세상에는 은순이가 없고 병서가 없고 애덕 여사도 없을 것이 당연한 일이다.

(1924년 11월 29일)

Tan-sil and Ju-yeong

I

For a weather in the early days of June, it was a blisteringly hot evening of late. The sunset, with its splendor of the golden ray now heatedly glared down at the crossroads of Seoul, Jongno.

The noxious-looking coal-black muck latched right onto the billboards of the store, scattered on every side of the street, in an intersection, which were boasting the name of each store.

It was at that time that the clock, like the hat of a German soldier, above the roof of Jongno police station was pointing right at 4. When the windows of the high second-floor house and one-storied house, along with the miniscule grain of a single molecule on the ground were all glimmering in the tedious sunshine, as if the splendorous symphony of light could be seen, the faces of people that should've ripened like the copper color clad in white clothes became drained of spirit and their movement slowed due to all the abuse they experienced from being weak. And so, a reddish light could not be seen from their wholly anemic faces and as the faces were sallow and black, they manifested a fruitless weak-willed powerlessness. Still, as if there was something that was up, they often frequented the crossroad, coming and going, here and there. In the middle of the road traversed by those clad in white clothes, the trams restlessly went by and passed by while ringing the bell. At present, a tram that was going back and forth from the northward side to the one-sided path picked up two people and dropped them off on the crossroads of Jongno. In the midst, a woman around 20, dressed in hemp clothes rarely seen among female students, holding a pongee umbrella, got off the tram with sharp force like the blade of a knife.

Also, opposite to this, even at the southward side, the tram picked up a number of people and dropped them off on the crossroads of Jongno. In the midst, while a young man dressed in gray suit of medium height and a willowy young man clad in black suit, holding a black book, were talking about something, they crossed the complicated intersection of the tramline sidewards and came to stand in the station to take the tram bound for Seodaemun. While the female student in sobok (white clothes) was also walking to the station on the other side, she bent her back.

Upon cursorily seeing her, she seemed to be a strikingly beautiful and smart woman. Also, no matter how much one would indifferently see her face that had an agile expression, she did not appear to be an ordinary female student.

Among the two young men standing in the station and waiting for the tram, the young man dressed in black suit who first got off the tram bound for Namdaemun took off his hat and greeted the female student in sobok face-to-face. And when the female student dressed in sobok was coming closer, he said hesitatingly,

"Miss Tan-sil, I'm now on my way to Mr. Kim's residence. Would Mr. Kim be there in the residence? I hope he'd be there just in time"

while stealing a glance at the female student's facial expression that did not seem like it was going to instantly open the tightly shut mouth. The female student merely was abashed for a moment and said,

"I don't know"

and greeted, but as if she did not want to speak, she took three or four steps back. And, while looking eastward, she only waited for the tram to come.

As if the young man in black suit was disappointed with the young man in gray suit, he said,

"I've got it all wrong. One has to look at the sky to reach for the stars."

The young man in gray suit spoke as if it was natural,

"Hmph, what I'm saying is to instead take a nap. It is natural for someone worthy of a human not to latch onto the devil even if he feels that he would be abandoned by God."

As if the young man in black suit did not have a clue what his friend meant, he tilted his head and then, just in time, he got on the tram that came and stopped over in front of him. The female student who was standing on the other side was waiting from afar and after the people all got in, she later ascended. Yet, as if she thought of something, when the tram rang the bell to leave right then, she hurriedly got off the tram. When carefully looking at the face of the person who got off, it was deadly pale to the point of somehow arousing the suspicion that a person who suffocated would also be like such. As if it had no choice, the tram dropped off the person that got on and carrying only the remaining people, it fled westward.

"Hmm," said the young man in black suit and as if he had a sour taste, he stood, gripping the leathered handle of the tram and then, sat down, letting out a deep sigh. The young man in gray suit, opening his mouth again, put a slight smile on the gentle but also rather idle face and said,

"That's what I'm saying. No matter how much you're an artist who creates and lives on the basis of love, if you tried to love, but failed once, you ought to firmly suppress your agitated emotions by holding on and dissect the failure you experienced all the way to the bone."

The young man in black suit spoke like he found his friend's words tiresome,

"Today, your preaching lacks taste. Try again tomorrow"

and as if he was sighing again, he swallowed the long breath that came spewing out. The young man in gray suit looked sideways like he was bored to some degree and again, as if he could not just let his friend stay the way he was, he said,

"Anyway, how old is Kim Jeong-taek's sister, Tan-sil? Hmm?"

and pointing at the book with a black cover in his friend's hands, he asked,

"Is she like the main character of the book, *Behind You*?"

2

The young man in black suit crossed his arms as if he was slightly displeased and was about to close his eyes, but as if he was moved by his friend's intent to make efforts in consoling him, he said,

"They are not entirely alike. Tan-sil is not a woman who's lived like Ju-yeong. She's still not someone that got out of the convention yet. I would like to guide her well on that⋯⋯."

and looked down at his tiptoes. The young man in gray suit turned his head as if there was a point where he could be defiant at these words and while turning his head, he asked over again,

"But how old is she?"

"I don't know exactly, but she's close to 30⋯⋯."

"What, she's close to 30 already? How does she look that age? When doing a quick-over of her, she looks rather pure and young"

and as if to say that he was clueless, he looked out the window. In the time that they were conversing like this, the tram reached Seodaemunjeong 2 Jung Mok (Location name during the colonial period, but the current location name is Sinmunno 2-ga) and stopped there. The two young men said,

"Here"

and got off. Yet, the young man in black suit, as expected, greatly faltered and like he did not know why he was going, he struck the ground with his footsteps and said,

"What do we do when we get there?"

The young man in gray suit stared at him like his behavior was embarrassing and admonished him,

"Now that we've come, let's meet Mr. Kim Jeong-taek and then, leave. While you may have despaired over a woman called Tan-sil, is there a reason why you shouldn't meet her brother?"

After dithering for a long while, they entered an alley that had the advertisement called 'Gwangje Hospital' plastered at the right side in front of the station. At the end of the alley, the two-floor Gwangje Hospital, which was built in a half-Western style, stood vacantly as if it was drowsy from being leisurely. When looking from the outside, there was no patient and the nurses and doctors appeared to be taking a nap. At this, the two people grabbed the handle of the hospital. The presence of people rung the bell of the doorway in a house that seemed to be dozing off. A 40-year-old doctor named Kim Jeong-taek who had been reading a newspaper in the hospital room came out to receive the two guests, grinning from ear to ear, with a good-natured attitude. And he asked a nurse coming out of the narrow wooden veranda on the other side,

"Hasn't the lady arrived yet?"

After carefully staring at the two guests, the nurse said,

"She hasn't come"

and went back inside.

Soon afterward, Kim Jeong-taek ushered the two guests into the hospital's reception room and said,

"Mr. Lee Su-jeong, Mr. Ji Seung-hak, have you been writing something interesting these days?"

and pulling out a fan, he laughed,

"Haha."

Among the two guests, the young man in black suit was called Lee Su-jeong and the young man in gray suit was called Ji Seung-hak. Here, the two people were youthful aficionados of literature, common in Joseon. The one in the black suit wrote poems and the one in the gray suit wrote novels.

Kim Jeong-taek greeted the two literary youths and as if it was rare to find a topic of conversation, he often searched for Tan-sil.

"If Tan-sil was here, she would've exchanged brilliant questions and answers with you guys and humbled all your pride"

and shaking his heavy build and reddish face, he said,

"Even if it's my little sister, there's something to compliment her as much as it's surprising. How come such an adorable woman got earmarked as the number one unfortunate even among the most unfortunate women?"

And he furtively looked out at the backyard that had a flower-bed. Ji Seung-hak stared at him as if to sympathize with his state and asked,

"By the way, a few years ago, did your sister not live in your house? When did she come over your house?"

"I finally brought her over in fall, last year. We have never grown up in the same house as we are half-sibling and because I could not exactly know her character, I let her do whatever she wanted to do and watched her from afar while suspecting, but not only is the misunderstanding she got from the world until now entirely futile, but also it is a trap laid by devious men and women. So, against the opposition of my aged parents, as I pleaded to them against their will, I brought her over and it seems like there would not be such a good girl like her ever again. While I would like to get her married somewhere nice, as soon as possible, as she herself is vehemently opposing it, I'm waiting for the time······ Her words of opposition are amusing as well. As long as she became the laughing stock of the world because of marriage issue, she says that trying to meld herself, a laughing stock with another person again is dirtying her sacred self. Alas. So, when I ask, how come you are the only one that sacred, for two and a half times, her answer was, 'Brother, it is only when we look at the peak of the mountain from below that it looks high. When climbing such a high place, we start to imagine that there is a higher place. Yet, somehow, if we accidentally slip and if it seems like we would plunge below the peak of the mountain, we come to think again that the peak of the mountain we climbed was high. That is, certainly, isn't it the case that a person yearns more for a high place when one is in a low place? The higher one goes, there is no limit to it being high and as people set their ideals, which they claim are sacred and lofty, if I could think of it like that, I am certainly sacred.' And as if she was also dumbfounded, she shed tears. How pitiful such a scene was." And, he spoke as if to sympathize with his sister.

3

After Ji Seung-hak carefully listened to Kim Jeong-taek's words, upon noticing his friend in black suit, Lee Su-jeong warily looking out at the bright-red poppy field of the backyard, he said,

"Your talk really makes us somber. Nowadays, my friend over there is having a nervous breakdown······"

and as expected, he looked back and forth between the widely grinning Kim Jeong-taek and his friend, then, once again, directed his gaze to Kim Jeong-taek, and said,

"Then, your sister must've really found herself. In that respect, she must be different from Ju-yeong who's in a novel called *Behind You*."

"Oh, right, the book called *Behind You* was written by a young Japanese man who rented a room in the guesthouse of my father's concubine. The main character sometimes portrays Tan-sil's behavior and way of speaking, but it's very different. Ju-yeong in the book is surely like a Japanese girl. How is she like Tan-sil? Still, while the author may say that the book's main character, Ju-yeong is a lot better than Tan-sil, first, starting with the fact, in the beginning, Tan-sil did not lose her virginity of her own accord and her virginity was taken not by a Japanese man but by a Korean man. Really, the man is certainly unspeakably vicious. While the youngster came to a place far away from home and at least trusts me, how come such an act was inflicted on her? The man is worse than Docheok (Notorious thief in the Warring States period of ancient Chinese history who was akin to the devil, because of his indiscriminate looting and infringement of human rights). To top it off, was she the one that went out with him because she wanted to? It was my uncle that so rashly did the matchmaking. Speaking of which, an adult like my uncle is ill-natured. If I speak all of it, as the flaws of my family would be gaping, I couldn't say it, but really, she is a woman that pitifully fell into an unfortunate fate. So, even at this point, if I could save her, I would rescue her from her fate, but would she ever listen? As she cursed, saying that she was averse to men even more than demons, while she originally was a good girl filled with a lot of compassion, when thinking of the time that she went corrupt, perhaps, she herself was not of sound mind. Yet, whichever side we see her, she is different from Ju-yeong."

Lee Su-jeong who had been next to him, listening to the talk unfolding like this, hastily cried out like he was talking to himself,

"Ah, ah, I miss Ju-yeong, Ju-yeong. I miss Ju-yeong who cried out, 'Advance on, advance on' and 'Forward, forward.' What I idealize is not a mere docile Korean woman abandoned by a man and remaining chaste for him, but rather a woman fighting on through thick and thin, and living a life, worthy of a human."

Dr. Kim smiled as if it was absurd and while smiling, he said,

"Mr. Lee Su-jeong, then, weren't you someone who also quite

wished to guide my sister? There are a lot of people who pounce on her by getting into the habit of foul-mouthing my sister like that. So, at night, instead of putting on a blanket and going to sleep, she stays up crying. Yet, Tan-sil is not a woman who would only be guided by others and she is also not a woman sordidly abandoned by a man nor does she remain chaste for him. As that is what the majority of people who fail after trying to get close to Tan-sil say as an excuse, she never tries to get close to a man, saying that it would taint her sacred self……"

While listening to Dr. Kim's words, the young man, Lee Su-jeong intervened, speaking as if he was spitting out his words,

"If you're considering me as one of those people, you're truly wrong."

As the young man, Ji Seung-hak heard the two people's words being at odds with each other, he said,

"Right, ultimately, it's no fun when speaking at odds with each other"

and looking straight at Lee Su-jeong, he admonished,

"Wasn't what you said and what the majority of young people say according to Dr. Kim the same?"

Here, as if he was very displeased, Mr. Lee Su-jeong found fault in order to rebel against what Dr. Kim and what even his friend said.

"Isn't what you're saying ludicrous? I said I missed Ju-yeong, but how come you drag in a woman named Tan-sil and compare what other men said about her with what I said? It's not like someone having an unrequited love was tossing a piece of letter."

"That's right. But my point is that because I've seen a couple of people saying such things, I talked about it out of suspicion. I didn't say it to mean you were really like that."

"Yes, while that is what you, Dr. Kim say, isn't you who's quibbling about others amusing? In the proverb, as there is a saying that goes, He that commits a fault thinks everyone speaks of it……."

"Ha, your words seem to be cornering me again……."

"Instead, give me a clear, conscientious answer. Did you think of or not think of the woman, Kim Tan-sil before coming over to Dr. Kim?"

"At least, initially, I didn't know that the woman, Kim Tan-sil went about saying something along the lines of being sacred and cursing every man all the same after being abandoned by him like that."

4

"If you just beat around the bush like that, what you say becomes very disrespectful. How can you speak of guiding her when you don't even know much about the woman's deep intention or even how she looks?"

"Instead, please speak up right away. Mr. Lee, don't you love my sister to a certain extent? Aren't you beating around the bush?

Please speak clearly. As Koreans all indiscriminately like to bluff, it is a huge weakness for one to shun something if the other person shuns it in the least bit. As it sounds too absurd that the thing that a person in the village hates is hated by everyone, it is common for the person hearing this not to feel good about it. But without being able to clearly explain why, a majority of people hates things, because others hate it, and has a heart of competition instead of negotiating. Speaking of my sister, it is really an old story of already 10 years ago. Without the strength to find new things in any ordinary thing, still, in order to do away with people's sordid bad-mouthing, she was about to be engaged to a short rat-like man who was showered with a pennyworth of praise, but her virginity was forcibly taken by the man. When that came to be known to the world, my young immature sister was held responsible, but the six-year older rat-like man vainly boasted of having good fortune in luring a beautiful woman. Having become an enemy of my sister, currently, he is said to be living well with another woman who's just like him. That being so, is there a reason for a young, immature person not to grow? Isn't it enough that my sister grew up and matured in the meantime? But it is not like that in the world and there are a lot of absurdities. When we think about it, as Tan-sil says, as we plunge downward, we're bound to realize the high place and so, we may think that the people in this world would understand that and help pull up the person under that circumstance. But if there is a person straying from falling into a water sediment a thousand miles deep, the superior that person is compared to the ordinary people, the more the world would refuse to save her and it would bury and hide her neck, the sole remnant in the water sediment, when almost drowning in it. Really, as the path that a small woman walked for 10 years is terribly frightening, even if there is a temptation, the temptation that comes striking at my sister is a different type. With the average brain, they cannot interpret this. Still, Tan-sil easily tells apart temptation from kindness. But who would know that? When she did not lose her virginity of her own accord but was raped by a clearly beast-like thing 10 years ago, even now, they don't hear this instantly and they think of only my sister as a dissipated woman······ How distraught Tan-sil was after the book, *Behind You* was published that I couldn't bear to see her. At the end of each sentence, she said, 'Brother, they'd think I dated a Japanese man. If so, they would say that I'm a woman that's like a prostitute. And they'd think that I had men around like Choi Seong-sik, Kim Seong-jun, and Shin Chun-yong' and she suffered and wept again. Now, as that also dwindled, she pretty much put it off her mind and is frequenting the Anguk-dong kindergarten, but······."

"Ah, Mr. Lee is now at a loss for words. It is a weakness for a person who's mostly thoughtful of others to not be able to contain his speech and beat around the bush. In my perspective, that is evidence of agitated emotions. And it is that such a person is not able to overcome destiny's trick, where one is incapable of putting one's thoughts together······."

"If you guys speak of it like that, I have nothing to say. In the meanwhile, I thought of one other thing. There is a big reason why Miss Tan-sil and Ju-yeong who's a character from the book are different. There is a difference between Ju-yeong who was abused by entirely foreigners and gnashed her teeth out of vengeance and Miss Tan-sil suffering for a long time from being abused by our countrymen, but who are Korean collaborators of Japanese······."

"Right, right. Mr. Lee, it's because my sister's desire for revenge being perfectly internal is different from Ju-yeong's case. Yet, Mr. Lee, isn't your regular way of speech contradicting your idealization of Ju-yeong? What are you proving by saying that an internal revolutionary (like Tan-sil) is inferior to an external revolutionary like Ju-yeong when you, Mr. Lee speak of poeticizing dreams on the basis of love?"

"Haha······Now, Mr. Lee's secret has been greatly divulged. Still, are you going to go on beating around the bush here and there?"

"Really, it's evidence that Mr. Lee's thoughts are in disarray or if not, it's deceit that is tricking him right before his eyes······."

5

In the reception room of Gwangje hospital, as the talk that had been held two hours ago still carried on, now and then, the sound of 'Tan-sil' and 'Ju-yeong' seeped all the way to the front of the flower bed of the backyard. At a time that the lifeline of the sunset for an entire day from far beyond the mountain with the Buddhist temple, was tranquilly ebbing, Tan-sil who was watering the flow-erbed in front of the bright-red poppy field and picking weeds out of a field shivered, hearing her name seeping out. And gradually plucking up the courage, she cautiously went to sit at the edge of the narrow wooden porch (running along the outside of a room) of the receptionist room, where she would not be seen.

Somehow, Tan-sil realized a vague feeling heavily stirring from her chest, like she had seen such a movement while dreaming.

In the sunlight where the evening wind was softly blowing, the jeoksam (unlined summer jacket) in ramie fabric she took out and wore seemed to little by little thoroughly roll up from the side-ways. The vague emotion gradually swelled and certainly, when the things she forgot came to mind again as she went back to the past memory, her whole body trembled like the poplar trees. And when she listened with strained ears,

"Write a novel with Tan-sil as the material. Really, it would be out of the ordinary······"

"Really. It would be different from Ju-yeong. While Ju-yeong to the very end was abused and deceived by Japanese people who were egoists, Tan-sil on the contrary was abused by Korean people who while being Korean, assimilated into the life and emotions of a Japanese. While Ju-yeong, when going to Japan, said that she would merely take revenge on the Japanese people by learning the law, when Tan-sil went to Japan, she said, 'Let's see how the Japa-nese are' and went there to test them, and as she did not worship the Japanese, she did not hope for any benefits, and she would not have been deceived by Namiki Akkio (Name of a Japanese person Ju-yeong met in *Behind You*) and even a Japanese rickshaw-puller. Not only that, but it's because Tan-sil herself is at times a far more of an egoist than a Japanese. When thinking of the time she crossed over to Japan, she was not a good girl like a baby sheep but a baby wolf or a baby tiger."

"If that seemed like it, the book, *Behind You* was never written to have a woman as the agent, but rather it was written by a Japanese man to see the error of his ways in the perspective of a Japanese, sympathizing with the entirety of Joseon."

"It could be that. Me saying that I assume the writer as being the young man who rented a receptionist room of the house of my father's concubine is not much proof. While Ju-yeong grew up bleakly in a below middle-class family, Tan-sil grew up in the most extravagant luxurious house in Taedong riverside. While the incident that happened near Aoyama and the father making his family go bankrupt after he collateralized others' debt is almost the same, and while depending on a Korean soldier serving Japan for one's living was similar, generally speaking, not only was Ju-yeong more pitiful than Tan-sil but incomparably, she became physically tainted. And whichever side would be seen, Ju-yeong was more foolish than Tan-sil. And, she did not have Tan-sil's haughtiness and greed.

When I think of Tan-sil lunging at the guy after losing her virginity, it gives me the shudders at how a mere woman could be that potent. As she did not love the man and didn't want to have a physical relationship with him ever again, she tried to whittle down the lifetime happiness of the man who forcibly took her virginity.

"Then, teacher Kim, what if I write a novel with your sister as the main character while depicting some portion about Koreans? If I do such a thing, as it was when Nakanishi Inosuke wrote about the cruelty of his countrymen when writing *Behind You*, he would as he pleases burrow into how our countrymen are crafty but filled with fear and foolish but vulnerable."

"I couldn't agree more."

"What? Are you saying that, because you think you could write that much?"

"What kind of gibberish is that? I get to write if I do write. It's just that what I write would not be the same. Do you think that the book (*Behind You*) was written quite well? Even if he looks down on Korean women, there's a limit to it. Who knew that for no reason, the Japanese saw themselves as superior to Koreans that a woman (Ju-yeong from the book, *Behind You*) who resolved to take revenge on the Japanese by conscientiously going to Japan and studying the law so readily followed a Japanese soldier all the way to the hot spring and lost her virginity? But is it just that? Speaking of Ju-yeong, isn't she one of the first Korean female students? Coming to think of it, they wouldn't have romance or whatever of the thing in their mind. While pretending not to, a woman firmly keeps her virginity, then, they get married to a man with prestige and property, and from there, they would have thought that living in comfort while idling is for the best. From our perspective, we would be against the book written by Nakanishi Inosuke. It's because while we were foolish, we didn't want to hide that. Isn't he boasting his superiority to us after writing the book? Yet, on the one hand, when thinking of it, he wondered if there would be a woman like Ju-yeong in Korea. It's because Korean women are lazy and cowardly but strong……"

"Joseon not being able to bring into the world a brave woman like Ju-yeong is attributed to the fact that Koreans curse and slander one another, being the ruin of each other."

"Well, coming to think of it, Ju-yeong is like a Japanese woman. It's because there is no woman like the Japanese who aren't picky about men's social status, has no sense of chastity, but on the one hand are spiteful……"

After listening to such a conversation, Tan-sil heaved her body with difficulty, then, returned to the courtyard, and went back to her room. There, her whole body and soul sank into daydreams of the past.

6

It was 28 years ago when the Pyeongyang castle was quite bustling after the first Sino-Japanese war.

The people in the Pyeongyang castle then rarely talked about the stories of being frightened and miserable during the war.

They tried to recover their property that was lost during other countries' war by losing no time in earning money.

However, that was a story of a family where the head of the household or the eldest son was alive, and unfortunately during the war, in a family where the husband or the son died, the young widow and the old widow, while making porridge instead of rice, worried so much about clothes and food to the point that despite eating, they could not gain weight.

On the contrary, if the head of the household or the son was alive, the family would soon be affluent and so, there was the case of being rich, without envy of a county governor or a provincial governor. So, the widows who were wage workers in sewing also lived well off joyfully.

The men generally learned the Japanese language, became translators for the Japanese, and while previously, only those from Yeongnam got the government position, after the war, the northerners attained a decent authority of an officer, wore hats on the topknot of their hair and dressed their twisted and crooked body in military uniform while showing off their piddling knowledge. So, during their first prosperity, they made gisaeng give service as mistress just the way they wanted and forced even married women from other houses to be concubines after depriving them of their rights. At the same time that it had been the privilege of the southerners which northern people had not enjoyed as they pleased so far, the northerners caught right onto the wicked behavior. How resentful and disappointed the northerners must have been at the atrociously corrupt behavior of those who had come as county governors or provincial governors? Yet, they could not let go of such people's wrongful behavior and after earning a good position with money, they engaged in tyranny even more than what the southerners had done, schemed against civilians, locked them up, killing and stealing their money.

At the time, Choi Sosa who lived in an old valley murdered his grown-up son over 20 in the midst of the mess and as he lapsed into a lonely state, he took in other family's daughters who were siblings. As an immature and ignorant woman came to decide, just as the lower-middle class families commonly did, she sold her daughters into gisaeng service (Gisaeng are women of low-class social background who entertained men of upper-class). So, later on, Choi Sosa set out to buy her two daughters who were sisters and lean onto them. The elder sister was called San-wol and the younger sister was called Yeong-wol. Yeong-wol was still young and the elder sister, San-wol, with her beauty, was called over here and there, but how so obstinate she was that even if she was told to dance, she wouldn't dance and if she was told to make a sound, she didn't make a sound and it was only when she wanted to that she let out a silvery voice. Hence, when calling San-wol over, it was like attending to a pampered lady master and serving her. Still, the men hooked by the radiant face and the refreshing eyes called San-wol over and tried to play cute tricks on her. At the time, it was when San-wol turned 15. It didn't seem like a lie to say that she was 18 when comparing her who was very promiscuous with other women in general. The governor of the valley called her over to make her give service as a mistress, but as if she thought of something, after sitting next to the governor, she made the excuse that she was going to the lavatory and ran all the way from the gate of the barracks to the old villa in stocking feet (one's feet with beoseon, traditional Korean socks on). Based on the subsequent story, the governor tried to make San-wol be seated, doggedly dragging her close to his body and through the crack of the window, the governor's concubine was said to have been glaring at them with her bright-red eyeballs. Afterward, San-wol earned the nickname, headstrong gisaeng and as she became the concubine of Ryu Ji-dong, a rich man, she didn't turn up anywhere. While San-wol went to a rich man, Ryu Ji-dong who was plain, archaic, had a lot of money, and adored her, the more Ryu Ji-dong was affectionate to her, the more it seemed to her that he was trying to assimilate her into his plain, archaic lifestyle that little by little, she became discontent. One day, as it was when thievery was at its worst, while moving the riches and gold coins buried here and there from place to place, as if she was thoroughly tired, while following Ryu Ji-dong, with money wrapped up in her skirt, she said,

"Why can't you just order your wife to do these things? Is it that I am the only one that could go die? It's because I'm just doing whatever you tell me to do"

and tossed away all the money she wrapped up in her skirt on the yard. Seeing her in such a state, Ryu Ji-dong fumed, but as if he found it absurd, he ended up smiling and said,

"I'm doing this, because I trust you. Would I do such a thing out of hatred to you? Even if I'd like to order my wife to do it, as she has a lot of poor dregs from her family, she's not trustworthy, which is why naturally, I'm ordering you to do it."

Yet, not lowering her swollen cheeks, she made a fuss, saying that she was going to her family. After he failed to reason with her, where he said he wouldn't do it again, he hid all her shoes and clothes. Still, in the spare time, San-wol folded up the blanket her mother made for her upon coming to Ryu Jidong's house, carried it, put on straw shoes that she got from a woman servant, and running for about 12 km (30 ri), came to her house, which was in the old valley of Pyeongyang.

<h1 style="text-align:center">7</h1>

Later, after some time, San-wol refused to go even when Ryu Ji-dong came over to take her and then, went to a person called Kim Hyeong-woo who lived as a county administrator in a certain district.

As for that even, San-wol headed there (as a concubine) not because she wanted to, but because after becoming so destitute, she went to support her mother and sister. There, in less than one year, San-wol gave birth to Tan-sil.

While in Kim Hyeong-woo's family, after raising a son as the only child, while it may seem like they would have been incredibly fond of having another child, due to San-wol's extreme desire for livelihood, it appeared that her authority in the family was becoming greater, and so, everyone was averse to Tan-sil coming out into this world. Yet, the child that came out and grew relentlessly burgeoned. Along with the growth of Tan-sil, the wealth of the family amplified more and more. So, Kim Hyeong-woo's aged mother said superstitiously,

"The household is growing richer, because the lump of luck was born."

And so, the entire family inevitably came to hold Tan-sil dear.

Yet, as San-wol's boasting steadily increased and as Kim Hyeong-woo's love for San-wol deepened day by day, San-wol looked down on the whole family and did not even see Kim Hyeong-woo's wife like a human. Hence, except for Kim Hyeong-woo, the family members bore a grudge against Tan-sil and her mother like they were an enemy.

At the time, Tan-sil grew up in the newest, most humongous second-floor house in Taedong riverside. Of course, they lived without serving the aged mother and Kim Hyeong-woo's wife, as if there were only three people in the family. Now and then, Kim Hyeong-woo's firstborn son, Jeong-taek came over and received all the instructions of his father.

As Tan-sil grew more and more, she turned into a gentle and intelligent child. Guided by his love for his young daughter, Hyeong-woo taught Tan-sil the Thousand-Character Classic and classical Chinese. The clear-headed Tan-sil wordlessly figured out ten letters when she was taught one letter like the child of a ghost. Somehow, since the past, while San-wol was not that fond of household work, when it reached up to the point where Tan-sil learned words and came to play all sorts of cute tricks, she did not release Tan-sil from her knees and saying,

"Tan-sil, my baby"

she spoke even to the house servants,

"Oh, if not for my Tan-sil, there would be no fun living in this world."

The young mother was not able to restrain the abundant desire for livelihood and was tired of Kim Hyeong-woo's family and her own family extorting money to the point that life got dull. As it was money collected by Kim Hyeong-woo for dear life and as it was money she tried hard not to fruitlessly use, she did not want to give even a single penny to others. Yet, overturning such a wish, the more money was amassed, the more Kim Hyeong-woo's mother came, saying, I heard there being a farmland somewhere, there being a grave somewhere, there being a pine grove some-where, there being a chestnut field somewhere. When she said that, without gripes, Kim Hyeong-woo purchased it and gave au-thentication under the name of Kim Jeong-taek. Of course, at the time, because San-wol did not know the classical Chinese char-acters, she was tricked every time, but instead, the receptionist person always snitched for San-wol. Whenever San-wol suffered from such things, she felt displeased to the point that her eyes reddened. At such times, she wondered why Tan-sil wasn't born a boy and even grumbled about her own child. And without notice, she cursed and swore at Kim Hyeong-woo. For lack of anything better, Kim Hyeong-woo bought one that was costlier than the one he bought for his firstborn son and gave authentication under the name of Tan-sil.

Then, when Tan-sil turned 8, as the Christian school flourished in Namsanjae of Pyeongyang (Mountain in Pyeongyang), the young female students knocked on doors from house to house, carrying a Christian church leaflet and proselytized,

"Please believe in Jesus. All the prosperity in the world is useless. In heaven, there is prosperity even for a beggar."

When such young band of proselytizers knocked on the grand gate of Kim Hyeong-woo, San-wol knitted the long slender eyebrows of her dazzling face and said,

"What are these girls? Even a gisaeng that is raised lowly like that would be of no use……"

And as if she did not find it right for young girls in a mob to knock on the door of someone else's house and cry out things they wouldn't even know, she said,

"I won't raise my child like that."

Yet, as if Kim Hyeong-woo was thinking of something, he said,

"Shall we send our baby to school around next spring? If we send her there, she would also perhaps be told to go around doing missionary work……"

and stared at San-wol's face. And he smiled as if to see what San-wol would do. Upon hearing such words, Tan-sil said,

"Father, I'll also be doing missionary work"

and leapt up immaturely.

Thinking that her daughter was going against her words, San-wol manifested dignity in her big black eyes and fumed,

"Kid, are you going to say that again? What would I do if I don't see you? I find this world tiresome, but even you are not listening to me?"

Yet, on the one hand, San-wol also wanted to send Tan-sil to school and make her study to the point that she would not lose to a boy. The only thing that San-wol was averse to was wandering around the street to proselytize.

8

In the year that Tan-sil turned 8, she pleaded to her mother on all sorts of things every day. First, having her mother attend a chapel with Tan-sil, Second, sending Tan-sil to school and every time her mother was leisurely sitting by, she came over and went on a tirade about not wanting to learn sewing. While that might have been like nonsense coming out of a young mouth, it had foundation.

Even when Tan-sil came over to play at the head family's house, her father's legal wife got into the habit of indiscreetly cursing at San-wol in front of Tan-sil.

"Such a wolfish bitch. What would it be like if that bitch died?

The bitch would die from getting struck by lightning"

and spewed out curses until the young mind was astonished. Thereby, Tan-sil at last came to know that her mother did something bad to others and that others bore a malicious grudge against her.

Still, as if something was not up to her liking, San-wol was quite reluctant to send Tan-sil to Christian school, but in late spring of the year, after quarreling with Kim Hyeong-woo for three days, she decided to donate 50 won to the school at the time and get Tan-sil enrolled in school.

Of course, Tan-sil was treated with dignity like a royal princess at school. She was envied in everything by all of the students. The teachers were affectionate to her as well, as if when it concerned Tan-sil, it wouldn't be painful even when something was shoved in their eyes. After being sent to the school, day after day, Tan-sil went there by crossing the mountain slope. Also, even after San-wol signed her up for school, as she found it pitiful that her daughter crossed the mountain slope to go to school, she hoped that Tan-sil would quit. Yet, as long as Tan-sil was enrolled in school, her father, Kim Hyeong-woo sought to make her study and witness prosperity to the very end.

At the time, Kim Hyeong-woo did a huge trading business at the side of Taedong river. Every day, in Tansil's house shed, thousands of seok (Korean unit of measurement, where 1 seok of rice is around 144kg) of rice came in and out.

And in San-wol's room, money bowls were placed everywhere.

San-wol used the money beyond measure. Even then, day after day, she called the servants over, making them stand in front of her, and cursed at them in her commanding voice, saying that such a good portion of money they had was disappearing. After Tan-sil started going to school, as she got tired of her mother's love, occasionally, when she came back from school, she slightly tossed the booklet at the wooden floor of the Western-style room and coming out to the reception room, she latched onto her father's pouch. Then, her father would say,

"You have a lot you could eat in the living room. Tell your mother to give them to you"

and appeased Tan-sil. Yet, Tan-sil shook her head and smiling sweetly, she said,

"I'm scared of mom."

Her father inevitably pulled out the money from the pouch, gave it to the servant boy so that San-wol wouldn't know and told him to buy something for Tan-sil.

As the wealth of Kim Hyeong-woo's house grew and San-wol's squandering increased, the bond between Tan-sil and her mother became gradually thinner. That was because the more Tan-sil made high achievement in her school academics, the more she received the lesson that the prosperity of the world was futile, that serving as someone's concubine was good for nothing, and that gisaeng was like the devil.

This all happened the following year after the Russo-Japanese war was fully waged. One day, a guest dressed in military clothes, riding a horse, came over to Tan-sil's house. Tan-sil was so scared of the guest that she went around, evading him, but got caught by the servants and was compelled to go to the front and bow to him. In any case, the person said that he was a soldier serving Japan who attended Japanese military academy. And he said that he was the uncle of Tan-sil. Even when the guest in military clothes said that he was an uncle while seeing Tan-sil for the first time, he did not even once give her a pat and said as a first greeting,

"It's not right to raise children in luxury like that. In the case of Japanese people, young girls who haven't yet married are raised rather frugally and when they get married, if we earn the money, they get to live in luxury. That kind of silk clothes. That kind of ring. We don't surround children with such things nor heaps of money. By all means, the Japanese raise their kids well. That, raising kids like that is improper"

and he did not clarify as to whether they were words spoken to his brother or to his sister-in-law, San-wol. At these words, already, furrowing her eyebrows, San-wol looked away and loaded tobacco on the long pipe and pointing the bowl of pipe toward Kim Hyeong-woo, she seemed to be waiting for him to strike the match and kindle it. As it must've been that Kim Hyeong-woo was flippantly pleased because his brother arrived upon graduating, he was slow to kindle the flame in San-wol's bowl of pipe. Yet, finally, Kim Hyeong-woo struck the match for San-wol's bowl of pipe. As if San-wol did not feel right, she dragged the thin skirt in ramie fabric while putting the tobacco pipe between her teeth, went over to the room on the other side and all the while, she called out to her child, as if she found her adorable,

"Tan-sil, Tan-sil."

9

Afterward, Tan-sil's uncle often submitted his opinion under the authority of San-wol and having earned the trust of Kim Hyeong-woo, he came to hold dignity in family affairs.

And while he pretended to deeply love Tan-sil, each time, he got a bunch of bills from her father's hands and put them in his pocket and was rumored to have regularly frequented the gisaeng room (Place where the gisaeng stayed to entertain men as a part of their occupation).

In the meanwhile, as Tan-sil's academics greatly improved, while it had been less than one year since she attended school, she came to be on par with the students who've been attending school for over three years, and was ahead of them to the point that she could instead teach classical Chinese text to other students.

While the relationship between the school and Tan-sil was quite close because the school endowed all sorts of love to the young student who excelled in her academics and young Tan-sil also donated much money, while sleeping, Tan-sil underwent paralysis and while praying, she came to have humongous grievances, where she sobbed. It was from that point that the Christian church came to have a fierce desire to promote the church in the land of beautiful scenery and as such, it made the young students forcefully drag the parents without faith to the chapel while in tears and saying,

"Please repent. Please repent. Confess all your crimes and let's have faith in Jesus starting from today"

all the believers followed blindly from the sound and while crying out, as if a mushroom continuously sprang up from the damp ground after the fall of rain, heaving to their feet,

"Any day and any time, I hated someone and prayed that he would be an evil person."

"I prayed for a month that my mother-in-law would die any month and as if the wish was heard, while my mother-in-law was eating, she passed away with her spoon held."

"As I thought of committing adultery with the preacher, I prayed for three years for the preacher's wife to die."

"I added lye in the food to kill my husband."

and letting out a sound that the ears could not bear to take, they sobbed and confessed,

"God, please forgive me. The Lord, Father, the Lord, please take a kind interest in us. The moment of repenting has arrived. Please save everyone"

and as if a huge mourning took place, they wailed.

At this time, one night, even Tan-sil's mother, San-wol was dragged to the chapel by her daughter. The deaconess and the bible women of the chapel flung themselves at her as if to greet their majesty, the queen and said,

"Please repent and have faith in Jesus. Everyone in the world has sinned. Would there be a person who has not sinned in this world? Please repent and have faith in Jesus starting from tonight"

and clinging to the lower end of San-wol's white silk clothes, they urged her to repent and have faith in Jesus with all their might.

As if she thought that coming to such a place was a mistake, she had an annoyed look on her face and in a bleak tone, she spoke what she said all the time,

"As the gods did not help me, when I turned 8, my father passed away and while my brother was there, nevertheless, when I turned 12, he got beaten up in the war and got killed by a Chinese man, and as I was left as the eldest, there was no way to support my single mother, which is why I became a gisaeng. So, as every one of you know, there is no way for a gisaeng to be someone's legal wife and so, naturally, I became someone's concubine. I also know that is a sin. But what could I do about it? Now, it's not just me, but since I have this young child, I couldn't get out of the house at once, right? It doesn't make a difference whether I repent or not. If everyone in the world is said to have sinned, even if it's god, wouldn't it be better for god not to count all of them?"

From which she at once cut off the bible women clingily throwing themselves at her and with all her might, flung open the chapel door, guarded by a gatekeeper who stood by, shut it, and getting ahold of Tan-sil who sprung at her, crying, San-wol let her precede and returned home.

Afterward, Tan-sil did not eat nor sleep and stepping into the three-compartment room, she prayed in front of the fulling-block day and night.

"God, God, please give my mother a repenting heart and make her believe in Jesus. If you don't, please send me to heaven as soon as possible. But please, don't send my beloved mother to hell"

and day and night, even while sleeping, she prayed, and while eating, she prayed.

One day, her mother asked Tan-sil whose appearance was becoming haggard,

"Tan-sil, shall I believe in Jesus? And shall I not serve as your father's concubine. Well? Then, you and I would be separated. Well? Baby, a person who believes in Jesus doesn't serve as someone's concubine."

At this moment, Tan-sil, even with her young heart, did not have a clue what to do. Afterward, she did not say the prayer again, 'please make my mother repent and have faith in Jesus.' Yet, as days passed by, this day, the next day, she grew so haggard to the point that it was conspicuous.

10

San-wol could not bear to see her young daughter's pain and so, if she could, she tried to pull her out of Christian school. So, she often felt Tan-sil's head and whenever she was setting off for school, she said desperately,

"Baby, your head is steaming, so don't go to school today. You should also take your mother's heart into account. Who do you think mother trusts solely, living in the world?"

and pleaded to her. At first for one to two times, Tan-sil reluctantly said,

"Mother, I'm not in misery, but because you're worrying, sure, I won't go to school today."

But knowing that her mother was saying such things frequently every day, she said,

"Satan has lunged at mother. So, she is trying to turn me into a slave of Satan"

and cried. San-wol had not known that her daughter who gave her stomach spasms of pain as she gave birth would be going all the way, saying such cruel words and she uttered,

"I'm not going to be looking at your pathetic state. Would there be a daughter who talks about her mother being taken over by Satan? Disgraceful child," and then broke down into tears.

After seeing her mother like that, Tan-sil, on her way to school, also cried heaps of tears. All the while, when she went to school, it was not comforting even there. As Tan-sil was good at studying even when she was young, the other students, who were averse to her taking the upper-class after doing better than them, whispered stealthily,

"Daughter of a gisaeng, daughter of a concubine, she's bound to turn out nothing better than that."

"Besides, as she has such an air of lowliness about her, what would she become later on?"

"Her father does business with a Japanese. Before that, when he was a county administrator, he was said to have ruined so many men of great affluence."

"Ah, he's identical to a thief. A daughter of such a thief has gone up to the 3rd grade like that and is merely paying a snug hoard of money and behaving distastefully."

When Tan-sil came to know such words being spoken, her round, pure, but prideful heart got squashed and it was painful as if to draw out blood. While she had heard vaguely that her father got on formerly as a county administrator, she did not know that he even committed acts of tyranny and while he might on occasions associate with the Japanese, she had no idea that he got so close to the Japanese that he was doing the same type of work as them. Such a criticism was a huge pain that struck, gouging out the body and mind of this young Tan-sil who prayed day and night to be the greatly sacred daughter of God.

As a young mind, she was in such a misery that she came to hate even her father and mother.

To Tan-sil, who tried to be a sincere daughter of God that wouldn't lose out to Virgin Mary, her biological parents were too much of deep sinners. The daughter of a concubine, the daughter of a gisaeng, the daughter of a Japanese spy, the daughter of a tyrannical player. She could not help but be astonished to the point that she would pass out from the filthy pronouns that rang in her ears. All the while, when she came back home, San-wol who lost even the love of her daughter ceaselessly lorded over others and so, the entire house was all abuzz, boiling hot like the water boiling. Also, day after day, Kim Hyeong-woo invited guests and opened a banquet. His brother, Kim Si-woo behaved to all the guests like the master of the house while feigning a magnanimous facial expression and took the plunge in spending money without knowing how valuable it was. Already, from that time, San-wol was not in the circumstance of being able to put money in every corner and spending it beyond measure.

In the receptionist room of her house, day and night, the obscene sounds of a Japanese gisaeng and Korean gisaeng were ceaselessly heard. In the midst of it, there was the shortest man with a dark face who entertained the whole room like a clown. Each time, the man became the guest of honor and procured all the Japanese gisaeng, Korean gisaeng, and every prostitute there was in Pyeongyang. And he alone watched playful tricks by the gisaeng who showed off all sorts of flattery. It was where he looked like a grotesque rock in the flowerbed engirdling him by his side. When peeping at him through the door, it was absurd to the point that scoffs arose. Any guest that was gathered there yielded to the man who was like the grotesque rock and if a giseang came to their side, they all pushed her over to his side. Upon glance, it seemed like the man had great power that other people in the room did not have. Everyone called the man, 'Elder, elder,' and served him.

Yet, San-wol cursed at the man, saying that he was a goblin. And she said, "Is it because you're smart that you're treated like a human? It's because the Kim household has a bountiful of money that they could afford to treat someone like you as a human. If you could make Kim Hyeong-woo a governor with your own hands, burn up my tongue" and cursed as much as the man could hear her when he passed by. All the while, on the day that Tan-sil's father and uncle spent money thoughtlessly at the end of the banquet, as they asked San-wol to borrow money for them, a huge ruckus took place in the whole house. San-wol said to Kim Hyeong-woo all the time,

"This is my house. Get out of my house. Why would you gather all sorts of things in someone's house and put on all sorts of dissipated act? You should also have some shame. How could you act like that to me when I'm 20 years younger than you? Wouldn't the village be humiliated? Wouldn't our young daughter be ashamed? It's enough that you have that much money and authority. Besides, what would you do if you become a governor? A person is supposed to have some awareness after the age of 40. Do you think there would be any huge glory in indecently becoming a governor, all rotten to the core, with the helping hand of your little brother's friend?"

And at certain times, San-wol stirred up an uproar, saying that she was going to leave and, on some occasions, Kim Hyeong-woo caused a tumult, saying that he was going to run off.

11

In the summer, the house of Kim Hyeong-woo's head family (Kim Hyeong-woo's legal wife's family) cooked up a huge scheme. It was a scheme, where coming to terms with Tan-sil's wants, they would beguile her into coming to the head family's house by attending the chapel. Previously, when Tan-sil went to the chapel on Sundays, she boundlessly envied other friends sitting next to their mother and grandmother and displaying their winning ways. And she felt unbearably lonely for sitting alone next to such friends and still having to act like the daughter of the biggest house in Pyeongyang.

In the meantime, she met her grandmother as well as her father's legal wife, and even her sister-in-law in the chapel. Her sister-in-law was the wife of Kim Jeong-taek. At the time, Kim Jeong-taek already was married.

It was not a disagreeable thing to refer to Tan-sil as one's daughter or granddaughter or sister, whom others gazed at for two to three times for her beauty and academic excellence.

Still, if someone asked them, Kim Jeong-taek's new wife said, "Daughter of my father-in-law's concubine" and Kim Hyeong-woo's legal wife said, "The one that San-wol gave birth to" and the grandmother said, "My concubine daughter-in-law's child."

When thinking of such things, Tan-sil felt the urge to have her youthful body snuck into a hole, but from that moment on, she did not hear the discriminatory words in the church, such as, 'You are the daughter of an outsider.' It dawned on Tan-sil that this alone was fortunate. Yet, knowing that they were acting much more gratefully than before, albeit being a bit flawed, she nit-picked,

"Mother (Word choice that Tan-sil used for endearment and not referring to her real mother but rather the legal wife of her father), why do you refer to me as a daughter that San-wol gave birth to?"

As Kim Jeong-taek's mother had been waiting for such an opportunity, she placated her,

"Then, would you come to our house and act as my daughter? How can I call you my daughter when you don't even do so?"

It was a time when young Tan-sil had been thinking that it was fortunate she met a relative she knew in the chapel. Also, she found the mother of Jeong-taek (Legal wife of her father) pitiful for not only having her husband taken by her mother but also for not being able to spend money as she pleased and for being chastised by San-wol every time they gathered in one house.

So, it occurred to her that it would be good to be kind to her father's legal wife, at least out of a sense of justice. So, when she had the opportunity, Tan-sil regularly frequented the head family's house, which was in the street of the new highway up Taedong-mun, outside of the house in Dongpiru.

San-wol who came to know this was enraged as if the world went dark. Kim Hyeong-woo also said to Tan-sil, "Don't visit the head family's house regularly." Yet, Tan-sil heard Kim Hyeong woo's wife whining day after day as she went there and picked up on all sorts of sins of her mother. The more Tan-sil heard the whining of her father's wife, the more she came to think of her mother as an unspeakably evil person and it seemed like her father's legal wife was a female saint who intactly received the will of God in the bible.

There, after one year, Tan-sil briefly let go of her concerns that she had day and night, and day after day, visited the head family's house, listened to the past stories from her grandmother, and found some joy in hearing the whining of her father's wife that she heard almost every day. And she treated her mother coldly, as if she was not the daughter of San-wol.

However, the dark concerns at the very bottom of Tan-sil's narrow chest, 'My mother would be going to hell' did not dissipate.

San-wol flew into a burning rage as Tan-sil frequenting the head family's house was said to have been attributed to a wicked scheme to entice Kim Hyeong-woo by dragging in Tan-sil and making her stay there. And she told her young daughter, 'If I find out about you going to the head family's house, I'll soon be running off somewhere else."

As Kim Hyeong-woo found it unpleasant to wreak all sorts of trouble, every time he saw her, he told Tan-sil not to go to the head family's house. Yet, the more they did so, the more the head family's house set up all sorts of schemes to cajole Tan-sil. There, while young Tan-sil was drawn to the affection that was fabricated to seem like it had justice and while avoiding the intense affection that came from her own mother's love, she once again was concerned. Not only that. A huge turmoil occurred that was incomparable to the past when it had still been a peaceful family despite the occasional almost ceaseless uproar of San-wol till' now. That was as Kim Hyeong-woo came to whore in the gisaeng house, guided by the short man that San-wol referred to as a goblin. So, while in the past, if San-wol lost her temper, Kim Hyeong-woo immediately quit whatever it was that he was doing, now, not only did he not do that but occasionally borrowing the words of his brother who returned from Japan and his brother's friends, he retaliated, "It's only right for a woman not to lose her temper. Are there any woman out there who dares to go around giving commands like in our house?"

There, on certain days, San-wol browbeat Kim Hyeong-woo, but on some days, she was like a defeated castellan and placated her daughter. Yet, rather, Sanwol had a lot more benefits in browbeating Kim Hyeong-woo. In accordance with the words of her father's wife, Tan-sil came to linger in the head family's house and seldom came back home.

12

From that time on, Kim Hyeong-woo regularly frequented the head family's house, greeted his mother, and left after patting Tan-sil. Kim Si-woo, knowing that his brother's love slanted too much to Tan-sil that it couldn't be helped with the usual power, said,

"I cannot understand you, brother. You don't know how to love your son, but as your love is only for your daughter as if it assumes serious proportions, maybe, it's because San-wol gave birth to her. It's when a girl has something to be ogled at that she could be treated with affection. And it is an inexplicable thing that you, brother, are firmly in San-wol's clutch."

Even so, he bought a suit that appeared dazzling and dressed up Tan-sil.

All the while, on some occasion, San-wol tried to intimidate Tan-sil who was stubborn about staying in the head family's house and at certain times, she barely managed to clearly write letters in the cursive handwriting of Korean alphabets she solely learned. Yet, Tan-sil who inherited the obstinacy right from her mother and learned cleanliness and righteousness from the bible was not immediately moved. Yet, in Tan-sil's young heart, the bleak thought did not dissolve, 'My mother would go to hell in the future and burning in the midst of hot fire, she would go begging for a drop of water.' She dreamed every night. The one that she dreamed the most was such. ⋯⋯ When her grandmother, her father's wife, and her sister-in-law were frolicking around, holding onto each other's wrist, they would be taking the sturdy path to heaven. Yet, her mother was shrouded in tattered, beaten silk-clothes and harassed here and there by innumerable servants of the devil, while pushed back into a corner, incapable of making any sound. Tan-sil followed her and said, Mother, mother, I'm here, mother, can't you see me now? I won't go back to the head family's house ever again⋯⋯After having such a dream, her slumber grinded to a halt.

How miserable the youth straying in such a dream must have been! From that moment, she thought that a person ought not to do evil things to others. Even more than that, first, she thought that it was not right for one to serve as someone's concubine. And as if she had seen from many tales of her future, she daydreamed establishing a Gothic-style abbey and living in the midst of it. And she wanted to wait for it to happen.

Already, she made a eulogy that yearned for heaven in the Korean alphabets and gave it to her friends. Among them, there were such things.

> *As I do not know*
> *the way to heaven*
> *please guide me,*
> *and even if my mother comes after me,*
> *please don't chase her away.*

> *As I do not know*
> *what is so great about my Lord's grace,*
> *My Lord, please see to it until I get it,*
> *and even if I commit an unforgivable crime,*
> *please don't write it on the afterworld list of the righteous.*

From that point on, she saw a strange, lovely seed in her heart that would turn her into an 'inscrutable person' in the future.

While hoping that she would go to heaven fair and square, in her heart, she silently doubted even her faith and the rewards of heaven. Even so, the confidence that she was a good person was quite solid. When praying at school successively, there was a time when she had made many old students and teachers laugh after such a prayer. That was a very simple prayer.

"My Lord, My Lord, please guide us who are like the young sheep. We could become good or evil depending on the strength of the Lord. My Lord who has great ability, please don't let us down. Please make heaven present in our minds. The glory of the Lord is in heaven."

Tan-sil herself was not conscious that it has become peculiar that her prayer deviated from every precedent done at school or church. When her teachers and the students teased her prayer for being amusing, a vague doubt cropped up, 'I must've prayed incorrectly.' She did not even want to reflect on the right and wrong of her prayer.

Yet, when seeing the facial expression of the upper-grade students and teachers, she caught sight of an intentionally deceitful smile that regarded her as a toy. The young Tan-sil bristled with bright-red fury when those who idealized heaven could not refrain from deceiving – and further, taunted her with the ferocity of regarding others as a toy.

Afterward, as her prayer became very different from many people, at certain times, she tried to fully lean on the strength of the

Lord while on some occasions, she tried to take all the responsibility for her life. Also, in some moments, she believed that the heaven fully belonged to the Lord and at other times, she reckoned that everything belonged solely to her. There, for that one thing, the seed of her young ideology made her miserable, and so, the heart-bursting depths of anxiety she had for her mother since the past seemed to be penetrated by something vague and thinning day by day.

While saying that she shouldn't be like that and shaking her young head, she dolefully tried to suppress something that was somehow unknowable.

13

The youthful days of Tan-sil were swept by heart-bursting, humiliating pain and vague doubt.

Yet, as precocious Tan-sil turned 11, she became a slender lady with hair whose length was one ja and a half (one ja = 30.3 cm, the Korean foot).

Her desire for knowledge expanded day by day. And her curiosity to see something strange that she had not seen grew heavily day by day. Now, she wore the silk clothes that her mother made for her without furrowing her eyebrows in the least bit. And she even thought of wanting to be more lavish. So, she wore the suit that her uncle made for her and she came to like following around her father, uncle, and her brother who was about ten years older than her.

As the people in the street of Pyeongyang South Gate saw Tan-sil attending school every morning in pink skirt that seemed to smile harmoniously, yellow jeogori (Korean traditional jacket) that appeared to have the mist rising or in yellowish green jeogori with a young female servant behind her, they all swallowed their saliva, coveting her as their future daughter-in-law. Yet, everyone could not dare wish for it. At the time, there were clamorous rumors over Kim Hyeong-woo who had the ability to make even the flying birds fall in Pyeongyang castle that he might become the governor of Hwanghae-do in the near future······

Thereupon, as the entire house of Kim Hyeong-woo's head family made a fuss over it for more than a year, Kim Hyeong-woo had a change of heart and so, even when he visited Tan-sil, he did not stay, but instead came over briefly and left after patting just Tan-sil. And sometimes, he dispatched the rickshaw, taking only Tan-sil and occasionally San-wol merely sent food she made. So, the head family was disappointed as they were not able to achieve what they had anticipated from having Tan-sil over. They who weren't of good nature wound up finding it tiresome to have Tan-sil over in their house and look after her any longer. Not only that but because with the money that was used up from Kim Hyeong-woo's campaign for governor, they have become gravely hard-pressed, which did not give the head family room to afford things as it had been in the past. And so, instead of holding a grudge against Kim Hyeong-woo, they harassed Tan-sil.

All the while, Kim Hyeong-woo used up a great sum of money until it would not be an exaggeration to say that he squandered almost all of the house property outside of San-wol's possessions. Also, he surreptitiously had his document on the rights over house and farmland caught by a Japanese, where he paid his debts, got a huge mortgage that was several times larger, and gave it to the person called goblin. A great sum of money that was 60,000 won went into the fees of campaigning for governor. Kim Hyeong-woo who fearlessly put a great sum of money into the campaign for governor went to Kyeongseong for ten times a month. He did not seem to work to find all sorts of joy for San-wol and her daughter like previously, but seemed to be sacrificing all of the fun at present, out of a greed to make his wife and son prosper by becoming a governor in the future. He did not go to the head family's house to search for Tan-sil like before and did not dispatch the rickshaw. Not only that but every day, some gisaeng who meddled with him was completely immersed in writing letters to him while lying down. Although Kim Hyeong-woo did not seem to be too immersed in her, he went to the gisaeng's room and stayed there until night once every three days.

San-wol herself did not take pains to do only housework like before and vacated the house, playing around with the same flock of young women with oily hair and powdered face. San-wol who went out in the morning and came back home in the evening stopped over at the head family's house on her way back and wrapping something up in the handkerchief, gave it to Tan-sil. That was usually a sweet cookie most favored by a young child.

And then, because at the head family's house, Jeong-taek's wife delivered a baby, every day, they got ahold of the servant who had been sent to accompany Tan-sil on her way to school and ordered the servant to sit next to the baby while making Tan-sil go to school alone. Not only that but also the love that had been directed to Tan-sil was all transferred to the youngster. No matter how smart and precocious she was, a plaintive emotion that could not help but desire compassion was there. Now, she came to miss being by her mother's side. While she could not endure the misery just based on that, after a long time, the head family's attitude toward her changed day by day, and there was unbearable hardship in going to school and coming back home from school. Not only did the street people slow her way by effortfully being pretentious and asking her questions, but when passing by a remote alley, some rude lads of thirteen or fourteen years of age stormed at her and tried to cling to her while teasing,

"I've staked out a claim on you."

"I have my eyes on you."

"My future bride."

While Tan-sil spoke about this once to her grandmother, she turned a deaf ear. It appeared that once again, she did not care about what Tan-sil thought.

Tan-sil's small chest was deceived for the first time by compassion that turned out to be ferocious. Even then, Tan-sil did not want to promptly go back home and soon call San-wol, mother, mother. Somehow, she was reluctant to soon call San-wol her mother. Yet, it was never the case that Tan-sil genuinely hated her mother, but rather she did not want to hear the words, daughter of a concubine, daughter of a gisaeng. Ever since she was young, she was a lady brimming with self-esteem.

14

Ever since she was a child, Tan-sil who had so much dignity thought that even if anyone was born in a rather exasperating home, it would be fine as long as one studied well and was respectable. Somehow, this child was averse to not being respectable. Even when playing with her friends, when it seemed like someone would be making her do a wrongful request for something, her complexion became flushed and even while trying to display a nonchalant look, she was gravely distressed, as if it didn't turn out the way she wanted. Such a disposition became more vivid as she grew. She never had forgiveness for a base action. One day, after suffering from such an incident at the house of Taedongmun, she very much regretted staying there for more than a year and ended up coming back home, outside of Dongpiru.

It was a clear spring day at the time. During winter, as the lake water that seemed like the thick glass board fence was laid over it was going downward or upward, like a blue silk roll already spread out lengthily, the ripples were soothingly chaffing with the warm spring scenery. Even on this day, Tan-sil left the young female servant called 'Jak-eunne,' who looked after her, at home and on her way back home after school, while going down the slanted hill with several friends, when hearing a friend say,

"While we used to go to Taedong river and play in Tan-sil's house, skating during winter, these days, we haven't been able to go there at all"

Tan-sil immediately said,

"Then, let's gather at our house today. From there, let's head to the Ryongwang Pavilion to dig up herbs."

There, going down the Namsanje hill (Name of a scenic hill in Pyeongyang), her friends were about to hurriedly part to busily get back home and leave the book bundle there. Yet, Tan-sil soon put on a dark face and said,

"Guys, let's meet in front of Ryongwang Pavilion. From there, let's go to my mother's house, which is outside of Dongpiru"

and called the children that were a couple of steps or three or four steps ahead, halting them. Upon hearing what Tan-sil said, all of the children leapt up, out of joy, saying,

"Sure. I like your mother."

They asked, "Why aren't you staying in her house?"

Tan-sil said hesitatingly,

"It's because there are some issues."

The youngsters did not even give any thought to this again and without examining their friend's complexion, they hastily parted once more and at the thought of meeting again soon, moved their footsteps forward and forward.

Tan-sil ploddingly walked alone and thought,

'When I come back to the head family's house, what kind of face would they wear again in greeting me? Jak-eunne is my person, but why do they take over her? How come that many people among my grandmother, my father's wife, sister-in-law, the foster daughter, the maid could not fend for one baby and make a fuss, ordering Jak-eunne to clean the poo and change the diapers? Today, when I go there, I'm going to take Jak-eunne out and play for a bit.'

Tan-sil hurried on her way back. Like it was usually, her brother did not return from the agriculture and forestry school, her grandmother was spindling the strip of silk cloth at the edge of the wooden floor of the reception room, her father's wife kept rattling in the kitchen to make something, and her sister-in-law in the opposite room was thoughtlessly sewing a picturesque, absurd piece of thread to put a sash around the baby's waist for one's first birthday. No one spoke a word to Tan-sil even when she returned. Oppressed by the lonely thought, Tan-sil called out, as if trouble stirred up,

"Jak-eunne, Jak-eunne."

While her sister-in-law in the opposite room could not have done so if it were from another family, as Tan-sil was the daughter of her father-in-law's concubine, she asked,

"Tan-sil, what's up with you? Jak-eunne is carrying the child.

What's the matter?"

and lost her temper, crying out, "If you go about making a fuss like that, the baby's going to fall off." As if Tan-sil was displeased, she said,

"What would've been the matter? I was going to rub my shoes a bit and hang them out in the sun."

At these words, her sister-in-law was speechless and then, murmured to herself inaudibly,

"What would be the use of raising a girl like that? What would she turn out to be later on?"

In the spare moment, her father's wife who had been doing something in the kitchen all at once ran out and groundlessly cursed at her,

"Why did you say, Jak-eunne, Jak-eunne? She was just carrying the baby. A child like you is of no use behaving like that. You should have some simple-minded side. If you go on, only making a fuss, saying, 'Do things for me', 'Do things for me,' would there be someone that likes you? As the saying goes, a person with a foul family background ends up with no better character. No matter how much I tell you, you ought to be listening to my words in order to be cultivated."

As Tan-sil was dumbfounded, she stood, her face having paled and when her grandmother stepped into the inner gate and said,

"Why are you all like this?"

she ended up sobbing. At this moment, her father's wife and Jeong-taek's wife in cooperation said,

"She was throwing a tantrum just because Jak-eunne was carrying the baby and so, when we told her not to do that, she's crying like that,"

scoffing and tattling on her. Still, the grandmother merely said,

"Would you be of any use when you're like that?"

and did not bother to fathom Tan-sil's words.

15

Tan-sil's ill-temperedness hit the roof. She thought that it was utterly against what was right to have someone small and young that she had taken away and the whole family heavily cooperating to suppress her. Until now, even when San-wol set a commotion in the whole house like boiling water, she had not seen uproar over an unrighteous thing. Even in her young mind, somehow, she thought that it was a bit unfair for them (Head family's house) to go to heaven but for only her mother to go to hell. At last, due to the sorrow, which was close to despair stemming from the emotion of being deceived by others, she vehemently cried until her narrow windpipe seemed to burst with a snap.

'I saw those people in vain. How could those people be different from my mother? While they don't even think of me as a relative, I trusted them because I was foolish. ······ They took away my Jak-eunne and are not letting me make her do an errand······How is it certainly different from my mother taking my father not from the head family's house but from a gisaeng's house in the street? When comparing these two things, their side is forcibly blocking Jak-eunne when she wants to follow me around and my father is only at my mother's side, because he himself wants to be there. By all means, I need go to my mother today and tell her. I'm not going to let Jak-eunne stay in this house just like that.'

Thinking of it like this, she shed tears. Even when Tan-sil cried like that, they merely said shamelessly,

"Why are you crying? That is a tad strange. Did someone hit you or curse at you?"

Now, at such a place, she could not find any justice or compassion. At the edge of the wooden floor, she held the damp cloth and scrubbed the soles of her shoe that were wet with her perspiration with her own hands. Jak-eunne who saw this from the main room came out, carrying the baby on her back and saying,

"Lady, let me scrub it. If I don't, your mama outside of the fortress would get worried"

and tackled it as if a huge trouble arose. It was at this moment that she realized a peculiar compassion that she had not experienced until now. How much did the young heart shed tears of joy when the two of them who had been on close terms were separated by something and then, got close again after defeating everything? She ended up crying as she gave to Jak-eunne the sole of the shoes that she was about to scrub with clenched teeth. And thinking of going back to her mother and talking about the past incidents in the head family's house, she cried even more. They were soft and light shameful tears aroused by an emotion that was all close to regret.

She stood, holding the book bundle and cried heavily as she wore the shoes that Jak-eunne, bending over with the baby at her back, was scrubbing for her. It was at this point that Jeong-taek's wife released her baby from the waist of young Jak-eunne. Jak-eunne scrubbed the shoes in a hurry and making Tan-sil put them on, she consoled her,

"Let's go to the house outside of the fortress. Lady, why are you staying here? You're worrying your mama who's living outside of the fortress."

After crying, Tan-sil answered with a nod of her head and wordlessly set out to leave the gate of the head family's house. When she was coming out of the gate, her grandmother fretted,

"Kid, don't rat us out to your mother again like someone did something."

Upon glance, it seemed that her grandmother did not have even a half pennyworth of feelings for Tan-sil that she had for her grandson. It was merely that her grandmother was pretending to do so as she set up a scheme to beguile her son who loved Tan-sil into coming to her family. As if Tan-sil was not going to step back into the gate ever again, she firmly held the book bundle and set out of the gate. Jak-eunne turned a deaf ear to the sound of Kim Hyeong-woo's wife who said,

"Hey! You stay here"

and went with Tan-sil in haste.

Holding the wrist of Jak-eunne, while setting out to the alley, Tan-sil thought of the promise she made earlier with several friends below the school hill. While swiftly moving her footsteps forward and forward, she said,

"Jak-eunne, let's move on quickly. I promised to meet everyone in front of Ryongwang Pavilion while we were parting in school a little while ago. I forgot about it while crying. By heaven. My friends would be cursing at me"

and she started running. In the spring when snow melted and in the warm spring scenery, when the spring soil lifted the heat haze, as a lark rose up to the high sky from the far field, like the newly made cotton this year hanging out, unfurled, the white clouds, which seemed like they would softly melt upon being touched, were scattered around the entire sky. Tan-sil and Jak-eunne narrowly went beyond the Eryundang (Name of village school in Taedongmun of Pyeongyang) all the way to the rice seedbed, where on the unwashed road, different from now, what with the snow-melted ground, the shoes sank down into the ground, and through the Taedongmun, they ran, facing the Ryongwang Pavilion. Panting for breath, they went after glancing at the picturesque young maidens playing on the other side.

16

Tan-sil's friends, who saw her running, came dashing to her, face-to-face, and said in Pyeongyang words,

"Now, you're here."

"Hey, kid, we've waited for quite a while. Does even a child come that slowly? We've waited for an hour."

"Hey, you've been crying."

"The thin eyebrows thickly swelled"

and held her.

After having been running along this path while sniffling until this moment, Tan-sil held her friends in an embrace and wept again. While she tried to speak soon, her mouth would not open as sobs welled up from the beginning.

It was the first time that she received the cold treatment from a person and was awfully sad.

Even when she later received abuse that was several times worse, she did not think that it would ever be as sad as this moment. While she may have heard the usual criticism from her friends until this moment, it was because she took the first place instead and snatched their prestige by being so good at her studies. This was because whoever it was, they would be very disappointed if someone who was 3 years behind them started studying, but instead trampled on their heads, exceeding them⋯⋯While crying, Tan-sil who had a lot of pride did not open her mouth right away even as her friends asked her why. The words confessing that the entire head family was giving her the cold treatment could not bear to roll out of her mouth. When her friends obstinately asked for the reason, she said,

"It's because my mother doesn't believe in Jesus. She doesn't have faith no matter how much I tell her to have faith⋯⋯"

and cried loudly again. It was that her old sorrow welled up from her new sorrow.

As if repressed by a somehow dark atmosphere, her friends, thinking that their friend's mother would be going to hell in the future from not believing in Jesus, pondered on their young faiths again, and after musing over the phrases in the bible, 'It is very difficult to go to heaven,' they all had the untimely thought in the broad daylight of vibrant spring until it gave them goosebumps.

At the time, a 17 to 18-year-old neat maiden, holding a book bundle, busily passed by them to head to the Taedongmun port. The children said to her who had been rushing off, calling her and stopping her.

"Sun-sil sis, Sun-sil sis."

"Sun-sil sis."

"Sun-sil sis, sis."

"Sun-sil sis"

She was the daughter of Governor Choi who lived across the Taedong river.

While hurriedly passing by with a flushed face, hearing the children calling her, she stood, facing the other side and as if she found it welcoming, she said,

"Why are you all gathered here?"

and afterward, she said,

"Tan-sil, you're also here. Why did you cry?"

and again, carefully asking Tan-sil who was mixed in with the children, put a halt to her busy steps. At this point, Tan-sil stopped shedding tears and occasionally sniffled, but upon seeing the student called Choi Sun-sil, as if she was abashed, she turned her head.

Choi Sun-sil was the first graduate from Namsanje Elementary School two years ago and now, she was a big student attending girls' middle school outside of the West Gate. As she was the daughter of Kim Hyeong-woo's friend, even before attending school, she and Tan-sil knew each other. Also, as things, such as their mothers and family traditions were generally similar, they could not help but be close. As the children were aware of such a relationship, they informed her,

"This kid is crying, because her mother doesn't believe in Jesus."

"Even when she keeps suggesting faith in Jesus, her mother doesn't have faith."

Still, as if the big student did not hear this instantly, she said,

"Would you be crying because of that? I heard that you were at your head family's house and they must have severely neglected you. Look at you. If you're not with your mother, sin would be bound to come crashing down on you. Do you know how many times your mother came over our house and cried after talking about you? There is no way for someone born as an only child to disobey like that. Look at me. Despite being so busy in my studies, aren't I going home in a hurry because tomorrow is my mother's birthday? What have your mother done wrong that you're acting like this? There's no mother like yours in the world who's smart and distinguished. Others all say, what would be the use of hating such a mother when being born as the only child. For those who are going to heaven, they are said to go there even when they don't believe in Jesus. Do you think that everyone goes to heaven if they believe in Jesus?"

and thoroughly and strongly admonished her.

The children crept closer to Choi Sun-sil and said,

"Sis, we could go to heaven even though we don't believe in Jesus as long as we're good, right?"

"I like Tan-sil's mother. Her face is like a lump of moon. I don't know how she's like that."

"Haha, this kid, why are you studying her face?"

"When we go there, she behaves so gratefully······"

"The wife of this kid's father is weird. Even we're there to play, she says, what have you all come here for? Tan-sil's not here."

And doing away with the melancholic atmosphere that had been there until now, the children talked while laughing. Choi Sun-sil replied to any child's words,

"Of course,"

and later, she said,

"Tan-sil, come over our house with your mother tomorrow. I made the clam-shaped songpyeon (Half-moon rice cake) that you like. Please come" and, "I'm busy and so, I have to be on my way."

Then, she again hastily walked the path that she had been taking.

17

Sun-sil walked on for a long while and as if she was incredulous again, she turned around, saying,

"Girls, please bring Tan-sil all the way home outside of the fortress. I'm requesting you"

and walked swiftly again, slipping through Taedongmun.

As if the young girls' hearts had instantly become lighter, they each leapt up and said,

"What Sun-sil sis says is correct, right?"

"Kid, didn't teacher also say so? That it doesn't mean that everyone goes to heaven just by believing in Jesus."

"Doesn't inaction when one knows of it entail a deeper sin and doesn't inaction when one is oblivious to it entail a smaller sin?"

and they chatted away boisterously. With the sniffling and deep sigh brought about in the aftermath of crying, Tan-sil said,

"Then, let's go to my house. We could come again tomorrow to dig up the herbs a bit, but today, let's go to my mother and play. I want to ride a boat. I would like to ride a boat and······right?"

"Wow."

"Sure, let's do that."

"It would be a lot more fun to do that."

"Right. It looks like you're doing exactly what Sun-sil sis has told you to do."

"Of course."

"I know."

"Then, let's all go to my mother. But⋯⋯what should I say when I go to my mother now⋯⋯Girls, what should I now say when I go to my mother⋯⋯The truth is I quarreled with my entire head family today."

"Hey, didn't the Ten Commandments tell you not to lie?"

"Then, should I say everything just as it is? Even then, there would be huge trouble if my mother gets so mad that she gives me a sharp scolding."

"Don't do that, but rather say that you came because you missed your mother. Then, wouldn't your mother like it and wouldn't the household also be comforting?"

"Right, right."

"It's settled. If you do just that, it wouldn't be an excuse nor a lie."

The children had such a discussion and quickening their footsteps, they stepped on the spot that toppled over the chaos that had been around for a while and walked on totteringly.

Even on this day, Kim Hyeong-woo had gone off to Seoul and from holding a big banquet, while San-wol had been taking care of things in the kitchen, she stepped on the blade of a knife for scraping away the fish bones and so, the sole of her foot got severely cut and blood poured out. On this day, even when the servant had come from her friend's house, she could not go there and had been conversing with the seamstress while sitting forlornly in a profoundly, ornately designed Western-style floored room.

"It's clearly spring now. Right, I need to dispatch the rickshaw to bring Tan-sil. Word got around that these days, she's going to school alone without Jak-eunne accompanying her."

"I already dispatched the rickshaw. The child is now 11 years old, right? Days go by really fast. Wouldn't she get married in just a few years from now?"

"Haha, what's it about being in a few years? Last time, didn't the matchmaker come and leave?"

"Right, what to do about that? Do you just let go of that good opportunity?"

"Well, according to my old man, as it's easy for a person to be lost under the circumstance of serving a widowed mother-in-law, perhaps, he's determined not to send her off there. ······As for me, I'm not supposed to be intervening even in that matter."

"If you as a mother don't intervene, then, who would? Still, you need to step in. What do you think the men know about this?"

"Even then, the entire family wouldn't let me interfere. Hmph, it's when my old man and my child become the father and daughter of a commoner's family (Throughout Joseon until the early 20th century, a social hierarchy existed, where below the Yangban, upper-class and Chungin, middle-class, there was the commoner class, which was higher in social status than the concubine and gisaeng in the lowest rung of society) that it could be a matter where they could intervene. The old man himself says that his work is the only right thing and while the child herself came out of me, as if it had not been so, she's gone over to the head family's house and so, what am I to do? Everyone's self-righteous. Still, it's only my child I could trust and no matter how much I make my old man subservient to me, it only gets clamorous."

"As for that, you're saying that because the child is too distinguished. If you say that the relationship between you and the old man isn't trustworthy, would there be anywhere to trust? It is a needless complaint."

When San-wol had been smoking and the seamstress had been picking out the newly scissored cloth of Tan-sil while conversing, Tan-sil dragged her friends and stepped into the courtyard, lined up. San-wol had been sitting vacantly from having shed a lot of blood with her pale face and upon seeing Tan-sil, she said,

"Child, I dispatched the rickshaw, but did you come on foot?"

and showed a burst of anger on her face, but looking at the face swollen from crying, she said,

"Baby, why did you cry? It looks like Jak-eunne also cried."

Tan-sil's pure black eyes were again streaked with tears and she called,

"Mother."

She turned her head for a long while and then, straightening it, she saw the bandaged foot of her mother and said,

"Did you get your foot hurt?"

and lowered her head.

The young friends opened their eyes as wide as a bell and after merely seeing the interaction of the mother and daughter, when San-wol said to the seamstress,

"Please get these children something to eat. And for us to eat something different for dinner together……"

their faces all reddened and they said,

"No."

"No"

and staring at each other's faces, they all shed tears from the feelings of others.

18

Even as Tan-sil came back home, everything did not seem to be what she wanted and she was miserable.

Firstly, as she shared the distress of her mother, the young Tan-sil could not help but shoulder it.

Now and then, San-wol stayed up all night, making Tan-sil's clothes with her own hands. By the middle window where the long lake tranquilly flowed, in the peaceful moment when everything was asleep, the sound of the waterway being split up from the rapids of the lake was dimly heard. It was the dead of night of a spring day. Tan-sil was sleeping peacefully under a radiant blanket and next to her, San-wol had been sewing and smoking when as if something came to mind, she threw open the sliding door and called, "Seamstress, seamstress." At the sound, Tan-sil opened her eyes in a flash. Yet, as if she was concerned that her mother would see her, she immediately closed her eyes. …… But

⋯⋯She spoke such words in her heart.

'Mother, mother wants to cry again. Instead, please get under my blanket⋯⋯'

As if the body had been wrapped up in the soft silk blanket in and out, her heart was swept up in sorrow. From that moment on, she could not fall into a deep sleep from the household affairs and her mother's concerns. On some occasions, there was a time when she clearly opened her eyes and said, "Mother, why aren't you sleeping?" At this time, her mother had been crying and upon hearing her daughter's voice, the tears dropped, trickling down and she said,

"Baby, why have you woken up?" and laid the blanket over her again and amiably tapped her chest. And she was very sorry as if she had woken up her sleeping baby because of something that she had done wrong. Tan-sil did not want to inflict such a concern on her mother. As a matter of fact, as far as she knew, her mother who was a young woman of 27 to 28 years of age had so much of a huge concern.

Her father could not promptly be a governor and could not contain the displeasure in having to pay interest on a loan in the bank every month. Yet, as if it was difficult for him to bear such a responsibility alone, he fretted in the house day after day and when San-wol reprimanded him face-to-face, he was out for a whole day and during the break of dawn, he returned, still inebriated and called out, "Tan-sil, Tan-sil."

Even on this night, Kim Hyeong-woo complained about San-wol refusing to borrow money for him and got out, not returning even after twelve o' clock. Even though San-wol had not been waiting, she was so anxious that she called the seamstress out of what seemed to be worries, as if it was difficult to instead shoulder alone the concerns that faintly came everywhere,

"Even today, he's coming in late again. If I lived alone instead, won't I know it would be like that and not wait around?"

and complained. Not having had a deep sleep yet, the seamstress awoke and feigning a yawn, she replied,

"Oh, the old man must've gone out from a burst of anger what with having a lot on his mind. Would he have gone out because you and your child have something disagreeable? You yourself are so understanding and vivacious and the child herself is that smart……"

As if San-wol found it pitiful that the seamstress was sleepy, she said,

"Ah, pitiful. While I do think that it is not right for my concern to make others miserable as well, as I naturally have my concern, there are times when I couldn't sleep"

and talked about all sorts of concerns the seamstress was familiar with.

First, more than half of San-wol and her daughter's property had gone into Kim Hyeong-woo's campaign for governor. If it seemed like he could earn the governor post, Kim Hyeong-woo was determined to spend all of the money. Yet, according to San-wol, not only was that action very much wrong, but also it was a gravely dangerous thing in the world now. During that period, upon the return of a country person's son from studying in Japan, not only was it babbled all over town and the countryside that his father having combined the interests, recovered the property stolen by a gentleman from Seoul in the old days, but the person that was bribed and sold the government post was jailed and ended up doing drudgery.

19

Tan-sil barely managed to get out of her youthful faith. Around this time, she did not avoid her mother in the least bit, but hoped that her mother would trust her more to tell her specifically what was going on in the house. Somehow, she thought that she could've been walking the dream route for two to three years. At this time, unfortunately, a huge tumult arose in the chapel.

······The preacher of the chapel who appeared to infuse new life as he spoke God's truth to thousands of Christians, with inflamed face, wholly drawing the blood of the deity, while rapping on the table with his fist and echoing the pulpit with his feet, got caught committing adultery with a widow······

Many Christians were disheartened. Someone erased her name, saying that she would never come back to the chapel ever again and someone altogether took one's child away from the school. At this opportunity, in order to completely pull Christianity out of her daughter's mind, San-wol thoroughly admonished her.

"Look at that. What reward is there in attending a chapel? Didn't the preacher who babbled about having the greatest faith in church commit such a misdeed? What would you believe in? That's all a means to lure people. The preacher who said, 'A concubine could not go to heaven even if she believes in Jesus. Confess all your crimes,' himself ended up not confessing his sins. And that man who pretentiously sat up above everyone was in a pathetic state, where he abandoned his wife and children, and fled. And so, I don't have to say the rest to know what happened. What would be decent about him······Baby, you should also stop going to the Christian school. Instead, go to Seoul and attend a different school. On the day that you still attend the Christian school in Pyeongyang, harm would be inflicted on you in the future. As a matter of fact, as your mother is not from a commoner class, there'd be a lot of tiresome things, but if you also attend such a horrid church school, how would others think of you? You could settle down in the house and learn to sew or if not, you could set off for Seoul and study there······If you go there, how much your grandmother and aunt (Maternal) would welcome you ······How could you study in Pyeongyang now?"

As a matter of fact, Tan-sil, who heard these words spoken by San-wol, had been wanting to go to Seoul and study there, and all of a sudden, she was seized by a greater urge to study in Seoul. While such words could not bear to come out when thinking of her mother being disappointed, as she simply could not overcome her urge to study, she said,

"Mother, then, I'd go to Seoul. A lot of big eunnis (Korean word referring to non-relative females that are her senior) who studied in Namsanje school are there."

And as if she wanted to go there so much that she could not bear it, she spoke while writhing.

About one month later, not being able to go on compelling Tan-sil to not study and teach her sewing, San-wol sent her to Seoul.

In the station, San-wol was apprehensive about what would happen after Tan-sil would venture to Seoul.

"As your uncle (Tan-sil's father's younger brother) and I are on bad terms, don't think that he would take you into his house, but as you're bound to stir up trouble if you only go over to your aunt's (Tan-sil's mother's sister) place, go to your uncle's place if he comes to take you. But don't go there too often······."

When San-wol helped Tan-sil get on and be seated, and the tram was about to wildly belch out a noise, she said,

"Tan-sil, I'll be there one month later. Please be well on your way and study"

and as if she was soon on the verge of breaking down, she held onto the pillar of the station and wept. Tan-sil whose eyes were streaked with tears said,

"Mother, please don't cry"

and Kim Hyeong-woo who was bringing along Tan-sil also said,

"Please don't cry there"

and as he thought of the parting between mother and daughter, he shed tears.

When the tram was just departing, the mother insanely went dashing to the tram window and afterward, clinging to the tram station employee, she pleaded in a choked voice,

"Old man, please don't send the kid to a Christian school."

It was a time when the heat of the tedious autumn season of September was waning in a day or two. In Jinmyeong Girls' School of Seoul, Bukjangdong, an 11-year-old Pyeongyang maiden newly arrived and was fleeing around under the shades, hiding in every corner, and shedding tears as she wept over nostalgia.

20

The maiden who once upon a time wept in Jinmyeong Girls' School in Changseong-dong was today's Kim Tan-sil.

At the school, she was maltreated like an animal and grew up, being trapped in a cage like an animal. Her uncle requested it to be like that to the school's dorm inspector and strictly forbid her from going out to visit her maternal family. How envious must she have been at the dorm students going out of the dorm gates when it was the Sundays. After being trapped in the dorm each year, when it was summer vacation, she went to Pyeongyang and played around in the Pyeongyang fortress. She truly despised having to live apart from her parents.

As she considered the long two-month vacation as too quick, she thought bitterly of time passing by. Yet, all the while, she was preparing in advance for the studies she would be doing in Seoul. Not only that but if talk of marriage that would keep her from going to Seoul surfaced, she plucked up the courage and vehemently opposed it. Somehow, after Tan-sil set off for Seoul to study, she became ill-natured day by day.

She wasn't gentle and nimble like before and became overly narrow-minded and bad-tempered. Whatever it was, if it was something in the name of competition, by all means, she fought to achieve victory for life or death.

She went on to become a jealous and ill-natured maiden. While her mother said that it was attributed to her depression becoming worse and tried to make her get freedom and the permission to go out of the dorm at least on Sundays, her father objected to it and believed only in his younger brother's words.

Kim Hyeong-woo looked up to his younger brother, Si-woo's knowledge and put the utmost confidence in him. Whatever it was, if it was what his little brother said, he obeyed even when it was tiresome. Yet, not only did he not see any efficacy, but he also experienced a huge failure. While it was quite unfair for him to experience a huge failure after putting a great sum of money into campaigning for governor, he did not speak a single word of it to his younger brother and each time, he thoughtlessly lavished spending huge sums of money when it concerned his younger brother. Yet, Kim Si-woo never once said good things about his older brother to his friends. And when he opened his mouth, he definitely laid out the faults of San-wol in the midst of strangers and made her a laughingstock.

Yet, Kim Si-woo was a highly regarded patriot among Korean soldiers at the time. He said that he was holding the banquet to support national affairs, but danced and frolicked with the gisaeng. Also, in order to do politics, he swindled his older brother out of his property and was about to buy the title of a governor by bribing the public servant, but he ended up spending all the money on hooking up with a gisaeng. As such, Kim Hyeong-woo gave up on all of his contacts with his younger brother. Yet, Kim Si-woo said eloquently,

"Brother, what would you do as a governor in these degenerate days? It's beneficial to stay in the province just as it is"

and lured him.

When Kim Si-woo was in Japan, he hoped to do a lot of things upon returning to Korea. Yet, eventually, after coming back, not only did the Korean government not place any confidence in them, including him but was really miserly about giving out the wages to the lowest positioned soldiers of the government.

The disheartened soldiers who had gone abroad to Japan indulged in debauchery as much as they could, because there was nowhere to displace their anger or disappointment. Yet, as they could not afford the cost with their low wage, they indiscreetly lured the people who tended to have a lot of money and were gullible. So, after they won the hearts of people by expressing their concerns for Korea and cursing at their superior in words, while saying that they would make the people become governors by enlisting the help of the resident general, they heavily lusted after the campaign funds, using it up and made the excuse that it was because the country was corrupt.

In the meanwhile, the first person who was sacrificed was Kim Hyeong-woo. There were many times where he paid not only for the fees of his younger brother's prostitute but also for the prostitutes of the person whom San-wol referred to as goblin and additionally for the expenses of the prostitutes of the goblin's friends. Yet, all the while, after two years, Kim Hyeong-woo could not manage it with the money he had. Later on, no matter how valuable campaigning for governor was, due to not having the money, he could not pay for all the costs that came from the goblin's friend frequenting the prostitute's house. One time, the young drunkard named Gil Ju-euck who was like a younger brother to the goblin deliberately came over by train and asked for money from Kim Hyeong-woo but was rejected.

21

In two years since such incidents took place, word got around from far and near that Kim Hyeong-woo's house went bankrupt, without anything left. All the while, there were whispers about San-wol being the only one that hid her money separately and was refusing to bring it out.

In the meantime, the so-called patriots were locked up in jail or sought asylum abroad. During the time that they frolicked around day and night, due to it being quite a covert matter, while it was not known exactly as to whether they also meddled in the affairs of the state, there were people who got sued for swindling, cornered into debt on all sides, and ended up fleeing. The person called goblin was one of them. As such, Kim Hyeong-woo was in a circumstance, where he could not help but pay for the debt in the person's stead, even when he regretted having to pay his debts as he put his property up as a collateral for the goblin's default.

Everything disappeared like it was a dream. The independence movement of the patriots and Kim Hyeong-woo's campaign for governor all vanished more readily than the foam disappearing. As for the remainder, there was nothing left except Kim Hyeong-woo's debt, where his document on his house and farmland was stuck at a dirt-cheap price even less than one-tenth. What was left was utter mistreatment that was even more sorrowful and bitter than this. In all corners of the street, while he used to hear the chatters, 'chatta matta' (Religious term meaning 'sinner'), the topknot of his hair got yanked and he got slapped on the cheeks. As the sound of leather shoes lessened, the sound of clogs circulated in the street of Seoul in broad daylight and came to be heard.

As the remainder of every wicked scheme, every gambling, every obscenity, and every treacherousness all turned into debts, the house, the farmland, the sky, the land was sold, and only idleness was left in a coffin-like room.

Even before getting on with a diligent campaign, as everyone went rambling about, they ended up wearing bright red, blue prison uniforms and trapped in a cage where they would indulge utterly in idleness, they blankly, absurdly waited only for the moment they would be inflicted a severe punishment.

Without clearly having any zealous righteousness, as if they were ignorant of the fact that they were the subjects of the country, with the mere thought that their country would be lost, that their king would be ill-treated by the foreign king, that their empress would lose chastity and be humiliated, they fled while kicking up a fuss and were locked up. All the while, they did not forget to scheme and curse at each other. They already even set up their accused friend and put him in jail so that he would get all sorts of inhumane abuse from a Japanese prison officer under the Japanese Empire's new constitution during the reign of Ito Hirobumi.

How ignorant the subjects of the last era of Daehan Jeguk (Korean Empire, 1907~1910) were and what's more, how much they've suffered a cruel punishment for two, three years, before and after Ito Hirobumi died in Harbin.

As God was decisive, suppose it was the case that no punishment existed, due to there being no sins for the ignorant. If then, the Korean subjects and their descendants ten years ago may have not been put through such a distress and may instead have been rewarded. However, the sin of being ignorant was sizeable. As they made a fuss only through their mouth that they believed solely in Jesus, they were ignorant and memorized the words that there was no sin for inaction, and because they did not consider the life of the subjects, in other words, their lives precious, they wielded tyranny and habitually schemed at each other and merely from being ignorant of their foolishness that spawned a disgraceful behavior, they eventually lost their freedom and lost themselves. A person who lost oneself could not lead an independent life. It was as if while a lunatic was wandering the street at will and putting on all sorts of free disgraceful behavior, one was so akin to a filthy slave that one already was a filthy nobody that lost oneself······ Still, as long as they became a slave of insanity, where they could not help but call it themselves, they lost their self, instead turning into a slave of themselves and so, as long as they did all sorts of dishonest behavior, no matter how much freedom they had, that wasn't freedom but a severe punishment.

That was because if they got caught by a person of sound mind who did not lose oneself, the person would not restrain them and would not leave them just the way it is.

Yet, in the perspective of a person who was restrained, the mind of the restrainer was unknowable. That being so, the mind of the restrainer also could not know the mind of the person under restraint from the very beginning.

Therefore, people who did not know one another were enemies to each other.

Insane person, Sane person, foolish person, knowledgeable person, destitute person, wealthy person, there is no understanding between sides polarized from each other.

The relationship between a strong and a weak person is also like such. Hence, a strong person fails to understand the mind of a weak person and shackles the weak, and the weak person gravely misunderstands the strong. In short, in the relationship between strangers that are polarized from each other, there is no such thing as understanding.

22

It was the year of the Korea-Japan annexation. Tan-sil's head family and her mother, the concubine's family came together in one house. As the country was weak, they could not stand alone. Having collateralized someone's debt, Kim Hyeong-woo repaid it instead, and as they could not manage two households, they came together in one place. Failing to be a governor that he aspired, out of what may have been a burst of rage, Hyeong-woo suffered from a lingering illness and passed away. It was the time of spring when Tan-sil turned 14. At the edge of the wooden floor of the dorm, pressing her face, which could not but turn as red as a beet, with her fingertips, Tan-sil who had just taken the 3rd semester exam asked the students,

"Why did my face become flushed like this?"

Among them, one student, as if she had grievance over something, snidely said,

"It's bound to be the case when you study too well. It's enough that you clinch first place from excelling at just studying despite flunking needlework. What is there to be even worried about your flushed face on top of it?"

"That's right. She'd probably beat Hye-sook sis this time."

"Of course."

"How could someone beat such a tenacious person? Hey, walking dictionary, good for you."

'Walking dictionary' (Dictionary for Hanja, Chinese characters) was a nickname she got from figuring out whatever Chinese character she was asked in her class. Upon hearing this, Tan-sil blushed even more as if she was displeased and flew into rage,

"Why do you tease me like that just because I talked about my flushed face? There really are a lot of odd things. Do you get to strike gold if you tease just me in one classroom like that?"

At the time, at this school, whoever it was, the female students were quite fond of acting surly and getting into fights. No matter how gentle a maiden was, in around one month since she attended this school, she became a remarkably grumpy person. And they usually got into fights. When it was time for exam, they reviewed with reckless abandon, as if they could not hide such admirable jealousy and envied with all the strength they had. In the midst of such people, as Tan-sil's uncle spoke to the dean of Jinmyeong Girls' School,

"She's the child of my brother's concubine, but her maternal family is all a bunch of gisaeng wastes. Please don't give her the permission to go out and as the uniforms have been too lavish so far, if such uniforms arrive, please don't dress her in them."

Such words of request spread around school and so, whenever she received hate, her peers taunted her,

"Daughter of a gisaeng bitch."

"That kid's mother is such a beauty. She doesn't even seem to come from the commoner class (Throughout the Joseon period, a strict class hierarchy existed, which was divided into Yangban/ scholar-gentry, Chungin/ upper-middle class, Commoner class, which is higher than Cheonmin, the lowest class that includes gisaeng)."

"I wish I could be that pretty, haha."

"Kid. You ought to be a gisaeng as well. Then, if you plaster makeup and dress up in silk clothes, you'd become pretty, haha."

Even on this day, as her inflamed head seemed to be boiling again from hearing such words, she held the pillar on one side and stood all alone forlornly. At this moment, the school dean, holding the telegram, rushed into the dorm and said,

"Tan-sil, look at this telegram. Your father passed away."

Tan-sil had already been standing as if she was about to faint and then, as she was stunned, she collapsed, crying out,

"Oh no"

and had nosebleed pouring out.

This spring, she suffered a malicious blow mentally and physically. The country went through annexation, because it was powerless. As they were shorn of money, the families who could not stand being with each other had come together in one place and stirred up grievances toward each other. Her peers cornered her multiple times, saying that she did something that she didn't do. Even then, when it was test day, they certainly came over to her and copied her answer sheet word for word. While the teachers, knowing her ability, did not suspect that Tan-sil could have copied other student's answer sheet, each time, the teacher, roaming near her, made a student coming to her sit far away. At such times, the ignorant students with heaps of jealousy fumed that Tan-sil was trying not to show them her answer sheet by ratting them out to the teacher. Among them, the harassment by the daughter of Si-woo's friend, a short student whose face was dark with bloodthirst was much worse. It was from this time that Tan-sil was mistreated. Also, as she had good grades to the extent that she excelled in the class, she suffered the biggest blow when the studies lessened due to the change of the educational system.

23

When Tan-sil went to Pyeongyang, Kim Hyeong-woo was reclining on the plank (Before placing the body in the coffin, the deceased lay on the plank). The whole family cried as if the sky collapsed. While crying, the family sent to Jeong-taek and Tan-sil, who had been studying far away, their father's will which said,

"If possible, excel in your studies and collect money."

There, like an unfortunate dream, Tan-sil lost her father and came to be entrusted a duty by herself to support her single mother. Following this, Tan-sil who came back to school continued to study day and night and thought of her duty to support her single parent. At last, she realized that her father's love was also in vain. Her father who used to be affectionate only to her passed away, leaving inheritance solely to his son, Jeong-taek and put all of Tan-sil's belongings as a collateral. It was just that at the time, he called out two words,

"Tan-sil, Tan-sil"

and closed his eyes. While it was not known what calling out Tan-sil several times meant, it came to be known that the money that was put into the life insurance company under the name of Tan-sil was not Tan-sil's but the name of Jeong-taek. Not many months since Tan-sil's father passed away, San-wol moved to Kyeongseong (Name of the capital in Korea during the colonial period). At last, Tan-sil got out of the hell-like dorm and bought a house in Gyedong with her mother and commuted. In such a way, the relationship between the mother, daughter and the aunt they visited every other day was harmonious without the space for a crack. If it went just like this, what trouble would surface again? Yet, even in the midst of such harmony, the abuse that could not help but be received, due to weakness, crowded on all sides. First, Tan-sil had nothing to learn with the change of the educational system. While during the period of the annexation, she had been in the 1st year of middle school, the following year, even if she skipped a grade to the third year of middle school, there was utterly nothing to put efforts in learning. The students at school all were enraged. Even if what they learned were not Korean words, when it was what they had already covered a few years ago, the dissatisfied feeling that went, 'What a trifling thing' did not disappear. Besides, as it included only the technical skills of needlework, embroidery, making floral design on pottery, and handicraft workmanship, which were bitterly tiresome for the students studying, it gave them utter misery. The students, whoever it was that studied hard in their major, were roused to anger and wished to study abroad. If it had been like before, Tan-sil would have been able to readily take action when wishing to go abroad, but as she could not do so now, she was idle in all of her needlework and read books that she wanted to read, while hearing the nickname, 'lazy student' at school. Yet, when even the students who did not have better grades than her set off for Japan, China, or America to study, she was not at ease. Not only that but ever since she was a child, she brimmed with the hope to fulfill all her aspirations that were felt to the very marrow of her bones. She always thought,

'I was terribly looked down on for being the daughter of a gi-saeng or the daughter of a concubine in an inferior circumstance. The country that I'm growing up in is weak and ignorant, the times that it historically outcompeted others were scant, and it was always looked down on by strong countries. But I need to get out of this circumstance. I need to get out. During the time that a maiden from another country is playing after learning five letters, I cannot but think of learning twelve letters without frolicking around. When others are finding honor on the surface, I cannot but foster my inner skills. In order for the one line of insult and the one inch of hatred to turn to glory in the future, by learning and thinking with all my energy, I have to become a woman of virtue who above all wouldn't hear the despicable name, 'concubine.' To do so, I cannot but excel in my studies alone and hide my flaws instead, as I'm not the daughter of a virtuous woman, unlike maidens from other households.'

Yet, now, she was burdened with all sorts of things that she ended up not being able to study. She truly did not want to merely learn a couple of Japanese words and carelessly put on airs over it. Rather than fruitlessly wasting the days on learning a bit of Japanese language, needlework, and the work of using scissors, she wanted to go to Japan and study properly with the Japanese maidens. And at some time, in whichever school it would be, she wanted to keep all of the students in class on their toes with her strength. She thought to the utmost, 'Okay, while these cannot all pay off the debts, on the day that I, one person start having such will, which would eventually pass on to other people who would come to have such determination, not long after, we would free ourselves from the oppression of others while beating a drum······.' She truly wanted to go to Japan. There, she wanted to study until she outcompeted everyone and thereby, pay off the debts. Even if it would entail a single line of curse, one-time laughter, one-time compliment, or multiple whipping and all sorts of mistreatments, she wanted to pay off all of the debts. She absolutely despised debts.

24

Tan-sil who hated debts was burdened with debt that was not of small amount. That was what San-wol borrowed from here and there in order to repay the interest in the bank when Tan-sil's father was living. While San-wol spoke about such things to Jeong-taek, as Jeong-taek's family was left with not a small inheritance, they did not respond and entrusted it solely to San-wol. San-wol was truly cornered as now, up to this point, it felt like her body had broken shoulder joints. All the money left in her hands was just barely 8000 won. Still, the world thought that she had a lot of inheritance set up. The people who were owed money when Kim Hyeong-woo was living followed them all the way to Seoul and put San-wol and her daughter through misery. And when San-wol and her daughter talked about their circumstance of not being able to quickly pay off their debt, they admonished,

"Make Tan-sil a gisaeng."

"If you turn her into a gisaeng, she's bound to be known as a celebrated, good-natured gisaeng. Her face is lovely, she has talent. Why don't you sell her into gisaeng service?"

When Tan-sil heard such things, she flew into rage like fire. She was not the good child that solely listened to other people and willingly obeyed, laughing it off like the time in the past when she had grown up in the dorm. As the days long passed by, she became a maiden that wanted to make amends for everything, whatever it was. She wanted to pay back the single line of insult with hundred lines. Reaching up to this point, she did not even have a seed of religion that had been embedded in her heart since she was a child. As she was bloodthirsty, she scolded them,

"You people become a gisaeng if you want to or don't become one if you don't want to. Why are you telling others to become a gisaeng? Despite holding us accountable for owing you money, are you at ease when you disdain people like that?"

San-wol hid the bravado somewhere, which in the former days, had curdled in the whole house and as if to plead to her daughter who dared to scold the guests, she said,

"Tan-sil, it's improper to do that. Child, would you be of any use if you behave like that"

and putting on a half-smile, she looked at the guests' faces and begged,

"Please don't do that to the child. What sin does she have? If there's a sin, it belongs to the deceased father and the mother who has lived to turn out like this. What would that child know?"

At such time, the guests could not help but concede and the following day, having obtained the interest and the servants, they headed to Pyeongyang.

One year after Tan-sil's mother came to Seoul, Tan-sil was the

4th graduating class from Jinmyeong Girls' school. She flunked all of her handicraft. Tan-sil's mother was happy, wondering if it was a dream. Yet, as Tan-sil who barely turned fifteen still could not suppress the heaps of desire for knowledge, she was in great agony. Contrary to this, now that Tan-sil graduated, her mother thought that Tan-sil would help with the living by serving as a lady teacher at some small school in Seoul. Yet, after the spring passed by and even when the summer came, she refused to listen so far when her school teacher requested multiple times that she become a lady teacher in her alma mater, while her fresh cherry-pink face turned blue and red twelve times a day. One day, she said these words in front of her mother.

"Mother, I would like to have just 50 won."

"What would you do with that money?"

"My shoes have worn down. All the female students in Seoul wear white shoes, but only I'm wearing black shoes. And while others' watches are all gold watches, mine are the silver watches that my uncle exchanged with my aunt. I would like to switch that to a gold watch."

"Would 50 won be enough to do all that?"

"While it wouldn't be enough when switching it to a new gold watch, as a friend who has a gold watch is suggesting just in time to exchange hers with my watch, I could give a little bit more to her and exchange. It's because telling her to exchange watches, just as it is, would be shameless."

In four days since they had such a conversation, her mother

said,

"I'm giving it to you so that you could get things to make your garments in the future. So, you ought to buy your clothes with the money you earn"

and gave her 50 won. Tan-sil who received the 50 won muttered to herself,

"We don't know what would happen to a person. Maybe it has turned out to be that my mother cannot help but be concerned about me using that much money"

and sniffled.

Afterward, for a few days, she couldn't sleep, saying that she was in pain and with a pale face and a quivering voice, she said,

"Mother, I'm going to visit Kim Jeong-wi's house. As the daughter of that family, Sook-hee is heading to Japan, I'm going to visit her so that I could also lend her my leather bag. She wants to borrow the bag for just five months. Before, Sook-hee and I were not on good terms but now, we've gotten quite close."

According to her mother, as Kim Jeong-wi was cousins with the person called goblin and as he was wealthy, Tan-sil did not have to be that kind and so, she said,

"Hey, Tan-sil, your father also bonded with the members of that family and yet, ended up experiencing failure, but even you······"

but halted.

Yet, day after day, Tan-sil discussed something as she frequented the house of her uncle whom she had been estranged from for a while.

Her uncle was attending the king's military attaché in Kyeongseong. After his brother passed away, while all of a sudden, he ceased visiting San-wol's house, he did not dare despise Tan-sil.

25

It was the morning of early autumn ten years ago. As the students who were returning to their hometown in the north were caught going back home and so, were getting off the Namdaemun station, on the contrary, there were two female students flurriedly fleeing to a platform, holding something plentily in their hands. One student was short with a dark azure face and pupil with long eyelashes that were about to come loose, but seemed to have the white and black pupil of the eye forcibly apart. The other student had chubby cheeks with back that seemed like it would break and rather round, fresh pupils. The student who was short with an azure face was 17 years old and the student whose face and eyes were round was at the maximum around 16 years old. After these two students swarmed in one place and wavered, as if twistingly tied up, the young tall student was going to soon run away first, ahead of her. The short student was in such a bad temper that she called out to her,

"Hey, Tan-sil, are you going to be like that even in Japan? How come you're going ahead of me?"

As if she was sorry, the tall student had cheeks that flushed beet red and saying,

"I'm going to go first and grab the seats"

and ran, taking a couple of steps. The short student in her choked voice called out again, saying,

"Tan-sil, I really didn't know that you were going to be like this. How could you do this?"

The tall young student helplessly took a couple of steps back and said,

"You don't know, because you've never taken a train. But if we don't grab the seats first, we might be standing while going all the way to Busan and so, what would you be doing that for? If we walk totteringly like you, someone would……"

As if the short student forgot something, she was taken by surprise and said,

"Hey, kid, then go first and grab the seats. How come you have such wits? I was mistaken."

As the tall student's two cheeks were sunken, a well was caved in her cheeks and smiling sweetly, she said,

"Okay"

and edging herself between people, she broke into a run first and grabbed the seats on one side of the third-class Gyeongbu-line. This student was Kim Tan-sil. She didn't dare tell her mother that she was going to Japan and with a resolve to flee with a friend, she got on the Gyeongbu-line.

All this time, she discussed matters with her uncle on what to do after she would go off to Japan.

Her uncle wrote a letter to her, saying that there······in Tokyo was a soldier named Gil Cham-ryeong who was a heavy drinker and a student called Tae-mo with academic honors and upright behavior.

When they reached the Shinbashi Station, Jeong Hee-soon, the brother of Tan-sil's companion went out to meet them. Upon glancing at him, he seemed to be a young, dignified 24- to 25-year-old man.

Not long after they've been to Tokyo, the student named Jeong Hee-soon attended Commerce School and Tan-sil went to Sang-ban Girls' School in Shibuya to get into university by getting through the stages.

Before coming to Tokyo, right in the summer, Tan-sil came to know a young man in her uncle's house. He was a student at a Japanese Military Academy named Tae Yeong-sae. Before, he had been in Kyeongseong as a working student, but from steadily excelling in his studies, as he caught the eye of his landlord, he was able to go all the way to Japan. Somehow, when requests for marriage to the soldier student piled up together, they were said to be as bountiful as there being mountains of them. Upon hearing such things, Tan-sil whose youthful heart was fond of competition was readily taken aback. While it was not known what kind of maiden would be selected among the innumerable people and become his wife, she thought that the person who would get to take such a spot would definitely be superior to the ordinary people.

Even so, she couldn't figure out what her uncle was up to as he introduced Tan-sil to Tae Yeong-sae when she was shabby among that many competitors. After she came to Tokyo, she thought about a lot of matters regarding Tae Yeong-sae and babbled about it. There was talk of marriage with the daughter of the rich, the daughter of a minister, the daughter of a viscount, and with the daughter of a baron. However, Tan-sil thought that he was like a bumpkin that happened to enter government office. That was because upon instantly seeing Tae Yeong-sae, Tan-sil did not find him that distinguished······

While inwardly, Tan-sil came to Tokyo to study, at last, based on the circumstance, she appeared to have come here to wallow in her anxiety.

26

One week after Tan-sil went into the dorm of Sangban School, on some holiday, Tae Yeong-sae, clad in military uniform, came to visit Tan-sil. Tan-sil's hand that received the name card, 'Tae Yeong-sae' trembled without reason. After wondering as to whether or not she should open the door of the reception room, she mustered up all of her youthful courage and opened the door.

A small soldier with short height and round, flattish face stood in the middle. Upon seeing the short soldier, her body quivered like an earthquake with the terrifying thought she had not experienced until now. Somehow, he gave off closeness, where he could not be spoken of as a complete stranger while stirring up a suspicion that a butcher dragging a beast to a slaughterhouse would be like that. A suspicion on whether each individual cell of the man was made up of entirely iron or rock materialized. As the thin small eyes gathered more and more energy that was on the verge of bursting, they appeared to be pierced with a reddish, black hue. The face was that of a 24 to 25-year-old man and was quite undersized, but the head whose top was spread out like an earthenware was utterly huge. Tan-sil was scared, but could not show contempt for the head and savage beast-like eyes of this tiny, tiny man who was seemingly immature but was 6 years older than her. All the while, the man's attitude was overly patient and cold, but every time he changed the subject, he gave off a sense of closeness in each wording. Further, the man conveyed a smiling expression with his eyes.

While at last, the man was neither distinguished nor gentle, he fully deserved to pass the test in grabbing the heartstrings of a naive country girl. If the honor coming from his academic excellence and the popularity, where he was showered with marriage requests, had been scant, Tan-sil would not have been content with him. Yet, for some reason, Tan-sil found the man called Tae Yeong-sae terrifying. His adroit way of speaking that seemed to give off a bit of closeness, his honor, and his popularity could not whittle down the terror Tan-sil felt from him. Even then, she was boundlessly frightful of how it seemed like he would lure a person with his coldness and patience and end up tossing the person away.

"I came over as your uncle wrote me a letter."

"When did you leave Seoul? Did you leave on the 25th of August in Namdaemun station? If so, you must've come one day later than me······."

"When you left without the consent of your mother like that······ weren't you scared? You plucked up courage that is difficult even for men to muster."

"As I'm at the school that your uncle has been before, if something's up, please send me a letter there."

Such words he spoke were slightly commanding, but when thinking of how they welled up from the gigantic head and rolled out of his unnatural mouth, it was cold and ferocious to the point that it gave her the shudders.

While putting aside this complicated impression after Tae Yeong-sae for the first time came and left, a welcoming thought also surfaced in Tan-sil. That was the feeling of a person who set out to a foreign place seeing someone from home. All the while, she did not have the opportunity to frequently meet Jeong Hee-soon who accompanied her possibly due to their schools being different. It was just that Jeong Hee-soon with his overly dignified face and with the attitude of a big brother dealing with a young sister came over every other day or every third day and said,

"As you must be so lonely, I came over, wondering if you might be crying again"

and for a long while, he talked about clothes to wear, combing the hair, and the mannerism of dealing with a Japanese and left. A little while before this, Tan-sil's heart softened, having come to Tokyo. There were a lot of causes for that. First, the Japanese people were greatly kind. Whoever friend or teacher, if it was something to do with Tan-sil, they lent a helping hand even if it was a difficult matter. And they took her anywhere and let her go on a sightseeing. Among them, someone called her, 'Adorable child' and another person called her, 'Beautiful child.'

She earned a feeling of warm compassion that she had not experienced once in Jinmyeong Girls' School of Seoul. Up to this point, she came to realize the great beauty of her mother's affection and thought that it would be good for Tae Yeong-sae to be a bit kinder. Yet, such an emotion did not stir up easily without tears and without consideration.

27

Each time she opened and looked at the letter that came from her mother or her uncle, Tan-sil, who had gone far away from home, could not help but be moved to tears twice.

Her mother's letter was written with the words in repetition that told her to study hard, excel, and come back after achieving success, now that she had already gone there, which left a heavy burden on Tan-sil and stirred a heavy thought that she'd have to cross a long uphill path. And as her uncle's letter was written with Tae

Yeong-sae's words as much as possible, such words made her feel close to him and she realized that it was difficult to be suspicious and fearful of Yeong-sae any longer. Swept by a lonely and forlorn thought, with the lonely days, far away from home, becoming prolonged, she missed the affection of a person. In her childhood, how her mother held her in her embrace, how her father guided her wrist, how her brother carried her on his back, and when she was in Seoul, how her maternal grandmother occasionally gave her food that she packed, and all the pleasant thoughts she had as a child softly and dryly came out, seasoned from the chest of a maiden that longed for a warm and sweet thing like the tangerine peels, wholly loaded with honey.

As Tan-sil thought of all the past incidents, it was like roaming the golden path when walking into the palace garden of Seoul. Up to this point, every one of her past incidents were all a brilliant movie to her.

In fact, the financial concern she had now was not few. While she was not in the circumstance of delaying the payment for the monthly school fee or the food expenses, there were so many times that she was pressed for pocket money that she secretly washed her tears through the Japanese sleeve. Even if she set out to study, as she carried a huge burden on her back and for the first time thought about the opposite sex, all the while, constantly getting kindness and consolation from the Japanese, the determination she had in Joseon to take vengeance on the Japanese and her begrudging hatred toward the head family's house and the creditors readily dimmed.

She did not study with gritted teeth, like she had done in Joseon. No, instead of saying that she did not, it would be correct to say that she could not. When she held the book to study, Tae Yeong-sae's language and behavior unfolded before her eyes again and again to the point that there were many times that she ended up shutting the book. It was at this time that she could not but see no flaws in him and incredibly miss the man who did not seem to have any beauty and further, was strikingly short even in height. Tan-sil thought about how she had retorted to the statement that it was easy for the daughter of a gisaeng to lead a dissipated life; asserting that as a young maiden, she could not meet men altogether, but only if it seemed like she would be getting married, she wouldn't be frequenting many places and would rather settle in one place that was to her heart's content, and if not, she would live single her entire life. Tan-sil who used to think such things now merely wanted to blindly hold right onto the short, good-for-nothing Tae Yeong-sae. Yet, at the very bottom of her heart, she still wanted to study. She wanted to study for life or death as she had been entrusted all sorts of things from all that studying and to pay off the debts.

Yet, she went through the experience without having any clue that studying was in fact, a bit of a leisurely play. It was just that the words that seemed to come from a deep reflection, 'I've become lazy. I am going corrupt,' continuously spun around from her heart all the way to the very peak of her head until it seemed like they would at the slightest slip move the shape of her lips in front of someone. On a holiday, when Tae Yeong-sae came over, she ended up spitting out such words. While dragging below her armpits the long tresses of her hair hanging down to the heels, tied up in three bundles, and stroking them, she said,

"I don't think I can study. I can't study like it was before possibly because I went corrupt."

When having a new taste of the new letters, 'corrupt,' Tae Yeong-sae's face abruptly reddened and he said,

"Tokyo really is wide. Who would know that such a Joseon woman would be here in this place? Does your friend's brother that looks like a bulldog come over these days?"

At these words, even as Tan-sil realized that it was out of the ordinary, she said quickly,

"Oh, he comes over. At certain times, as he comes over at night, he walks on eggshells around the dorm inspector."

At this time, the man smacked his lips, as if the taste was sour and said,

"I have to be on my way, because I have somewhere to go to"

and stood up. Even when Tan-sil certainly did not know why the man was forlornly standing up like that, before the words began, she intactly took in what the man spoke and said,

"Aren't you going to Gil Cham-ryeong's house? I've been there once, but the direction isn't clear."

Yet, the man still bleakly said,

"Then, let's go"

and even when abruptly rising to his feet, he put on a dull face. While Tan-sil found such behavior of Tae Yeong-sae strange, there was no way for her to know why. However, after several years, when a huge mishap between Tan-sil and Yeong-sae took place, everything was exposed. She bore a weak heart and she alone took all the responsibility. The world even cornered her into doing so.

How much of a weeping maiden Tan-sil has turned out to be? For a brief time period, she developed a mental disorder.

28

It was······the spring when Tan-sil turned 18 years old. In the village called Shibuya of Japan, as she had suffered during the time of graduation from a high school called Sangban Girls' School, even when she had not made a slip-up in a single letter in her exam, she was gossiped as being quite deviant in each newspaper, and as the person in charge hid somewhere, she was not given the graduation certificate and the teachers took a complete turn as they went to the press, asked questions and even detected the dormitory where the student was in. The more they inspected one fact and the more they dredged it up, the hideous things that were at odds with what the student usually was regarded as came out, rearing their ugly head. The school teachers ended up removing the student's name from the list of graduates' names. The student's name was Kim Tan-sil.

One year prior to this, in winter, there was a time when Tan-sil was at Gil Cham-ryeong's house due to issues with paying for her school fees. When comparing to the things that the lonely daughter of a widow had, everything in the house of Gil Cham-ryeong was extravagant like a palace. The wife of Gil Cham-ryeong was a witch-like Japanese beauty that was barely 30 years old. Her skills of speaking that were sharply adroit did not make slip-up in even one syllable, the figure like the willow listlessly roamed around, and her attitude was such that she did not remain still without leading everyone in everything. Even as the elders of the village pouted, they said to her,

"Okusan, Okusan (Japanese word respectfully referring to Madam)"

and lowered their heads. Only having heard of such, the merchants looked down on her even more for being a Japanese woman that lived with a Joseon man, but after meeting her, they ended up bowing to her. Also, in the beginning, when the Joseon students who came to Tokyo to study abroad only heard of such, they said,

"What would be distinguished about a woman married to a good-for-nothing Gil Cham-ryeong?"

and after carelessly gossiping about her, as their friends complimented her so much, they were driven to visit Gil Cham-ryeong's house and upon coming back, they chimed together in praising her to the skies,

"A woman is of use when she's a Japanese. Eh, what are they Joseon women? They're in such a foul state and besides, how stiff they are"

and cursed at their sisters, mothers, and grandmothers. Initially, when Tan-sil was in tears from the concerns about the school fees, having received the letter from her mother that told her to return soon, due to not being able to send her the money, Gil Cham-ryeong and his wife let her stay in their house as in the beginning, they immensely loved Tan-sil. Gil Cham-ryeong's wife and Tan-sil who came to be in one house together became so close that on some days, the wife played the piano and Tan-sil sang in her mild voice. Also, on some occasion, during the evening dusk, just the two of them strolled around the Poetry Monument Park and Azabu (name of region in the vicinity of Tokyo). The wife of Gil Cham-ryeong liked to introduce Tan-sil to many people while bringing her along. Tan-sil also absolutely did not dislike being in a relative-like relationship with such a beautiful woman.

They were on close terms even as the whole winter passed by. Yet, in the spring, Gil Cham-ryeong's wife decided to bring in her niece and take care of her after the wife's brother committed suicide as he failed at something and became debt-ridden. The name of the girl was Hanakko and she was a maiden with white skin and portly eyes, of the same age as Tan-sil.

This maiden was born in Osaka and in Osaka, she barely graduated from middle school. While it may have been a natural thing for the maiden, it seemed like she was trying to earnestly catch the eye of the Madam (Gil Cham-ryeong's wife). Even while Tan-sil thought that it couldn't be helped, when seeing the maiden try to slander her, she was so unbearably lonely that she shed tears.

While Tan-sil sent a letter to her uncle and requested that he help with the school fees after the passing of winter until the coming of spring, there was no definite reply. While Tae Yeong-sae, sympathizing with Tan-sil's haggard state, wrote to her uncle for him to send her the school fees, there was no definite response and instead, came the reply that hinted at a request for Tae Yeong-sae to marry Tan-sil.

The hope to get engaged to Tan-sil could not arise at all in Tae Yeong-sae what with possessing that prestige and that prosperity. It was merely that he wanted to study like Tan-sil inwardly wished to. Due to his bursting desire for knowledge and the prosperity that he would certainly earn later on, he was so self-entranced that like the young concubine his landlord had in the past, he idealized a comely girl who was 20 years younger than him. As such, he was a bit averse to Tan-sil for being only 6 years younger than him and what was more, for being taller with long bone joints. Also, it was a time in the world when people considered a short, slender woman beautiful.

[June 14th~ July 15th, 1924]

탄실이와 주영이

1

6월 초승의 요사이 일기로는 아주 더운 어느 날 오후였다. 석양은 지금 황금빛같이 찬란함으로 조선 서울 종로 네거리에 뜨겁게 내리비친다.

열십자로 갈라진 전후좌우 길거리에 널려 있는 상점의 광고판들은 독기 있어 보이는 시꺼먼 먹으로 바짝 붙어서서 각각 그 이름을 자랑하고 있다.

종로경찰서 지붕 위의 독일 병정의 모자 같은 시계가 바로 4시를 가리켰을 때이다. 드높은 이층집 유리창과 단층집 창, 그리고 땅 위의 한 분자 분자의 작은 알맹이가, 모두 지루한 볕에 반짝거릴 때, 마치 빛의 찬란한 심포니를 보는 것 처럼 구릿빛으로 무르익어야 마땅할 흰옷을 입은 사람들의 얼굴은 저들이 약함으로써 받는 모든 학대 때문에 기운이 쇠침해지고 행동이 느려져서 전체로 빈혈된 얼굴에는 붉은빛이라고는 없고 누렇고 검어서 부질없이 의지 약한 힘없음을 보인다. 그래도 그들은 무슨 일이 있는지 네거리를 이리 가고 저리 가고 자주 왕래한다. 이 흰 옷 입은 이들이 걸어 다니는 길 가운데로는 전차들이 쉴 틈 없이 종을 치면서 지나가고 지나온다. 지금 북쪽에서 외쪽 길로 왔다 갔다 하던 전차 하나가 두어 사람 실어다가 종로 네거리에 내려놓는다. 그 가운데 여학생으로서는 흔히 볼 수 없는 베옷 입은 스무 살 안팎의 여자 하나가 산동주(중국의 산둥 지방에서 나는 명주) 양산을 들고 칼날 같은 날카로운 기세로 전차에서 내렸다.

또 이와 반대되는 남쪽에서도 사람을 많이 실어다가 종로 네거리에 내려놓았다. 그 가운데 회색 양복 입은 중키나 되는 청년과 검정 양복 입은 호리호리한 청년이 검정 책 한 권을 들고 무엇이라고 이야기하면서 서대문으로 향해 가는 전차를 타려고 얼키설키한 십자가의 전찻길을 옆으로 건너서 정류장에 와 섰다. 마침 소복을 한 여학생도 그 편 정류장을 향하고 걸어가다가 허리를 굽혔다.

그는 언뜻 보기에 대단히 아름답고 영리해 보이는 여자 같았다. 또 그의 민첩한 표정을 한 얼굴은 아무리 무심히 보더라도 다만 하나의 보통 여학생으로는 보이지 않았다.

정류장에 서서 전차를 기다리던 두 청년 중에 남대문 편으로 오던 전차에서 먼저 내린 검정 양복 입은 청년이 모자를 벗어서 소복한 여학생에게 마주 인사했다. 그리고 그 소복한 여학생이 점점 가까이 갔을 때,

"탄실 씨, 시방 댁으로 가던 길이올시다. 김 선생이 댁에 계실까요? 마침 계셨으면"

하고 탄실이란 여학생의 그 꼭 다문 입이 얼른 열릴 것 같지도 않을 표정을 엿보면서 머뭇 말했다. 여학생은 다만 잠깐 낯을 붉히고,

"모르겠어요"

하고 인사는 하였지만 말은 하고 싶지 않다는 듯이 서너 발자국 다시 물러섰다. 그리고 동쪽을 바라보면서 전차 오기만 기다렸다.

"다 틀렸네. 하늘을 보아야 별을 따지"

하고 검은 양복 입은 청년이 회색 양복 입은 청년에게 낙망한 듯이 말했다. 회색 양복 입은 청년은 그것이 당연한 일이라는 듯이,

"흥, 그러기에 낮잠이나 자란 말이지. 사람이란 가령 하느님에게 내버려질 것 같으면 악마에게도 가 붙지 않는 것이 당연한 사람다운 일일세"

하고 말했다.

검정 양복 입은 청년은 그러한 친구의 말이 무슨 의미인지 알 수 없는 듯이 고개를 기울이다가 때마침 그 앞에 와서 머무는 전차 위에 올랐다.

저편에 섰던 여학생도 멀리서 기다리다가 사람이 다 오른 뒤에 나중으로 올라섰다. 그러나 그는 무엇을 생각했는지 전차가 막 떠나려고 종을 칠 때 급히 전차에서 내렸다. 그 내리는 이의 얼굴을 유심히 볼 것 같으면 무엇인지 숨이 콱 막힌 사람으로 의심이 날 만치 새파랗다. 전차는 할 수 없는 듯이 올랐던 사람을 다시 내려놓고 남아 있는 사람들만 싣고 서쪽으로 서쪽으로 달아났다.

"음"

하고 입맛이 쓴 듯이 검정 양복 입은 청년이 전차의 가죽 손잡이를 쥐고 섰다가 앉으면서 한숨지었다. 회색 양복 입은 청년은 다시 입을 열면서 약간의 미소를 그 온화하고도 몹시 게으름이 나는 듯한 얼굴에 띠고,

"그러기 내 말이, 아무리 사랑을 기본으로 창작하고 생활하는 예술가일지라도 사랑을 하려다가 한번 실패를 했거든 참아서 들뜨는 마음을 꽉 누르고 자기가 경험한 실패를 그 뼛속까지 해부해보란 말이야"

했다. 검정 양복 입은 청년은, 그 친구의 말이 귀찮은 듯이,

"오늘은 자네 설교가 안 먹히니. 내일이나 또 해보세"

하고 다시 탄식하듯이 밖으로 뿜어 나와지는 긴 숨을 삼켰다. 회색 양복 입은 청년은 사뭇 무료한 듯이 옆을 바라보다가 다시 그 친구를 그대로 둘 수는 없다는 듯이,

"그런데 아까 그 탄실이라는 김정택의 누이가 몇 살인고, 음"

하고 그 친구의 손에 있는 검정 표지인 책을 가리키며,

"이 『너희들의 등 뒤에』라는 책의 주인공과 같은가?"

하고 물었다.

2

검정 양복 입은 청년은 좀 불쾌한 듯이 팔짱을 끼고 눈을 감으려다가 그 친구의 애써 위로하려는 뜻에 감동된 듯이,

"전부 같지는 않아. 저 탄실이야 주영이같이 산 여자는 아니지. 아직 그 사람은 전형을 못 벗어난 사람이야. 그것을 내가 잘 인도하고 싶단 말이지…"

하고 발끝을 내려다본다. 회색 양복 입은 청년은 그 말에 불복할 점이 있는 듯이 고개를 돌리다가,

"그런데 몇 살이냐?"

하고 다시 재차 물었다.

"나도 자세히 모르지만 삼십 가까웠지……"

"뭐야, 어느새 삼십이 가까워? 어디 그렇게 보이나, 얼른 보기에 퍽 순수하고 어려 보이는데"

하고 알 수 없다는 듯이 창밖을 내다보았다. 이같이 이야기하는 동안에 전차는 서대문정 2정목에 와서 정거했다, 두 청년은,

"여기로세"

하고 내렸다. 그러나 역시 검정 양복 입은 청년이 대단히 주저하며 갈 바를 모르는 듯이 발길로 땅을 치다가,

"가면 무얼 하노?"

했다.

회색 양복 입은 청년은 그 행동이 난처하다는 듯이 바라보다가,

"이왕 왔으니 김정택 군을 만나고 가지. 탄실이란 여자에게 절망했기로서니 그 오라범까지 만나지 말란 법이야 어디 있나"

하고 타일렀다.

저들은 한참 머뭇거리다가 정류장 앞 바른편에 '광제병원'이라고 광고 붙

인 골목으로 들어갔다. 그 골목 막다른 곳에는 반 서양식으로 지은 광제 병원이 한가해서 졸린 듯이 우두커니 이층으로 서 있었다. 밖으로 보기에 환자도 없고, 간호사나 의사는 낮잠이나 자는 듯하였다. 이에 두 사람은 그 병원 핸들을 잡았다. 조는 듯한 집에 사람의 인기척이 문간 종을 울렸다. 병실에서 신문을 보던 김정택이란 40여 세 된 의사가 사람 좋은 태도로 빙글빙글 웃으며 두 손님을 나와 맞았다. 그리고 저편 쪽마루로 나오는 간호부에게

"작은아씨 아직 안 오셨니?"

하고 물었다. 간호부는 두 손님을 유심히 바라보다가,

"안 오셨어요"

하고 다시 안으로 들어갔다.

김정택은 이윽고 병원 응접실로 두 손님을 인도하고,

"이수정 군, 지승학 군, 요새 재미있는 창작 좀 하셨소?"

하고 부채를 내놓으면서,

"하하"

하고 웃었다.

그 두 손님 중에 검정 양복 입은 청년을 이수정이라 하고, 회색양복 입은 청년을 지승학이라 한다. 여기 두 사람은 조선에 흔히 있는 문학청년이었다. 검정 양복 입은 이는 시를 짓고, 회색 양복 입은 이는 소설을 짓는다.

김정택은 두 문학청년을 맞아놓고, 이야깃거리가 흔하지 않은 듯이 자주 탄실을 찾는다.

"우리 탄실이가 있었으면 자네들하고 훌륭한 문답을 해서 자네들의 높은 코를 다 낮추어놓을 터인데"

하고, 부대한 몸집과 붉은 얼굴을 흔들면서,

"내 누이동생이라도 어떤 일은 놀랄 만치 칭찬할 일이 있어. 그렇게 귀여운 여자가 무슨 일로 가장 불행한 여자들 중에도 첫 손가락을 꼽히게 되

었는지"

하고는 슬며시 화단 있는 후원을 내다본다. 지승학은 그 모양을 동정하는 듯이 바라보다가,

"그런데 영매께서 연전에는 댁에 안 계셨지요? 언제 댁으로 오셨나요?"

하고 물었다.

"작년 가을에 비로소 데려왔지요. 나와는 이복형제인 고로 같이 한집에서 자라본 적이 없었고 또 그 성질을 자세히 알 수 없어서, 의심하면서 제가 하는 대로 내버려두고 멀리 바라만 보았더니, 그 애가 지금까지 세상에서 오해를 받은 것은 전부 허무한 일일 뿐 아니라 악한 남녀의 모함입니다 그려. 그래서 노친은 반대하시는 것을 억지로 빌다시피 해서 데려왔더니 그런 착한 여자가 다시는 없을 것 같습니다. 나는 하루바삐 어디 좋은 곳에 심어주고 싶지만 당사자가 극력으로 반대하니까 때를 기다리고 있지요.……그 반대하는 말이 또 우습지요. 한번 결혼 일 땔에 세상의 웃음거리가 된 이상에 그 웃음거리 된 몸을 다시 다른 사람과 결합하려고 하는 것은 신성한 자기를 더럽힌다는 거지요. 참. 그래서 어째 하필 너만 그렇게 신성하냐고 물을 것 같으면, 두 번가웃에 그 대답이, '오라버니, 산봉우리를 아래서 쳐다볼 때만 높게 봅니다. 그 높은 데 올라갈 것 같으면 다시 더 높은 곳이 있듯이 보입니다. 그러나 어찌하다가 잘못 미끄러져서 산봉우리 아래 떨어질 것 같으면 다시 자기가 올라갔던 산봉우리가 아주 높았던 듯이 생각이 됩니다. 그러니까 확실히 사람은 낮은 데 있어야 높은 데를 더 그리는 것 아닙니까? 올라갈수록 높은 것이 한정 있는 것은 아니고, 그 사람들의 이상을 규정하고 신성하다 고상하다 하는 것이니까, 그렇게 따지고 보면 확실히 저는 신성합니다' 하고는 저도 기가 막히는 듯이 웁디다. 그 정경이 참 딱하지요" 하고 그 누이를 동정하는 듯이 말한다.

3

지승학은 김정택의 말을 유심히 듣다가 검정 양복 입은 친구 이수정이 후원의 새빨간 우미인초虞美人草 밭만을 풀 없이 내다보는 것을 보고,

"자네의 이야기가 참 숙연하게 만드네 그려. 저 친구는 요새 신경쇠약에 걸려서……"

하고 역시 풀 없이 빙그레 웃는 김정택과 그 친구를 번갈아 보다가 다시 김정택에게 시선을 향하고,

"그러면 영매께서는 아주 자기를 찾으신 모양이십니다 그려. 그 점에 있어서 저 『너희들의 등 뒤에서』라는 소설 속 주영이와는 다르실걸요"

했다.

"오, 참, 그 『너희들의 등 뒤에서』라는 책은 우리 서모 집 사랑 채에 셋방을 빌려가지고 있던 일본 청년이 쓴 것이라지. 그 주인공은 탄실의 행동과 말하는 것을 더러 묘사했다지만 아주 다르지요. 그 책 가운데 주영이는 꼭 일본 여자지 어디 탄실이 같습니까? 그래도 그 작가는 탄실이보다는 그 책의 주인공인 주영이가 훨씬 낫다고 할지 모르지만 우선 사실부터 탄실이는 처음에 동정을 자기 스스로 깨뜨린 것이 아니고 빼앗긴 것도 일본 사람에게가 아니라 조선 사람에게 그랬으니까요. 참 말 못 할 패악한 사람이지요. 그 어린것이 멀리 타향에 가서 그래도 저를 믿는데, 차마 그런 행동이 어떡해서 가해졌는지, 도척(중국 춘추시대 도둑의 두목)이 보다 더하지요. 그것도 본인이 원해서 사귀게 된 것 입니까? 내 삼촌이 아주 경솔하게 맺어준 것이지요. 말하자면 내 삼촌이란 어른이 심사가 고약하지요. 그것을 다 말하면 집안 흉이 날 테니까 채 말은 못 하지만 안타깝게도 탄실이는 참 불행한 운명에 빠진 여자입니다. 그래서 나는 지금이라도, 혹시 구할 수만 있으면 탄실이를 그 운명에서 구해주려고 하지만 어디 말을 들어요? 남자란 악마보다 더 거리긴다고 저주하니까. 본래는 아주 인정 많고

착한 여자였지만 그 타락하던 당시를 생각하면 아마 자기도 온전치는 못한 모양이었어요. 하나 어느 편으로 보든지 주영이와는 다릅니다."

이같이 이야기하는 것을 옆에서 듣던 이수정은 급히 소리를 질러서,

"아아, 주영이가 그립다, 주영이, 주영이. '전진, 전진' 하고 '앞으로, 앞으로' 하며 부르짖는 주영이가 그립다. 내가 이상화하는 것은 남에게 버려지고 수절하는 그냥 순응하는 조선 여자가 아니고 어디까지나 싸워나가면서 사람답게 사는 여자다"

하고 혼자말같이 부르짖었다.

김 의사는 어처구니없는 듯이 웃으면서,

"이수정 군, 그럼 자네도 내 누이를 은근히 지도하겠노라고 원하던 사람이 아닌가. 탄실에게 대해선 그렇게 입버릇으로 달려드는 사람이 많지. 그래서 그 애가 밤이면 이불 쓰고 잠자는 대신 울어서 밤새우지. 그러나 탄실이는 남에게 지도만 받을 여자는 아니고 구구하게 버려져서 그 사람을 위해서 수절하는 여자도 아니고. 대개 사람마다 핑계가, 탄실이와 친하려고 하다가 실패를 하면, 말을 그렇게 하니까 그 애가 신성한 자기를 더럽힌다고 남자를 절대로 가까이하지 않으려고 하는거고……"

하였다.

이수정이란 청년은 김 의사의 말을 듣다가 가로막으며,

"나를 그런 사람들 가운데 하나로 치면 참말 잘못이십니다"

하고 말을 뱉어냈다.

지승학이란 청년은 두 사람의 말이 서로 어긋나는 것을 듣고,

"그렇게 말씀을 서로 어긋나도록 하시면 결국 재미가 없어지지요"

하고, 이수정을 똑바로 보며,

"사실 자네 말하던 것과 김 의사께서 일반 청년이 말한다는 것과는 똑같지 않은가"

하고 타일렀다. 여기서 이수정 군은 아주 불쾌한 듯이 김 의사의 말과

그 친구의 말까지 반항하려고 트집을 내었다.

"자네들 말이 우습지 않은가? 내가 주영이가 그립다고 하는데 하필 탄실이란 여자를 끌어다가 이러니저러니 내게 비길 것이 무엇이야? 누가 외짝 사랑이나 해서 편지 장을 던져준 것도 아닌데."

"그야 그렇지. 내 말은 그러는 사람을 한 사람 두 사람 보았으니까 미심쩍어서 한 말이지 무슨 자네를 꼭 그렇다고 한 말은 아닐세."

"그래 김 의사의 말씀은 그런데 탄하는 자네가 우습지 않은가? 속담에 도적이 발치다는 말이 있느니……"

"하, 또 자네 말이 나를 모는 것 같으니……"

"그러지 말고, 자네 양심에 물어서, 분명히 말해보게. 자네는 이 김 의사를 찾아올 때까지 김탄실이란 여자를 마음에 생각했나 안했나?"

"나는 먼저까지, 적어도 김탄실이란 여자는, 그렇게 사람에게 버려져가지고 자기가 신성하니 어쩌니 하면서, 모든 남자를 똑같이 저주할 줄은 몰랐네."

4

"그렇게 말을 돌려대기만 하면 자네 말은 아주 무례하게만 들리네. 아주 쉽게 그 여자의 심지라든지 또는 외양도 잘 모르면서야 어떻게 남을 지도한단 말을 할 수 있단 말인가."

"그러지 말고 바로 말하게. 이 군, 자네가 내 누이를 얼만큼이라도 사모하지 않는가? 그런데 이리저리 돌려대보는 것 아닌가? 똑바로 말해보게. 조선 사람은 다 마찬가지로 허풍 치기를 좋아해서 조금이라도 다른 사람이 꺼리는 것이면 자기도 꺼려보는 것이 큰 병이야. 가령 한 동리에 한 사람이 싫어하는 것을 다른 사람이 다들 싫어한다면 말이 너무 허황해서 들는 사람도 좋은 감정을 안 가질 것이 예사로운 일이지. 하지만 대개는 그 분명히 말도 못하는, 남이 싫어하니까 나도 싫어한다는, 다른 사람과 타협 하는것이 아니고 경쟁하는 마음을 가지고 있지. 내 누이로 말하면 10년 전에 벌써, 참 옛 이야길세. 어떤 평범한 아무런 일에도 새로운 것을 찾아 낼 힘이 없으면서, 그래도 구구히 사람들의 군 입내를 없이 하기 위해서 칭찬 푼어치나 듣는 쥐 같은 작은 남자와 약혼하려다가 그 남자에게 절개 까지 억지로 앗기고, 그나마 그것이 세상에 알려졌을 때, 어리고 철없는 내 누이의 책임이 되어서 그보다 6년이나 위 되는 쥐 같은 남자가 염복 (아 름다운 여자가 잘 따르는 복) 있다는 헛자랑을 얻고 또 내 누이와는 원수같이 되어서 현재 저와 꼭 같은 다른 계집하고 잘 산다 하네. 그러기로서니 어 리고 철없던 사람이 자라지 말라는 법이야 어디 있나. 그동안에 내 누이가 자라고 철들었다고 할 것 같으면 그만이 아닌가. 그렇지만 세상은 그렇지 않고 기막힌 일이 많아. 우리가 생각할 땐, 참 우리 탄실이가 말하는 것같 이, 아래로 떨어질수록 높은 것을 알 터이니까 세상 사람도 그것을 알아주 고 그 경우에서 끌어올려줄 것같이 생각하지만. 몇 천 길 깊은 해감에 빠 져서 헤매는 사람이 있다고 하면 그 사람이 보통 사람보다는 우월優越할수 록 반드시 세상은 그것을 건져주기는 고사하고 해감 속에 거의 빠져서 모 가지만 남은 것을 마저 해감 속에 넣어 숨기려고 하니까. 참 작은 한 여자 의 10년 동안 걸어온 길이 지독히도 무서워서, 유혹이 있더라도, 내 누이 에게 닥쳐오는 유혹은 종류가 다르지. 얼마만 한 두뇌로는 그것을 해석도 못 하지. 그래도 탄실이는 능히 유혹과 친절을 분간해 나가지만. 하나 누 가 그것을 아나? 그 애가 10년 전에 동정을 제 마음대로도 아니고 분명한 짐승 같은 것에게 팔 힘으로 앗겼다 하면, 시방도 바로 듣지 않고 내 누이 만을 불량성을 가진 여자로 아니……때맞춰 『너희들의 등 뒤에서』란 책이 난 뒤에도 탄실이는 얼마나 염려를 하는지 그 꼴을 차마 눈으로 볼 수 없 었어. 말끝마다 '오빠, 내가 일본 남자와 연애했던 줄 알겠구려. 그러면 내가 창부같은 계집이라겠지. 그리고 내게도 조성식이라든지, 김성준이라든지, 또 신춘용이라든지 그런 남자들이 있던 줄 알겠구려' 하고 번민을 하고 또 울고 하더니 이제는 그것도 사그라져서 제법 잊어버리고 저 안국동 유치원에 다니지만……"

"아, 이제야 이 군은 말이 없어졌지. 대대로 남을 생각하는 사람이 그 말을 참지 못하고 이리저리 둘러다 대는 것은 병이야. 그것은 내 생각에 마음이 들뜬 증거 같아. 그리고 마음을 한데로 꼭 모을 수 없는 운명의 장난을 이기지 못하는 것이야……"

"자네들이 그렇게 말하면 할 말이 없네. 그동안에 나는 또 한가지 생각한 일이 있네. 탄실 씨와 책 속의 주영이가 다른 것은 큰 원인이 있네 그려. 주영이란 여자가 전부 다른 나라 사람들한테 학대를 받고 원수를 갚는다고 이를 가는 것과 탄실 씨가 우리나라 사람들 그러나 친일파들한테 학대를 받고 오랫동안 번민하는 것은 다를 것이지……"

"옳소, 옳소. 이 군, 내 누이의 복수하려는 마음이 온전히 내적인 것은 주영이의 경우와는 다른 것이 원인이오. 하나 이 군의 평상에 말하는 주의로 보면 또 주영이를 이상하는 마음과 몹시 모순되지 않나? 사랑을 기초로 하고 그 꿈을 시화詩化한다는 이 군이 온전히 내부적 혁명가를 외부적 혁명가인 주영이만 못하다고 하는 것은 무엇을 증명하는 것인가?"

"하하……이제 이 군의 비밀이 아주 폭로되었네. 그래도 이러고 저러고 말을 둘러댈 터인가."

"그것은 참 이 군의 사상이 통일되지 않은 증거거나 그렇지 않으면 자기를 눈앞에 속이는 거짓일세……"

5

    광제병원 응접실에서는 두어 시간 전부터 하던 이야기를 계속하는지 이따금 '탄실이'니 '주영이'니 하는 소리가 후원 화단 앞까지 새어 들린다. 석양은 아주 서산 너머로 온종일의 목숨을 호젓이 지울 때, 새빨간 우미인초 밭 앞에서 꽃밭에 물을 주고, 김을 매던 탄실은 새어 들리는 제 이름에 간담을 녹이다가 차츰차츰 용기를 내서 응접실 툇마루 끝으로 제 모양이 보이지 않으리만큼 조심스럽게 가 앉았다.

    탄실은 무엇인지 이러한 동작을 꿈결에라도 어찌 본 듯한 아련한 감정이 그의 가슴속에서 모락모락 일어나는 것을 깨달았다.

    저녁 바람이 산들산들 불어서 된 햇볕에 꺼내 입었던 모시 적삼이 그 옆에서부터 위로 점점 달달 말려 올라가는 것 같다. 아련하던 감정이 점점 불어서 분명히 옛날 추억에 돌아가서 잊었던 것을 다시 또 생각해 낼 때, 그의 온몸이 사시나무같이 떨렸다. 또 그 귀를 기울이면,

    "탄실이를 재료로 소설을 써보게. 확실히 심상치 않은 것이 될 터이니……"

    "확실히 주영이와는 다를 것일세. 주영이는 끝내 이기주의자인 일본 사람들에게 학대를 받고 속았지만 탄실이는 그 반대로 조선 사람이면서 일본 사람의 생활과 감정에 동화된 조선 사람들에게 학대를 받았네. 주영이가 일본으로 갈 때는 다만 법률을 배워서 일본 사람에게 원수를 갚겠다고 갔지만, 탄실이가 일본 갈 때는 '어디 일본 사람은 어떠한지 보자' 하고 시험 격으로 간 것이요, 그리고 일본 사람을 숭배하지도 않았으니까 아무 이익을 바라지 않고, 나미키 아키오이든지 심지어 일본 인력거꾼에게까지 속아넘어가진 않았을 것 일세. 그뿐 아니라 탄실이 자신이 어떤 때는 일본 사람 이상 이기주의자이니까. 그 애가 일본 건너갈 때를 생각하면 그건 양의 새끼 같은 착하기만 한 여자가 아니고 마치 이리 새끼나 호랑이 새끼

같았지."

"그럴 것 같으면『너희들의 등 뒤에서』라는 책은 한 여성을 주인으로 쓴 것이 결코 아니고, 조선 전체를 동정해서 일본 사람인 나카니시 이노스케 가 일본 사람의 처지에서 반성하노라고 쓴 것일 것입니다."

"그런지 모르지요. 내가 그 작자를 서모 집 사랑채에 세를 들어 살던 청 년인가 보다고 말하는 것도 무슨 증거가 있던 것은 아니고. 주영이는 중 류 이하 가정에서 초라하게 자라났지만 탄실은 대동강가에서는 제일 호사 하는 호화로운 집에서 자라났으니까요. 그러나 그 부친이 남의 빚 담보를 했다가 패가를 한 것은 거의 같은 일이고, 또 아오야마(도쿄 도미나토구에 위 치해 있는 동네) 근처에 있던 일과 조선 사람인 일본 군인의 집에 부쳐 있던 일도 근사하지만, 대체로 말하면 주영이는 탄실이보다 더 불쌍할 뿐 아니 라 또 비교하지 못하리 만큼 육체가 더러워졌습니다. 그리고 어떤 편으로 보아도 주영이는 탄실이보다 더 어리석습니다. 그리고 탄실의 교만함과 욕 심스러움을 못 가졌습니다.

탄실이가 정조를 잃고 그 사나이에게 달려들던 생각을 하면 어찌 한낱 여자가 그다지 지독한지 치가 떨려집니다. 결코 그 남자를 사랑도 하지 않 고 다시는 육체적 관계도 맺지 않으려면서 강제로 한 남자의 일평생의 행 복을 흐지부지하게 만들려고 했던 것입니다."

"그러면 김 선생, 내가 영매를 주인공으로 하고 소설을 지으면서 조선 사 람의 일부를 그려내보면 어떨까요? 그러할 것 같으면 나카니시 이노스케 가『너희들의 등 뒤에서』를 쓸 때, 저희 나라 사람의 잔학함을 쓴 것과 같 이 우리나라 사람의 간사스럽고도 겁 많고, 어리석고도 약한 것을 마음대 로 들추어 볼 것입니다."

"대찬성입니다."

"무얼, 자네가 그만치 쓸 것 같아서 그러나."

"그런 말이 어디 있나? 쓰면 쓰는 것이지, 비록 같지 않다 뿐일 것이지.

그 책은 그리 잘 쓴 것인 줄 아나? 조선 여성을 무시해도 분수가 있지. 아무 이유도 없이 조선 사람보다 그들이 얼마나 높이 보여서, 허투루 안 가고 꼭 법률을 공부해서 일본 사람에게 원수를 갚겠다고 결심한 여자가, 그렇게 쉽게, 하필 일본 군인을 온천에까지 따라가 자기 동정을 깨트릴 줄 누가 알았나? 그리고 그 뿐인가? 주영이로 말하면 우리나라 제1기의 여학생 아닌가. 그러고 보면 주영이는 연애고 무엇이고 염두에 없었네. 그들은 아닌 체하면서도 여자는 절개를 꼭 간직했다가 명예 있고, 재산 있는 남자에게 시집가서 거기서 손끝에 물 튀기면서 호강하는 것을 제일로 알았을 것일세. 나카니시 이노스케가 그 책을 쓴 것은 우리 처지로 보아서 찬성 못함일세. 우리는 못났지만 그것을 감추고 싶지 않으니까. 그는 그 책을 쓰고 자기의 우월함을 우리에게 자랑하는 것이 아닌가. 그러나 한편으로 생각하면 주영이 같은 여자가 조선에 있을지를 생각해 본 것 일세. 조선 여자는 게으르고 겁쟁이면서도 강인하니까……"

"조선이 주영이같이 용기 있는 여자를 못 낳는 것은 조선 사람은 자기네들끼리 서로 저주하고 모함해서 서로 망하는 탓일세."

"참, 그러고 보면 주영이는 꼭 일본 여자같아. 그들같이 남자의 계급을 가리지 않고 정조 관념이 없고 또 한편으로는 그렇게 독한 여자가 없으니까."

탄실이는 이러한 이야기를 듣고는 간신히 몸을 일으켜서 안뜰로 돌아서 자기 방으로 돌아왔다. 그는 거기서 그 옛날 감상에 그 온몸과 온 영혼이 잠겼다.

6

지금부터 28년 전에, 청일전쟁(1894년) 지나고 나서 평양성 안이 제법 홍

성거려졌을 때다.

평양 성안 사람은 지금은 그 전쟁 당시에 무섭던 이야기와 괴롭던 이야기를 드물게 하였다.

그들은 하루바삐 돈벌이를 해서 남의 전쟁 틈에 잃어버린 재산을 도로 회복하려 하였다.

그러나 그것은 한 집안의 가장이나 장자가 살아 있는 집 이야기이고, 불행히 전쟁 틈에 남편이나 아들이 죽은 집에서는 젊은 과부와 노년 과부가 밥 대신 죽을 하면서 그날 그날의 옷 근심, 밥 근심을 먹어도 살이 찌지 않도록 몹시 하였다.

이와 반대로 한 집의 가장이 살았거나 아들이 살아 있으면 급히 부자가 되어서, 군수나 관찰사 부럽지 않게 부자 되는 수가 있었다. 그래서 과부들의 바느질 품팔이하기도 재미나리 만치 흔전흔전해졌다.

남자들은 대개 일본말을 배워가지고 일본 사람의 통역도 하고 또 전에는 꼭 영남 사람만 벼슬하던 것을 전쟁 이후로는 북쪽 사람들도 웬만한 무관의 지위를 얻어서 상투 위에 모자를 쓰고 구부러지고 일그러진 그 몸에 군복을 입고 주적거리게 되었다. 그래서 제일 첫 영화로 기생을 마음대로 수청 들이고, 또 남의 집 유부녀라도 권리로 뺏어다가 첩을 만들었다. 그것은 지금껏 북선의 사람들이 마음대로 하지 못하던 남선 사람들의 권리인 동시에 행악을 고대로 배운 것이었다. 북선 사람은 한 고을에 군수나 또한 도의 관찰사로 온 사람들의 무도한 행악을 얼마나 원망하고 서러워하였을까? 그러나 그들은 그 사람들의 행악을 버리지 못하고, 돈을 들여서 좋은 지위를 얻어서는 남선 사람들이 하던 이상 학정질을 해서 양민을 모함하고 가두고 죽이고 돈을 빼앗았다.

그때 구골 사는 최 소사는 난리 틈에 20이 넘은 장성한 아들을 죽이고 딸 형제를 데리고, 외로운 신세가 되었다. 그러므로 철없고 아는 것 없는 여편네 생각에 그 고을에서 흔히 중류 이하 가정에서 하는 것처럼 딸 형제를 기생에 넣었다. 그래서 최 소사는 나중껏 그 딸 형제를 의지하고 살려 하였던 것이다. 형을 산월이라하고 아우를 영월이라 하였다. 영월은 아직 어리고, 형 산월은 그 아름다움으로 이리저리 불리어 다니게 되었으나, 어찌 고집스러운지, 춤추라고 해도 춤도 안 추고 소리를 하래도 소리도 안 하다가는 꼭 자기가 하고 싶은 때만 옥을 굴리는 듯한 소리를 내뽑았다. 그런고로 산월이를 부르는 것은, 응석받이 상전 아가씨를 모셔다가 시중드는 일 체였다. 그래도 그 환한 얼굴과 시원스러운 눈매에 홀린 남자들은 산월을 불러다가 재롱을 보려 하였다. 그러할 동안에 산월은 열다섯 살이 되었다. 몹시 조숙한 그는 보통여자와 비기면 열여덟 살이라 해도 거짓말 같지는 않을 것 같았다. 그 고을 관찰사가 그를 수청 들이려고 하여서 불러 갔으나 산월은 무엇을 생각했는지 관찰사 옆에 앉았다가 뒷간에 간다고 핑계하고 버선발로 영문 앞에서 구골까지 달아왔다. 뒤에 그 이야기를 들으면 관찰사는 부득부득 산월을 자기 몸 가까이 끌어 앉히려고 하고, 저편 창틈으로는 관찰사 내항(관찰사의 첩)이 눈알이 새빨개져서 노려보았다 한다. 그 후에 산월은 고집쟁이 기생으로 별명을 얻고, 류지동이란 큰 부자의 첩이 되자 그 모양을 아무 곳에도 나타내지 않았다. 산월은 동촌 사는 돈 많고도 질구한 류지동이란 사람에게 가서 귀염을 받게 되었으나 산월은 그 류지동이라는 부자가 산월이를 귀애할수록 그 질구한 생활에 동화시키려고만 하는 것 같아서 점점 불평을 갖게 되었다. 하루는 도적이 심한 그때 일이라, 온종일 이곳저곳에 묻었던 재물과 금전을 이리 저리로 옮기다가 그는 몹시 피곤했던지 류지동의 뒤에서 돈을 치맛자락에 싸가지고 따라가다가,

"이런 일은 왜 큰마누라를 좀 못 시켜요. 나만 죽을 사람이란 말이오? 가만히 하라는 대로 하니까"

하고, 치마 앞에 쌌던 돈을 뜰에 다 털어버렸다. 류지동은 그 꼴을 보고 화를 내었다가 그만 어처구니없는 듯이 웃으면서,

"내가 너를 믿는 탓으로 이러지 낸들 네가 미워서 이러겠니? 큰마누라에게 시키고 싶어도 그 사람은 빈한한 친정 떨거지들이 많아서 미덥지가 않으니까 자연히 너를 시키게 되는 것이 아니냐"

하고 일렀으나 그는 부은 볼을 낮추지 않았다가 친정으로 간다고 떼를 썼다. 류지동은 다시는 그러지 않으마고 타이르다 못해서 신발과 옷을 다 감추었다. 그래도 산월은 어느 틈에 자기 어머니가 류지동의 집으로 올 때 만들어준 이불을 돌돌 말아서 이고, 또 행랑어멈의 짚세기를 얻어 신고, 30리나 달아나서 자기 집인 평양 구골로 왔었다.

7

그 후 얼마쯤 지나서 산월은 류지동의 집에서 데리러 와도 가지를 않다가, 어느 고을 군수로 있던 김형우라는 사람에게로 가게되었다.

그것도 산월이가 가고 싶어서 간 것이 아니고, 몹시 빈한해진 고로 그 어머니와 동생을 거두려고 갔었다. 거기서 산월은 1년이 못되어 탄실을 낳았다.

김형우의 집에서는 외아들만 기르다가 서자나마 또 하나 생겼으니, 대단히 좋아할 듯하였으나 산월의 과도한 생활욕生活慾 때문에 그의 가정에 대한 권세가 커지는 것 같아서 누구나 다 탄실이가 이 세상에 나온 것을 꺼렸다. 하나 나와서 자라는 아이는 거침없이 자랐다. 그 집 재산은 탄실이가 성장함을 따라서 점점 불었다. 그래서 김형우의 늙은 모친이 미신으로,

"복동이가 나와서 집안이 늘어간다"

고 말하기 때문에 온 집안도 할 수 없이 탄실을 중히 알게 되었다. 하나 산월의 자랑은 점점 늘어가고 또 김형우의 산월에게 대한 사랑도 날이 갈수록 깊어감을 따라 산월은 온 집안사람을 모두 눈아래로 보고 또 큰마

누라를 사람같이 보지도 않았다. 그러므로 그 집 사람은 누구나 김형우를 제하고는 탄실의 모녀를 원수같이 원망하였다.

그때 탄실은 대동강가에서는 제일 새롭고 큰 이층집에서 자랐다. 물론 그들은 일가 세 사람뿐인 듯이 늙은 모친과 큰마누라는 모셔오지 않고 생활하였다. 이따금 김형우의 맏아들인 정택이가 와서 그 아버지의 모든 지도를 받았다.

탄실은 점점 커감을 따라서 유순하고 총명한 아이가 되었다. 김형우는 어린 딸의 사랑에 이끌려서 탄실에게 천자문도 가르치고 한문도 가르쳤다. 말없이 정신 맑은 탄실은 귀신의 아이같이 한자를 가르치면 열 자를 알아냈다. 산월은 전부터 무엇인지 집안일에는 그리 좋아하는 일이 없었으나 탄실이가 글을 배우게까지 되어서 온갖 재롱을 다 피우게 된 때는 탄실을 그 무릎에 놓지 않고,

"탄실아, 내 아기야"

하면서 집안 하인들에게까지,

"아이구 내 탄실이가 아니면 이 세상을 살아갈 재미가 없지"

하였다. 어린 어머니는 그 풍부한 생활욕을 억제치 못하고, 큰집에서 뜯어가는 것 또는 자기 친정에서 뜯어가는 것, 세상살이가 재미없도록 귀찮았다. 그는 할 수만 있으면 자기 남편이 죽을힘을 다 들여서 모은 돈이고 또 자기가 애써서 헛용으로 안 쓴 재산이니 한 푼이라도 남에게 주고 싶지 않았다. 그런데 그러한 소원을 뒤집어 넘기고 돈이 모이면 모일수록 김형우의 모친이 와서 어디 어디 논밭이 있다더라, 어디 꾀가 있다더라, 어디 솔밭이 있다더라, 밤밭이 있다더라, 하면 김형우는 두말없이 그것을 사서 김정택의 이름으로 증명을 냈다. 물론 그 당시는 산월은 한문을 모르니까 언제든지 속았으나 그 대신 사랑 사람이 언제든지 산월에게 일러바쳤다. 산월은 그런 일을 당할 때마다 눈이 빨개지도록 불쾌하였다. 그런 때는 탄실이가 왜 아들이 되어 나오지 않았는고 하고 자기 자식에 대한 불평까

지 일어났다. 그리고 다짜고짜로 김형우에게 포달을 부렸다. 그 남편은 하는 수 없이 그 큰아들에게 사는 이상 값 많은 것으로 사서 탄실의 이름으로 증명을 냈다.

그러자 탄실이가 여덟 살 되었을 때, 평양 남산재에는 예수교학교가 흥왕 하게 되어서, 어린 여학생들이 예수 탄일에 예수교회 선전지를 들고 집집마다 문을 두들기면서,

"예수를 믿으십시오. 이 세상 모든 영화가 쓸데없습니다. 하늘나라에는 거지에게까지라도 영화가 있습니다"

하고 전도하였다.

그러한 나이 어린 전도대가 김형우의 굉장한 대문을 두들기게 되었을 때, 산월은 그 화려한 얼굴의 아미를 찌푸리고,

"계집애들이 저것이 뭐야? 기생도 저렇게 천히 길러서는 못쓰는 법인데……"

하고 처녀들이 몰켜서 알지도 못하는 남의 집 문을 두들기고, 무어라고 알지도 못할 말을 부르짖는 것이 맛갑지 않아서,

"우리 아기는 그렇게 기르진 않을 것이다"

하고 말했다. 하나 김형우는 무엇을 생각하는지,

"우리 아기도 내년 봄쯤 학교에 넣을까? 거기 넣으면 그 애더러도 아마 전도 다니라고 할걸……"

하고 산월의 낯을 바라보았다. 그리고 산월의 하는 양을 보려는 듯이 웃었다. 탄실은 그런 말을 듣고,

"아버니, 저두 전도할 테여요"

하고 철없이 날뛰었다.

산월은 내 딸이 내 말을 어긴다는 생각으로 그 검은 큰 눈에 위엄을 띠고,

"이 계집애, 그런 말을 또 할 테야? 어미가 네 꼴을 안 본다면 어떡하려고 그래? 도무지 이 세상이 귀찮기만 한데 너까지 내 말을 안 들어?"

하고 노했다.

　그러나 그 한편으로는 산월도 탄실을 학교에 넣어서 사내아이에게 지지 않으리 만치 공부시키고 싶었다. 단지 그가 꺼리는 것은 전도하노라고 길바닥으로 돌아다니는 것이었다.

8

　탄실은 여덟 살 되던 해로는 그 어머니에게 대해서 여러 가지 일을 매일같이 졸랐다. 첫째는 그 어머니가 탄실이와 같이 회당에 다닐 일, 둘째는 탄실을 학교에 넣으라는 일, 바느질은 배우기 싫다는 일을 그 어머니가 한가하게 앉았기만 하면 그 옆에 가서 들입다 졸랐다. 그것은 어린 입으로 나오는 군소리 같은 말일것이었으나 뿌리가 있는 것이었다.

　탄실이가 혹시 큰집에 놀러 가더라도 탄실의 적모가 입버릇같이 탄실에게 산월을 함부로 욕했다.

　"이리 같은 년, 그년이 죽으면 무엇이 될꼬. 벼락을 맞아 죽을년"

　하고 어린 마음이 놀랍도록 욕질을 했다. 그러므로 탄실은 비로소 그 모친이 남에게 좋지 않은 일을 하는 줄 알게 되고, 또 남의 몹쓸 원망을 입는 줄 알게 되었다.

　그래도 산월은 무엇이 그리 싫은지 탄실을 예수교 학교에 넣기를 심히 꺼리다가 그해 늦은 봄에야 사흘 동안이나 김형우와 다투다가 학교에 그때 돈 50원을 기부하고 탄실을 입학시키기로 했다.

　물론 탄실은, 그 학교에서는 왕녀와 같이 위엄을 받았다. 모든 일에 모든 생도들에게 부럽게 보였다. 선생들도 탄실이라면 눈 속에 집어넣어도 아프지 않을 듯이 귀애했다. 탄실은 그 학교에 든 이후로는 매일같이 산비탈을 넘어서 학교에 다녔다. 또 산월은 탄실을 학교에 넣고도 산비탈을 넘어 다니는 것이 애처롭다 하여 그만두기를 바랐다. 하나 그 아버지 김형우는 이 왕 학교에 넣은 이상에는 끝끝내 공부를 시켜서 영화를 보고자 하였다.

그때 김형우는 대동강 변에서 큰 무역상을 했다. 매일 탄실의 집 곳간에 서는 몇 천 석의 벼가 나갔다 들어왔다 하였다.

그리고 산월의 방에는 구석구석이 돈 그릇이 놓여 있었다. 산월은 돈을 헤아리지 않고 썼다. 그러면서도 그렇게 흔한 돈이 없어진다고 산월의 호령기 있는 음성이 매일같이 그 앞에 하인들을 불러 세우고 욕했다. 탄실은 학교에 든 이후로는 그 모친의 사랑이 지겨워져서 때때로 학교에서 돌아오면 책보만 살짝 양실 마루에 던지고 사랑으로 나가서 그 아버지의 주머니에 매달렸다. 그러면 그 아버지의 말이

"안방에는 너 먹을 것이 많지, 엄마더러 달래라"

하고 탄실을 달랬다. 하나 탄실은 고개를 돌리면서 생끗생끗 웃고는,

"엄마 무서워"

했다.

그 부친은 하는 수 없이 그 돈주머니에서 돈을 꺼내서 안방아씨가 모르게 상노에게 주며 무엇을 사다가 탄실을 주라고 하였다.

탄실 모녀의 정은 김형우의 집 재산이 늘어가고 산월의 호사가 늘어갈수록 점점 엷어갔다. 그것은 탄실이가 학교에서 공부를 잘하게 될수록 세상 영화가 쓸데없다든지, 또 남의 첩 노릇을 해서는 못쓴다든지, 기생은 악마 같은 것이란 교훈을 듣게 된 탓이었다.

이런 일은 전부 러일전쟁(1904~1905년)을 치르고 난 그 이듬해의 일이었다. 하루는 탄실의 집에 말 타고 군복 입은 손님이 왔다. 탄실은 그 손님이 무서워서 이리저리 피해 다니다가 하인들에게 붙들려서 하는 수 없이 그 앞에 가서 절을 했다. 하여튼 그 사람은 일본가서 사관학교에 다니던 일본의 군인이라 하였다. 그리고 탄실의 삼촌이라 하였다. 그 군복 입은 손님은 처음으로 탄실을 바라보고 삼촌이라면서도 한번 쓰다듬어보지도 않고

첫인사로,

"저 애들은 저렇게 호사시켜서 기를 것이 아니에요. 일본 사람들을 볼 것 같으면 아주 시집가지 않은 계집애 때는 아주 검소하게 기르다가 시집 가서 저희들이 돈을 벌면 호사를 하거든요. 저런 저 비단옷 같은 것, 또 반지 같은 것, 저런 돈 많은 것을 애들 몸에 감지 않거든요. 암만해도 일본 사람이 애들은 잘 길러. 저, 저렇게 기르면 못쓰는 법이에요"

하고 그 형에게 하는 말인지 또는 형수인 산월에게 하는 말인지 분명치 않게 하였다. 산월은 그 말에 벌써 눈살을 찌푸리고 외면을 하고, 긴 담뱃 대에 담배를 실어서 담배통을 김형우 앞에 향하고 성냥을 그어 붙여달라 는 듯이 기다렸다. 김형우는 실없이 그 동생이 졸업하고 돌아왔대서 그런 지 좋아하면서 산월의 담배통에 불붙이기를 더디 하였다. 그러나 기어코 김형우는 산월의 담배통에 성냥을 그어 대주었다. 산월은 맛갑지 않은 듯 이 담뱃대를 물고 가는 모시 치마를 질질 끌면서 건넌방으로 건너가서 그 와중에도 아이가 귀여운 듯이,

"탄실아, 탄실아"

불렀다.

9

그 후에 탄실의 숙부는 자주 산월의 권리 안에 의견을 넣게 되고, 또 김 형우의 신임을 얻어서 일 가문에 위엄을 받게 되었다.

그리고 탄실을 몹시 사랑하는 체하기도 하면서 언제든지 그 아버지의 손에서 지폐 뭉치를 받아서는 호주머니에 넣고, 자주 기생방에 든다는 소 문이 들렸다.

그동안에 탄실의 공부는 심히 늘어서 학교에 들어간 지 1년이 못 되었건

마는, 그 학교에 3년 넘어 다니는 학생들과 같이 어깨를 나란히 하고, 한문 같은 것은 도리어 다른 학생을 가르치리 만치 앞섰다.

그 학교에서도 이같이 공부 잘하는 어린 학생에게 온갖 사랑을 다 베풀고, 어린 탄실도 학교에 대해서는 언제든지 적지 않은 돈을 기부도 하여서 학교와 탄실 사이가 지극히 친밀하였으나, 탄실은 잠을 자다가도 가위를 눌리고, 기도를 하다가도 소리쳐 우는 큰 근심을 갖게 되었다. 그것은 자못 그때부터 예수교회에서는 그 교회를 이 금수강산 안에 선전할 욕망이 맹렬하여져서 사뭇 어린 생도의 믿지 않는 부모를 어린 생도로 하여금 울며불며 억지로 교회당에 끌어오게 하고,

"회개하시오. 회개하시오. 모든 죄를 자복하고 오늘부터 예수를 믿읍시다"

하고 모든 신자들이 그 소리에 뇌동해서 울며 부르며 비 온 뒤에 음습한 땅에 버섯이 일어나듯이, 연달아서 일어나며,

"나는 아무 날 아무 때 누구를 미워하고 그가 악한 사람이 되라고 기도 했습니다."

"나는 아무 달에 시어머니를 죽으라고 한 달 동안이나 기도를 했더니 과연 그 소원이 들어졌는지 우리 시어머니가 밥 잡수시다가 숟가락을 쥔 채이 세상을 떠났습니다."

"나는 목사를 간음하는 마음으로 생각하게 되어서 그 목사부인을 죽으라고 3년이나 기도했습니다."

"나는 남편을 죽이려고 밥에 양잿물을 탔습니다"

하고 차마 귀로는 듣지 못할 소리로 엉엉 울면서 자복하고.

"하나님 용서하십시오. 주여, 주 아버님이여, 굽어살피시옵소서. 회개할 때가 왔습니다. 모든 사람을 구원하소서"

하고 큰 상사나 일어난 듯이 통곡을 했다.

이런 때 하룻밤에는 탄실의 이머니인 산월이도 그 딸에게 끌려서 회당에 갔었다. 회당의 권사나 전도 부인들은 여왕 전하를 맞듯이 그 앞으로

달려들어서.

"회개하고 예수를 믿으십시오. 세상 사람은 누구든지 죄를 가졌습니다. 이 세상에 죄 없는 사람이 어디 있습니까? 회개하시고 오늘 저녁부터 예수를 믿으십시오"

하고 산월의 그 하얀 비단 옷자락에 매달려서 그가 회개하고 예수를 믿게 되라고 있는 힘을 다해서 권했다.

산월은 이러한 곳에 온 것이 불찰이라고 생각하는지 귀찮은 얼굴을 하고 그 처량한 기운을 띤 음성으로 언제든지 하던 말을,

"내게는 신명이 돕지 않으셔서 여덟 살 나자 아버지가 돌아가시고, 오라버니가 계시더니 그나마 내가 열두 살 되었을 때 전쟁 틈에 청인에게 맞아 죽고, 내가 제일 위로 남아서 홀어머니를 봉양할 길이 없어서 기생이 되었습니다. 그러니 여러분이 아시다시피 기생이라는 것은 남의 큰마누라가 되는 법이 없으니까 자연히 나도 남의 첩이 되었습니다. 그것이 나도 죄악인 줄은 알지요. 그러나 어찌합니까? 지금은 내 한 몸도 아니고 이런 어린 것이 있고 보니 금시로 그 집에서 나올 수도 없지 않습니까? 자백은 하나 안 하나 거진 비등한 일이지요. 이 세상 사람이 죄다 죄악이 있다고 할 것 같으면 하나님이실지라도 그것을 일일이 헤아리시지 않는 편이 좋지 않을까요?"

해서, 전도 부인이 끈적끈적하게 달려드는 것을 단번에 꺾어 넘기고, 문지기가 지키고 섰는 회당문을 힘껏 열어 닫치고 울며 달려드는 탄실을 붙잡아 앞세우고는 자기 집으로 돌아왔다.

그 후로 탄실은 먹지도 않고 자지도 않고 밤낮 세 칸 방에 들어가서는 방망잇돌 앞에서 기도했다.

"하나님이시여, 하나님이시여, 우리 어머니에게 회개하는 마음을 주셔서 예수를 믿게 하소서. 만일 그렇지 않으면 저를 하루바삐 천당으로 불러가소서. 그러나 사랑하는 어머니를 지옥으로 가게는 맙소서"

하고 밤이나 낮이나 자다가도 기도를 하고 먹다가도 기도를 했다. 하루는 형용이 초췌하여가는 탄실에게 그 모친이,

"탄실아, 내 예수를 믿으랴? 그리고 너희 아버지의 첩 노릇도 하지 말랴 응? 그러면 나와 너와는 떨어지게 된다 응? 애기야, 예수 믿는 사람은 남의 첩 노릇을 안 하는 법이란다"

하고 물었다. 탄실은 이때에 어린 마음에라도 어찌할 바를 몰랐다. 그는 그 후로는 다시 '우리 어머니에게 회개하고 예수를 믿게 하소서' 하고 빌지는 않았다. 그러나 그는 날이 감에 따라서 오늘 내일 눈에 보일 만치 수척해갔다.

10

산월은 그 어린 딸의 고통을 차마 보다 못 보아서 할 수만 있으면 그를 예수교 학교에서 끌어내 오려고 했다. 그래서 자주 탄실의 머리를 짚어보고는 학교에 가려고 할 때마다 간절히,

"애기야, 오늘은 네 머리가 더우니 학교에 가지 마라. 어미의 마음도 헤아려주어야지. 어미가 누구만 믿고 세상을 사는 줄 알고 그러니?"

하고 사정했다. 탄실은 하는 수 없이 처음에 한두 번은,

"어머니, 나는 괴롭지 않아도 어머니가 걱정하시니 고만두지요"

하였으나 번번이 매일 그러는 것을 알고는,

"어머니에게는 마귀가 달려들었어요. 그래서 나를 마귀의 종을 만들려고 그래요"

하고 울었다. 산월은 자기의 배를 아프게 하고 낳은 자기의 딸이 그런 매정스러운 말까지는 할 줄을 몰랐다가,

"나는 네 꼴을 안 보겠다. 어미더러 마귀 들렸다는 딸년이 어디 있단 말

이냐? 이 괘씸한 애야"

하고 울었다. 탄실도 어머니의 그 모양을 보고 학교에 가는 길에서 들입다 울었다. 그런 중에 학교에 가면 거기서도 편하지는 않았다. 탄실이가 어리면서도 공부를 잘해서 자기들을 이기고 윗반이 된 것을 꺼리는 학생들은 은근히,

"기생의 딸, 첩의 딸, 저것도 그렇게 밖에 더 될라구."

"게다가 천한 태가 저렇게 나니 쟤가 나중에 무엇이 될꼬."

"저 애 아버지도 일본 사람 앞으로 장사를 한다지. 그전에 어디 군수로 있을 땐 아주 큰 부자를 몇 사람 망쳤는지 모른대."

"원, 도적이나 마찬가지지. 아주 그런 것의 딸이 저렇게 3년급이 되어가지고, 돈푼이나 내고는 아니꼽게 구는구나"

하고 속살거렸다.

그런 말을 탄실이가 알았을 때는, 그의 순하고도 자존심 많은 둥그런 마음이 찌브러져서 피를 뽑는 듯이 아팠다. 그는 그 아비지가 전일에 군수를 지냈다 한 것은 어렴풋이 들었으나 그렇게 학정질까지 한 줄은 몰랐고, 또 일본 사람과 드문드문 상종은 할지라도 그렇게까지 친밀해져서 동사 (동종업) 를 하는 줄은 몰랐었다. 이 어린, 아주 거룩한 하나님의 딸이 되려고 밤낮 기도하는 탄실에게는 그러한 비평이 몸과 마음을 찍어 에이는 큰 고통이었다.

그는 어린 마음에 괴로워 하다 하다 못해서, 그의 아버지와 어머니를 싫어하게까지 되었다.

이 마리아에게 지지 않으리 만치 진실한 하나님의 딸이 되려고 하는 탄실에게는 그 육신의 부모가 너무나 깊은 죄인이었다. 첩의 딸, 기생의 딸, 일본 스파이의 딸, 학정꾼의 딸. 그는 자기 귀에 들리는 이 더러운 대명사에 기절을 하도록 놀라지 않을 수 없었다. 그런 중에 집에 돌아오면 그 딸의 사랑까지 잃은 산월은 호령을 끊일 새 없이 해서 온 집 안은 물 끓이듯

술렁술렁 끓었다. 또 김형우는 매일같이 손님을 청해다가 연회를 차렸다. 그 아우 김시우는 모든 손님에게 주인같이 행동하면서 배포 큰 얼굴을 하고 돈 아까운 줄 모르게 써버렸다. 벌써 그때부터 산월의 방에는 돈을 구석구석이 놓고 헤이지 않고 쓸 형편은 못 되었다.

그의 집 사랑에는 밤낮으로 일본 기생, 조선 기생의 음란한 소리가 쉬지 않고 들렸다. 그 가운데 어릿광대같이 온 방 안을 웃기는 제일 키 작고 얼굴 검은 아저씨가 있었다. 언제든지 그 사람이 주빈이 되어서는 일본 기생, 조선 기생, 평양 안의 창부란 창부는 깡그리 모아 왔다. 그리고 그 옆에 빙 돌려놓고 꽃밭 속의 고석(괴상하게 생긴 돌) 모양으로, 온갖 아양을 떨어 보이는 것들의 재롱을 혼자 보았다. 그 모양을 문틈으로 엿보면 그것은 코웃음이 나도록 어처구니없었다. 거기 모인 손님들은, 누구든지 이 고석 같은 아저씨에게 사양을 해서 그 옆으로 오는 기생이면, 다 그 옆으로 밀어 넘겼다. 보기에 그 사람은 그 방 사람이 가지지 못한 큰 세력을 가지고 있는 듯하였다. 모두 그 사람을 '영감, 영감' 하고 불러 모셨다.

그러나 산월은 그 사람을 도깨비라고 욕했다. 그리고 "네가 잘나서 사람이라더냐, 김가네집 돈이 많아서 너 같은 것을 사람이라고 대접하지. 네 손에 김형우가 관찰사를 얻게 되면 내 헛바닥에 뜸을 놓아라" 하고, 그 사람이 지나갈 때 들리리 만치 욕을 했다. 그러다가 탄실이 아버지나 삼촌이 연회 끝에 함부로 써버린 모자라는 돈을 산월에게 돌려달라고 하는 날이면 온 집 안에 큰 야단이 일어났다. 산월은 언제든지 그 남편에게,

"이것은 내 집이오. 내 집에서 나가요. 무슨 일로 남의 집에서 온갖 것들을 모아다 놓고 온갖 작태를 한단 말이오? 당신도 염치가 있지요. 20년이나 아래 되는 처에게, 그런 행세를 어떻게 한단 말이오? 동리가 부끄럽지 않소? 어린 딸이 부끄럽지 않소? 그만치 돈 있고 지위 있으면 고만이지. 게다가 관찰사는 하면 뭘 한단 말이오? 사람이 40이 넘으면 지각이 나야 하는 법이야요. 점잖지 못하게 동생의 친구의 손에 다 썩어진 관찰사나 얻어

하면 무슨 큰 영광이나 될 줄 아시오?"

했다. 그리고 어떤 때는 산월이가 나간다고 야단도 하고 어떤 때는 김형우 나간다고 야단도 했었다.

11

여름에 김형우의 큰집에서는 큰 수단을 내었다. 그것은 탄실의 마음을 헤아려서 회당에 다니면서 점점 탄실의 마음을 이끌어서 큰집으로 오게 하려는 수단이었다. 그전에 탄실은 주일날 회당에 가면 다른 동무들이 그 어머니 옆이나 할머니 옆에 앉아서 어리광을 부리는 것이 한없이 부러웠다. 그리고 자기 혼자 그런 동무들 옆에 앉아서 그래도 평양 안에 제일 큰 집 딸 행세를 해야 할 것이 참을 수 없이 쓸쓸했다.

그런 틈에 그는 그 회당 안에서 할머니와 또 적모(서자가 아버지의 정실을 이르는 말)와 새언니까지 만나게 되었다. 새언니라면 김정택의 아내를 이름이었다. 그때 김정택은 벌써 장가를 들었다.

그들도 회당 안에서 얼굴도 아름답고 공부도 잘해서 남들이 두 번 세 번씩 바라다보는 탄실을 자기 딸이라든지 손녀라든지 또는 동생이라고 하기는 싫지 않은 일이었다.

그래도 그들은 누가 물으면 김정택의 새아씨가 "우리 서모의딸……" 하고, 김형우의 본처가 "산월이가 낳은 것" 하고, 할머니는 "우리 첩며느리 딸" 하고 말했다.

탄실은 그것을 생각하면 어린 몸이 어느 구멍으로라도 기어 들어가고 싶었으나 그때부터는 너는 '외인의 딸이다' 하는 차별있는 말은 교회 안에서 안 들었다. 탄실이는 그것만이라도 다행하다고 생각했다. 그러나 좀 부족하지만 그들이 전보다는 매우 고맙게 구는 것을 알고,

"어머니(적모), 왜 나더러 산월이가 낳은 딸이라고 그러세요?"

하고 따졌다. 김정택의 모친은 그런 기회를 기다리던 판이라.

"그럼 너는 우리 집에 와서 내 딸 노릇을 하려므나. 그러지도 않는 데야 딸이라고 하겠니?"

하고 달랬다. 어린 탄실은 회당에서 아는 사람인 친척을 만난 것이 다행하다고 생각하던 때이다. 또 정택의 모친은 자기 어머니 땜에 남편도 빼앗겼을 뿐 아니라, 돈도 마음대로 못 쓰고 어느 때든지 한집에 모이게 되면 산월에게 구박만 받는 것이 불쌍하게 생각되었다.

그래서 의리로라도 그 큰어머니에게 친절히 해야만 좋을 듯이 생각이 들었다. 그래서 기회만 있으면 탄실은 동피루 밖 집에서 대동문 위 신작로 길거리에 있는 큰집에를 자주 왕래하게 되었다.

이것을 알게 된 산월은 이 세상이 캄캄해진 듯이 노여웠다. 김형우도 탄실에게 "큰집에 자주 다니지 마라" 하고 일렀다. 하나 탄실은 그 적모의 하소연을 들어 매일같이 가서 자기 모친 산월의 갖은 죄악을 들었다. 탄실은 그 적모에게 하소연을 들을수록 그 모친이 말 못 할 악한 사람같이 생각되고, 그 적모가 아주 성경 속에 있는 하나님의 뜻을 그대로 받은 듯한 성녀 같았다.

탄실은 거기서 1년 넘어, 일야로 해오던 근심을 잠깐 놓고, 매일같이 큰집에 가서 그 할머니에게 옛이야기를 듣고, 그 적모에게 매일같이 듣는 하소연을 듣고는 얼마큼 재미를 붙였다. 그리고 그 어머니에게는 산월의 딸이 아닌 듯이 쌀쌀스럽게 굴었다. 그러나 그러한 탄실의 좁은 가슴속 맨 밑에는 '우리 어머니는 지옥으로 가겠지' 하는 어두운 근심이 없어지지 않았다.

산월은 탄실이가 큰집에 다니게 된 것은 큰집에서 탄실을 끌어다가 거기 있게 하고 김형우의 마음을 끌어보려는 흉계라 하여 불같이 성내었다. 그리고 "만일 탄실이가 큰집에 가는 것을 알기만 하면 곧 어디로 나가버리겠다" 하고 어린 딸에게 을렀다.

　김형우도 온갖 말썽을 일으키는 것이 불쾌해서 탄실에게 큰집에 다니지 말라고, 그를 볼 때마다 일렀다. 하나 큰집에서는 그러면 그럴수록 탄실의 맘을 끌도록 온갖 수단을 다 부렸다. 거기서 어린 탄실은 의리가 있을 듯한 꾸민 정에 끌리면서 그 어머니의 애정으로 오는 격렬한 정을 피하면서 다시 다시 근심을 하게 되었다. 그뿐 아니라. 지금까지 이따금씩 산월의 야단이 끊일 새 없을지라도 오히려 화평하던 가정에는 전일에 비기지 못할 큰 파란이 생겼다. 그것은 김형우가 산월의 말과 같이 도깨비라는 키 작은 아저씨에게 이끌려서 기생집으로 오입을 하게 되었다. 그래서 전일 같으면 산월이가 성을 내면 김형우는 언제 아무런 일일지라도 뚝 그쳤으나 지금에는 그러지 않을 뿐 아니라, 때때로 일본서 돌아온 그 동생과 또 그 친구들의 말을 빌려서, "여자는 성을 내지 않아야 옳다. 우리 집같이 여자가 집안에서 호령질을 함부로 하는 곳이 어디 있으랴" 하고 대들었다.

　어느 날은 김형우를 을러대다가 어느 날은 산월은 패한 성주가 되어 그 딸을 달래었다. 그러나 산월은 그 남편을 을러대는편이 오히려 이익이 많았다. 탄실은 그 조모의 말대로 큰집에 머물러 있게까지 되고 드물게 그 집에 돌아왔다.

12

　그로부터 김형우는 큰집에 자주 드나들게 되어서 그 모친도 뵙고 탄실을 쓰다듬다가 갔다. 김시우도 형의 사랑이 탄실에게 무척 치우쳐서 여간한 힘으로는 어찌할 수 없는 것을 알고.

　"나, 그 형님의 맘을 알 수가 없어. 아들도 귀애하실 줄 모르고 딱 딸만 큰일이 난 듯이 귀애하니 아마 산월이가 나은 것이라서 그런지. 계집애가 어디 볼 데가 있어야 귀애하지. 그리고 나는 형님이 그 산월이 손에 꾹 잡힌 것도 알 수 없는 일이지"

하면서도 보기에 눈이 부신 양복을 사다가 탄실의 몸에 입혀주기도 하였다.

그동안에 산월은, 큰집에 가서 거기 있겠다고 고집부리는 탄실에게 어떤 때는 을러도 보고 어떤 때는 흘림 글씨로만 배운 언문 글씨를 겨우 분명써서 편지도 하였다. 하나 그 고집스러움을 그 모친에게 그대로 받고, 깨끗하고 의리 있음을 성경에서 배운 탄실은 얼른 움직여지지 않았다. 하나 탄실의 어린 마음에는 결코 '내 어머니는 장차 지옥으로 가서 뜨거운 불 가운데 그 몸이 타면서 내게라도 물을 한 방울 달라고 애걸하겠지' 하는 암담한 생각이 없지 않았다. 그는 밤마다 꿈을 보았다. 제일 많이 보는 것은 이러하였다. ……할머니와 큰어머니와 새언니가 탄탄한 길로 손목을 잡고 놀며 놀며 천당길을 갈 때, 그 모친이 찢어지고 매진 비단옷을 몸에 감고 수많은 데빌(악마)의 부하에게 이리 부대끼고 저리 부대끼면서 아무 소리도 하지 못하고 뒤몰리어 갈 때, 자기가 그 뒤를 따라가면서 어머니 어머니 나 여기 있소, 어머니 지금은 내가 눈에 선하지 않소? 나는 이제 다시는 큰집에 가지 않을 테요……

그는 이런 꿈을 보고는 잠을 깨친다.

이토록 꿈 속을 헤매는 어린 몸이 얼마나 괴로웠을까! 그는 그때부터 사람이 남에게 악한 일을 할 것은 아니라고 생각했다. 그보다 첫째 남의 첩 노릇을 해서는 못 쓴다고 생각했다. 그리고 자기의 장래에는 많은 동화에서 본 듯이 고딕식의 수도원을 설시하고 그 가운데서 생활하리라는 공상을 그렸다. 또 그러하게 기다리고 싶었다.

그는 어느때부터 언문으로 하늘나라를 사모하는 찬미를 지어서 동무들에게 주었다. 그 가운데는 이러한 것이 있었다.

내가 하늘나라에
갈 길을 모르니
주여 인도하소서,
내 어머니가 쫓아오더라도
쫓아버리지는 마시고.

내가 주 은혜에
아주 좋음을 모르니
주여 그때까지 보소서,
용서치 못할 죄를 짓더라도
생명록에 쓰지도 마시고.

그때부터 그의 마음에는 그를 장차 '알 수 없는 사람'을 만들어낼 이상한 고운 싹이 보였다.

그는 공명정대히 자기가 천국에 갈 것을 바라면서도 그 마음속으로는 가만히 자기의 믿음도 하늘나라의 보수도 의심하였다. 그러면서도 자기는 착한 사람이거니 하는 자신이 심히 굳세었다. 그는 학교에서 번차례巡番 기도를 할 때 이런 기도를 하고 나이 많은 생도와 선생들을 웃긴 일이 있었다. 그것은 아주 간단한 기도였다.

"주여, 주여, 어린양과 같은 우리들을 잘 인도하소서. 우리들은 주의 힘에 인해서, 착해도 지고 악해도 집니다. 능력이 많으신 주여, 우리들을 저버리진 마옵소서. 하늘나라가 우리 머리에 임하게 하소서. 주의 영광이 하늘나라에 있습니다."

그의 이러한 기도가 학교나 교회에서 하는 모든 사람의 전례를 벗어나서 이상하게 된 것은 탄실이 자신도 의식하지 못하였다. 그는 그 선생들과 생도들이 자기의 기도가 우습다고 놀릴 때, '내가 기도를 잘못 했나 부다'

하는 분명치 않은 의심이 일어났다. 그는 자기 기도의 잘잘못을 반성하고 싶지도 않았다.

하나 그는 윗반 생도와 선생의 고의로운 표정을 볼 때, 자기를 장난감같이 보는 거짓 웃음을 보았다. 어린 그는 천국을 이상화하는 저들이 그렇게 삼가지 못하고 거짓-게다가 또 남을 장난감같이 보는 사나움으로 자기를 놀릴 때 불같이 성을 냈다.

그 후로 그의 기도는 여러 사람들의 그것과는 아주 달라져서, 어떤 때는 주의 힘에 온전히 매달리려 하고 어떤 때는 자기의 삶에 모든 책임을 지려 하였다. 또 어떤 때는 하늘나라가 온전히 주에게 있는 듯이 믿고 또 어떤 때는 모든 것이 오직 자기에게 있다고 헤아려졌다. 거기서 또 한 가지로 어린 사상의 싹이 그를 괴롭게 하였으니 그의 전부터 하여오던, 가슴이 터지는 듯한 어머니에 대한 남모를 수심이 어렴풋한 그 무엇에 꿰뚫려서 나날이, 엷어져가는 듯하였다.

그는 어린 머리를 흔들면서 그래서는 안 되리라고, 무엇인지 알 수 없는 무엇을 암연히(슬프고 침울하게) 누르려 하였다.

13

탄실의 어린 날은 가슴이 터지는 듯한 부끄러운 아픔과 어렴풋한 의심에 싸여 있었다.

그러나 조숙한 탄실은 열한 살이 되어서 머리가 자가웃(한 자 반쯤) 길이나 되는 날씬한 처녀가 되었다.

그의 지식욕은 나날이 늘어갔다. 그리고 이상한, 보지 않던 것을 보고 싶어 하는 호기심도 나날이 물씬물씬 자랐다. 그는 지금은 그 어머니가 지어주는 비단옷을 눈살 하나 찌푸리지 않고 입었다. 그리고 그는 자기가 더 사치하고 싶은 생각도 있었다. 그래서 그 숙부가 지어준 양복을 입고 그 아버지나 삼촌을 따라다니기와 또 여남은 살 위 되는 그 오라버니 따라다니기를 좋아하게 되었다.

오순오순 웃는 듯한 분홍 치마에 안개가 일어나는 듯한 노랑 저고리나 연두 저고리를 입고 어린 계집 하인을 뒤에 세우고 아침마다 학교에 다니는 탄실을 보는 평양 남문 거리 사람들은 모두 침을 삼키면서 장래 며느리로 삼고 싶었다. 하나 누구든지 감히 바라지는 못하였다. 그때 평양성 안에서는 나는 새라도 떨어뜨릴 능력을 가진 김형우는 오늘이나 내일이나 황해도 관찰사가 된다고 짝자글(소문이 널리 퍼져 떠들썩한 모양)했으니까……

그러자 김형우의 큰집에서는 1년 넘어나 온 집안이 떠들어서 탄실의 시중을 들었어도 김형우는 마음이 돌아서 오지 않고 다만 잠깐잠깐 와서 탄실만을 쓰다듬다가 가기도 하고, 어떤 때는 인력거를 보내서 탄실만을 데려가기도 하고, 어떤 때는 산월이가 음식을 해서 보낼 뿐이었다. 그러므로 그들은 탄실을 데려다가 두고 기대하는 바를 얻지 못하고 낙망하였다. 심사 곱지 못한 그들은 탄실을 더 집에 두고 시중들기는 귀찮게 되었다. 그뿐 아니라 김형우가 관찰사 운동 하느라고 써버린 돈 뒤(경제사정)가 대단히 곤란해져서 전일같이 큰집에 여유를 주지 못하매 그들은 김형우를 원망하는 대신 탄실을 귀찮아 했다.

그동안에 김형우는 산월의 소유 밖의 집 재산을 거의 낭비하였다 해도 과언이 되지 않도록 큰돈을 써버리고, 또 산월이 몰래 집 문권과 전답 문권을 일본 사람에게 잡히고 빚을 내고, 또 그보다 배나 되는 큰 빚 담보를 해서 도깨비라는 사람에게 주었다. 6만원이란 큰돈이 관찰사 운동비에 들어갔다. 큰돈을 두려움 없이 관찰사 운동비에 넣은 김형우는 한 달이면 열 번씩은 경성 출입을 하게 되었다. 저는 전일과 같이 산월 모녀만을 위해서 온갖 재미를 보려고 무슨 일을 하는 것 같지 않고, 그러노라고 하기는 하는 것이 장자 관찰사를 해서 자기 처자를 영화롭게 하리는 욕심 때문에 지금의 모든 재미를 회생하고 마는 듯하였다. 저는 전일과같이 탄실을 찾아서 큰집에 가지 않고, 인력거도 보내지 않았다. 그럴 뿐 아니라 지와 상관한 어떤 기생은 머리를 싸매고 누워서 매일 편지질을 했다. 김형우는 거기 아주 빠진 것 같지는 않아도 사흘에 한 번씩은 거기 가서 밤들도록 있다 왔다.

산월은 산월이대로 전일같이 살림만을 하려고 아득바득하지 않고 자기와 같은 무리되는 유두분면(기름을 바른 머리와 분칠을 한 얼굴)의 젊은 여자들과 같이 집 안을 비우고 놀러 다녔다. 아침에 나가서 저녁때나 집에 돌아오는 산월은 그 돌아오는 길에는 반드시 큰집에 들러서 손수건에 무엇을 싸 들어다가 탄실에게 주었다. 그것은 대개 달고 단, 어린애로서는 제일 좋아하는 과자였다.

그리고 탄실의 큰집에서는 정택의 아내가 해산을 한 고로, 날마다 탄실이가 학교에 다닐 때 데리고 다니라고 딸려 보낸 하인을 붙잡아서 어린애 옆에 앉았게 하고, 탄실을 혼자 학교에 다니게 하였다. 그뿐 아니라 탄실에게 향해 주던 사랑은 전부 어린 것에게로 옮겼다. 아무리 영리하고 조숙한 아이일지라도 인정을 몰라라 할 수 없는 애처로운 감정이 있었다. 그는 지금 그 어머니의 옆을 그리게 되었다. 그뿐만으로도 괴로움을 참지 못하겠는데 큰집에서 그에 대한 태도는 날이 오램을 따라서 나날이 달라가고, 또 그가 학교 내왕하는 길은 참을 수 없는 고난이 있었다. 길가 사람들이 애써서 알은체하고 말을 물어서 길을 더디게 할 뿐 아니라 외딴 골목을 지날 때는 우악스러운 열서너 살의 사내아이들이 어떤 것은 그에게 달려들어서 붙잡아보기도 하고,

"침 발라놓았다."

"점찍어놓았다."

"내 장래 색시"

하고 놀렸다. 탄실은 이런 말을 그 할머니에게 한번 말해보았으나 그 할머니는 들은 체 만 체하였다. 다시 탄실의 생각은 염두에 없는 모양이었다.

탄실의 작은 가슴은 처음으로 사나운 인정에 속았음을 느꼈다. 그렇다고 탄실은 얼른 집으로 돌아가서 산월을 어머니 어머니 하기는 선뜻 내키지 않았다. 그는 산월이를 무엇인지 어머니라고 부르기가 꺼려졌다. 하나 탄실은 결코 그 모친을 진심으로 싫어하는 것이 아니고, 다만 첩의 딸, 기생의 딸이란 말이 듣기 싫었다. 그는 어릴 때부터 자존심 강한 처녀였다.

14

이렇게 명예심 많은 탄실은 어릴 때부터 생각하기를 누구든지 퍽 피곤한 집에 태어났을지라도 공부만 잘하고, 점잖기만 하면 좋을 줄 알았다. 이 아이는 무엇인지 점잖지 못한 것을 몹시 꺼렸다. 그는 동무들끼리 놀다가도 누가 무슨 일을 잘못 청하게 할 것 같으면 낯빛을 붉혔다가 아주 예사로운 빛을 보이려 하면서도 여의치 못한 듯이 몹시 괴로워했다. 그런 성질은 그가 자라감에 따라서 한층 더 선명하여갔다. 그는 절대로 비열한 행동에 대해서는 용서성을 갖지 못하였다, 하루는 대동문 안 집에서도 그런 일을 당하고 거기 1년 넘어나 붙어 있던 것을 심히 후회하고, 그만 등피루밖 집으로 돌아오게 되었다.

그때는 완연한 봄날이었다. 겨울 동안에 두꺼운 유리 판장을 깔아놓은 것 같은 강물은 어느덧에 푸른 비단 필을 길게 펴놓은 듯이 아래로 가는지 위로 가는지 잔물결이 따뜻한 봄빛과 잔잔히 회롱하고 있었다. 탄실은 이날도 그의 시중드는 '작은네'라는 계집 하인을 집에 남겨놓고 학교에 갔다 돌아오는 길에 여러 동무들과 같이 언덕 비탈을 내려오다가 어느 동무의,

"우리는 겨울 동안에는 대동강에 가서 얼음지치기를 하면서 탄실네 집에 가 놀기도 하였지만 요새는 도무지 가보지 못했다"

하는 말을 듣고, 탄실은 얼른,

"그럼 오늘 우리 집으로 모이자. 그래서 나물 캐러 연광정 앞에 가자"

했다. 거기서 그의 동무들은 바삐 자기 집으로 돌아가서 책보를 두고 오려고 남산재 언덕 아래를 내려서면서, 총총히 헤어지려 하였다. 하나 탄실은 급히 어두운 얼굴을 하고,

"얘들아, 우리 연광정 앞에서 만나자. 그래서 우리 동피루 밖 엄마 집에 가자"

하고, 혹은 두어 발자국 앞에 혹은 서너 발자국 앞에 앞서간 아이들을 불러 세웠다. 아이들은 누구든지 탄실의 말을 듣고 좋아서 날뛰며,

"그러자. 나는 너의 어머니가 좋더라. 너는 왜 그 집에 있지 않니?"

하고 물었다. 탄실은 머뭇머뭇,

"무슨 일이 있어 그래"

했다.

어린 그들은 다시 아무런 생각도 하지 않고 동무의 낯빛도 살피지 않으면서 다시 총총히 어서 헤어졌다가 어서 또다시 만날 생각에 앞으로 앞으로 발걸음을 옮겼다.

탄실은 혼자 타박타박 걸으며,

'오늘 돌아가면 또 어떤 얼굴로 나를 맞아주려노? 작은네는 왜 내 사람인데 저희들이 차지하노? 할머니, 적모, 새언니(정택 오빠의 아내), 수양딸, 어멈, 몇 사람이서 어린애 하나를 거두지 못하고, 작은네 더러 똥을 쳐라 기저귀를 갈아대라 하고 야단인가. 오늘은 가면 내가 작은네를 데리고 좀 놀러 나갈 테야'

하고 생각했다. 그 길로 탄실은 급히 돌아왔다. 평시와 같이 오빠는 농림학교에 갔다가 아직 돌아오지 않고, 할머니는 사랑마루 끝에서 명주가

락을 헤고, 적모는 부엌에서 무엇을 만드느라고 대그락거리고, 언니는 건넌방에서 어린애 돌띠(돌을 맞은 아기의 허리에 매어주는 띠)라고 울긋불긋 당치도 않은 실올을 함부로 꿰매고 있었다. 아무도 탄실이가 돌아와도 말을 건네지 않았다. 탄실은 쓸쓸한 생각에 눌려서.

"작은네야, 작은네야."

야단이 난 듯이 불렀다. 건넌방에서 새언니가 다른 집 같으면 그렇지 못하건만 서모의 딸이라서 그런지,

"탄실이 너 왜 그러니? 작은네는 아이 업었다. 무슨 일이 났니?" 하고는 "그렇게 야단을 떨다가 애 떨어지게 해라" 라고 부르짖으면서 성을 냈다. 탄실은 불쾌한 듯이,

"무슨 일이 나기는. 내 신 좀 문질러 볕에 널라고 그래요"

했다. 그 말에 그 오라범댁은 아무 말 없다가 혼자서 잘 들리지않게,

"계집애를 저따위로 길러 뭘 해, 나중에 무엇을 만들려누"

하고 중얼중얼했다.

그 틈에 부엌에서 무엇 하던 적모는 와락 밖으로 내달으며,

"왜 '작은네야 작은네야' 하니? 어린애 좀 업혀주었는데. 애가 그래서 못 쓴다, 좀 어수룩한 데가 있어야지. 그렇게 '내 해, 내 해' 하고 앙탈만 부리면 너 좋다고 할 사람 어디 있겠니? 황 개꼬리 3년 묻어도 황 개 꼬리대로 있다더니. 그렇게 일러도 말을 들어야 길러 먹지"

하며 턱없는 욕을 했다. 탄실은 기가 막혀서 파랗게 되어 섰다가 그 할머니가 중문 안으로 들어오며,

"너희들 왜 그러니?"

할 때, 그만 소리쳐 울었다. 그때 적모와 정택의 처가 협력해서,

"작은네에게 애 좀 업혔다고 악을 악을 쓰기에 그러지 말라고 했더니 저렇게 운다우"

하고 이르면서 비웃었다. 그래도 할머니는,

"그래서 쓰나"

할 뿐이고 탄실의 말을 헤아려주지는 않았다.

15

탄실은 심술이 머리끝까지 났다. 어리고 작은 자기의 것을 빼앗고, 온 집 안이 크게 협력해서 그를 눌러버리려는 일은 아주 도리에 닿지 않는 일이라고 생각했다. 그는 지금까지 산월이가 온 집 안을 물 끓이듯 술렁술렁거릴 때일지라도, 그런 도리에 닿지 않는 일을 떠드는 것을 본 때가 없었다. 무엇인지 그 어린 생각에도 저들이 천당을 가고 자기 어머니만 지옥을 간다면 좀 불공평하리라고 생각해졌다. 그는 비로소 한 절망에 가까운, 남에게 속았다는 감정으로 받는 설움 때문에 좁은 숨통이 탁탁 미어지도록 격렬히 울었다.

'공연히 저 사람들을 그렇게 보았다. 저 사람들이 우리 어머니보다 무엇이 다르랴! 저 사람들은 나를 친척 같이도 생각지 않는데 내가 못나서 저들을 믿었다. ……저들이 내 작은네를 빼앗고 내 심부름도 못 시키게 하는 것이나…… 어머니가 우리 아버지를 확실히 큰집에서가 아니라 길바닥 같은 어느 기생의 집에서 데려온 것이나 무엇이 다르랴? 이 두 가지 일을 비기면 작은네는 나를 따라다니고 싶어 하는 것을 저편에서 억지로 막는 것이고, 아버지는 자기가 가 있고 싶어서 어머니에게만 가 있는 것이다. 아무려나 오늘은 어머니에게 가 일러야 하겠다. 작은네를 이 집에 그대로 두지는 않겠다.'

이렇게 생각하고 그는 눈물을 흘렸다. 탄실은 그렇게 울어도 저들은 뻔뻔스럽게,

"너 왜 우니. 그거 원 이상하구나. 누가 너를 때렸니, 욕했니?"

할 뿐이었다, 그는 지금은 그런 곳에서 아무런 의리도 인정도 찾을 수 없었다. 그는 마루 끝에서 걸레를 들어다가 자기의 땀 밴 신바닥을 손수 문질렀다. 이것을 안방에서 보던 작은네는 아이 업은 채 밖으로 나오며,

"아가씨, 제가 문질러드려요. 그러지 않으면 성 밖 마마님께 걱정 들어요"

하고 큰일이 난 듯이 덤볐다. 그는 그때 지금까지 지녀보지 못하던 이상한 인정이 느껴지는 것을 알았다. 두 친한 사이가 무엇 땜에 헤어져 있다가 다시 모든 것을 물리치고 친해질 때 어린 마음은 얼마나 기쁜 눈물을 흘릴까? 그는 자기가 이를 악물고 문지르려던 신바닥을 작은네에게 주면서 그만 울었다. 그리고 그 어머니 앞에 돌아가서 큰집에서 지난 일을 이야기할 생각을 하고 더욱 울었다. 그것은 모두 뉘우침에 가까운 감정에서 우러나는 보드랍고 연한 부끄러운 눈물이었다.

그는 책보를 쥐고 서서 작은네가 아이 업은 채 구부리고 문질러주는 신을 신고 들입다 울었다. 그때야 정택의 아내는 자기의 아이를 어린 작은네의 허리에서 풀어놓았다. 작은네는 부리나케 신을 문질러서 탄실에게 신기고,

"성 밖 집으로 갑시다. 아가씨, 여기 무엇 하러 계셔요? 성 밖 마마님 걱정이나 시켜드리지"

하고 달랬다. 탄실은 울다가 머리로 끄덕 대답하고 아무 말도 없이 큰집 문을 나섰다. 문밖을 나설 때,

"얘, 또 너 어미한테 누가 어떡한 듯이 이르지나 마라"

하고 할머니가 짜증을 냈다. 보기에 할머니는 탄실에게 반 푼어치도 손자 같은 감정을 가지지 않은 듯하였다. 그는 단지 탄실을 귀애하는 그 아들을 이끌어 오려는 수단으로 지어서 하는 체하였던 것이다. 탄실은 다시는 그 문 안을 들어서지 않으려는 듯이 책보를 단단히 쥐고 그 문밖을 나섰다. 작은네는 부리나케,

"야! 너는 여기 있거라"

하는 적모의 소리를 귓등으로 듣고, 탄실을 따라나섰다.

탄실은 작은네의 손목을 잡고 골목 밖으로 나가다가 먼저 학교언덕 아래서 여러 동무들과 약속했던 것을 생각했다. 그는 발걸음을 앞으로 앞으로 빨리 옮겨놓으며,

"작은네야, 어서 가자. 아까 학교에서 헤어져 오며 여럿이서 모두 연광정 앞에서 만나자고 약속하였다. 그것을 우느라고 잊어버렸다. 큰일 났다. 동무들이 욕하겠다"

하고 그는 달음박질하기 시작했다. 눈 녹은 봄 흙은 따뜻한 봄볕에 아지랑이를 올리고, 종다리 먼 들에서 구천久天에 오를 때 햇솜을 펴서 넌 듯이 만지면 하박하박 녹아질 듯한 하얀 구름이 온 하늘에 널려 있었다. 탄실과 작은네는 그때는 지금과 달라서 닦아놓지 않은 울퉁불퉁한 길 위에 눈 녹은 땅이라 신발이 푹푹 빠져 땅속으로 들어가는 것을 애련당 못자리까지 간신히 넘어서 대동문 통으로 연광정을 바라고 달아났다. 그들은 숨이 턱에 닿아서 저편에 울긋불긋한 어린 처녀들이 노는 것을 바라고 갔다.

16

탄실이가 달음질해 오는 것을 본 탄실의 동무들은 마주 달음질해서 오며 평양말로,

"너 지금에야 오네."

"얘야, 우리는 퍽 기다렸단다. 웬 아이두 그렇게 더디오니? 한 시간이나 기다렸단다."

"얘, 너 울었구나."

"그 얇은 눈까풀이 통통이 부었네"

하고 그를 붙들었다.

탄실은 지금까지 흑흑 느끼면서 길로 달음질해 와서는 그대로 동무들을 얼싸안고 또다시 울었다. 그는 얼른 말을 하려 하였으나 울음부터 북받쳐서 입이 열리지 않았다.

그는 처음으로 사람에게 냉대를 느끼고 대단히 슬펐던 것이다.

그 이후에 그는 이보다 몇 배 되는 학대를 받았을 때도 결코 이때와 같이 슬프다고 생각하지는 못하였다. 이때까지 동무들에게 여간한 비평은 들었을지라도 그것은 자기가 너무 공부를 잘해서 그들의 수석과 따라오는 명예를 다 빼앗은 탓이었다. 누구든지 3년이나 자기들보다 뒤떨어져서 공부를 시작해가지고 오히려 자기네들 머리 위를 밟아 넘긴다면 퍽 원망될 것이니까…… 자존심 많은 탄실은 울면서 그 동무들이 연고를 물어도 얼른 입을 열지 않았다. 그는 차마 큰집 일가가 전부 자기를 냉대한단 말이 입 밖에 나오지 않았다. 그는 동무들이 굳이 연고를 물을 때,

"우리 엄마가 예수를 안 믿어서 그래. 아무리 믿으라고 그래도 믿지를 않아……"

하고 또다시 크게 울었다. 새 설움에 옛 설움이 북받쳤던 것이다. 그 동무들은 무엇인지 어두운 기운에 억눌려서 동무의 어머니가 예수를 안 믿다가 장차 지옥으로 갈 생각을 하고, 또 자기네들의 어린 믿음을 생각하고, '하늘나라에 들기가 지극히 어렵다'는 성경 속의 문구들을 생각하고는 모두 이 양기로운 봄날 대낮에 때아닌 생각을 소름이 끼치도록 했다.

이때 17, 8세 된 단정한 처녀가 책보를 끼고, 대동문 나루를 향해 가노라고 분주히 그들의 앞을 지났다. 아이들은 분주히 가는 그에게,

"순실 형님, 순실 형님."

"순실 형님."

"순실 형님, 형님."

"순실 형님"

해서 분주히 가는 그를 불러 세웠다. 그는 대동강 건너 사는. 최군수의

딸이었다.

얼굴이 빨개서 급히 가다가 아이들의 부르는 소리를 듣고, 그 편을 향해 서며 반가운 듯이,

"너희들 왜 여기 모여 섰니?"

하고 말하다가,

"탄실이 너두 있구나. 너 왜 울었니?"

하고 아이들 틈에 섞인 탄실에게 다시 찬찬히 물으며 그는 바쁜 길을 멈추었다. 탄실은 이때는 눈물을 그치고, 때때로 흑흑 느끼기만 하다가 최순실이라는 생도를 보고 부끄러운 듯이 고개를 돌렸다.

최순실은 2년 전에, 남산재 소학교를 제1회로 졸업하고, 지금은 서문 밖 여중학교에 다니는 큰 생도였다. 그는 김형우의 친구의 딸인 고로 학교에 들기 전에도 탄실이와는 아는 사이였다. 또 그 모친이며 가풍이 탄실이와 대동소이한 고로 서로 친하지 않을 수 없이 되었다. 아이들은 그 사이를 아는 고로,

"이 애 어머니가 예수 믿지 않는다고 울어요."

"이 애 어머니는 예수를 믿으라고 자꾸 권고해도 믿지 않는대요"

하고 일렀다. 그래도 큰 학생은 바로 듣지를 않는 듯이,

"그래서야 울겠니? 너 큰집에 있다더니 거기서 몹시 굴던 것이로구나. 너 보아라. 어머니하고 있지 않으면 죄가 내리는 법이네라. 어머니가 우리 집에 오셔서 네 말을 하고 얼마나 많이 우신 줄 아니? 남의 외딸로 태어나서 그렇게 말을 어기는 법은 없단다. 나 봐라. 이렇게 공부가 바빠도 내일이 어머니 생신이어서 부리나케 집에 가지 않니? 너희 어머니가 무엇을 잘못해서 그러니? 세상에 너희 어머니같이 똑똑하고 잘난 사람은 없다더라. 남이 다 그러는데 네가 남의 외딸로 태어나서 그런 어머니를 싫다고 해서야 쓰겠니? 예수 안 믿어도 천당 갈 사람은 간다더라. 예수 믿으면 다 천당 가는 줄 아니?"

하고 곰곰이 힘 있게 타일렀다.

아이들은 최순실의 앞으로 바싹바싹 다가들며,

"형님, 예수 안 믿어도 착하기만 하면 천당 가지요?"

"나는 탄실이 어머니가 좋아요. 얼굴이 달덩이 같으세요. 어쩌면 그러신지 모르겠어요."

"하하, 그 애는, 얼굴은 왜 들추어."

"아주 우리들이 가면 고맙게 구셔요……"

"이 애 큰어머니는 사람이 별해요. 우리들이 놀러 가도 너희들 뭘 하러 왔네? 탄실이 없단다 해요."

하고 아이들은 지금까지 침울한 기운을 없이 하고 웃으며 이야기했다. 최순실은 아무 아이의 말이나

"그렇고 말고"

하고 대답하다가 나중에

"탄실아, 내일 어머니하고 같이 우리 집에 오너라. 너 좋아하는 조개송편 했단다. 부디 오너라" 하고, "나는 바빠서 간다" 하면서 다시 가던 길을 총총히 걸어갔다.

17

그는 한참이나 걸어가다가 다시 못 미더운 듯이 돌아서서,

"얘들아, 탄실이를 성 밖 집까지 데려다주어라, 부탁한다"

하고 다시 급히 급히 걸어서 대동문 통으로 빠져나갔다.

어린 처녀 아이들은 금시로 마음이 가벼워진 듯이 제각기 날뛰면서,

"순실 형님 말이 옳다 응?"

"얘, 선생님도 그러지 않던? 예수 믿는다고 다 천당 가는 것이 아니라고."

"알고 안 행하는 것은 죄가 더 깊고, 모르고 못 행하는 것은 죄가 가볍다지 않던?"

하고 짝자글하게 떠들었다. 탄실은 운 뒤의 흐느낌과 한숨을 한데 내쉬며,

"그럼 우리 집에 가자. 나무새기는 내일 좀 캐러 또 오고 오늘은 우리 엄마한테 가서 놀자. 배 타고 싶거든 배도 타고……웅?"

"오"

"웅 그러자."

"그러는 것이 더 재미나겠다."

"그래. 너는 순실 언니 말대로 하려고 하는구나."

"얘는, 그럼 그렇지 않구."

"그러게 말이야"

"그럼 우리 엄마한테 다들 가자. 그래도…… 이제 엄마한테 가서 무엇이라구 하나…… 얘들아, 이제 엄마한테 뭐라구 할까…… 실상은 오늘 큰집 사람들하구 모두 싸웠단다."

"얘, 너 십계명에 거짓말하지 말라구 하지 않았던?"

"그럼 있는 대로 다 말할까? 그렇더라도 엄마가 노해서 온통 야단을 하면 큰일이 날걸."

"그러지 말고 엄마가 보고 싶어 왔다고 하렴. 그러면 너희 어머니께서도 좋아하고 집안도 편하지 않으냐?"

"옳다 옳다."

"되었다. 그만하면 핑계도 되지 않고, 거짓말도 되지 않는다."

어린아이들은 이 같은 의논을 하고 발걸음을 빨리해서 그간의 혼돈을 무너뜨린 그 자리를 밟고 배틀배틀 걸어갔다.

김형우는 이날도 서울 가고 산월은 큰 연회를 차리느라고 찬간에서 돌보다가 잘못 생선 뼈 빼는 칼날을 밟아서 발바닥을 몹시 베고 피를 쏟았다. 그는 이날은 동무의 집에서 하인이 와도 가지를 못하고 심심히(깊고 깊이) 화려하게 지은 서양식 마루방에 쓸쓸히 앉아서 침모하고 이야기를 하고 있었다.

"인제 완연한 봄이구려. 참, 탄실이 데리러 인력거를 보내야 하겠군. 요새는 저 혼자 작은네도 안 데리고 학교에 다닌단 말이 있어."

"인력거는 벌써 보냈어요. 애기도 인제는 열한 살이 되었지요? 세월이 참 빠르긴 해요. 인제 몇 해 있으면 혼인하겠지요?"

"하하 몇 해가 뭐야요. 일전에 중매가 왔다 가지 않았소."

"참, 그것 어떡하셔요? 그런 좋은 자리를 그대로 내버리세요?"

"글쎄, 영감 말씀이 홀어머니 시하에 사람 버리기 쉽다고 하시니까 아마 안 보내실 작정이시지. ……나야 그런 데까지 참견하진 않아야 할 터이니까."

"어머니께서 참견을 안 하시면 누가 합니까? 그래도 참견하셔야지. 사내들이 무얼 아는 줄 아십쇼?"

"그렇더라도 온 집안이 다 내 간섭을 허락지 않을 터이니까. 흥! 영감도 자식도 여염집 부녀 되고야 다 참견할 수 있는 일이야. 영감은 영감대로 제 일만 옳다고 하고, 자식은 자식대로 내 속에서 나왔어도 그렇지 않은 듯이 큰집에 가 있으니 내가 무엇이 좋겠소? 다 독불장군이지. 그래도 마음은 내 자식만 믿어지지 영감 같은 것은 아무리 내게 복종을 하더라도 싱크럽기만 (시끄럽기만) 해."

"그야 애기가 하도 잘났으니까 하시는 말씀이시지. 마마님 내외 같은 사이를 미덥지 않으시다면 믿을 곳이 어디 있겠습니까? 공연한 불평이시지요."

이와 같이 산월은 담배를 피우고 침모는 새로 마른 (자른) 탄실의 옷감을 추리면서 이야기를 할 때 탄실이가 동무들을 끌고 울레줄레 안뜰에 들어섰다. 산월은 피를 많이 쏟고 얼굴이 해쓱해서 우두커니 앉았다가 탄실을 보고,

"얘, 인력거 보냈는데 걸어왔니?"

하면서 얼굴에 화색을 띠었다가 울어서 부은 그 얼굴을 바라보고,

"애기, 너 왜 울었니? 저 작은네도 울었구나"

하였다.

탄실은 그 검은 순수한 눈에 눈물을 다시 띠고,

"어머니"

부르고 한참 얼굴을 돌렸다가 고개를 바로 하고 그 모친의 발 처맨 것을 보고,

"발을 다치셨어요?"

하고 고개를 숙였다.

어린 동무들은 눈을 방울같이 뜨고 모녀의 행동만 바라보다가 산월이가 침모에게,

"저 애들 먹을 것 갖다주시오. 그리고 저녁에도 맛 다른 것 해서 같이 먹도록……"

할 때는 다 얼굴을 붉히면서,

"아니요."

"아니요"

하고 얼굴을 서로 쳐다보면서 남의 느낌에 모두 눈물을 지었다.

18

탄실은 자기 집에 돌아와서도 모든 일이 마음 같지 않고 괴로웠다.

그는 첫째로 그 모친의 고충을 나누어서 그 어린 몸에 감당하지 않으면 안 될 것이었다.

산월은 이따금씩 탄실의 옷을 손수 지으면서 밤을 새웠다. 긴 강물이 잔잔히 흐르는 중간 창가에 모든 것이 잠들어 고요한 때에 여울턱에 물길 갈리는 소리가 그윽히 들려왔다. 봄날의 깊은 밤이었다. 탄실은 찬란한 이불 속에 고요히 잠자고 산월은 그 옆에서 바느질을 하다가 담배를 피우다가 무엇을 생각하였는지 미닫이를 드윽 열어젖히고, "침모, 침모" 하고 불러본다. 탄실은 그 소리에 눈을 반짝 떴다. 그러나 그 모친이 볼까 봐 염려되는 듯이 얼른 눈을 감았다. ……하나…… 그 마음속으로는 이런 말을 했다.

'엄마, 엄마는 또 울고 싶은 것이구려. 그러지 말고 내 이불 속으로 들어오세요……'

그 몸이 보드라운 안팎 비단 이불에 싸인 것같이 그 마음은 설움에 메여 있었다. 그는 이즈음으로 집안일과 그 모친의 근심 때문에 깊은 잠을 들지 못하게 되었다. 어떤 때는 눈을 분명히 뜨고, "어머니, 왜 안 주무세요?" 하고 불러볼 때도 있었다. 이런 때 그 모친은 울다가 그 딸의 음성을 듣고 눈물을 뚝뚝 떨어뜨리며, "아기, 왜 깼니?" 하며 이불을 다시 폭 덮어주고 사분사분 그의 가슴을 두들겨준다. 그리고 자기가 무엇을 잘못해서 잠든 애기를 깨운 듯이 심히 미안해한다. 탄실은 그런 염려를 그 어머니에게 시켜드리고 싶지 않았다. 그러지 않아도 그가 알기에 그 모친인 27, 8세의 젊은 여인에게는 너무나 큰 근심이 있었다.

그 부친은 얼른 관찰사도 되지 못하고 매월 은행 변리(대출이자)를 내기에 불쾌한 심지를 누를 수 없었다. 그러나 더는 그런 책임을 혼자 지기 어려운지 매일같이 집 안에서 짜증을 내다가, 산월이가 마주 야단을 하는 때면 온종일 나가서 있다가 날이 샐 때에 아직도 술이 깨지 않아서 돌아와서는, "탄실아, 탄실아" 부른다.

이날 밤에도 김형우는 산월에게 돈을 빌려 대주지 않는다고 트집을 일으키고, 나가서 열두 시가 지나도 돌아오지 않았다. 산월은 그렇게 초조해서 기다리지는 않으나 희미하게 여러 곳으로 오는 근심을 홀로 대신 부담하기가 어려울 듯한 염려로 그럼인지 침모를 불러서,

"오늘도 또 늦게 들어오시는구려. 차라리 나 혼자 살 것 같으면 그런 줄이나 알고 기다리지 않을 것 아니오"

하면서 불평을 말한다. 침모는 단잠을 못다 자고 일어나서 선하품을 하면서,

"아이구, 영감께서도 염려되시는 것이 많이 있어 홧김에 나가계신 것이지요. 마마님께나 애기에게 마땅치 않은 일이 있어 그러시겠습니까? 마마님께서는 그렇게 늡늡하시고(성격이 너그럽고 활달하시고) 애기는 애기대로 그렇게 영리하신데……"

하고 대답한다.

산월은 침모의 졸려 하는 것이 가엾은 듯이,

"아이구 안되었구려. 내 근심에 남까지 괴롭게 하는 것은 좋지 않은 일이라고 생각은 하면서도 자연히 내 근심이 있어서 잠 못들 때는 이렇구려"

하고 온갖 근심에 익숙한 침모에게 이야기한다.

우선 산월 모녀의 재산은 이번 관찰사 운동에 반 넘어 들어갔다. 만일에 김형우는 관찰사를 얻게 될 것 같으면 그 재산을 전부 뽑아낼 결심이다. 하나 산월의 생각으로 보면 지금 세상에 그런 일은 아주 옳지 않은 일일 뿐 아니라 심히 위험한 일이었다. 그 세월에 어떤 촌사람의 아들은 일본 가서 공부를 해가지고 돌아가서 그 부친이 어느 옛적에 서울 어떤 양반에게 빼앗긴 재산을 이자까지 합해서 도로 돌이켰다는 말이 경향 간에 너무나 와자지껄할 뿐 아니라, 뇌물을 받고 벼슬을 판 사람은 거진 감옥에 들어가서 고역을 하게 되었다.

19

　탄실은 겨우 어린 믿음에서, 그 몸을 빼어내게 되었다. 그는 이때에 이르러서는 조금도 그 모친을 꺼리지 않고 좀더 그 어머니가 자기를 신용해서 집안 이야기를 자세히 해주기를 바랐다. 무엇인지 자기가 2, 3년 동안 꿈길을 걷고 있었다고도 생각해보았다. 이런 때에 불행하게도 회당 안에서는 큰 풍파가 일어났다.

　……완전 신의 피를 끌어가며 얼굴에 열을 올려가면서 주먹으로 탁자를 두들기고 발로 강단을 울리고, 몇 천 명 되는 신자의 귀에 하나님의 진리를 말해서 새 생명을 불어넣어주는 듯하던 성신을 받은 회당 목사가 남의 집 과부를 간통하다가 발각되었다고……

　여러 신자들은 실심(근심 걱정으로 맥이 빠지고 마음이 산란해짐)했다. 어떤 사람은 다시는 회당에 안 온다고 이름을 지워 가고 어떤 사람은 자기의 자식을 학교에서 아주 데려갔다. 이 틈에 산월은 예수교를 그 딸의 머리에서 아주 빼내도록 하려고 곰곰 타일렀다.

　"그것 보아라. 회당에 다니더라도 무슨 보람이 있나? 회당안에서 제일 성신 받았다고 뒤떠들던 목사가 그런 좋지 못한 행동을 하지 않았니? 믿기는 무엇을 믿겠니? 그것이 다 사람을 꾀어들이는 수단이지. 남의 첩은 예수를 믿어서 천당에 가지 못하느니라, 죄를 다 자백해라, 하던 목사가 저는 자백도 안 하고, 잘난 듯이 모든 사람 위에 올라앉았던 것이 그 꼴을 하고는 처자를 버리고 달아났으니 그 나머지야 말하지 않아도 알 일이지 무엇이 변변하겠냐……애기 너도 고만 예수교 학교에는 다니지 말자. 차라리 서울로 가서 다른 학교를 다니면 다녔지. 평양서 그 회당 학교에 그대로 다니는 날이면 장래 네 몸에 해가 미친다. 그러지 않아도 너는 어미가 여염 사람이 아니어서 성가신 일이 많을 터인데 게다가 그런 흉난 교회학교에까지 다니면 남이 너를 어떻게 알겠니? 집에 들어앉아서 바느질이나 배우든지 그러지 않으면 서울로 가서 공부를 하든지…… 거기 가면 외할 머니나 이모가 너를 좀 반가워하겠니…… 이제 평양서야 어떻게 공부를 하겠니?"

이러한 산월의 말을 들은 탄실은 그러지 않아도 서울 가서 공부하고 싶던 판인데 불현듯이 더욱 서울로 가서 공부하고 싶었다. 그는 그 모친이 섭섭하여 하는 것을 생각하면 차마 그런 말이 입 밖에 나오지 않지만 다만 공부하고 싶은 마음을 이길 수 없어,

"어머니, 그럼 저는 서울로 가요. 거기 가면 남산재 학교에서 공부하던 큰언니들이 많아요"

하고 정말 가고 싶어서 참을 수 없는 듯이 그 몸을 비비 꼬면서 말했다.

그 뒤에 한 달쯤 지나서 산월은 탄실을 더 공부시키지 않고 바느질이나 가르치려고 이르다 이르다 못해서 서울로 보냈다.

정거장에서 산월은 탄실에게 서울 간 뒤에 일어날 일을 염려했다.

"필경 너의 숙부가 나와 불합하니까 너를 집에 데려다 둘 생각은 아니하리라마는 네가 이모 집에만 다니면 말썽을 일으킬 터이니, 숙부의 집에서 데리러 오거든 가보아라. 너무 자주 가지도 말고……"

산월은 탄실을 차에 올려 앉히고 차가 막 소리를 지르려 할 때

"탄실아, 내 한 달 후에 가마. 부디 잘 가서 공부해라"

하고 이내 쓰리질 듯이 정거장의 기둥을 붙들고 울었다. 탄실도 눈에 눈물을 가랑가랑 띠고,

"어머니, 울지 마세요"

하고, 탄실을 데리고 가던 김형우도,

"거기서 울지 말아요"

하고 이르면서 모녀의 떠나는 정리를 생각해서 눈물을 흘렸다.

차가 막 떠날 때 그 모친은 미친 듯이 차창에 달려들다가 철도역원에게 붙들려서 목멘 소리로,

"영감, 그 애를 예수교 학교에는 넣지 마세요"
하고 당부했다.

때는 추구월의 지루하던 더위가 산들바람에 하루 이틀 식어가는 때였다. 서울 북장동 진명여학교에는 열한 살 된 평양 처녀가 새로 들어와서 그늘 그늘로 피해 다니며 구석구석에서 숨어서 눈물을 짓고 향수鄕愁에 울었다.

20

그때 한 옛적에 창성동 진명여학교에서 울던 처녀는 지금의 김탄실이었다.
그는 그 학교에서 마치 동물과 같이 괴로움을 받고 동물처럼 우리에 갇혀서 자랐다. 그의 숙부는 학교 기숙사감에게 그같이 부탁하고, 일절 그의 외가에 출입하는 것을 엄금하였다. 그가 얼마나 기숙사 학생들이 공일이면 기숙사 문밖에 나가는 것을 부러워하였을까? 그는 1년 동안이나 꼬박 기숙사에 갇혀 있다가 여름방학이면 평양에 가서 평양성 안을 돌아다니며 놀았다. 그는 참으로 부모를 떠나있는게 싫었다.
두 달 동안의 긴 방학이 빠르다고 생각하면서 세월 가는 것을 원수같이 알았다. 하나 그러는 동안에도 그는 서울 가서 할 공부를 미리 준비하고 있었다. 그뿐 아니라 서울 가지 못할 혼인 말이 일어나면, 그는 용기를 가다듬어서 극력으로 반대하였다. 어쩐지 탄실은 서울 가서 공부하게 된 이후로는 그 성품이 나날이 황폐해져갔다.
그는 전일같이 유순하고 민첩하지가 못하고, 심히 옹졸하고, 심술스럽게 되어갔다. 무엇이든지 경쟁이라고 이름 짓고 하는 일이면 죽을지 살지 모르고 기어이 승리를 얻기까지 다투었다.

그는 질투심 많고, 심사 곱지 못한 처녀가 되어갔다. 그 모친은 그의 우울증이 도져서 그래지는 것이라고 기숙사에서 그가 자유를 얻고 공일날이라도 외출하도록 허락하게 하려 하였으나 그 부친은 반대하고 그 동생의 말만 믿었다.

김형우는 그 아우인 시우의 학식을 태산같이 우러러보고 믿었다. 그는 무엇이든지 그 아우의 말이라면 귀찮은 일까지라도 복종하였다. 그러나 그는 아무 효험을 보지 못할 뿐 아니라 큰 실패를 보았다. 저는 많은 돈을 들이고 관찰사가 되려는 운동을 하다가 큰 실패를 한 것이 심히 억울한 일이건만 그런 말 한마디 그 동생에게 하지 않고, 언제든지 그 동생의 일에는 무턱으로 큰돈을 아끼지 않고 내었다. 그러나 김시우는 그 형의 말을 그 친구 사이에도 한번 좋게 하여본 때가 없었다. 그리고 입을 열면 반드시 산월의 흉질을 알지도 못하는 사람들 가운데서 펼쳐놓고 웃음거리를 지었다.

그러나 김시우는 그 당시 한국 군인들 가운데 손꼽히게 든다는 애국지사였다. 그는 나랏일을 도모한다고 연회를 차리고, 기생들과 같이 춤추고 놀았다. 또 정치를 한다고 형의 재산을 속여다가 대신에게 뇌물을 주고 벼슬을 사려다가 기생의 해우채(기생들과 관계를 가지고 그 대가로 주는 돈)를 주느라고 소비해버렸다. 그러므로 김형우는 그 동생과 연락하던 모든 일을 단념하였다. 하나 김시우는 언변 좋게,

"형님, 이런 말세에 벼슬은 하면 무엇을 하십니까? 그대로 시골 계신 편이 유익하지요"

하고 꾀었다.

저는 일본 있을 때는 한국에 돌아오면 많은 일을 하려고 바랐다. 그러나 결국 돌아와보매 한국 정부는 저들에게 아무런 신임도 하지 않을 뿐 아니라, 형식과 같이 미관말직微官末職의 봉급까지 무척 아꼈다.

적이 실심한 일본 유학생 군인들은 분풀이인지 낙담인지를 향할 곳 없

어서 되는대로 방탕에 몸을 맡겼다. 그러나 저들은 적은 봉급으로는 그 비용을 감당할 수 없어서 경향京鄕의 돈 있고 어수룩한 사람들을 함부로 꾀어내도록 했다. 그래서 입으로 한국을 근심하고 상관을 욕해서 그럴듯이 인심을 사놓고, 이등통감을 빌려서 벼슬 시킨다고 하고는 운동비를 무척 탐해서 소비해버리고 나라가 글러서 그렇다고 핑계해버렸다.

그 틈에 제일 첫째로 희생된 사람은 김형우였다. 저는 그 동생의 유흥비뿐 아니라 산월이가 도깨비라고 이름한 사람의 유흥비까지 내고, 또 그 친구의 그런 비용까지 낸 일이 많았다. 그러나 그러는 동안이 2년이 되매 김형우가 가진 재산으로는 그것을 담당할 수 없었다. 나중에는 아무리 관찰사 운동이 귀중할지라도 돈이 없는 연고로 도깨비의 친구의 갈보 집 다닌 비용까지 다 낼 수는 없었다. 한번은 도깨비라는 이의 의동생 길주억이란 청년 주정꾼이 일부러 기차를 타고 가서 김형우에게 돈을 청구하다가 거절을 당하였다.

21

그런 일들이 있은 지 두어 해 만에 김형우의 집은 남는 것 하나 없이 패가를 하였다고 경향 간에 소문이 들렸다. 그런 중에도 산월만은 자기의 돈은 따로 감추고 내놓지 않는다고 수군수군하였다.

그동안에 애국지사라던 이들은 혹은 감옥에 갇히고, 혹은 외국으로 망명하였다. 그들이 밤낮을 바꾸어서 노는 동안에 국사에도 간섭하였는지는 극히 비밀한 일이어서 자세히 알 수 없었으나 사면으로 빚에 몰려서 사기 취재로 고소를 당하고, 그만 달아나버린 사람도 있었다. 도깨비라는 사람은 그 하나였다. 그러므로 김형우는 그 사람의 빚 담보를 후회하면서도 할 수 없이 그 빚을 대신 갚지 않으면 안 될 경우였다.

모든 일은 꿈결과 같이 사라졌다. 애국지사들의 독립 운동도, 또 김형우의 관찰사 운동도 모두 다 물거품보다 쉽게 사라졌다. 그 나머지라고는 집 문권, 밭 문권을 깡그리 10분의 1도 되지 못할 헐가로 잡힌 김형우의 빚밖에 남은 것이 없었다. 그리고 이보다 더 섧게 남은 것이라고는 참으로 학대밖에 없었다. 길거리마다 상투를 튼 조선 사람들이 무엇이라고 떠드는 말을, '하따라 마따라'(종교에서 범죄자로 간주한다는 의미)라고 듣다가는, 상투를 꺼들리고 뺨을 맞았다. 징신(가죽신) 소리가 줄고, 나막신 소리가 대낮에 서울 시가를 돌아 들리게 되었다.

모든 흉계, 모든 노름, 모든 음란, 모든 간악의 나머지가 모두 빚이 되어서 집을 팔고, 전답을 팔고, 하늘을 팔고, 땅을 팔고, 관 같은 방 안에 게으름만 남겼다.

모든 사람은 착실한 운동도 해보기 전에 횡설수설하다가 홍바지 청바지(홍색청색의 죄수복)만 입고, 게으름을 완전히 부려볼 철창 속에 갇혀서 우두커니 턱없이 악형 당할 때만 기다렸다.

그들은 아무 열성스러운 의의義意도 분명히 갖지 못하고, 다만 나라를 잃겠다, 임금이 외국 왕에게 학대를 받겠다, 황후가 정절을 잃고 욕을 보겠다, 하는 맘으로, 나라 즉 백성들인 것을 알지 못하는 듯이 뒤떠들며 달아나고 갇혔다. 그런 중에서도 서로 음모하고, 서로 욕하기는 잊지 않았다. 그들은 벌써 이토 히로부미 통치하에 일본제국의 새 헌법의 일본 간수에게 갖은 인정 없는 학대를 받으라고 자기의 친구이던 혐의 있는 사람을 모함해서 감옥에 집어넣기도 하였다.

이토 히로부미가 하얼빈서 죽기 전후 2, 3년 동안에 융희(대한민국의 마지막 연호, 1907-1910년)의 백성들은 얼마나 모르고 게다가 악형을 당했을까? 만일 하늘이 분명하셔서 모르는 사람에게는 죄가 없어서 형벌이 없다고 할진대 지금부터 10여 년 전 한국 백성들과 및 그 자손을 지금껏 이런 도탄 중에 넣지 않고 도리어 상을 주셨을지도 몰랐을 것이다. 그러나 모르는 것의 죄는 큰 것이다. 그들은 예수만 믿는다고 입으로만 떠들기 땜에 모르고 안 행하는 것에는 죄가 없단 말을 외우고, 백성 즉 자기의 생명을 귀중히 여기지 않기 때문에 서로 학정질하고 서로 무함하는 것만 일삼다가, 그 여러 가지 추태醜態를 낳아놓은, 단지 무식한 것을 모른 탓에 드디어 자유를 잃고 자기를 잃었다. 자기를 잃은 사람은 독립생활을 못 한다. 마치 정신병자가 길바닥을 마음대로 헤매면서도 온갖 자유스러운 추태를 다 하면서도 무엇의 더러운 종인 것과 같아, 이미 자기를 잃은 아무것도 아닌 더러운……그래도 자기라고 부르지 않으면 안 될, 미침의 종이 된 이상에 자기를 잃고 오히려 자기의 종이 되어 온갖 올곧지 못한 행동을 다 하는 이상에는 아무리 자유가 있더라도 그것은 자유가 아니요, 심한 형벌이다.

그것은 정신 있는, 자기를 잃지 않는 사람의 눈에 들키면 분명히 그를 속박지 않고 그대로 두지 않을 것이니까.

그러나 속박을 받는 사람의 견지로 보면 속박하는 사람의 마음은 알 수 없다. 그것과 같이 속박하는 사람도 속박받는 사람의 마음을 애초부터 알 수 없다.

그러므로 서로 모르는 사람은 서로 원수이다.

미친 사람, 안 미친 사람, 무식한 사람, 유식한 사람, 빈한한 사람, 풍부한 사람, 서로 반대되는 사이에는 아무런 이해도 없다.

그와 같이 강한 사람과 약한 사람 사이도 그러하다. 그러므로 강한 자는 약한 자의 맘을 이해치 않고 그를 구속하고, 약한 자는 강한 자를 무척 오해한다. 요컨대, 서로 반대되는 모르는 사람 사이에는 이해라고는 없다.

한일합방 하던 해였다. 탄실의 큰집과 작은집은 한집에 모이게 되었다. 그들은 나라가 약해서 홀로 서 있을 수 없음과 같이 김형우의 집에는 남의 빚 담보를 하였다가 대신 갚고, 두 집을 거느릴수 없으므로 한곳에 모였다. 그 홧김인지 형우는 시름시름 앓다가 바라던 관찰사도 해보지 못하고 세상을 하직하였다. 때는 탄실이가 열네 살 나던 봄이었다. 3학기 시험을 치르고 난 탄실은 기숙사 마루 끝에서 새빨갛게 상기된 얼굴을 어찌할 수 없는 듯이 두 손끝으로 꼭꼭 누르면서 학생들에게,

"나는 왜 이렇게 얼굴이 달아오를까?"

하고 물었다. 그 중에 한 학생은 무슨 불평이 있는지 아무 몰풍스럽게 (성격이나 태도가 정이 없고 냉랭하며 퉁명스러운데가 있다는 뜻),

"너무 공부를 잘하면 그런 법이야. 재봉에 낙제를 해도 공부만 잘해서 일등만 하면 그만이지, 거기에 얼굴이 다는 것까지야 그리 염려될 것 있나?"

"그러게 말이지, 이번에 저 애는 아마 혜숙 언니를 이겨놓을걸."

"그렇고 말구."

"저런 독종에게 누가 이길 수가 있나. 애 자전아, 너는 참 좋겠다."

'자전字典'(한자 하나하나의 발음과 뜻을 적어놓은 책)이라 함은 탄실의 반에서 무슨 글자든지 탄실에게 물으면 다 알아내는 고로 별명을 얻은 것이었다. 탄실은 이런 말을 듣고 불쾌한 듯이 얼굴을 더 붉히며,

"왜 얼굴 단다고 그랬다고 그렇게 사람을 놀려요. 참 별일도 다 많다. 그렇게 한 반에서 나만 놀려대면 무슨 별수나 나나"

하고 성을 내었다.

그때 이 학교에서는 여학생들이 누구든지 심술 잘 부리기와 싸움 잘하기를 퍽 좋아하였다. 아무리 유순한 처녀 아이라도 이 학교에 든 지 한 달

만 될 것 같으면 훌륭한 심술쟁이가 되었다. 그리고 싸움질하기를 예사로 하였다. 그리고 시험 때가 되면 그 장한 질투심을 감출 수 없는 듯이 복습은 아무렇게나 하고, 시기는 힘있는 대로 다 했다. 그런 사람들 가운데 탄실은 그 삼촌이 진명여학교 학감에게,

"저 애는 우리 형님의 서자인데, 자기 외가라고는 죄다 기생 찌꺼기들뿐이니, 외출을 시키지 말고 의복도 지금껏 너무 사치하니, 만일 그런 의복이 올 것 같으면 입히지 말도록 해주시오"

하고 부탁한 말이 학교 안에 퍼져서 그가 미움을 바칠 때마다.

"기생의 딸년."

"저 애 이모는 참 예뻐, 여염 사람 같지 않아."

"나도 좀 그렇게 예뻐 보았으면, 하하."

"참 애는. 너두 기생이 되어보렴. 그래서 분 바르고 비단옷 입으면 예뻐진단다, 하하"

하고 놀렸다. 그는 이날도 그런 말을 듣고 상기되었던 머리가 다시 끓어 넘는 것 같아서 한편 기둥을 잡고 외따로 쓸쓸히 서 있었다. 이때 전보를 든 학감은 달음질해서 기숙사 안으로 뛰어오며,

"탄실아, 이 전보 보아라. 너의 아버지께서 세상을 떠나셨단다"

했다. 탄실은 그러지 않아도 졸도할 듯이 서 있다가, 아뜩해서 쓰러지며,

"아이구"

하고는 코피를 들입다 쏟았다.

그는 이 봄에는 그 정신상에나 육신상에 몹쓸 타격을 받았다. 나라가 힘이 없어 합병을 했다. 같이 있지 못할 집이 돈이 없어 한데로 모이고 서로 불평을 일으켰다. 동무들이 몇 번이나 안 한 일을 했다고 몰았다. 그러면서도 시험 때면 반드시 그의 옆에 와서 그의 답안을 그대로 베꼈다. 이런 일은 선생들이 그의 실력을 아니까 설마 탄실이가 다른 학생의 답안을 베꼈으리라고 의심은 받지 않았으나 언제든지 선생이 그 옆으로 빙빙 돌

며 그 옆에 오는 학생이면 멀리 앉혔다. 그런 일이 있을 때 우매한 질투심 많은 학생들은 탄실이가 선생에게 일러서 그들에게 답안을 보이지 않으려 함이라고 노했다. 그 중에 시우의 친구의 딸이라는 키 작고 얼굴 검은 살기가 등등한 학생은 그런 행패가 더욱 심했다. 그는 이때부터 학대받는 신세였다. 또 한 반에서 뛰어나도록 성적이 좋았는 고로 학제 변경으로 공부가 줄어진 것이 제일 큰 타격이었다.

23

탄실이가 평양 갔을 때는 김형우는 시상판(입관하기 전에 시신을 눕혀놓는 널) 위에 누워 있었다. 온 가족은 하늘이 무너진 듯이 울었다. 그들은 울면서 멀리 공부하느라고 가 있던 정택과 탄실에게,

"아무쪼록 공부 잘해서 돈 모으라"

고 하더란 그 아버지의 유언을 전하였다. 거기서 탄실은 불행한 꿈과 같이 그 부친을 여의고, 홀로 그 편모를 봉양하여야 할 의무를 갖게 되었다. 이로부터 학교에 돌아온 탄실은 밤낮으로 공부를 계속해서 그 편친을 봉양할 의무를 생각했다. 그는 비로소 부친의 사랑도 허사였던 것을 알았다. 자기만을 귀애하던 부친이 그 아들 정택에게만 재산을 남기고, 탄실의 것은 다 전당에 넣은 채로 운명했다. 다만 그 당시에,

"탄실아 탄실아."

두어 마디 부르고 눈을 감았다 한다. 무슨 뜻으로 탄실을 두어 번 불렀는지 모르나 탄실의 이름으로 생명보험회사에 돈을 넣었다던 것도 탄실의 이름이 아니고 정택의 이름인 것을 알았다. 산월은 그 부친이 죽은 지 몇 달 되지 않아서 경성으로 이사를 왔다. 비로소 탄실은 그 지옥 같은 기숙사를 벗어나서 그 모친과 같이 계동에 집을 사고 통학하였다. 이렇게 모녀

와 또 하루건너 왕래하는 이모의 집 사이는 물 샐 틈 없이 단란하였다. 이대로만 가면 무슨 풍파가 또다시야 생기랴마는, 이러한 단란한 중에도, 약함으로써 받지 않으면 아니 될 학대가 사면으로 몰려들어 왔다. 우선 탄실은 학과 변경에 배울 것이 없어졌다. 그는 한일합병 당시에 중등과 1년급이던 것을, 그 이듬해에는 중등과 3년으로 월반을 했어도 도무지 힘들여 배울 것이 없었다. 학교 학생들은 모두 성냈다. 그들이 벌써 몇 해 전에 배워 넘긴 것을 다시 배울 때는 비록 조선말은 아닐지라도 불만인 '이까짓 것' 하는 감정이 사라지진 않았다. 게다가 공부하는 학생들에게는 원수같이 귀찮은 침공, 자수, 조화 또 츠마미(수예 세공의 종류)만 넣어서 참으로 학생들에게 괴로움을 주었다. 학과를 열심히 하는 학생들은 누구나 성을 내고, 외국으로 공부 가기를 원했다. 전일 같으면 탄실도 외국 가고 싶을 때 선뜻 나서지 못할 형편이 아니었으나 지금은 그렇지 못해서, 온 학교에서 게으른 학생이란 별명을 들으면서 모든 수공을 게을리하고, 보고 싶은 책이나 보았다. 그러나 자기보다 성적 좋지 못한 학생들도 일본이나 청국이나 또는 미국으로 공부하러 출발할 때는, 심지가 편안하지 못했다. 그뿐 아니라 어릴 때부터 골수에 사무친 모든 결심을 달할 가망이 아득하였다. 그는 늘 마음속으로,

'나는 남만 못한 처지에서 나서 기생의 딸이니 첩년의 딸이니 하고 많은 업심을 받았다. 그리고 내가 생장하는 나라는 약하고 무식하므로 역사적으로 남에게 이겨본 때가 별로 없었고, 늘 강한 나라의 업심을 받았다. 그러나 나는 이 경우에서 벗어나야 하겠다, 벗어나야 하겠다. 남의 나라 처녀가 다섯 자를 배우고 노는 동안에 나는 놀지 않고 열두 자를 배우고 생각하지 않으면 안 된다. 남이 겉으로 명예를 찾을 때 나는 속으로 실력을 기르지 않으면 안 되겠다. 지금의 한마디 욕, 한 치의 미움이 장차 내 영광이 되도록 나는 내 모든 정력으로 배우고 생각해서 무엇보다도 듣기 싫은 '첩' 이란 이름을 듣지 않을, 정숙한 여자가 되어야 하겠다. 그러려면 나는

다른 집 처녀가 가지고 있는 정숙한 부인의 딸이란 팔자가 아니니 그 대신 공부를 잘해서 그 결점을 감추지 않으면 안 되겠다'

하고 생각하였다. 그러나 지금에 이르러 그는 그렇게 온갖 일을 떠안은 채 그 공부를 할 수 없이 되었다. 그는 참으로 일어 몇 마디나 배워가지고 허투루 꺼덕거리기는 싫었다. 그는 차라리 일어 조금 배우고 바늘과 가위로서 헛되이 시일을 허비할진댄 일본으로 가서 일본 처녀들과 같이 제대로 공부하고 싶었다. 그리고 어느 때 어느 학교에서든지 그래본, 그 힘을 내서 전 반 생도를 꾹 눌러놓고 싶었다. '오냐, 모든 품갚음을 다하는 것은 못 될망정 나 한 사람이 이러한 의지가 종금 다른 사람으로 이어져 그러한 결심을 갖게 되는 날이면 우리는 며칠이 안 되어 남의 압제 아래에서 북을 치며 벗어날 것이다……' 하고 생각하기를 마지않았다. 그는 참으로 일본으로 가고 싶었다. 거기 가 모든 사람을 이기도록 공부해서 품갚음을 하고 싶었다. 한마디의 욕, 한번의 웃음, 한번의 칭찬, 또 여러 번의 매, 여러 가지의 학대일지라도 다 품 갚고 싶었다. 도무지 빚이라고는 싫었다.

24

빚을 싫어하는 탄실에게 적지 않은 빚이 부담되어 있었다. 그것은 그 부친 생시에, 은행 이자를 갚느라고 산월이가 여기저기서 꾸어다 댄 것이었다. 이러한 것을 산월은 정택에게 말했으나 유산을 적지 않게 남긴 그들은 대답하지 않고 산월에게만 떠밀어 말겼다. 산월은 지금에 이르러 부러진 죽지를 단 몸 같아서 참으로 난처하였다. 그의 수중에 돈이라고는 도무지 남은 것이 8천원 가량 될까 말까 하였다. 그래도 세상이 알기에 많은 재산을 장치한줄 알았다. 평양서 김형우 생시에 빚을 지운 사람들은 서울까지 따라와서 산월 모녀를 괴롭게 했다. 그리고 속히 갚지 못할 형편을 말할

때는,

"탄실이를 기생이나 부치지요"

하고 타일렀다.

"기생에 넣을 것 같으면 담박 명기 소리 듣게 되리다. 얼굴도 고와, 재조도 있어, 왜 저 애를 기생에 넣지 않아요?"

했다.

탄실은 이런 말을 들으면 불같이 성을 냈다. 그는 전일에 기숙사에서 자랄 때처럼 남의 말만 듣고 허허 낙종(기쁜 마음으로 복종함)하는 **좋은** 아이도 아니었다. 그는 날이 오램을 따라서 무엇이든지 다 바로잡고 싶은 처녀가 되었다. 한마디의 모욕을 백 마디로 갚고 싶었다. 이때에 이르러 그의 마음속에는 어릴 때부터 그 속에 뿌리박은 종교는 싹도 없었다. 그는 살기가 등등해서,

"당신네들이나 기생이 되려거든 되고 말려거든 말지 왜 남더러 기생이 되란다는 말이에요? 아무리 돈푼이나 남에게 지웠기로 그렇게 사람을 멸시하고 마음이 편하시오?"

하고 야단을 했다. 산월은 전일에 온 집 안을 끓이던 호기를 지금은 어디로 감추고 손님에게 함부로 야단하는 딸에게 빌듯이,

"탄실아, 그래서는 못쓴다. 저 애가 원, 그래서야 쓰나"

하고 반은 웃으면서 손님의 낯을 쳐다보고,

"저 애보고는 그러지 마세요. 저것이야 무슨 죄가 있겠소? 죄가 있으면 죽은 아비에게나 살아서 이렇게 된 어미에게나 있지. 저것이야 무엇을 알겠소"

하고 사정했다.

손님은 이런 때는 할 수 없이 양보를 하고, 그 이튿날 얼마간 이자와 노비를 얻어가지고 평양으로 갔다.

탄실의 모친이 서울로 온 지 1년이 된 뒤에 탄실은 진명여학교를 4회로

졸업했다. 그는 수예는 모두 낙제였다. 탄실의 모친은 꿈이 아닌가 하고 기뻐했다. 하나 겨우 열다섯 살 된 탄실은 아직도 산 같은 지식욕을 제어할 수가 없어서 몹시 번뇌하였다. 탄실의 모친은 이와 반대로, 탄실이가 졸업을 했으니 지금은 서울 어느 소학교에서 교원 노릇을 해서 살림을 도울 줄 알았다. 그러나 그 봄이 지나고, 여름이 왔어도, 그는 선 앵두 빛 같은 얼굴을 하루에 열두 번씩 푸르게 붉게 변하면서 학교 담임선생이 몇 번이나 모교 교원이 되어달라고 청했어도 종래 말을 듣지 않았다가 하루는 그 모친 앞에서 이런 말을 하였다.

"어머니 나 돈 한 50원만 있으면 좋겠어요."

"그 돈은 뭘 하게?"

"내 구두가 헐었는데 서울 안에 여학생들이란 여학생은 다 흰 구두를 신었지만 나만 검정 것을 그대로 신었어요. 그리고 시계도 다들 금시계인데, 나만 그때 작은아버지가 작은어머니하고 바꾸어준 은시계예요. 그것을 금시계로 바꾸었으면 좋겠어요"

"그런 것을 다 하려면, 50원쯤 가지고야 되겠니?"

"시계를 새 금시계로 바꾸려면 모자라겠지만 마침 금시계 가진 동무가 내 시계와 바꾸자니까, 얼마 좀더 주고 바꾸면 되겠지요. 그대로 바꾸자하기는 염치 없으니까요"

했다. 그런 이야기가 있은 지 사흘 만에 그 모친은,

"네 장래 옷가지나 지어두어야 할 것을 그만 네게 준다. 그러니 옷은 네가 벌어서 장만하도록 하자"

하면서 돈 50원을 주었다. 그 돈 50원을 받아 든 탄실은,

"사람의 일이란 알 수 없어요. 어쩌면 내가 이만 돈을 쓰는 데 어머니께서 염려를 하시지 않으면 안 되게 되었는지"

하고 혼잣말같이 중얼거리다가 흑흑 느꼈다.

그러고 그 며칠 동안은 몸이 괴롭다고 잠을 못 자다가 해쓱한 얼굴에

치가 떨리는 듯한 음성으로,

"어머니 내 김 정위 댁에 다녀오리다. 그 집 딸 숙희가 일본을 간다니 저 내 가죽 가방도 좀 빌려줄 겸 다녀오리다. 저 가방을 꼭 다섯 달 동안만 빌리자는데요. 전일에는 숙희와 나와 의가 좋지 못했지만 지금은 퍽 친해졌어요"

했다. 그 모친은 생각하기를 김 정위네라면 도깨비란 이와 사촌 형제였고, 또 부자였으니까 탄실이가 그렇게까지 친절하지 않아도 좋을 것인 고로,

"애 탄실아, 너의 아버지도 그 집안사람들하고 사귀었다가 실패를 하였는데 너까지……"

이런 말을 이르려다가 그쳤다.

하나 탄실은 그동안 절교 상태에 들어 있던 그 숙부의 집에를 매일같이 왕래하면서 무슨 일을 의논하였다.

그 숙부는 경성서 어느 왕의 부무관을 다니고 있었다. 그 형이 죽은 뒤에는 산월의 집에는 아주 발을 뚝 끊었으나 감히 탄실을 미워하진 않았다.

25

지금부터 10여 년 전에 초가을 아침이었다. 북선北鮮 방면으로 귀성하였던 학생들이 들켜서 남대문역에 내릴 때, 그 반대로 플랫폼을 향하여 무엇을 손에 잔뜩 들고 갈팡질팡 달아나는 여학생 두 명이 있었다. 한 학생은 키가 작고 검고 푸른 얼굴에 살눈썹 긴 눈동자가 휘 풀어지려다가 억지로 푸르고 검게 흰자위 검은자위를 갈라놓은 듯한 눈을 가지고, 한 학생은 끊어질 듯한 허리에 오동통한 뺨과 극히 둥글고 맑은 눈동자를 가졌다. 키 작고 얼굴 푸른 학생은 열일곱이나 되고, 얼굴 둥글고 눈 둥근 학생은

많이 나야 열여섯 살이 났을까 말았을까 하였다. 이 두 학생은 한데 뭉켜서 비틀어 맨 것처럼 갈팡질팡하다가 나이 어리고 키 큰 학생이 얼른 앞서서 먼저 달아나려 했다. 키 작은 학생은 심술이 통통이 나서,

"얘 탄실아, 너 일본 가서도 그러련. 어찌 너가 먼저 가니"

하고 불렀다. 키 큰 학생은 미안한 듯이 그 뺨을 새빨갛게 물들이고

"내 먼저 가서 자리 잡아놓으마"

하고 다시 두어 발자국 달아났다. 키 작은 학생은 다시 목멘 소리로

"탄실아, 나는 네가 이럴 줄은 정말 몰랐다. 어쩌면 이러니"

하고 다시 불렀다. 키 크고 어린 학생은 할 수 없는 듯이 서너 발자국 돌아서 오면서,

"너는 기차를 타보지 않아서 모르는구나. 그렇지만 자리를 먼저 잡아놓지 않으면 부산까지 서서 갈지도 모르는데 어쩌자고 그러니? 너처럼 뒤뚱뒤뚱 걸어오다가 누구를……"

키 작은 학생은 무엇을 잊었던 듯이 깜짝 놀라며,

"이 애야, 그럼 먼저 가서 자리를 잡아놓아라. 너는 어쩌면 그런 꾀가 나니. 내가 잘못했다"

하였다. 키 큰 학생은 그 두 뺨에 옴폭하니 우물을 지우고 쌍끗 웃어 보이면서,

"그래"

하고는 사람들 틈에 끼어서 먼저 달아나서, 경부선 차 3등실 한편에 자리를 잡았다. 이 학생은 김탄실이었다. 그는 차마 그 모친에게 일본 갈 것을 말하지 못하고, 어떤 동무와 같이 달아날 작정으로 경부선에 올라앉았다.

그는 그동안에 그의 숙부와 같이 일본 간 후의 일을 의논하였다.

거기……동경에는 길 참령이라는 술 잘 먹는 군인이 있고, 또 태모라는 학력 우등이고 품행 방정한 학생이 있다고 그 숙부가 편지를 써서 주었다.

그들이 신바시新橋역에 이르렀을 때, 정희순이라는 탄실과 동행한 친구

의 오라버니가 마중을 왔다. 저는 보기에 24, 5세 되는 준절한(위엄있고 정중한) 청년 같았다.

　그들이 동경에 간 지 며칠 안 되어서 정희순이라는 학생은 상업학교에 들고, 탄실은 단계를 밟아서 대학에 들려고 시부야滿谷에 있는 상반여학교에 들었다.

　탄실은 동경 오기 전에 바로 그 여름에 그 숙부의 집에서 어떤 청년을 알게 되었다. 태영세라는 일본사관학교 학생이라 하였다. 전일에는 고학생으로 경성에 왔으나, 차차 공부를 잘해서 주인의 눈에 들어 일본으로까지 가게 되었다. 무엇인지 그 군인 학생은 혼인하자는 곳이 모아 쌓으면 산더미라도 되리 만치 많다고하였다. 탄실은 그런 말을 듣고 경쟁을 좋아하는 어린 마음이 선뜻 놀라졌다. 그런 많은 사람들 가운데 어떤 처녀가 뽑혀 그의 부인이 될지는 모르지만 그런 자리에 앉게 되는 이는 보통 사람보다 반드시 우월優越하리라고 생각했다.

　그러면서 그렇게 많은 경쟁자가 있는 사람에게 그중 초라한 자기를 소개한 그 숙부의 마음이 알 수 없었다. 그는 동경을 온 뒤로 태영세의 일을 많이 생각하고 떠들었다. 어떤 부자의 딸과도 혼인 말이 있고, 어떤 대신의 딸과도 혼인 말이 있고, 어떤 자작의 딸, 남작의 딸과도 혼인 말이 있다고 하였다. 그러나 탄실의 생각에 그는 관청 안에 들어온 촌닭 같다고 생각하였다. 그것은 탄실이가 태영세를 언뜻 보기에 그리 잘난 것 같지 않았으니까……

　탄실은 맘으로는 동경에 공부하러 왔지만, 형편으로는 필경 근심하러 온 모양이었다.

26

 탄실이가 상반학교 기숙사에 든 지 1주일 지나서 어떤 공일날 태영세가 군복을 입고 탄실을 찾아왔다. '태영세太英世'란 명함을 받아 든 탄실의 손은 연고 모르게 바르르 떨렸다. 그는 응접실도어를 열까 말까 하다가 어린 용기를 다 내서 문을 열었다.

 그 가운데는 키 작고 얼굴 납대대한 작디작은 군인이 서 있었다. 탄실은 그 작은 군인을 보았을 때 지금까지 경험해보지 못한 무서운 생각으로 그 몸이 지진같이 떨렸다. 무엇인지 아주 남이라고는 말할 수 없는 듯한 친함을 주면서 도수장에 짐승을 이끌고 가는 백정도 저렇지 않을까 하는 의심을 일으켰다. 그 남자의 세포 하나하나가 전부 쇠나 돌로 되어 있지 않나 하는 의심을 일으켰다. 가늘고 작은 그 눈은 넘치는 듯한 정력을 모으고 또 모아서 빨갛고 검게 꼭 찔러놓은 듯하였다. 얼굴은 24, 5세의 남자의 것으로는 극히 왜소하였으나 머리통은 오지동이같이 위가 퍼진 것이 지극히 컸다. 탄실은 이렇게 미숙한 듯한데 자기보다 6년이나 위 되는, 작디작은 남자의 머리와 눈이 맹수의 그것과 같이 무서우면서도 경멸할 수 없어 보였다. 그런 중에 그 남자의 태도란 지극히 침착하고 냉정하면서도 말끝 돌릴 때마다 한마디씩 친함을 주었다. 게다가 또 그 남자는 눈웃음을 지었다.

 그 남자는 필경 잘나거나 곱지는 않았을지언정, 어수룩한 촌 처녀의 마음을 끌기로서는 전부가 합격되어 있다고도 할 만하였다. 거기 따라오는 공부 잘한다는 명예와 혼인하자는 곳 많다는 인망이 적었을 것 같으면 그가 탄실의 마음에는 들어 보이진 않았을 것이다. 그러나 태영세라는 남자는 어쩐지 탄실의 마음에는 무시무시하게 생각되었다. 그 조금씩 친함을 주는 듯한 말솜씨도, 그 명예, 그 인망도 결코 탄실의 무시무시한 생각을 감해주지는 못했다. 그러면서도 그 냉정함과 침착함으로 사람을 이끌어 동댕이쳐버릴 듯한 것이 한없이 무서웠다.

"삼촌님께서 편지를 하셨기에 찾아왔습니다."

"어느 날 서울서 떠나셨습니까? 8월 25일 날 남대문역에서 떠나셨어요? 그럴 것 같으면 나보다 하루 뒤져서 오셨군……"

"그렇게 어머니 승낙도 없이 떠나오시느라고……무섭지 않으셨어요? 남자도 내기 어려운 용기를 내셨습니다그려."

"나는 전일에 삼촌님께서 계시던 학교에 있으니, 혹시 무슨 일이 있거든 그리로 편지해주시오"

하는 말들이 약간 명령적이면서, 그 큰 머릿속으로 우러나서 멋쩍은 입속을 굴러 나오는 것을 생각하면 치가 떨리도록 차고 매웠다.

탄실은 태영세가 처음으로 왔다 간 뒤에 이 복잡한 인상을 제치고 반가운 생각도 들었다. 그것은 타관에 나선 사람이, 고향 사람을 보는 듯한 감정이었다. 그런 중에 동행한 정희순은 학교가 다른 탓인지 자주 만날 기회가 없었다. 다만 정희순의 지극히 준절한 얼굴과 큰 오라버니가 어린 누이에게 대하는 듯한 태도로, 하루건너 혹은 이틀 건너 찾아와서,

"하도 외로울 터이니까 또 울지나 않나 하고 찾아왔소"

하고 한참 동안 옷 입는 것, 머리 빗는 것, 일본 사람 대하는 태도를 말하고 갔다. 이보다 조금 전에 이미 탄실은 동경에 와서 그 마음이 누그러졌다. 거기는 많은 원인이 있었다. 첫째 일본 사람들은 대단히 친절했다. 동무들이고 선생들이고 탄실의 일이라면 아무리 어려운 일이라도 손수 도움을 주었다. 그리고 아무 곳이든지 데리고 가서 구경시켰다. 그들 중에 어떤 사람은 '귀여운 아이'라고 부르고, 또 어떤 사람은 '아름다운 아이'라고 불렀다.

그는 서울 진명여학교에서는 한 번도 경험해보지 않은 따뜻한 인정을 받는 느낌을 얻었다. 그는 지금에 이르러 그 모친의 애정이 극히 아름다운 것인 줄을 알게 되고, 또 태영세가 좀더 친절해도 좋을 줄 생각했다. 그러나 이러한 감정이 눈물 없이 사려 없이 술술 일어나지는 않았다.

27

멀리 고향을 떠난 탄실은 그 모친에게서나 그 삼촌에게서 온 편지를 뜯어 볼 때마다 도저히 눈물 없이는 지날 수 없는 두 가지의 감격을 받았다.

그 모친의 편지는 이왕 간 바에는 열심히 공부를 잘해서 성공해 가지고 오라고 하는 말이 거듭거듭 적혀서 탄실에게 무거운 짐을 지고 긴 고개를 넘어야 할 무거운 생각을 일으키고, 그 삼촌의 편지는 할 수 있는 대로 태영세의 말을 씨서 저에게 친함을 갖도록 함으로 태영세에게 향한 의심과 두려움에 더 이상 시달리기가 지난한(지극히 어려운) 것을 알게 되었다. 탄실은 쓸쓸하고 적적한 생각에 쏠려 먼 타향의 외로운 날들이 오래됨에 따라 사람의 정이 그리웠다. 어리던 때에 어머니가 품어주던 것, 아버지가 손목을 이끌어주던 것, 오빠가 업어주던 것, 서울 있을 때에 그 외조모가 틈틈이 먹을 것을 싸다가 주던 것, 어렸을 때에 반갑던 생각이란 생각은 모조리 꿀에 재었던 밀감 껍질같이 따뜻하고 달콤한 것을 그리는 처녀의 가슴속에서 하박하박 절어서 나왔다.

탄실은 모든 옛일을 생각할 때, 어느 날 서울 비원秘苑 안을 걸을 때 같은 황금빛 길을 배회하는 것 같았다. 지금에 이르러 그에게는 그의 옛일이 모두 다 훌륭한 영화였다.

그는 실상 지금은 금전상으로 받은 곤란도 적지 않았다. 매삭 내는 월사나 식비를 밀리도록 내는 형편은 아니었지만, 용돈에 몰려서 남몰래 긴 소데(일본 옷소매)로 눈물 씻을 때도 많았다. 공부는 하노라고 해도, 큰 번민을 등에 지고 또 처음으로 이성에 대해서 생각하게 된 그는 늘 일본 사람에게 친절을 받고 위로를 받으면서 조선서 결심한 일본인에 향한 복수, 또 그 큰집과 빚쟁이에게 품었던 원혐까지라도 쉽사리 흐려졌다.

그는 조선 있을 때같이 입술을 깨물고 공부하지 않았다. 아니 그런 것이 아니라 못했단 말이 옳을 것이다. 그는 공부하려고 책을 들면, 태영세의 언어 행동이 또다시 또다시 눈에 벌어서 책을 그만 덮게 될 때도 많았다. 이때가 되어 아무 아름다운 곳도 없는 듯한, 게다가 키까지 무척 작은 듯한 남자를 아무 결점도 보지 않고 무척 그리기를 마지않았다. 처녀의 - 통히 남자를 보지 못하고, 단지 혼인을 할 것 같으면, 여러 곳에 이르지도 말고 꼭 마음에 맞는 한곳에 일렀다가 되면 하고 되지 않으면 평생을 독신으로 지내서, 기생의 딸로서 난봉이 나기는 쉬우리라고 한 말대꾸를 하려고 생각하던 탄실의 마음이 다만 맹목적으로 키 작고 보잘것없는 태영세를 꽉 붙들고 싶었다. 하나 그 마음속 맨 밑에는 여전히 공부하고 싶었다. 모두 그것으로 온갖 일을 부탁하고 보수하려고 죽도록 공부하고 싶었다.

그러나 공부란 것은 사실 좀 여유 있는 연극인 것을 그는 전혀 알지 못하고 경험했다. 다만 '내가 게을러졌다. 내가 타락하여간다' 하는 깊은 반성에서 나오는 듯한 말이 자칫하면 사람 앞에서도 그 입모습을 움직일 듯이 그의 마음속에서 머리 꼭대기까지 계속 돌았다. 그는 어느 공일날 태영세가 왔을 때 그만 그 말을 입 밖에 내었다. 발뒤축까지 세 묶음에 묶어서 늘어뜨린 머리채를 겨드랑이 아래로 끌어다 쓰다듬으며,

"저는 아마 공부를 못 할 것 같아요. 타락한 까닭인지 전같이 공부가 되지를 않아요"

하고 타락이란 새 문자를 써보는 새 맛을 볼 때 홀연히 태영세는 그 얼굴이 빨개지며,

"도쿄가 넓기는 넓어. 이런 곳에 이런 조선 것이 있을 줄 누가 알까? 요새도 그 동무의 오라비라는 불도그같이 생긴 것이 오오?"

했다. 이 말에 탄실은 예사롭지 못한 것을 깨달으면서도 얼른,

"아이, 와요. 어느 때는 밤 든 때에 와서 기숙사감의 눈치를 보아요"

했다. 그때에 남자는 입안이 쓴 듯이 입맛을 다시다가,

"나는 가볼 데가 있어 가요"

하고 일어섰다. 탄실은 그 남자가 무슨 연고로 그렇게 쓸쓸히 일어서는지

는 분명히 모르면서 그 말이 시작되기 전에 남자가 한 말을 그대로 받아서,

"저 길 참령 댁에 안 가세요? 저는 한 번 갔지만 길이 분명치 않아요"

했다. 하나 남자는 그대로 쓸쓸하게,

"그럼 갑시다"

하고 문득 일어서면서 재미없는 얼굴을 하였다. 그러한 태영세의 행동을 탄실은 이상하다고 생각은 하면서도 그 원인을 알 길이 없었다. 그러나 이후 몇 해가 지나서 탄실과 영세 사이에 큰 변이 일어났을 때, 모든 일이 발각되었다. 그는 약한 가슴을 움켜지고 모든 책임을 그 한 몸에 졌다. 세상도 그러하도록 그를 몰았다.

탄실은 얼마나 눈물 많은 처녀가 되었는지. 일시는 정신 이상까지 생겼다.

28

그것은…… 탄실이가 열여덟 살 나던 봄이었다. 일본 시부야라는 동리에 있는 상반여학교라는 고등학교에서는 졸업식 할 때를 당해서 시험을 한 글자 헛하지 않고도 각 신문지에 아주 이상히 떠들리고, 또 당인이 어디로 숨어버린 고로 졸업장을 주지 못하고 선생들이 일변으로 신문사에 가서 묻기도 하고, 그 학생이 있던 기숙사에 탐지도 하였다. 하나 사실을 살필수록 그 학생의 평시로 보면 어울리지 않는 추악한 일이 들출수록 쳐들리어 나왔다. 학교 선생들은 그만 그 학생의 이름을 졸업생 명부록에서 지워내었다. 그 학생의 이름은 김탄실이었다.

탄실은 이보다 1년 전 겨울에 학비 곤란으로 길 참령 집에 가 있은 일이 있었다. 길 참령 집에는 모든 것이 과부의 외로운 딸의 것으로 비교해보면 왕궁과 같이 호사하였다. 길 참령 처는 삼십이 될락 말락 한 독부 같은 일본 미인이었다. 한마디도 헛하지 않는 날카롭도록 민첩한 말솜씨, 나른나

른 걸어 다니는 버들 같은 몸매, 모든 것으로 모두 사람을 이끌지 않고는 가만있지 않는 태도였다. 동리의 늙은이들은 입을 삐죽하면서도 그에게,

"옥상, 옥상 (부인을 예우하여 부르는 일본어)"

하고 머리를 숙였다. 장사들도 밖에서 말만 듣고는 조선 사람하고 사는 계집이라고 한층 내려다보다가 그를 만나보고는 그만 허리를 굽혔다. 또 동경 와서 공부하는 조선 유학생들도 처음에 말만 듣고는,

"그까짓 것 길 참령 같은 것에게 태운 여자가 무엇이 잘났을꼬"

하고 함부로 말짓거리 하다가는 동무가 하도 칭찬하는 바람에 이끌려서 길 참령 집을 방문하고 돌아와서는 기어이 이구동성으로 입에 침이 마르도록 칭찬하면서,

"여자는 일본 것이라야 쓰겠다. 에, 우리 조선 여자들 그것이 뭐야? 더러운 꼴들을 하고 게다가 뻣뻣하기는 왜 그렇게들 뻣뻣한지"

하고, 자기들의 누이와 엄마와 할머니들을 욕했다. 처음에 길 참령과 길 참령 부인은 탄실을 심히 사랑해서, 그가 학비 곤란으로 그 어머니의 돈 보내지 못할 터이니 속히 돌아오라는 편지를 받아 들고 울 때, 그 집에 와서 머물게 하였다. 한집에 있게 된 길 참령 부인과 탄실은 퍽 친해서 어떤 때는 길 참령 부인이 피아노를 치고 탄실이가 순한 음성으로 노래를 했다. 또 어떤 때는 시비공원과 아자부(도쿄 인근의 지명)를 어스름 저녁때 단둘이 산보하였다. 길 참령 부인은 탄실을 이끌고 다니면서 여러 사람에게 소개하기를 좋아했다. 탄실도 그와 같이 아름다운 부인과 친척 사이같이 하고 다니는 것이 결코 싫은 일은 아니었다.

그들은 그 겨울이 다 지나도록 사이가 좋았다. 하나 그 봄에 길 참령 부인은 그 오라버니가 무슨 실패를 하고 빚에 몰려서 자살한 뒤에 그 조카딸을 데려다 돌보기로 했다. 그 여자는 이름을 '하나꼬'라 하고, 살색 희고 눈이 우둥퉁한 탄실과 같은 또래의 처녀였다.

이 처녀는 대판에서 나서 대판에서 겨우 고등소학교를 졸업했다. 그 처

녀는 당연한 일이겠지만 그 아주머니의 눈에 알뜰히 들려고 하는 것 같았다. 탄실은 그것을 어찌할 수 없는 일이라고 생각은 하면서도 이따금 이따금 그 처녀가 자기의 말을 해치려고 하는 것을 보면 참을 수 없이 쓸쓸해서 눈물을 흘렸다.

그는 겨울 동안이 지나고 봄이 오기까지 수십여 차나 그 삼촌에게 편지를 해서 학비를 좀 도와달라고 청구하였으나, 아무 분명한 답장이 없었다. 태영세도 탄실의 초췌하여 하는 양을 동정해서, 탄실의 삼촌에게 학비를 보내도록 편지를 하였으나, 분명한 대답은 없고, 속히 태영세가 탄실과 결혼하기를 빙빙 돌려서 청구했다.

태영세는 그런 명망을 이고, 그런 영화를 지고, 도저히 탄실과 약혼할 희망은 도저히 일어나지 않았다. 저는 탄실이가 마음속으로 바라는 것같이 단지 공부하고 싶어 했다. 그는 너무나 넘칠 듯한 지식욕과 그 후에 반드시 얻어질 자기의 영화 때문에 스스로 황홀해서, 한 옛적에 자기 주인이 하던 젊은 첩같이 아리따운, 자기보다 20년 아래나 되는 계집을 이상화했다. 그리하여 저는 자기보다 겨우 여섯 살 어린 탄실이가 게다가 키도 크고, 뼈마디가 늘진늘진한게 좀 꺼리었다. 또 그때는 세상 사람들이 키 작고 가는 여자를 아름답게 보던 때였다.

(1924년 6월 14일~7월 15일)

Seonrae

The afternoon sky of August cleared up, devoid of clouds.

As the breeze gently slipped in between the poplar leaves, fringed by the body of wall at Gijareung (Tomb in Pyeongyang), the round shadows of light and shadows of leaves frisked about hoveringly above the sports grounds and the spur of hill spotted with white.

As if it was an evening scenery of the school sports grounds, students gathered in the school yard without teachers around, due to not being able to fight off boredom while on vacation and amidst serenity and loneliness, they absent-mindedly leapt around to hide their subtle emotions when no one saw them.

Up to this point, while nature seemed to say something to life, as a person has had a history of having aged already, one ended up not asking nature to teach the person any secret as one refused to lend an ear.

The story that started here was a funny incident, where people sat together and decided to talk about what they had hid from each other.

At one side of the flat sports grounds, in the office of the empty school whose area was made higher through the layers of the stone over-bridge, the exchange of laughter of a man and a woman at times mingled and was heard as it got carried by the wind.

The teachers that gathered here opened a workers' meeting ahead of the new semester. Then, they put together the desk they each owned and in a place, where the cool wind swept in and out, partly to forget the heat, they set the table in a rectangle and the eight teachers sat around, beginning their conversation in the order that they took a seat.

In the third time, at last, after being pestered by teacher Park, the school's music teacher found his story, which was one he shared since a long time ago. As he did so, he sniffed his nose and rolled his bright eyes with a soft expression, a habit of his that could be frequently seen.

Anyone sitting in this office jested about it being luck, luck when teacher Han and teacher Park first talked about fishing and hunting, but now, as teacher Kim put on a silent and solemn demeanor again, they tucked up their collar and showed their intent to listen carefully. Eventually, at the table of eight with two people each facing, the music teacher drank the ice-water poured by the school's errand boy and as if to put off the apprehensive expression that was becoming sizeable, he once bent his chest, looking down at the table with seemingly wretched eyes like a man intending to take his own life. Then, he straightened his chest and once again, manifested the radiant luster of his eyes and with such lustrous gaze, he said,

"Ah, I remember her name being Seonrae, but the first time I met the inscrutable woman was once in the middle of the road going from Karasuma Station of Kyoto in Japan to Kumanoshi Station.

(Though I'm not sure if among you, Mr. Park has a rough assumption on this.)

While it was spring, as it was seriously a capricious weather, on a certain day, it was warm like the shiny eyeballs of a cat and some other day, it was cold to the point that even my joints ached from the chill. I was at a loss as if I'd forget to eat and sleep, asking at the time, Should I be a musician or an artist? as I stood at a crossroad, divided into two. Already, as I diverged from the old belief, the vague thought of becoming a conventionally good man of service to society dissipated. And merely, I was indecisive over whether to shoot high in a music concert or an art exhibition, like a young sheep that couldn't hear the sound of its master's flute, wondering where to be drawn to. So, at some time, the orchestral music that assembled a variety of sounds resonated with my heart and at other times, I was infatuated with the eye-opening shapes.

At the time, finally, in Tokyo, as it was when I was researching with great passion about expressionism, newspapers and magazines advertised such an ism and opened art exhibitions of the same artistic style here and there, which brought astonished looks by everyone. And thus, new praises were bestowed to Gough and Gaugin and shifted to catch the attention of even those who read only the Sunday supplement to newspapers with prints of Ukiyo-e (Type of Japanese art that used to flourish between the 17th and 19th century, which involved a creation of woodblock prints or paintings of historical scenes and folk tales). As such, it was a time of struggle when people who felt irritated with 'naturalism,' 'verism,' or 'realism' had their bodies plunged in the middle of huge chaos as midway through 'neoromanticism,' which they had tried to walk through, they turned their whole upper body away and failed to tread it.

Also, it was a time when while going from 'impressionism' 'post-impressionism', 'futurism' to 'expressionism,' one was shoved and dispersed around while not being able to deviate from the path.

All the while, as I was attracted to 'Variation' or 'Imagination' of Kandinsky, the color and line that was used was entirely like a musical structure, melody, and it was eye-opening. So, when attempting to paint something, I tried to get out of the former theory of naturalism and instead, learned nature, thought of a phrase to manifest nature, scoffed, got mad, pondered on the Greek art, ruminated on the greatest history of mankind, and became so ecstatic that I would go leaping around. Yet, in reality, when I held the brush to paint, all the thoughts left me and it was as if they didn't even turn around and look back. All the more, because every line that was borrowed from music could not be captured by my fingers, while I was trying to use the cries of the great man Beethoven, sadly, a line even inferior to the cries of a donkey was drawn and the considerable sorrow of Chopin turned out to be a line even lowlier than the moaning of a drunkard that left one breathless. Ah, later on, even the drowsy melody of Mozart that was like the white frost-like feathers did not listen to my words. While I felt extreme anger and sorrow there, as even that wasn't pure, there was nothing I could keep under control. At such time, on some day of March when the snow came and melted, without ever having the time to fall to the ground, as if I got mad at how my ideas could not come together and my poor painting skill, even when I had nothing to prepare, I went all the way to Sanjo of Karatsu. On that particular day, as the day was gloomy and my head was spinning, the obnoxious heat from my entire body was on the verge of profusely lifting its steam through the top of my ragged Japanese clothes.

With my head spinning in such a shape like an entangled hemp thread, I went all the way to Sanjo without it being clear as to whether or not something happened in the morning. Then, I was on my way back, riding a tram, and reached a station."

After speaking up to this point, the music teacher let out a deep sigh. His eyes blurred like the spring sky that was about to rain. As the teachers that sat around listening to the story were allured by the wide plaintive musicality of the music teacher, they appeared merely hoping for the long unreleased, stashed clues to be released even more gently and neatly.

"It would all occur to you that she was so beautiful as you could see from how even now, I couldn't translate her appearance into words. No matter what it is, it was a face I have once seen before. While it was not really clear if it was from a dream unspoken yet that only I saw, when she got on the tram of the Kawabata Station, the three women who had been standing together in the station bent their heads all the way to the tip of their toes and bowed. Upon brief glance, she looked like a woman from a house of an imperial family or a duke or a marquis. Yet, she didn't seem to be a completely oblivious maiden.

In the midst of getting on the tram that is like a faint dream at the time, it is vague as if I am thinking back to a dream and while I constantly ponder on it like my own breathing, which I ought to always be conscious of, I seem to also forget it. At the time, Seonrae was certainly sitting in front of me obliquely.

I realized that my entire body was becoming invigorated at that moment. The big shape of her eyes that seemed to be clearly flowing and that upright, well-suited long, slender figure. It was merely that the cool tune I had not heard for a long time seemed to be flowing into my ear. Even so, as the thought that I had once before seen such a person somewhere was rather vivid, I closed my eyes in front of her and reflected on all the women I had met in the middle of all the streets and houses, and examined them one by one. At the time, no matter how absorbed I was, it would not dawn on me instantly. All the while, my cheeks seemed to get some kind of ray and I felt like I was in agony. My eyes blinked wide open. At that moment, in the middle of the street, the woman (Seonrae) met my gaze and it was as if a big flamelet was being stoked. After that one moment, her eyes gradually became cold again, then changed to an expression that was on the verge of smiling, and shifted to a derisive look. It also struck me that she seemed to be greeting me like she knew me.

Ah, ah, even now, there are numerous times that such a cool expression alone brightly lights up the way wherever I go. Yet, it is merely to that extent and afterward, even as I close my eyes and think of her face, I could not at all conjure it up. It is just that her behavior seemed to leave me with a wide array of plaintive tunes. Even now, the moment I think of her, instead of a fixed shape, a tune that seems to be flowing would just burst out of my mouth.

The second time I met her was at the entrance of an art exhibition near Kyoto university. Everyone, could you presume what I would now say about seeing how she stood as I entered the art exhibition? Would the woman perhaps have stood in front of her beautiful portrait, putting on all sorts of coquettish behavior? If not, would she have stood shimmeringly in front of a goddess or a saintess that was just like her? Do you think of her doing such things? It wasn't this or that. I submitted my artwork to the art exhibition. I called the artwork 'Dancing Woman' and had drawn a dancing Japanese gisaeng (Woman of low-class social background who entertained men of upper-class with music, conversation, and poetry). I set out to significantly change the ideology and technique into musical ones. Please don't be surprised. The beautiful woman was wearing a cold expression in front of my painting and wrapped up in light clothes that flapped, she stood, looking with cool eyes for some time. She stood staring at my painting for a long while like that and while she may have known or not known that I was standing behind her, she poured these words over my painting in very precise Korean words.

'A great deal of tricks must've gone in here. But pitifully, it looks like someone who's rather lost her way.'

Everyone, how shocked must I have been at that moment? As it was May, while it was when the heat intensified, I felt like an icy water had been poured over the top of my head all the way to the tips of my toes on the 11th and 12th month of the lunar calendar. When I was so bewildered that I was standing as if I was rid of my soul, she seemed to look back once and in no time, she was out of the art exhibition. The moment I came to my senses, from outside, the sound of the car turning its wheels could be heard. That day, I returned home and as it felt like my head had rammed into a rock, with the look of a half-wit, I lapsed into illness, which dragged on for several days. It was a few days later. A letter asking if I would sell the painting came from the teacher who recommended my painting to the art exhibition. Conscientiously speaking, at the time, I would've turned it down as I already lost the confidence to send others the painting. But as the contents of my life did not live up to the extent that others looked up to me as the child of a rich family, I could not bear it, out of my destitute circumstances. And so, I replied to the teacher that it was okay to sell with a greatly modest intention. Later, after some time, as I received with my own hands an exorbitant sum of money that was several times greater than the value of the painting, a rather shameful thought cropped up and so, I asked the art teacher as to who paid such a huge sum of money to buy the painting. At the time, the teacher said that his friend purchased it and it may have been bought as a gift for someone. I didn't find the need to ask anymore. So, when the money came into my hands, I considered it to be reasonable, bought a lot of painting materials and canvas, and made a sketch of the nature by a brook in Kamogawa of Kyoto. One day, after quite studiously painting a picture of the Kamogawa bridge, when I looked at it, it was merely a space that had been scrubbed black with a brush, casting into doubt as to whether or not I was in the right state of mind painting it. There was not a single clear line that could be seen. As I found it to be so strange, I suspected as to whether I was going insane. But still, no matter how much I inspected, I could not find anything of suspicion in my body. The following day, once again, the ferocious assiduousness was aroused and as if to hope for a strange miracle, I went to the same place, set up the easel, and painted. And to test my strength, I assessed the line one by one and after painting the bridge, the forest, the path to the forest through the bridge, as well as the outstanding villa of the Roman architecture in the forest, this time, the villa that I had painted a moment ago was erased completely white. At that moment, it was so absurd that even if I tried to cry, I'd cry over reasonable things. Tears wouldn't even spring up. So, I folded what I had been drawing, slung it over the top of my shoulder, and without even turning back, returned home.

The following day, still, I could not help but go back to paint. So, just as ever, I started painting at the same spot, overlooking the same place. Ah ah, everyone, please don't get surprised. Beyond my shoulders, a long brush came over and when I was frantically painting for a while, it erased all that I had painted. I looked back abruptly. What would have been there? My body was immobile, as if it had frozen for thirty to forty minutes with my back turned to look behind. In the middle of the beautiful path, she was the woman who even on that day was dressed pleasantly plain and much like someone who had followed me, she had been deceiving the eyes of people who were passing by from behind. She also had the brush held and with a pitiful face, like it was smiling or fuming, she stared at me. The woman who looked that refined and dignified seemed to be only around 18 upon close look. At the time, I was 23 years old. After standing like that for a long time, she said, 'Forgive me' and spoke to me like she was someone close to me. I barely managed to say, 'No problem.' And then, I shut my mouth again and could not say anything. Next, she opened her small lips again that trembled, 'You think of me as a rather suspicious woman, right? Even I think of myself as quite a suspicious thing······After seeing you in the tram at that time, the thought of my childhood stirred up like fire. While there is no need to speak of such an incident on purpose, have you ever seen me somewhere by any chance? About 5 to 6 years ago, there was a time when I had spent the midwinter in Pyeongyang······' Right then, the thought occurred to me. In one windy winter, on my way out of the West Gate, while passing by the Pyeongyang Christian Hospital, I had seen a 15- to 16-year-old slender girl with braided hair in gray, plain clothed silk-skirt and in jeogori (Upper garment of

Korean traditional clothes), made out of white silk go into the hospital. Yet, how much more noble the woman now standing in front of me was than the girl? While at that time, the girl was quite beautiful, still, an atmosphere of a bud that did not bloom yet had been abounding. So, I said ambiguously, 'Yes······it just occurred to me now. Wasn't it in front of Pyeongyang Christian Hospital outside of the West Gate in Pyeongyang······?' And the woman's face flushed momentarily and she communicated her affirmation through her eyes. That day, after setting aside the easel and tucking the painting materials into the box in front of the woman, I could not make the attempt to paint again. That day, with the look of a person cast under hypnosis, I followed the woman and went wherever she was off to. Everyone, please don't be surprised again. The villa across the Kamogawa bridge that I was trying hard to paint was her house. When she entered the house, the male and female servants in Joseon clothes came out, received me, and followed inside. At the time, as I was dressed in my rather slovenly school uniform, it was awkward for me to step inside the extravagant place. While I wouldn't speak about all the extravagant things as the story would last too long, when I was following her and going up the over-bridge that was twisted around and around, she asked me as to whether I liked painting. So, I was going to reply in the affirmative, but when I ended up saying that I didn't like it as much as music, the woman said that it seemed like it. And then, even after she spoke, she asked me as to whether I was going to paint again. So, of course, needless to say, while I was about to say that I was going to paint again, I unwittingly ended up saying that I would never paint, as if I was averse to something or as if to speak of it as a farce."

After speaking up until here, teacher Kim let out a long sigh. As if to still wait for what would come later, many teachers' eyes flashed with burning curiosity. Kim Nam-suk, the female teacher who sat next to teacher Kim pitifully had her eyes lit up with the long glossy eyelashes and furtively held up her thin face that radiated a purple color, staring at the shape of the mouth of teacher Kim who had been talking. Teacher Kim who had been sharing his story directed his eyes at Nam-suk's eyes as if to say, 'I will speak again of what comes later' and then, continued his words. All the while, he let out a long, pathetic sigh again and said,

"Ah, as I come to think of it, it was why I was not able to do painting, which my teachers had hoped for and fostered in me, and I ended up as a school teacher like this. At the time, for a long-while, I turned around and around, and with the woman, I stepped into one of the rooms that seemed to be ornately adorned. The room was somewhat similar to a study and slightly resembled an indoor receptionist room. The piano, the bookshelf, and of course, the sofa was placed there as well. The woman entered the room and wordlessly, turned on the lovely lamp that was placed on the table. It was all the more peculiar that the light was turned on in a room where a red wardrobe was arranged and even when it was daytime. As expected, the light of the lamp let out a reddish hue. Soon after, as the woman's delicately textured hand hit the lamp, in no time, the lamp shattered on the wooden floor, oil flooded out, and horrifying flames rose up on the floor. Doesn't every one of you assume that there, I would have made a fuss about how the fire would blaze up? But it was a fact that I was not able to do such a thing. While it is the case even now, what was more, the woman at the time ruled over me like I was a servant. I could only gaze at everything that the woman did just as it was. The fire left a black spot on the floor and was extinguished with a snap. Ah, everyone, now that I think of it, the woman directed passion to me, which ended up coming to fruition.

That is right. Like the main character of a dream whose flames gradually blazed up and after fully catching fire, became extinguished, Seonrae enlightened me. No. Rather, it is correct to say that she tempted me. Her passion started as the song of spring. And the coolness of summer made one forget the past days and from the serenity and solemnity of winter, as if 'Seonnyeo (Taoist fairy) came down to the well side and left abruptly,' at least, just as it is when it appears and stays fleetingly in a dream, she vanished into thin air.

Everyone, I dreamed a dream that I could not awaken from.

Everyone, I lapsed into illness, which I could not be cured from.

Despite trying to talk about my past experience, I still couldn't find the agreeable words, though that may not be even a suitable thing to say. Yet, from my experience, my eyes opened to some degree. From there, I returned to the music room of the Kyoto Young Men's Association dormitory where I laid the groundwork for my life in the past, settled down completely, and opened the collection of elementary school songs with skills that did not work at discretion and saw myself familiarizing myself with it. In the midst of the chaos of the ruins of the old life, I found in myself a not fully grown blood-stained child practicing his first walk, as he took the first step and the second step.

That is definitely me, Kim ○○.

Every one of you would be guessing how much I had lapsed into the middle of disappointment and despair at that point. Yet, with my own power, what could I do about the huge fate where the bygone times turn into each verse's melody and perpetually vanish in the eternal, humongous sea?

Seonrae was like a tune with a spell. Ah, could a person do a greater work in one's lifetime than creating a beautiful syllable?

The flowing current momentarily smiles with its eyes at the surrounding hill that it fleetingly meets and merely goes its way, even without dreaming and making a fuss. The hill that sends the water flowing cannot move eternally and as it ages, it would look ahead, as if all the times were the one time when it had been the strongest and the most beautiful.

Up to this point, to start off, what I said about Seonrae tempting me becomes very much a lie.

Ah, then, it must've been that Seonrae merely passed by me. One time, I thought that a person could not but flow. Yet, tragically, my thought did not reap the right behavior and I realized that even when the water of the swamp sloshed every time the wind blew, it could not dare flow.

To me, Seonrae is the only one that is beautiful. It is just that Seonrae is the only woman with vigor. Through the things of this world that inexhaustibly flow and through every flowing tune, I envision only Seonrae.

Everyone, it is when a person forgets all of one's selfish interests and desires that with fairness in mind, one could beautifully compliment even one's enemy to no end.

Seonnyeo, which is a common name in the vicinity of Pyeongan seems to have been rolled and modified to Seonrae for it to sound good to call in Japanese.

While I also do not specifically know the origin of Seonrae, somehow, it seems to be that her father was an entertainer from Yeongnam and her mother was a Pyeongyang gisaeng (Woman of low-class social background who entertained men of upper-class with music, conversation, and poetry). If the following is true, there would be no one who wouldn't know them. That is if the mother is gisaeng Bae Yeong-weol who had a huge remarkable wealth. And for those of you who are sitting here, you would remember it as a memory of your earliest childhood or as a quaint, strange incident about a rumor on pregnancy, where the Pyeongyang gisaeng gave birth as the concubine of a minister, instead of the entertainer and hid the baby somewhere. Yet, it is the least difficult thing for the entire truth of a person to be passed on falsely.

However, the place where Seonrae grew up was in Gyeongdo. There, at a school where the noble attend, she was respectfully treated like the daughter of the noble and raised preciously with the most prolific hobby.

I absolutely have no idea where Seonrae is now. It was just for a year that I knew Seonrae. But I don't ask the world about matters on Seonrae. Who would know her? Even if one were to know her, would it be believable that someone would love her more than me?

Everyone, it seems that here, one would have awakened from the dream that made one intensely grind one's teeth out of insanity. But could I really ever forget the one clear dream in my life?

The trace of a footprint of a youthful step that I am familiarizing myself with would have certainly been embedded in the form of a troubled heart thinking of Seonrae. Yet, even though this youthful step may take off, it would definitely move forward and forward. In the meantime, I was able to paint a picture which tried to unify the tune, color, and movement.

Everyone, every livelihood of a person ought to be rooted in the flowing tune. The artwork called 'Dancing Woman,' which I had painted while greatly daydreaming to be an artist for the first and last time had deeply gone into Seonrae's belongings as an item that reaped success in producing longing and would disperse into every quietly secluded place of the entire world like a possessed spirit. At this time, the composition of Kandinsky comes to mind."

Teacher Kim finished his words like this. Thinking of the path filled with the ups and downs that their friend lived through, many teachers that were listening could not instantly come up with a single word. The eyes of teacher Kim who had been talking had the most pitiful look as he stared at the face of the female teacher, Kim Nam-suk. The face that had been gloomy and flushed turned bright yellow.

Her black eyes with glossy long eyelashes suspiciously dimmed. She shut her lips and put on an expression of barely managing to endure something and as if she went dizzy, she lowered her head at the desk.

It seemed to be that the entirety of her small body and soul were severely quaking as teacher Kim Nam-suk was the only one who listened attentively to the music teacher's story.

Oppressed by the meaning of the confusing story, many people shut their lips for a long time.

At this moment, in the yard of the Shinmyeong school sports ground, little by little, the shade lay askew, extensively obscuring the sunny spot.

[November, 1923]

선례

8월 오후의 하늘은 구름 없이 개었다.

산들바람은 빙 돌린 기롱(평양의 기자롱) 담 체두리(몸체의 둘레)의 포플러 잎들 사이로 솔솔 새어서 운동장 위에 그리고 해뜩해뜩한 모롱 땅 위로 동글동글한 빛 그림자와 잎 그림자가 아래 아롱 뛰놀린다.

그것이 마치 학교 운동장 안의 석경(저녁 풍경)인 듯 학교 생도들이 방학 동안에 무료함을 이기지 못해서 선생 없는 학교 뜰에 모여 와 하염없이 고요함과 외로움 가운데 남 보지 않을 사이 뜀뛰기로 미시미시한 기분을 감추려한다.

여기 이르러 자연은 인생에게 무엇을 말하려는 듯하나 사람은 벌써 나이 먹은 역사를 가지기 때문에 자연 그에게는 아무 비밀도 가르쳐달라고 귀를 빌리지 않게 되었다.

여기 시작된 이야기는 사람들끼리 모여 앉아서 서로서로 감추어두었던 이야기를 말하기로 결정된 재미스러운 일이다.

평평한 운동장 한편에 몇 층 돌 구름다리로 지대를 높인 이 빈 학교의 사무실에서는 때때로 남자와 여자의 엇바꾸는 웃음소리가 뒤섞여서 바람결에 전해 들린다.

여기 모인 선생님들은 개학날을 앞에 두고 직원회를 열었다가 각기 자기가 소유한 책상들을 잇대어 서늘서늘한 바람 드나드는 곳에서 더위도 잊을 겸 장방형의 탁자를 만들어놓고 여덟 사람이 둘러앉아서 앉은 차례대로 이야기를 시작하였던 것이다.

셋째 번에는 박 선생에게 부대끼다 못해서 이 학교의 음악 선생이 종종 이 보이는 버릇대로 그 애교 있는 코를 크크 하면서 유순한 표정으로 빛나는 눈찌를 굴려서 풀어본 지 오래인 이야기 끝을 찾는다.

누구든지 이 사무실에 앉았던 사람은 다 먼저 한 선생과 박 선생이 낚시질하던 이야기와 사냥질하던 이야기를 할 때는 운수 운수라고 놀림청을 댔으나 김 선생이 지금 다시 조용하고 엄숙한 태도를 가짐에는 다 옷깃을 여미고 잘 들으려는 뜻을 보였다. 드디어 음악 선생은 여덟 사람이 두 사람씩 마주 앉은 탁자에서 학교 사환이 따라놓은 얼음물을 마시고 너무 긴장하여지는 표정을 늦추려는 듯이 한번 가슴을 굽혀서 자결하려는 사람의 그것같이 비참한 듯한 눈찌로 탁자 위만 내려다보다가 가슴을 펴며 다시 휘황한 눈 광채를 나타내고 찬란한 눈찌로,

"아, 그 이름은 선례인 줄 기억하지만 아직 그 알 수 없는 여성을 처음으로 만난 것은 일본 경도 가라스마루 전차 정류장에서 쿠마노진자 정류장으로 향하는 한때 길 가운데서 입니다.

(이 중에 박 군은 대강 짐작이나 하시는지 모르겠지마는.)

때는 봄이라면서도 대단히 고르지 못한 날씨여서 어떤 날은 빛나는 고양이 눈알같이 따뜻하다가도 어떤 날은 뼈마디까지 으쓱으쓱하게 추웠습니다. 그때 저는 음악가가 될까, 화가가 될까? 하고 두 곳으로 갈라진 길머리에 서서 침식마저 잊은 듯 아득했었습니다. 이미 옛날 믿음세는 벗어나서 사회를 위하여 봉사하리라 전형적으로 착한 사람이 되리라 하던 어렴풋한 생각은 없어졌고 다만 음악회와 미술 전람장 사이에서 높이 떠보고 싶은 마음을 갈팡질팡시키면서 어느 곳으로 이끌릴지 주인의 피리 소리조차 못 듣는 어린양 같았습니다. 그래서 어느 때는 색색의 소리를 모아둔 관현악에 마음이 흐르고 또 어느 때는 눈이 깨일 듯한 모양들에 마음이 취하였습니다.

그때 마침 동경서는 표현주의에 대하여 대단한 열성으로 연구할때였던

고로 신문과 잡지는 애써서 그 주의를 선전하고 또 같은 파의 그림 전람회를 여기저기 열어서 모든 눈을 놀라게 하고 따라서 고흐와 고갱에게 새로운 찬사를 드리고 부세회浮世繪(우키요에, 일본 에도시대 서민 계층 사이에서 유행하였던 목판화) 판화들이 일요 부록으로 신문만을 보는 사람들에게까지 주의를 시키도록 돌려졌습니다. 그런 고로 지금까지 '자연주의'라든지 '진실주의'라든지 '사실주의'에 염증을 느끼던 사람들은 걸어가려던 '신낭만주의'의 중도에서 온몸의 윗동아리를 돌리고 미처발을 냅디지 못해서 큰 혼돈 가운데 몸을 빠뜨려 애쓸 때였습니다.

또 '인상파'에서 '후기 인상파'로 '미래파'로 '표현파'로 가다가 길을 어긋나지 못하고 밀려졌다 헤쳐졌다 할 때였습니다.

저는 그럴 동안에 칸딘스키의 바레숑이라든지 이미테숑 이라든지에 마음이 이끌려서, 그 색채色彩를 쓴 것이 선을 쓴 것이 완전히 음악적音樂的 구도構圖이고 선율線律인 데 눈이 깨어졌습니다. 그래서 저는 한 그림을 그리려 할 때를 당해서 전일의 자연주의의 학리에서 벗어나려고 하면서 오히려 자연을 배우자 자연을 나타내자 하는 구절句節을 생각해내고 비웃기도 하고 성내기도 하며 희랍의 예술藝術을 생각하고 인간의 가장 훌륭한 역사를 생각하고 마음이 기뻐져서 날뛰게도 되었습니다. 그러나 내가 그림을 그리려고 막상 붓을 들었을 때 모든 생각은 나를 버리고 뒤도 돌아보지 않는 것 같았습니다. 더욱이 음악에서 빌려온 모든 선이 제 손끝에는 잡히지 않아서 베토벤의 거인ㅌ人의 울음을 쓰려 할 때 참혹히도 당나귀 울음만도 못한 선이 그어지고 쇼팽의 적지 않은 슬픔이 술주정꾼의 숨 지우는 신음만치도 못한 선이 되어 그어집디다. 아, 나중에는 모차르트의 조는 듯한 상령한(서리같이 흰 빛깔의 날개같은) 선율도 제 말을 안 듣습디다. 저는 거기서 극한 분노와 설움을 느꼈지만 그것도 순전치가 못해서 걷잡아둘 만한 것이 없었습니다. 저는 그런 때 눈이 와서 땅에 내릴 새도 없이 녹아지는 3월 어느 날 모여들지 않는 구상構想에 그려지지 않는 솜씨에 성이 난 듯 준비할 일도 없는 것을 가라스마루 산조三条까지 갔었습니다. 그날따라 날은 구질구질하고 마음은 어지러워져서 불쾌한 열기가 제 온몸에서 일본 '누더기' 옷 위로 무럭무럭 김을 올릴 지경이었습니다.

그 모양으로 엉킨 삼실같이 어지러운 머리로 저는 그 아침에 무슨 일이 있었는지 없었는지 그도 분명치 않게 산조까지 갔다가 전차를 타고 돌아오다가 한 정류장에 이르렀습니다."

여기까지 말을 그치고 음악 선생은 한숨을 내쉰다. 그 눈은 비를 내리려는 봄 하늘같이 흐려졌다. 둘러앉아서 이야기 듣던 선생들은 음악 선생의 넓고도 처량한 음악성에 마음이 취해서 그 오래 풀지 않고 넣어두었던 실마리가 더 순순히 곱게만 풀리라고 비는 것같이 바라는 듯하다.

"그가 얼마나 아름다웠는지 지금도 이 입으로는 그 모양을 옮기지 못하는 것을 보시더라도 다 생각이 미치실 듯합니다. 아무렇든지 그전에 한번 본 듯한 얼굴이었습니다. 혹시 저만 보던 아직 말하지 않은 꿈속에서나 보았던지 심히 분명치는 않으나 그가 가와바다조란 정류장에서 전차 위에 올라설 때 정류장에 같이 섰던 여자 셋이 머리를 발부리까지 굽혀서 절을 합니다. 얼핏 보아도 그는 어느 황족이나 공후작의 집에서 나온 여성으로 보입니다. 그러나 아무것도 모르는 처녀로는 보이지 않습니다.

나는 그때 그 전차 안에 올라앉았던 일이 언제든지 어렴풋한 꿈가운데 꿈을 되돌아 생각하는 것처럼 희미하기도 하고 또 자기가 늘 의식하여야 할 자신의 호흡같이 늘 생각은 하면서도 잊는 것 같기도 합니다. 그때 선례는 분명히 나와 엇비슷하게 마주 앉았었습니다.

저는 그때 제 온몸에 다 기운이 나는 것을 깨달았습니다. 그 크고 맑게 흐르는 듯한 눈매 또 거기 반듯이 어울리는 길고 가는 몸매. 다만 그 기운 나는 오래 듣지 못하던 곡조가 내 귀에 흐르는 듯합니다. 그러면서도 그러한 사람을 어디서 한번 본 듯한 생각은 몹시 선연했었던 고로 저는 그이 앞에서 눈을 감고 모든 길 가운데 그리고 모든 집 가운데서 만났던 여성들을 생각 안으로 불러서 일일이 살펴보았습니다. 그때 아무리 골똘해도 얼른 생각이 튀어나오지 않습니다. 그럴 동안에 제 뺨은 무슨 광선을 받아서 재릿재릿해지는 것 같았습니다. 저는 눈을 번쩍 떴습니다. 그 순간에 그길 가운데 여성(선례)과 눈이 마주쳐서 큰 벌불(아궁이에 불을 땔 때 아궁이 밖으로 내뻗치는 불)을 일으키는 듯하였습니다. 그 한순간 후에 그의 눈은 점점 다시 서늘해지고 웃을 듯 말 듯한 표정으로 변하다가 홀연 비웃는 눈찌로 변해집디다. 그것은 마치 저를 아는 듯 인사하는 것 같이도 생각이 듭디다.

　아아, 그 시원한 눈찌만은 지금도 아무런 곳을 가더라도 환하도록 길을 밝혀줄 때가 많습니다. 그러나 겨우 그러할 뿐이지 그 얼굴은 도무지 그 뒤에 눈을 감고 생각해보아도 생각해낼 수 없는 것입니다. 그 행동은 다만 여러 가지 처량한 곡조를 내게 많이 남겨준 것 같습니다. 지금이라도 그이를 생각만 하면 고정固定한 모양보다 흐르는 듯한 곡조가 입속으로 우러날 뿐입니다.

　두번째 그이를 만난 것은 경도제국대학 근처의 어떤 미술 전람회장 어구에서였습니다. 여러분, 제가 지금 그 미술 전람장에 들어가서 그이가 어찌하고 섰던 것을 보았다고 말할 줄 짐작하십니까? 혹시 그 여자가 그 아름다운 자기의 초상화 앞에 갖은 교태를 짓고 섰더라고요? 그렇지 않으면 자기와 같은 여신女神이나 성녀聖女 앞에 아롱지게(또렷하지 않고 흐리게 아른거리는 모양으로) 섰더라고요? 그렇게 할 줄 아십니까? 그도 아니고 저도 아닙니다. 그 미술 전람장에는 제 그림을 출품했었습니다. 그 그림은 「춤추는 여인」이라고 이름 짓고 일본 기생이 춤추는 것을 그렸었습니다. 그것은 사상과 기교를 많이 음악적으로 변화해보았던 것입니다. 놀라지들 마십쇼. 그 아름다운 여자는 내 그림 앞에 냉정한 표정을 짓고 하드르르한 (가벼운 것이 날리는 듯한) 옷에 쌔여서 그 서늘한 눈으로 얼마간 보고 섰습디다. 그이는 그렇게 내 그림을 한참이나 보고 섰더니 내가 그 뒤에 선 것을 아는지 모르는지 아주 분명한 조선말로 이러한 말을 내 그림 위에 들씌웁니다.

'아주 한껏 재주를 피워보았다나. 그러나 가엾게도 아주 길을 잃은 사람' 같다 하고 말합디다.

여러분 그때 제가 얼마나 놀랐겠습니까? 그때는 5월이라 매우 더워졌던 때인데도 나는 마치 동지섣달에 얼음물을 머리 꼭대기에서부터 발뒤꿈치까지 들쓰는 것 같았습니다. 너무 얼떨해서 혼 잃은 듯이 섰을 때 그이는 한번 뒤돌아보는 것 같더니 어느덧 그 미술 전람장 밖으로 나가버렸습니다. 내가 바로 정신을 차렸을 때 밖에서는 자동차 바퀴 돌리는 소리가 납디다. 나는 그날 그때 집으로 돌아와서는 머리를 바위에 들이 조은 것 같아서 며칠을 얼빠진 사람 모양으로 시름시름 앓았습니다. 그, 며칠 후입니다. 제 그림을 그 미술 전람장에 추천해준 일인 선생한테서 그 그림을 팔지 않겠느냐고 묻는 편지가 왔습니다. 나는 그때 제 양심으로 말하면 벌써 그 그림을 남에게 전할 만한 자신이 없어졌노라고 거절했겠지만 기실 남은 다 날더러 부잣집 자식이라고 우러러보느니만큼 내용이 그렇지도 못하던 터이므로 군색(필요한 것이 없거나 모자라서 딱하고 옹색함)에 못 견뎌서 선생에게 대단히 겸손한 뜻으로 팔아도 무방하노라고 답장을 했습니다. 그 후 얼마 있다가 그림보다는 몇 배나 넘치는 큰돈을 제 손으로 받고는 좀 무색한 생각이 나서 그림 선생에게 누가 그런 큰돈을 내고 그 그림을 샀느냐고 물어보았습니다. 그때 선생의 말이 자기 친구가 샀는데 아마 누구에게 선물하려고 사는 듯 싶더라고 합디다. 나는 더 물을 필요가 없었습니다. 그래서 곧 돈이 손탁 (손아귀)에 들어왔을 때 그러하리라 하고 회구繪具와 화포를 많이 사놓고는 교토 가모가와京都下鴨川 개천가에서 사생을 했습니다. 하루는 그 가모가와 다리를 대단한 열심으로 그리고 나서 보니깐 제정신이 있어서 그렸는지 없어서 그렸는지 시커멓게 브러시로 문질러놓은 자리뿐이요 한 올의 분명한 선線이라고는 보이지 않습디다. 저는 하도 이상해서 스스로 미치지나 않았나 하고 의심하여도 보았습니다. 그래도 내 몸에 별로 의심할 만한 일이라고는 아무리 살펴보아도 찾을 수 없었습니다. 저는 그 이튿날 또 맹렬한 열심이 나서 이상한 기적을 바라는 듯이 똑같은 곳으로 가서 화가畫架를 뻗쳐놓고 그렸습니다. 그리고 내 힘을 시험하기 위해서는 한 줄 한 줄을 헤이며 다리를 그리고 삼림을 그리고 그 다리로 삼림에 가는 길을 그리고 삼림 속에 훌륭한 로마식 건축의 별장을 그려놓고 보니까 이번에는 금방 그려놓은 별장이 아주 하얗게 지워졌습니다. 저는 그때 하도 어이가 없어서 울려고 하여도 웬만한 일이라야 울지요, 눈물도 아니 나옵니다. 그래서 그림 그리던 것을 접어서 어깨 위에 메고는 뒤도 돌아보지 않고 집으로 돌아왔습니다.

그 이튿날 그래도 저는 또 그리러 가는 수밖에 없었습니다. 그래서 역시 꼭 같은 자리에서 꼭 같은 곳을 보고 그리기 시작했습니다. 아아 여러분 놀라지 마십시오. 제 어깨 너머로 기다란 브러시가 넘어와서 제가 한참 정신없이 그리려 할 때 그린 것을 죽 지웁니다. 저는 홱 뒤돌아보았습니다. 거기 무엇이 있었겠습니까? 제 몸은 뒤를 보느라고 돌린 채로 30분 40분 동안은 얼어붙었는지 움직일 수가 없었습니다. 그이는, 그 아름다운 길 가운데 여성은 그날조차 수수하게 차리고 아주 나를 따라온 사람같이 그 뒤에서 지나는 사람들의 눈을 속이고는 그리했던 것입니다. 그 이도 브러시를 쥔 채 웃는 듯 성내는 듯한 애처로운 얼굴로 나를 쳐다봅니다. 그렇게 점잖고 위엄 있게 보이던 여성은 가까이 보니 겨우 열여덟 살이나 되었을지 말았을지 합니다. 그때 나는 스물세살이었습니다. 그이는 한참 그렇게 섰다가 '용서합쇼' 하고 친하던 사람같이 내게 말을 걸칩니다. 나는 겨우 '아니오' 했습니다. 그러고는 또 입을 다물고 아무 말도 하지 못하였습니다. 그다음에 그이는 또 보르르르 떨리는 작은 입을 열어서, '저를 퍽 수상스러운 여자라고 생각하시지요. 저는 제가 생각해도 참 수상스러운 물건입니다⋯⋯그때 전차 안에서 당신을 뵈인 후로 어렸을때 생각이 불같이 일어났습니다. 그 일은 구태여 말할 필요가 없지마는 혹시 저를 어데서 보신 일이 없으십니까? 한 5, 6년 전에 저는 평양서 한겨울을 지낸 일이 있습니다……' 합디다. 그때 비로소 저는 생각이 납디다. 어느 바람 센 겨울에 서문 밖으로 나가다가 기휼병원(평양 기독교 병원) 앞을 지나노라니까 15, 6세의 날씬한 처녀가 머리를 충충 땋아서 늘이고 회색 무문 제병 치마에 흰 명주 안팎 저고리를 받쳐 입고 병원으로 들어갑디다. 그러나 그 여자보다 지금 눈앞에 섰는 여자는 얼마나 귀족 같았을까요? 그때 그 처녀도 한껏 아름다운 처녀였지마는 그래도 꽃 피지 않은 봉오리의 파르족족한 기운이 있었습니다. 그래서 나는 어름어름하면서 '네……지금 생각이 납니다. 평양 서문 밖 기휼병원 앞에서……가 아니었을까요?' 했더니 그 여자는 얼굴을 잠깐 붉히며 그렇다고 눈으로 말합디다. 그날 저는 그 여자 앞에서 화가를 접고 회구를 상자에 집어넣은 후로는 다시는 그림을 그리려고도 하지 못했습니다. 저는 그날 최면술 걸린 사람 모양으로 그 여자를 따라서 그가 가는 대로 갔습니다. 여러분 또 놀라지 마십시오. 제가 그 가모가와 다리 건너 애써 그리려고 하던 별장이 그이의 집이었습니다. 그가 들어갈 때에 조선 옷을 입은 남녀 하인들이 나와서 나를 맞아 따라갑디다. 나는 그때 참으로 구지레한 학생복에 쩨여서 그 화려한 곳에 들어가기가 서먹서먹합디다. 여기 그 화려하던 일들은 너무 시간이 오래질 터인 고로 말하지 않습니다마는 내가 그의 뒤를 따라 뱅뱅 돌려놓은 구름다리를 올라갈 때 그이는 내게 그림을 좋아하시느냐고 묻습디다. 그래서 저는 곧 그렇다고 대답하려다가 음악만치는 좋아하지 않는다고 했더니 그 여자의 말이 그러실것이라고 합디다. 그 다음에 또 그 여자의 말이 이후에도 그림을 또 그리려느냐고 묻습디다. 그래서 나는 물론 말할 것도 없이 또 그리겠다고 할 터인데 부지불식간에 무엇을 꺼리는 듯이 또는 웃음거리로 말하듯이 결코 아니 그리겠다고 말해버렸습니다."

여기까지 말하고는 김 선생은 긴 한숨을 쉬었다. 여러 선생은 아직도 그 뒤를 기다리는 듯이 불타듯 하는 호기심에 눈들이 반짝거린다. 더욱이 이야기하던 김 선생 옆에 앉았던 김남숙이란 여선생은 그 윤택한 살눈썹 긴 눈을 애처롭도록 빛내고 그 자줏빛 도는 갸름한 얼굴을 살그머니 들어서 김 선생의 입모습을 바라본다. 이야기하던 김 선생은 남숙의 눈에게 '이 뒤를 또 말하마' 하는 듯이 자기의 눈을 향했다가 말을 잇댄다. 그러면서 다시 긴 비창한 한숨을 한번 짓고,

"아, 생각하면 그때 그것이 제 선생들이 많이 바라주고 길러주던 그림을 못 그리고 이같이 교원 생활을 하게 된 원인입니다. 나는 그때 뺑뺑 한참이나 돌아서 그 여자와 같이 그중 화려하게 꾸민 듯한 한 방에 들어갔습니다. 그 방은 서실 비스름하고 내근한 응접실 비스름합디다. 피아노도 놓이고 책장도 놓이고 물론 소파도 놓였습디다. 그 여자는 그 방으로 들어가더니 말없이 탁자 위에 놓였던 고운 램프에 불을 켭디다. 나는 붉은 장을 늘인 방 안에 또 낮인데도 불을 켜놓은 고로 저으기 더 이상했었습디다. 램프의 불은 역시 불그레한 광채를 내입디다. 그러자마자 그 여자의 분길(분의 곱고 부드러운 결) 같은 손이 어느덧 램프를 탁 치니까 마룻바닥에 램프는 깨지고 기름이 쏟아져서 마루 위에서 무서운 불길이 일어납디다. 여러분은 제가 거기서 화재가 일겠다고 말을 하고 수선을 떨었을 줄 짐작하지는 않으십니까? 그러나 그러지 못한 것이 사실입니다.

그 여자는 시방도 그렇거니와 그때는 더군다나 나를 그 종과 같이 지배했습니다. 저는 모든 일을 그 여자가 하는 대로 다만 바라볼뿐이었습니다. 불은 마루 위에 컴컴한 자리를 남기고는 탁 꺼졌습니다. 아. 여러분 지금 생각하면 그렇듯이 그 여자는 내게 정열情熱을 향했다가 거두어갔습니다.

그렇습니다. 선례는 내 꿈의 주인공인 저 자신을 불길이 점점 타올라서 다붙은 다음에는 꺼지듯이 그렇게 깨어나게 했습니다. 아니요. 차라리 유혹했었더란 말이 옳겠지요. 그의 정열은 봄노래로 시작되었습니다. 그리고 여름의 서늘함으로 지난함을 잊게 하고 겨울의 고요함과 엄숙함으로 마치

'선녀가 우물가에 내려왔다 홀연 돌아가' 듯이 그것은 저의 꿈속에 잠시 나타나 머물다 자취도 없이 사라져버렸습니다.

여러분 저는 깨지 못할 꿈을 꾸었습니다.

여러분 저는 낫지 못할 병을 앓았습니다.

그조차 적당한 말이 아니올시다마는 저는 아직 제 지나온 경력을 말하려도 합의한 말을 못 찾습니다. 그러나 그 속에서 제 눈은 얼마큼 떴습니다. 거기서 저는 옛 생활의 터를 닦던 교토청년회관 기숙사 음악실로 돌아와서 푹 가라앉아서 임의로 움직여지지 않는 솜씨로 소학 창가집을 펴놓고 익히는 자신을 보았습니다. 옛 생활의 폐허廢墟의 혼돈混沌 가운데 다 자라지 못한 어린아이가 피투성이를 하고 한 발작 두 발작 첫걸음을 연습하는 저를 찾았습니다.

그것이 어김없는 나 김○○이올시다.

그때 제가 얼마나 섭섭함과 절망 가운데 빠졌다는 것을 여러분은 짐작하시겠지요. 그러나 지나가는 때들이 한 구절 한 구절의 곡조가 되어 영원에 영원의 큰 바다에 사라져버리는 큰 운명을 저의 힘으로 어찌하였겠습니까.

선례는 한 마력魔力 있는 조율調律이었습니다. 아, 사람은 그 일평생 한 아름다운 음절音節을 짓는 것 이상 더 위대한 일을 할 수가 있을까요.

흐르는 물결은 잠시 만나는 그의 환경인 언덕에게 잠깐잠깐의 눈웃음을 보내고 꿈도 꾸지 않고 수선도 피우지 않으며 다만 자기의 길을 갈 뿐이겠지요. 그 물을 흘려보내는 언덕은 영원히 움직이지도 못하고 저의 모양을 늙히면서 가장 힘 많던 가장 아름답던 자기네의 한때를, 모든 때가 다 그 한때이던 것같이 바라보겠지요.

여기 이르러 먼저 선례가 저를 유혹했더란 말은 아주 거짓말이 되어집니다.

아 그러면 선례는 저의 앞을 지나갔을 뿐이겠지요. 저는 한때 사람이 흐르지 않을 수 없다고도 생각하였습니다. 그러나 저의 생각은 비참하게도 옳은 행동을 얻지 못하고 소택沼澤(늪과 못을 아울러 이르는 말)의 물이 바람 불 때마다 출렁거리면서도 감히 흐르지는 못함을 깨달았습니다.

저에게는 선례만이 아름답습니다. 다만 선례만이 생명 있는 여자이올시다. 저는 이 세상의 무수히 유동流動하는 것들을 통하여, 흐르는 모든 음조音調를 통하여, 선례만을 상상합니다.

여러분 사람은 모든 사욕을 잊을 때 가장 공평한 생각으로 자기의 원수라도 아름다움으로 한없이 칭찬할 수가 있습니다.

선례는 평안도 부근에서 흔히 선녀라고 짓는 이름을 굴려서 일본말로 부르기 좋도록 고친 것 같습니다.

그러한 선례의 유래는 저도 자세히 모르지만 선례는 누구인지 그 부친은 영남 광대이고 그 모친은 평양 기생이라나 봅디다. 만일 그 말이 진정이면 누구든지 모르는 이가 없겠지요. 그 모친이 훌륭한 큰 재산을 가진 기생 배영월이라면요. 그리고 대신의 첩으로 광대를 상관해서 아이를 낳아서 어디로 숨겼더란 일도 여기 앉으신 분은 가장 어렸을 때 기억으로나 또는 태중 풍문쯤으로 들을 법한 진기한 괴변으로 기억하시겠지요. 그러나 사람의 진실은 전부 잘못 전해지는 것이 가장 어렵지 않은 일이올시다.

그러나 선례가 자란 곳은 경도京都올시다. 거기서 그는 어느 귀족들이 다니는 학교에서 가장 취미 깊은 귀족의 따님처럼 예우받고 귀하게 길러졌습니다.

그 선례는 지금 어데 가 있는지 저는 도무지 모릅니다. 제가 아는 선례는 다만 그 1년 동안뿐이올시다. 그러나 저는 선례의 일을 세상에게는 묻지 않습니다. 누가 그를 알겠습니까? 안다 한들 누가 그를 저보다 더 사랑할 줄 믿어지겠습니까.

여러분 여기 미쳐서 몹시 아득거리게 하던 꿈은 깨어졌을 듯합니다. 그러나 제가 제 일생에 한 분명한 꿈을 참으로 잊을 수가 있을까요?

제가 익히는 어린 발걸음의 한 발자국의 자취는 반드시 선례를 생각하는 아픈 마음으로 형상을 박았겠지요. 그러나 이 어린 발걸음은 비록 뜨더라도 반드시 앞으로 앞으로 나아갈 것이올시다. 그동안에 저는 음률音律과 색채色彩와 운동運動으로 통일하려던 저의 그림을 그리게 될 수가 있겠지요.

여러분, 사람의 모든 생활은 흐르는 곡조로 기초해야 합니다. 그때까지 제가 처음 그리고 마지막으로 화가가 되려고 큰 공상을 품고 그렸던 「춤추는 여인」이란 그림은 선례의 짐 속에 연戀의 승리품勝利品으로 깊이 들어서 사로잡힌 혼같이 온 세상에 모든 그윽한 곳을 편답할 것입니다. 이때에 저는 칸딘스키의 콤퍼지션構想이 떠올려집니다."

김 선생은 이같이 말을 맺었다. 듣던 여러 선생은 지나온 동무의 굴곡 있던 길을 생각하고 한마디도 얼른 말을 내지 못한다. 이야기하던 김 선생의 눈은 가장 가련한 빛을 가지고 김남숙이라는 여선생의 얼굴을 보았다. 그 얼굴은 그 캄캄하고 붉던 것이 샛노랗게 변하였다.

그 윤택하고 살눈썹 긴 검은 눈은 의심스럽게 흐렸다. 그는 입술을 다물고 간신히 참는 듯한 표정을 짓다가 아뜩해졌는지 책상에 머리를 숙였다.

마치 음악 선생의 이야기는 김남숙이란 선생 홀로 유심히 들어서 그 작은 온몸과 온 영혼이 몹시 흔들리는 것 같다.

여러 사람은 아리송송한 이야기 뜻에 억눌려서 오랫동안 입을 닫았다.

이때 신명학교 운동장 뜰에는 그늘이 점점 널따랗게 빗누워서 양지를 가려간다.

(1923년 11월)

2. POETRY

Nostalgia

When the pitiful daughter of a widow
bid farewell to her single mother
even for a little while
lightly kowtowing
exchanging eyes and puckering
she laughed while crying.

As she was lonesome
saying that she hated even a good home
solitarily she left
When she'd be ridiculed by the world
where should she direct
her grief and rage

When she descended into the garden
and would have planted again the red flower with buried roots
a woman wearing two faces
callously told her
that it stopped raining

In case you think of it as an eternal estrangement
let go of the clothes sleeves
While immaturely waiting for
the one who left after giving a towel
for five months twelve times
my youth has all withered

It is said that as she was deceived
the maiden who sent a buddy
was soft like the grass leaf and
blushed like the Jonathan apple

An easily deceived young maiden
When would I see you again

You who can't be trusted as to whether you'd come or not, buddy nim (honorific address)
Even in the winter, with word of flowers blooming
on this day like a miracle
if it is an affection brimming with changes
let's sow the flower of spring again

(December 6th, 1925)

향수

불쌍한 과부 딸이
편친父親께 고별할 때
잠깐 동안이라고
가볍게 절하면서
눈 오건 쉬 오마고
울면서 웃었었다.

외로운 몸이기에
좋은 집도 싫다고
외따로 나왔거든
세상에 조소될 때
그 비탄과 분노를
무엇에게 이르랴

이심二心을 품은 여인
뜰 아래 내려설 때
뿌리 패인 빨강 꽃
다시 심어볼 것을
비나 멎건 가라고
냉랭히 일렀어라

영 이별인 줄 알면
그 옷소매 놓으랴
수건 주고 가신 님
철없이 기다리며
다섯 달 열두 번에
내 청춘 다 늙혀라

속아서 그렇다고
벗을 보낸 처녀는
풀잎같이 연하고
홍옥같이 붉었다

잘 속는 어린 처녀
어느 때에 또 보랴

온다고 안 온다고
믿을 수 없는 벗님
겨울에도 꽃소식
기적 같은 이날에
변화 많은 정이면
다시
봄꽃 피워요

(1925년, 12월 6일)

Start of Tan-sil's Dream

In the embrace of a mother with bursting strength

the maiden with a bountiful of hair laughed

pressing her small lips to

the benevolent cheeks and eyes

Intactly pulling her neck into an embrace

while listening to the sound of her laboring for breath.

In the chilled embrace of a mother

the maiden with a bountiful of hair cried

seeing the desolate mother

Mother mother

bellowing, why did you pass away

while crying out, who was it that you despised that made you do this.

Tan-sil who dozed off in the spring breeze

sniffled in the snowy wind

Tan-sil who was idle in love

was constantly on the move from the east to the west at being

mistreated

Now that she did not have money for a thatched cottage

she rested her head on the stone pillow and dreamed in a dream.

Like before, in a dream, she laid a silk blanket over her

Having fallen fast asleep and dreaming

thunder let out a cry

raindrops fell with a thud thud

Tan-sil abruptly heaved her body

Engulfed by the sound of the thunderbolt

she ran with all her might

the more she ran the rain and the snow

poured on her bare body

the thunderous sound lunged as if it had gone mad

then she hid herself in the shade of a tree.

The entire sky commanded her

"Advance, advance"

Like a young sheep

driven into a corner by fear

even while her bare body trembled

she ceaselessly ran

In the meanwhile the day cleared

In the azure path fringed by the deep blue summer cypress that
was planted

someone guided her hand

she was all alone however.

(1925)

탄실의 초몽初夢

힘 많은 어머니의 품에
머리 많은 처녀는 웃었다
그 인자仁慈한 뺨과 눈에
작은 입 대면서
그 목을 꼭 끌어안아서
숨막히시는 소리를 들으면서.

차디찬 어머니의 품에
머리 많은 처녀는 울었다
그 냉락冷落한 어머니를 보고
어머니 어머니
우왜 돌아가셨소 하고 부르짖으며
누가 미워서 그리했소 하고 울면서.

춘풍에 졸던 탄실彈實이
설한풍雪寒風에 흑흑 느끼다
사랑에 게으르던 탄실이
학대에 동분서주하다
여막에 줄 돈 없으니
돌베개 베고 꿈에 꿈을 꾸다.

꿈에 전前같이 비단이불 덮고
풀깃 잠들어 꿈을 꾸니
우레는 울어 오고
빗방울이 뚝뚝 든다
탄실은 화닥딱 몸을 일으키어
벽력소리에 몰리어
힘껏 달아났다
달아날수록 비와 눈은
그 헐벗은 몸에 쏟아지고
요란한 소리는 미친 듯 달려들다
그는 나무 그늘에 몸을 숨겼다.

온 하늘이 그에게 호령하다
"전진하라 전진하라"
그는 어린양같이
두려움에 몰리어서
헐벗은 몸 떨면서도
한없이 달아났다
그동안에 날은 개었더라
청靑 댑싸리 둘러 심은 푸른 길에
누군지 그의 손을 이끌다
그러나 그는 호올로였다.

(1925)

Curse

You, my love that rolls over the street
rolling out of the mouth of the famished
rocked the ears of person to person
You, a lie called 'love.'

You, a starving demon that plucks out blood from a maiden's
chest
crumbling in the hands of the blind
weaved the lament of good women.
You, a lie called 'love.'

You who isn't trustworthy, trustworthy
Some days I pray that I'd meet you
Other days I pray to Amitabha that I'd not meet you
You, a plain lie that deceives and deceives again

You that roll out of the mouth of the famished
and crumble in the hands of the blind
Be gone from my heart
Oh Oh you, a lie called 'love'!

(1925)

저주

길바닥에 구르는 사랑아
주린 이의 입에서 굴러 나와
사람 사람의 귀를 흔들었다
'사랑'이란 거짓말아.

처녀의 가슴에서 피를 뽑는 아귀야
눈먼 이의 손길에서 부서져
착한 여인들의 한을 지었다.
'사랑'이란 거짓말아.

내가 미덥지 않은 미덥지 않은 너를
어떤 날은 만나지라고 기도하고
어떤 날은 만나지지 말라고 염불한다
속이고 또 속이는 단순한 거짓말아.

주린 이의 입에서 굴러서
눈먼 이의 손길에 부서지는 것아
내 마음에서 사라져라
오오 '사랑'이란 거짓말아!

(1925)

Will

Joseon, when I bid my last farewell to you

whether slumping over a brook or plucking out the barnyard

grass of the field

please torture the dead corpse even more.

If that's not enough for you

next time a person like me comes out

torture again as much as you can

Then we who detest each other would be estranged for life

You ferocious place ferocious place.

(1925)

유언

조선아 내가 너를 영결永訣할 때
개천가에 고꾸라졌던지 들에 피 뽑았던지
죽은 시체에게라도 더 학대해다오.
그래도 부족하거든
이다음에 나 같은 사람이 나더라도
할 수만 있는 대로 또 학대해보아라
그러면 서로 미워하는 우리는 영영 작별된다
이 사나운 곳아 사나운 곳아

(1925년)

Fantasy

In the pond surrounded by a man-made towering castle
A gingko-colored lichen family clan grew and extended
faintly raising its strength······
challenging against a period with money lust

When people all bustling by the pond
lost blood and collapsed

Wind and waves lambasted every soul
Corruption dominated all bodies

When above the sky, insane wind instead
When above the ground, corruption still hasn't come to an end
a person made up of stone showed up
engulfing the whole world in the fantasy of purple

Here in a new world, spring comes
The moment women don't give birth and men aren't raised
 when the far or near, good or evil, and beauty or ugliness is
abolished

comes from within our heart

Here, the pleasant moment of a new spring comes

The moment the dark undercurrents of the cave sing to the sun

and the stream unites the song of the lark

comes from within our heart

(August, 1921)

환상

인공의 드높은 성으로 둘러싸인 못물에
은행색銀杏色의 태족苔族은 자라서 늘어서
은은히 힘 길러서는……
동록銅綠의 시대에 도전하다

사람들은 다 못가에 아득거려
피를 잃고 넘어질 때

풍랑은 모든 영혼을 살아 쳐가고
부패는 모든 육체를 점령하다

하늘 위에는 오히려 미친 바람
땅 위에는 아직 부패 그치지 않았을 때
한 돌로 빚은 사람이 나타나서
자줏빛의 환상으로 온 세상을 싸 덮다

여기 새로운 세상에 봄이 오다
여인은 낳지 않고 남인男人은 기르지 않고
원근遠近 선악善惡 미추美醜를 폐지한 때가

우리들의 마음속으로부터 오다
여기 새로운 봄의 기꺼운 때가 오다
동굴洞堀의 암류暗流가 태양을 향해 노래하고
시냇물이 종다리 노래를 어우를 때가
우리들의 마음속으로부터 오다

(1921년 8월)

Consolation

Dear weeper
Dear my friend
Wash your tears
See the beauty of the spring sky
that drew our fantasy

Dear friend
We first
promised silence –
that was kept by every great figure
on the olden road teeming with lichen.

Yet, my friend
we've chattered too much
While my blabbermouth
became tongue-tied again,
your mouth
could barely contain it.

Dear friend

Do you, my friend

believe that your heart is the pinwheel of the wind?

Do you think of it as foam

that floats on water and then disappears?

Yet, my friend

Don't we see

our paradise

towering above the spring sky?

The focal point where our gazes converge.

(April 10th , 1923)

위로慰勞

우는 이여
나의 벗이여
벗의 눈물을 씻겨
우리들의 환상을 그린
봄 하늘의 아름다움을 보라.

벗이여
우리는 먼저
침묵을 약속하였었다 —
모든 거인ㅌㅅ들이 지킨 것을
우리는 이끼 그윽한 옛길 위에서.

그러나 벗이여
우리는 너무 말했다
가벼운 내 입이
또 무거우나 참기 어려운
벗의 입이

벗이여
벗은 벗의 마음을
바람의 팔랑개비인 줄 믿느뇨?

물 위에 떴다 사라지는
물거품인 줄 아느뇨?

하나 벗이여
우리는 보지 않는가
봄 하늘 위에 솟은
우리들의 낙원을?
우리의 시선에 모이는 초점을.

(1923년 4월 10일)

To a friend heading to the abbey

My friends are heading to the mountain

Following the spring sunshine, the shade of trees, the fresh wind
and bright moon

   heading to the abbey to forget this world

   Upon entering the abbey, cutting hair and becoming a nun

   throwing away all of the world's idle thoughts and

   burning incense on the burner in the morning and evening

   while ringing the bell with a clang, clang, they set off to make
silent prayers with sacred heart

   hereby, to reach one's end in the world

   Yet, my friend

   instead of heading to the place where the worshippers of hell,
the comrades of death, and spoiled corpses are in clusters

   come

   come to us where the worshippers of life, the pioneers of life
have gathered

   come, bring all of your parents, wives, children, and younger
siblings, and come

to our workplace where we adamantly march forth, blowing the
trumpet of life

to our battlefield where we're pioneering a good world

(July, 1933)

수도원修道院으로 가는 벗에게

벗들은 산으로 가네
춘광春光을 따라 녹음을 따라 청풍명월을 따라
이 세상을 잊어버리려고 수도원으로 가네

수도원에 가서 머리를 깎고 중이 되어서
모든 세상의 잡념을 다 던져버리고
아침저녁 향로에 향을 피우고
종을 땡땡 울리며 거룩한 마음으로 묵도默禱를 하러 간다지
이로써 한세상을 마치려고

그러나 벗이여
지옥의 예찬자 사死의 동지 썩은 송장들이 뭉켜 있는 그곳을 가지
말고
오게
생의 예찬자 생의 개척자가 모인 우리에게로 오게
오게 너희들의 부모처자 동생들을 다 데리고 오게
삶의 나팔을 불며 굳세게 행진하는 우리들의 일터로
좋은 세상을 개척하려는 우리들의 싸움터로

(1933년 7월)

In the Dead of Night

1

It's the dead of night
The surrounding is serene
As it has become a habit
I gaze at the bookshelf
piled up in heaps like a mountain
reminiscing the plight in buying each one of them

2

All of it
- could not help but make the circle of oblivion unfold -
it's what has been said
While gathering my energy and shaking my head
Mother! I serenely cry out
and let out a deep sigh, looking up at the ceiling

3

Your forehead that bespeaks divinity
beneath the black glasses, the turquoise gleam of your eyes
to make me forget the pain of kneeling down
You who put on a wide array of expressions
of dignity and love and integrity
I'm going to you. Also,
I'm waiting for you to come

4

When the divine scenery of the single spell of action passes
like it is when she was living, she wore white and
the round pupil below the long eyelashes
the beautiful nose and the shape of her lips were much more pu-
rified
   - My pitiful baby, how miserable you are -
like the affection of a flower, she manifests herself on the ceiling

5

In the beautiful flowerbed, in the merry banks of a stream
the time I cried out, brother, sister, friend

is all a past, but at least,

my mother who's gone now

she who shares my blood and flesh

seems to know my life and my love

At the sorrow coming from passing through the shadowy king-
dom of the dead

every night every moment

I shed tears

(April 23rd, 1938)

심야深夜에

1

심야이다
사위四圍 고요하다
버릇이 되어, 산같이 그득 쌓인
책장을 치어다본다
하나씩 사들이던 고난을 회상한다

2

그것이 모두
―무지無知의 원圓을 전개시키는 수밖에 없다―
일러온 것을
기氣를 가다듬고 머리를 흔들다가도
어머니! 고요히 부르짖고
천장天井을 우러러 한숨짓는다

3

신성神聖을 말씀하시는 그 이마
검은 안경 밑에 청록색의 안광眼光
나의 무릎을 잊게 하시려고
가지가지로 표정하시던
위엄과 사랑과 진실됨
당신에게로 내가 갑니다. 또한
오시도록 기다리옵니다

4

일장—場 거룩한 장면이 지나면
그의 생시와 같이 하얗게 입고
기다란 살눈썹 아래 둥그런 눈동자
아름다운 코와 입 모양이 한층 더 정화淨化되어
—애처로운 내 아기 그렇게 괴로워서—
꽃의 정情같이 천장 위로 나타난다

5

아름다운 꽃밭에 즐거운 시냇가에
오빠야 누나야 동무야 부르짖던 일
다 옛날이었고 그나마
지금은 안 계신 내 어머니
나와 피와 살을 나누신 그이가
내 생활과 내 사랑을 아시는 듯
유명계幽明界를 통하여 오는 설움에
밤마다 때마다
눈물을 짓는다

(1938년 4월 23일)

In the Glass Tube

Within the sorrow that seems or seems not to be visible

as the ensnared lifeline is still left

I endured the misery even today

Like a tiny, tiny creature

I am ensnared

What is this sorrow and what is this pain?

Like the prince of the past

who loved the forbidden woman,

trusting that I could live if I dance in the glass tube······

Within this faint sorrow

as they said I could live with joy

if I work, study, and love,

I have lived in the untrustworthy world.

Now in the tube where it seems or seems not to be visible

what should I do about this growing frustration?

Foolish me! Foolish me!

(May 24th, 1924)

유리관 속에서

뵈는 듯 마는 듯한 설움 속에

잡힌 목숨이 아직 남아서

오늘도 괴로움을 참았다

작은 작은 것의 생명과 같이

잡힌 몸이거든

이 서러움 이 아픔은 무엇이냐.

금단의 여인과 사랑하시던

옛날의 왕자와 같이

유리관 속에 춤추면 살 줄 믿고……

이 아련한 서러움 속에서

일하고 공부하고 사랑하면

재미나게 살수 있다기에

미덥지 않는 세상에 살아왔었다.

지금 이 뵈는 듯 마는 듯한 관 속에

생장生葬되는 이 답답함을 어찌하랴

미련한 나! 미련한 나!

(1924년 5월 24일)

Fight

There was an old soldier
who has fought for so long that
he had scars all over his body and having come to hate fights,
he replaced military tools with hoes and mattocks.

Yet, as the furrow was tough and
the landlord was ferocious
even as he planted seeds and picked weeds
there was no harvest.

At this, as the old soldier
was sleepy from the frustrating inner thoughts
he took a nap day after day and
one day he was paralyzed as if he was shot by a gun.

Ah - how strange this soldier is
Having thrown away his military tools and asleep
did he fight in the midst of dreaming?
He died with bruises all over his body.

People wrung their head

Whether one was asleep or awake, there were bound to be fights

Whether one was alive or dead, it was all bound to be the same

Everyone mustered the strength in their two arms

(1925)

싸움

늙은 병사가 있어서
오래 싸웠는지라
온몸에 상처를 받고는 싸움이 싫어서
군기軍器를 호미와 괭이로 갈았었다.

그러나 밭고랑은 거세고
지주는 사나우니
씨를 뿌리고 김을 매어도
추수는 없었다.

이에 늙은 병사는
답답한 회포에 졸려서
날마다 날마다 낮잠을 자더니
하루는 총에 쏘인 듯이 가위를 눌렀다.

아 ─ 이상해라 이 병사는
군기를 버리고 자다가
꿈 가운데서 싸웠던가
온몸에 멍이 들어 죽었다.

사람들이 머리를 비틀었다
자나 깨나 싸움이 있을진대
사나 죽으나 똑같을 것이라고
사람마다
두 팔에 힘을 내뽑았다.

(1925년)

Acknowledgements

Thank you, mother and father for always being a part of my journey and for being my best readers.

언제나 저의 여정의 일부분이 되어 주시고 최고의 독자가 되어 주셔서 감사합니다.